Two-Gun Witch

Two-Gun Witch

Bishop O'Connell

Charlotte, NC

FALSTAFF
BOOKS
WWW.FALSTAFFBOOKS.COM

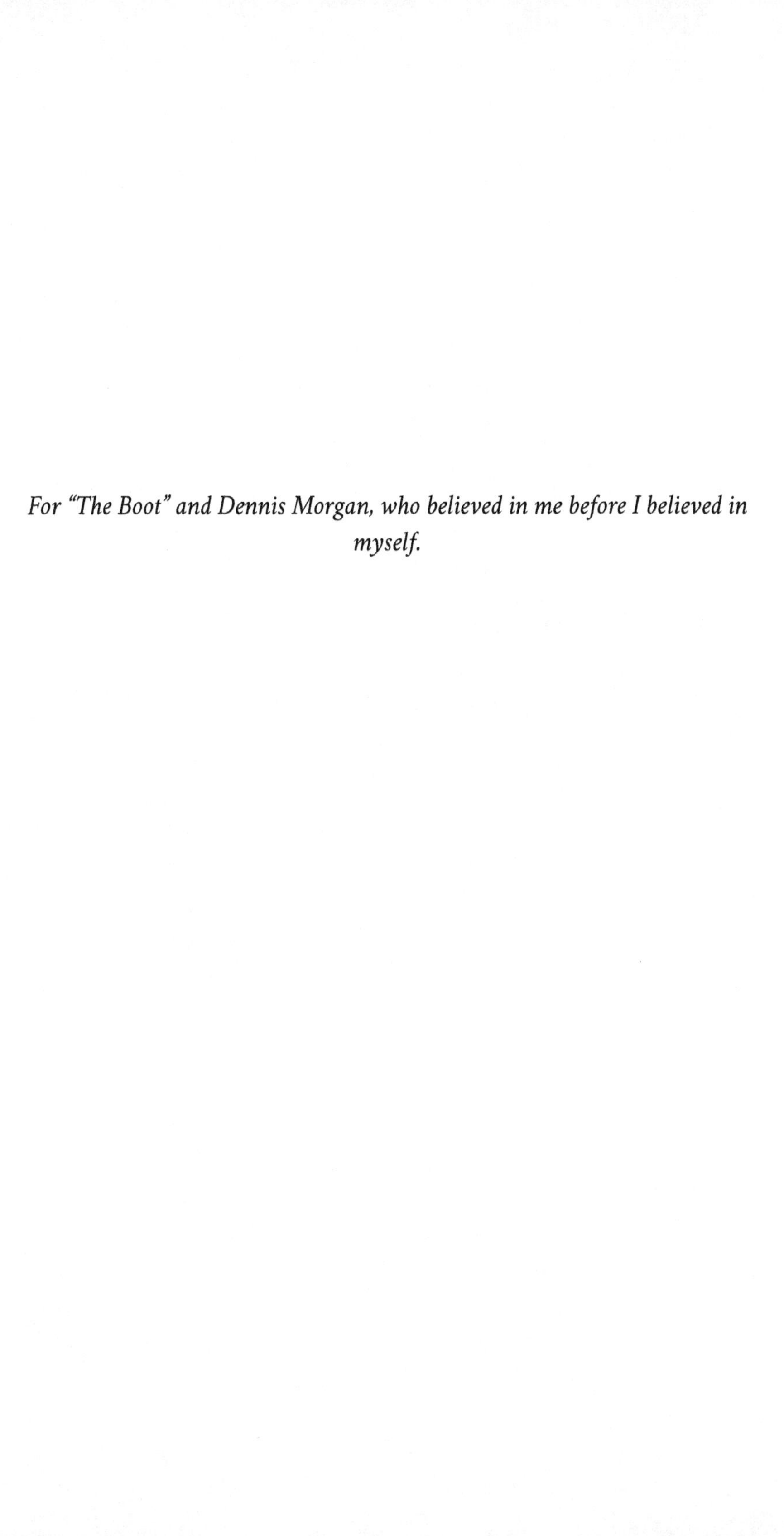

For "The Boot" and Dennis Morgan, who believed in me before I believed in myself.

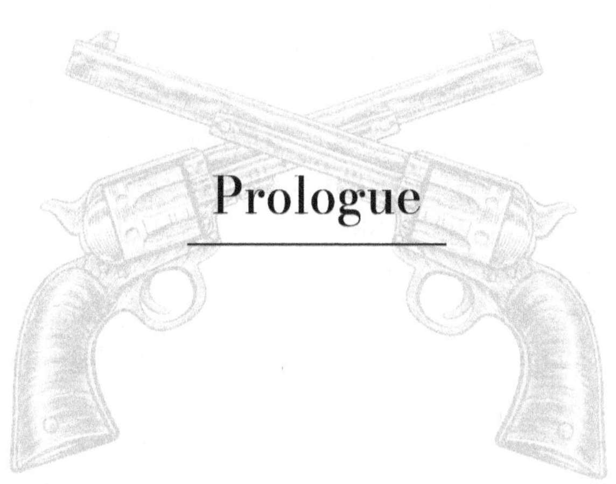

Prologue

Fort Pierre. Dakota Ter.
September 29th, 1863

My Dearest Annabelle,

I'm sure by the time this letter finds you, you'll know of our "glorious" victory at Whitestone Hill. No doubt the papers spoke with a poetic flourish I could never manage about our defeat of the Lakota and its confederacy, and how even their elven allies could not save them. How hollow those descriptors are compared to the awful truth of that day. I'm not a man of fanciful writings, nor am I a teller of tales, but I find myself compelled to tell someone the actuality of that day. There is no soul in this world I trust or rely on as you. As such, it is to you my dear that I impart the terrible truth. Know it is something that even many of my fellow soldiers will not speak of.

I do not exaggerate or play to drama when I tell you that our defeats had been so great that, even a week before, I did not believe I would ever look upon your gentle visage again. The Indians themselves were a fierce enough foe, but when the elves joined them, we all began to question the folly of Manifest Destiny.

The truth of the elves hardly compares to the fantastical fiction we all grew up hearing. It's true that the women are the warriors, the men serving as healers and the crafters of their magical wares. I use the term woman, but it is because of their biology, not their demeanor. There is nothing "womanly" about the demonesses who scythed down even the most hardened soldiers like so much wheat. These witches appeared from nowhere, seeming to step from the very shadows, and attacked before most even knew the battle had begun. I can attest that the most fearsome of the fiendesses can, as the stories tell, use a spell iron with their left hand as well as their right. Their skill and mastery flaunt the very laws of magic that we're told are unyielding. They are called two-gun witches by most, though few speak that name aloud. Even writing it sets my hands to shaking.

Forgive me, my dear, but I find myself requiring the fortification of spirits to settle my fractured nerves. I hope once I return to you that I can leave such weakness behind and live a life of peace. For I say true that I hope never to see another day of violence in my lifetime. There is bloodshed enough in my memories, and my nightmares, to last twenty score of men a dozen lifetimes. I am sorry. I beg you forgive my ramblings. I find I must work myself up to the retelling.

Our numbers had been so depleted by our continued defeats leading up to Whitestone Hill that a full two-thirds of our men were fresh recruits. Greener than the prairie grass, as the enlisted men would say. It was not even a week past, as I write this, that General Sully told us our defeats were at an end. Though we'd lost several battles, we were primed to win the war, once and for true. I do not have to tell you the doubt this was greeted with.

The shooting started not long before nightfall. It was as it can only be, a terrible and brutal affair, unfit for all but the worst demons in perdition. Even as we held the Indians at bay, the elven witches cut deep into our numbers. I said a prayer to God Almighty, asking for mercy and forgiveness of my trespasses, for I was certain I would stand in judgment before sunrise. That's when I heard it, when we all did. It was a sound that defies description, and certainly my words are lacking. I can only style it as a rolling thunder that does not end. So deep and powerful was this noise that it shook the very earth we stood upon. Even the Indians and elves paused in their attacks. I glanced at our general. He smiled, and I confess it perplexed me greatly. When I turned to follow his gaze, I saw the leviathans. The great iron monsters topped a nearby hill and rumbled toward us. "The dwarves!" our sergeant proclaimed over and over. I think I heard an officer chide that they took their sweet time.

These war machines covered ground at great speed, some rolling on spiked metal wheels, others crawling like low slung insects on multiple legs of strange articulation. They fired the massive cannons that covered their iron hides, and the sound deafened us even at a distance. Their shells exploded upon impact, sending dirt high into the air, along with the dreadful remains of any poor soul who'd been too close. I was filled with terror and relief in equal measure and was struck quite dumb by the sight.

The elves and Indians, for their parts, showed courage beyond any soldier ever I've heard spoken of, before or since. They attacked these metal beasts, though their bullets and spells did little to slow them. One particularly horrific monstrosity sprayed fire from a long tube like the dragons of legend. I will only say the stench and screams of the dying will haunt me the rest of my days. It was not a battle, my darling, it was a slaughter. I am shamed to say I felt excitement, even found myself cheering on the brutality. I can only ask the Lord, and you, for forgiveness. Men do terrible things when the specter of death is sent packing and they know they will live another day. However, my nightmares and haunted conscience remind me that such an explanation does nothing to excuse. Terrible enough was the battle, and I find myself longing to end my telling here, but I cannot in good conscience. I am deeply aggrieved that a woman is my only option to tell this tale, but then you were never like other women. It is because of your strength, compassion, and understanding that I continue.

The rage of men is a terrible thing. When it comes from men who feel aggrieved, it is so much worse.

The Indians and elves had set up camp nearby. Camp? No, it was a village, mobile as the tribes of these plains are known for. More than 500 called this place home, not counting the routed warriors. We followed them back to this village and caught them desperately trying to flee. Emboldened by the dwarven machines, we all, to a man, opened fire.

I would bear a heavy heart indeed if I could say only that no warrior survived the day. That much is true, but it does not tell the whole of the story. When the last shots were fired, nothing lived that did not wear a soldier's blue. The witches, the warriors, and more to my dishonor, the women and children, all lay dead or dying. Fouler still is that some few women survived the initial attack, only to be killed when the worst of our soldiers had satisfied their depraved desires on them. Surely that day the devil himself turned away in revulsion. I never had love for Indian or elf, but no one deserves what I saw that day.

I beg you forgive me, my dearest, for sharing these horrors, and for my part in them. It was not glorious. It was not even just or decent. Even when looking through the tinted lenses of war, it was the harshest of brutality and barbarism. And to think, we call them savages. I pray neither you, nor any living soul for that matter, will ever know the horrors I witnessed that day.

I'm sorry to retell this in a letter, but I fear I will never be able to speak aloud of what happened. And yet, your heart is too loving, your compassion too great. Surely you would see I was not the man who went west, and would beseech to know what had broken me. You deserve the truth and to lay whatever judgment upon me you see fit. Such will I accept as my just due.

There is talk now of pushing to the west, of taking the fight to the elves in the California forests. But for me it will not be. My term of enlistment is almost done, and despite the large bonus the Army is offering those of us with battle experience, I cannot continue. My soul can take no more.

I am coming home. I know not what I'll find when I arrive. But if you find the grace to forgive and the compassion to wait, I swear to you, no man alive will be so gentle, patient, or peaceful as I.

Ever and sincerely yours,
Will

Chapter One

Despite her dark, smoked lenses, Talen had to squint to see through the blowing dust and bright New Mexico sun. A battered, dirt-scoured wooden sign stood in the distance.

"Town of Agua Fria"

As if anyone in this town ever tasted cold water.

A moment later, she could make out a population number beneath the name: 587. But someone had crossed that out and carved 586. That had likewise been scratched out and after a series of corrections, 567 seemed to be the final tally. As if to punctuate the sign, the fetid smell of a stained soul washed over her.

Even this far from town, the putrid stench gripped her guts in a tight fist and left her feeling in need of a hot bath. She repositioned herself on the saddle and swallowed back the urge to vomit. Once certain the contents of her stomach would stay put, she squeezed the horse with her legs.

"Come on, Gaoth. Sooner done, sooner gone, and sooner we get paid."

At the small town's edge, something—apart from the growing stink—chilled her blood. She rode down the main street, passing the first few buildings, and knew the source of her anxiety. The town was just short of being literal ruins: broken windows, walls scorched black, and countless holes. Hell, it was a wonder anything remained standing. A handful of the structures had been reduced to nothing but charred, almost skeletal, remains.

Though terrible, the damage looked weeks old. Despite the putrid reek of dark magic's corruption, she couldn't help but wonder if she'd arrived too late to collect the bounty.

"Did you run off, Jack?" she whispered to herself. "Nah, you're still here, ain't you? You took this town. You wouldn't just up and leave it."

Between the damage and the smell, Talen knew why no one had taken this job. Her right hand drifted to the ensorcelled revolver, her spell iron, holstered on her hip. Without moving her head, she glanced from side to side, scanning the scene.

A subtle shifting of curtains as people peered out their windows caught her attention. When she turned her head, the hidden observers ducked out of sight.

Why the hell would anyone still live here? Were the cowards hoping for salvation? If so, they best keep hoping.

Whispering voices came from all around her, dozens—maybe a hundred—all too senseless or scared to leave. Hell, they hadn't even bothered repairing the damage. Dread permeated every inch of every building, banishing hope.

The warrant called this a ghost town. Turned out, rightfully so. Nothing remained but the tattered ghosts of murdered hopes and dreams. They haunted the shadows of this town full of dead souls just waiting for their bodies to catch up.

Not that she gave a damn.

I ought to turn around and leave this withered corpse of a town to Jack. Let the monster burn it all. Just like they did to us.

The faint, muffled sound of a crying child reached her ears; a young girl, trying hard to be quiet.

Something cold twisted in the remnants of Talen's heart and a quiet voice spoke from the shadows of her mind.

They're the monsters. They kill children. They let them suffer. Not you.

She drew in a slow breath, trying hard to ignore the scent of decay that filled the air and pushed the voice back into the darkness.

Was she a monster?

Would she even know if she were?

No, she decided. Not yet.

The oppressive hopelessness soaked in through her skin and warped her mind. She knew the profoundly stained had this effect. The recognition didn't stop the memories from coming. Not that they ever got far enough away to forget.

The rumble of the dwarven-forged, iron leviathans shook the earth, the air, and even her bones. The roar of cannons, exploding shells, and the screams of the dead and dying tore at her ears. The scent of the mangled and burning, sickly sweet and coppery, soaked the air.

Her stomach turned.

The reins shook in her hands, and despite the heat, a chill ran through her.

Coward, voices whispered from the darkest of her memories.

Yes, she'd run. They all had. What else could she do? What could any of them, those few who survived, have done?

"You could've died like the others," the whispers said.

The cold vast nothing of hopelessness wrapped around her and the faces of the dead stared accusingly.

No! Anger burst from her ruined heart. It rose like a pyre, filling her body, and burning away the corruption's influence.

The memories and shame were real, and well earned. Even so, she used the rage to shove them back down into the hole that had been her soul.

When she came back to herself, Gaoth had stopped. She got him moving and glanced about again, not bothering with subtlety. The cowed populace watched from near on every window. They likely thought the shadows and tattered curtains hid them from view, but she saw them all clearly enough, heard them too.

"A leafer," some whispered.

"Pointy-eared witch," said others.

The weight of their judgment settled over her. She hadn't bothered to disguise herself. She never did. Elven symbols covered her long, leather coat, and her leaf green hair hung loose to her shoulders, visible to the watching townsfolk. *Hate will thrive where hope dies,* she said to herself, recalling her mother's words. They'd been meant as call to patience and understanding, to withhold judgement. Now they struck Talen like an accusation.

"Or where humans live," she added in a whisper.

She sneered beneath the dusty kerchief that covered her nose and mouth. A tiny part of her wanted to feel sorry for these people. But the hope in her had been killed by humans, so the hate in her was of their own making. That hate stomped on even the whisper of empathy.

Whimpers and prayers reached her above the gentle clopping of her Gaoth's hooves. A few stared, impassive and waiting for the world to end.

Just do the job.

The index finger of her right hand tapped a mindless rhythm on the grip of her iron. A small smile emerged at the notion of taking Jack down. Destroying stained had been her job. Now it was all she had left. Truth to tell, succeeding where humans had failed meant more than the coin she earned; not that she wouldn't take the money.

In the center of town, she found the usual buildings: a telegraph office, a bank, a dry goods store, and three saloons. All of them were as battered and beaten, broken and soulless as the rest of town. The outer doors of one saloon swung back and forth, and a blackened human skeleton sat in a rocking chair to one side.

She slid from the saddle and led Gaoth to the hitching post. Feigning stretching her legs, she took in the surroundings.

Nothing stirred.

She draped the reins over the post and whispered, *"Quarisen."* As her fingertips slid over the well-worn leather, she poured magic into it. The symbols embossed along its length filled with green light and the tether drew itself taut.

She stretched again, this time for real, right hand never drifting far from her iron. She pulled down the kerchief and drew in a long breath. A soft breeze billowed her ankle-length coat behind her. The wind was a cool reprieve, refreshing on her dry skin. The faint promise of coming rain made it through the stench and brought her a measure of peace.

She climbed the porch stairs and glanced at the skeleton. The skull smiled at her, and the sun glinted off the melted remains of a brass star that clung to the rib bones. Someone had posed him, one leg crossed over the other.

Ignoring the latest example of human depravity, she closed her eyes and focused on the markings that covered her neck, face, and body. When the magic—and accompanying shadow cloak—settled over her, she continued on, making not a sound as she pushed through the small batwing doors.

The place managed to look even worse on the inside. Three tables were intact, all recently repaired. The remnants of others—and several chairs—lay piled in a corner.

Five men sat at one ramshackle table, small glasses of the local swill, cards, and coins in front of them. Two looked to be having the time of their life. The other three, well she'd seen a similar look on trapped animals, right before they chewed off their leg. Fear and hopelessness hung on the air, the same as outside but amplified, and distilled. The two smilers—they had to be Jack's boys—sipped it like their favorite belly burner.

She had another overwhelming urge to find hot water and lye soap.

No one took notice of her. But, as a Shadow Warden, if she didn't want anyone to see her, no one would.

A rotund man at the bar stuffed his face, spilling crumbs and bits of food down his very fine coat and vest. His corpulence, upturned nose, and bent ears all gave him the look of a pig someone had tried to teach to walk upright but hadn't quite succeeded. On the second story balcony, a couple of soiled doves stared into space. Unlike the men playing cards, these dead-eyed women had no fear. Like so many human women, they'd resigned themselves to a fate beyond their control. They couldn't be afraid because they had nothing left to fear losing.

None of the men were Jack. She'd memorized the mirage on the warrant, studied that wretched visage from every angle. She glanced at each of the three doors behind the women, not letting her hearing focus. If Jack were there, she did not want to hear that stained filth rutting away on some dead-eyed girl.

Left hand at her back, she cleared her throat, let the magic slip away, and stepped from the shadows.

No one gasped or jumped back in surprise. Instead, everyone looked over at her, blinking in confusion, as if she'd just been part of the background. A second later, the reality of her appearance settled in. Wide eyes went to her green hair and marked face, then to the iron on her hip.

"Ooh wee," breathed one of Jack's boys from the table. He leered at her and elbowed the man next to him. "Look at the bit of leafer fluff done blowed in."

Talen fought back a shudder, and the urge to cut the *shanzi fetsuian* down.

"You're a long way from home, leaf eater," said his compatriot.

The one at the bar turned a derisive, piggy-eyed glare at her. "If you can even call it a home anymore." He chuckled.

Neither of Jack's boys laughed, and the pig went back to shoveling food down his gullet.

The contempt and derision weren't new. She'd had the audacity to be born an elf. That was bad enough, but she was also a woman, one with a spine and a pair of spell irons no less. Among humans, that just could not be tolerated.

Juarchian, she swore to herself. That's what these humans were, an unrelenting ivy that just kept spreading.

The floor behind the bar creaked as a stout, bald dwarf stepped into view. He eyed her with even less charity than the humans.

It took every ounce of willpower she had not to drop him then and there.

She managed, but only just.

"We don't serve your kind here, leafer," he said in a thick accent, rough as the stones that birthed him. His ruddy face bore half a dozen scars, and a red beard—streaked with steel gray—hung past his belly.

The fury inside her churned and begged to be set free, to burn the town to ash.

I could kill you, stump. You're not human. No one would care.

Without consciously choosing to, she started walking toward the bar. Her right hand found the familiar grip of her iron, her fingers holding it firm and lovingly.

The dwarf looked from Talen's eyes to the pale markings on her dark brown face and neck, then finally to her spell iron.

He took a step back.

Her blood screamed to rend the flesh from his bones and—

One of Jack's boys got to his feet, knocking his chair over. "Hey, I was talking at you, leaf—"

Faster than a blink, Talen drew the second spell iron—the one she kept at her back—with her left hand. She pointed it at the man without looking from the dwarf. She poured magic into the iron, its runes and sigils lit with blue spell fire. "Sit down and shut up. I'll see to you in a minute, *juarchian*." For several heartbeats, no one moved. She could feel their gazes drifting from the spell iron in her left hand to the other still on her hip and back.

They sucked in breath as, she presumed, realization settled in.

Piggy forced nonchalance, continuing his meal, but his hand quavered.

Talen approached the bar. When the dwarf backed away again, she noticed his odd gait. A heavy thud and hiss accompanied each gimpy step down on his left leg. She leaned forward and saw a metal and leather artificer's leg, complete with whirling gears and a small steam generator. A satisfied smile settled on her lips.

"Must've been the war, huh?" she asked, holstering her left-hand iron. When she looked up, the dwarf's dark eyes blazed like a forge, and they tried to burn through her. But the beads of sweat on his pate betrayed him. Fear kept him still and silent. He knew what she was. They all did.

"You're a long way from home, witch," Piggy said through a mouthful of food.

"Why don't you hobble over and pour me a whiskey, stump?" she said to the dwarf, her voice dry as the miles she'd ridden. She dropped a silver dollar on the counter.

He hesitated for an instant, eyes lingering on the gleaming coin as he fretted his lower lip. After a moment, the allure of silver won him over. It always did. His leg hissed and whirred as he retrieved a glass, set it down, and filled it, never looking away.

She felt everyone in the bar staring.

To whoever took that leg, she toasted silently and tipped back the glass. The wretched stuff left a fiery trail down her throat and into her stomach. "I'm here on business." She nodded at the glass.

"Are you now?" the dwarf asked and poured. He shot a quick glance at Piggy.

The pig must be Jack's special pet. He didn't sport any charms or talismans, so she figured him as a crafter. Probably offering up his artificing skills to save his own ass.

Piggy wiped his plate clean with a piece of bread then shoved it into his mouth. "And what sort of business brings a two-gun bitch—"

Talen reached over and she drove the porcine dandy's face into the bar. Twice.

A sharp ammonia smell filled the air followed by a dripping sound. She glanced at the growing wet spot on the man's pants, doubtless the latest fashion; the pants, not the piss.

She slammed his head into the wood a third time.

"My business is none of—"

A click sounded from behind the bar, followed by the all too familiar whirring of a dwarven gun powering up.

"Turn 'em loose," the dwarf said. "'Fore I drop you where you stand, leaf eater."

"Still holding grudges, stump?" Talen didn't move or release the man. "War's years done now, and winners don't get to hold grudges."

The dwarf spit. "Tell it to my leg."

She let Piggy go.

He fell to the floor, blood pouring from his broken nose. He put a white handkerchief to his face which quickly turned scarlet.

She looked to the dwarf and met his gaze. Better than him had tried to stare her down. Besides, unlike his brothers at Whitestone Hill, this stump didn't have a leviathan to hide in. They both knew how fast elves were, and that two-gun witches were faster still. She could drop him before he could blink much less pull the trigger. And they both knew she wanted to.

"Just get," the dwarf said, trying to hide the fear in his voice and motioned toward the door with his flechette gun. "Run back to the redwoods and—"

Talen drew the badge from her coat and slammed it onto the bar. The spectral image of her face hovered over the tarnished brass star, smiling even less than she did now. Silence swept the room as everyone glanced at each other, then at the dwarf.

"You? A marshal?" the dwarf asked.

"Under contract. I'm a stalker."

The room went still.

The dwarf's face went pale and he lowered the rifle. The only sound was Piggy spitting teeth and whimpering.

"Didn't know you was, uh…" The dwarf swallowed. "A lawman, er, woman." He said the word uncertainly, which Talen enjoyed.

"World is full of strangeness these days, stump." She turned her back to him and considered taking his other leg.

Piggy tried to scoot away, but Talen kicked him in the face. He fell to the floor, spitting more teeth and blood. He inched away from her, and this time she let him.

She turned a hard glare on the men at the table. Jack's boys had slipped their hands out of sight. The other three looked at her with a mix of hope and uncertainty. She could almost read their thoughts. They wanted someone to save them, to kill the devil who'd taken their town. They just weren't sure they wanted it to be an elf, or a woman, much less both.

Pathetic.

"I'm here to collect a soul corrupted by dark magic," she said. "By order of the US Magistrate, the human known as Black Jack Collins is marked as stained." She turned to his boys. "And I mean to bring him in."

No one spoke, but the three men shot quick glances up to the balcony. The painted ladies exchanged a look then vanished into one of the rooms.

"Boss is busy at the moment," one of Jack's boys said through a smile of brown teeth.

Talen turned back to the dwarf and rapped the bar with the small glass.

He refilled it, not looking at her.

She stared at him.

It was you, you and your people. If you'd stayed out of it, kept to your mountains... But no. You sold us for gold.

The stump set the bottle on the bar, his gaze moving down to his flechette gun leaning against the wall.

Talen glanced at the humans, then back to the dwarf. "I've been wondering, stump." She tipped back the whiskey. "What's genocide run? I got me some gold saved up."

He ground his teeth and glanced at the rifle again.

Do it. Reach.

"You won't be the first stalker the boss done put down," said the smaller of the two lackeys.

The other chuckled. "Maybe he'll set you out there next to the last one who came looking. Make a matched set."

Talen kept staring at the dwarf, but her fingers twitched.

Why wait? Not like I never killed an unarmed man before. And this is a dwarf. If anyone has it coming...

Both men laughed, now feeding confidence to each other.

"Nah," said the first. "I reckon he'd find some other use for her first."

Talen felt them eyeing her and the need to bathe returned, this time with acid.

"Yeah," the first one continued, "I bet she'd be all kinds of—"

Talen spun, drawing the right-hand spell iron from her hip. She fed power into it and pulled the trigger, closing the magical circuit. Energy poured into the chamber, activating the spell components.

A blast of arctic wind roared from the barrel.

It blew the man out of his chair mid-sentence and filled the saloon with a dense fog.

When the mist settled to the floor, the outlaw was a statue of ice plastered to the wall. He still wore a bewildered look on his pinched face.

"Jesus, you killed him!" cried the other man, fumbling to pull the mundane shooter from his holster.

Talen drew down with her left-hand iron and leveled it at him as she rotated the cylinder of her right-hand iron to a fresh chamber.

"Not yet." She aimed the right-hand iron at the dwarf as he reached for his rifle. "Get a hearth stone or a crafter that can make one, and he'll thaw just fine." Of course, he'd need it in the next five minutes, and she'd never heard tell of anyone thawing without mental damage. Not as if anyone would notice.

The outlaw sputtered and glared at the other men who'd been sitting at the table. They'd dived away from the blast and were now huddled on the floor.

"Get out," Talen said to them. She turned to the dwarf and motioned with her right-hand iron toward the door. "You too, stump. Leave that sweeper where it is. We'll settle up later. I got business to tend to just now."

The men on the floor didn't wait. They got to their feet and sprinted out of the saloon, the evaporating mist swirling in their wake.

The dwarf hesitated.

Talen pushed power into the right-hand iron, igniting the runes in blue spell fire. "Or we can end it now, and I'll collect that bounty a few minutes later than—"

He raised his hands, gimped around the bar, and out the door. His leg hissed and whirred with each quick step.

The unfrozen outlaw just then seemed to remember he was heeled. He reached for his revolver to draw down—or tried.

It hadn't cleared leather before Talen let loose with her left-hand iron. A blast of pure force slammed into his chest, hammering him against the wall and almost through it. He fell to the floor, clutching at his crushed rib cage for a full second before he died.

"Wha—what about me?" Piggy asked from the corner. His handkerchief, now saturated with blood, still pressed to his face.

"You ain't worth the spell," Talen said and rolled the left-hand iron's cylinder to a fresh chamber. She turned her irons—both burning with blue fire—to the second-floor balcony and still closed doors.

Nothing moved, the only sound, Piggy's wheezy bawling.

She chided herself for letting the humans get to her. No way Jack didn't hear the ruckus. He'd had more than enough time to get dressed and grab his own iron. Now, the obvious move was to climb the stairs, kick open the door, and rain fire down on anything inside.

Which though? She knew which room the two whores had vanished into, and she doubted they took refuge with Jack. Fifty-fifty odds she picked the right one. Of course, Jack would like as not be lying in wait, ready to let loose dark magic as soon as she stepped near the door.

She narrowed her eyes. No, he wouldn't risk waiting for her to put some spells through the door or just setting the whole place on fire. He hadn't come out irons blazing when the shooting started. He'd likely slipped out.

She sniffed the air. Sure enough, the putrid stench of Jack's rotten soul had faded, just a bit.

"You've gone rabbit, Jack." She smiled and sprinted for the exit. She made the porch, pausing only long enough to kick Piggy in the face and send him sprawling to the floor in an unconscious heap.

Once outside, she took aim down both ends of the street, one iron in each direction.

The lane was empty, and nothing moved. Gaoth stood, still hitched to the post, entirely unperturbed. After giving a quick glance to the charred remains in the rocking chair, she moved along the saloon, scanning for movement, and listening intently to every sound.

"Shh, baby," a woman whispered from a window across the street. "It'll be okay. I promise."

Talen made for the corner of the building. She darted her head out and back, taking a quick scan of the alley between the saloon and the remains of a post office.

All clear.

"Gotta admit, I didn't believe y'all two-gun witches was real," said a voice, heavy with a drawl, from everywhere. "Not supposed to be possible to cast with the left hand. Figured y'all nothing but a spook story."

She rounded the corner and made for the rear of the saloon, left-hand iron pointed back, the other forward. As she walked, she kept her eyes moving and her ears open. The mouthpiece might cast Jack's voice far and wide, but he still had to speak into it. She only needed to hear past the illusion.

"In my opinion," Jack continued, "It ain't the dwarves to blame for you being beat. I say it's cause you leaf eaters send your women to fight while your men cower at home, tending to the children."

Between the auditory phantasm and the whispering of the cowering townsfolk, she couldn't pin Jack's location down.

That's it. Keep talking, rot. I'll find you.

"I got me ten pointed ears collected," Jack said. "Course none of them was two-gun witches. Seems fitting I'll be making it an even dozen with you."

Talen rounded the next corner and took aim down the empty street behind the saloon. She spotted an open window on the second floor. He must've fled onto the roof and made a run for it.

Jack started in again, taunting and mocking her. Talen ignored it. She stepped into an alcove and drew the shadows around her, vanishing from view. In that seclusion, she closed her eyes and reached out with her senses. She picked through the sounds, one by one, until she found what she was looking for.

"Mommy," a little girl said, only a hint of fear in her voice.

"Shh, sweetie, it's okay," a woman answered. "Please, I'm begging you, don't hurt my baby—"

"Shut the hell up," Jack hissed, "or I'll hurt you both in ways your nightmares get nightmares about."

Talen opened her eyes and sprinted—still without making a sound—back to the main street. She looked around, trying to figure the direction she'd heard the voices. She spotted an old hotel down the way and darted for the rear of the building. As she'd hoped, the place had a winding staircase and a door on each floor. Undoubtedly for those able to pay but not proper enough to come and go through the front.

She listened again, hoping to pinpoint which floor, but Jack had gone quiet.

A gust of wind blew through the alley and the third-floor door, not quite closed, tapped against the frame.

Spell irons at the ready, she bolted up the stairs, each step light to keep the wood from creaking. Her heart pounded, but she felt alive and filled with purpose. This was what she lived for now. When she reached the door, she took a second to steady herself. Soft breathing and whimpers came from inside but not close.

She waited, knowing the rot wouldn't be able to resist and sure enough, after a long minute, he started up again.

"This here is *my* town, you pointy-eared slommack!" he shouted. "Twenty stalkers came and nineteen fed the buzzards. Lucky number twenty was so pretty I left him to sit out in front of my saloon—"

Talen ignored the rest, letting his frothing rant give her cover. She slipped inside and made her way down the long hallway.

The third from the last door was open, just a hair, and Jack's rotten stink spilled out.

Still wrapped in her shadow glamour, Talen peeked inside. The heavy curtains, pulled almost all the way closed, let in only a sliver of sunlight. More than enough for her elven eyes.

A lanky man in his early twenties, with greasy black hair, crouched near the window. He held tight to a human girl, no older than twelve, his spell iron pressed into her side. A woman of middling years—the girl's mother, Talen presumed—huddled on the far side of the room, softly weeping.

Talen sneered at Jack's cowardice.

At the sight of his filthy, battered coat, her blood boiled. No mistaking the shade of blue or the gold epaulets on the shoulders. This rot was a cavalry soldier, or had been. She was really going to enjoy this.

"Damn it," Jack muttered. "Where you at, you leafer bitch?"

Talen stepped from the shadows and kicked the door wide. The darkened room filled with the blue light of her ignited spell irons, both aimed at Jack's chest.

"Here."

Jack pulled the girl up to shield him more completely. "I'll kill her. You know I will."

The smell of his rotten soul was almost unbearable, but the fire in Talen's chest burned it away.

"No, please!" the mother cried, tears running down her face.

"Let's make a deal, you and me," Jack said and flashed a grin of disintegrating, crooked teeth. Threads of black swirled behind his muddy green eyes.

"You got nothing I want, you blue-backed rot," Talen said. "You think I give two damns about a human? I'll just set you both ablaze and call it done."

"What?" The mother turned to Talen. "No, please!"

Jack narrowed his eyes and smiled wider. "Nah. You can't play that stone-hearted killer with me, leafer. If you didn't care about this pretty little flower, you'd have cooked us both straight away."

One side of Talen's mouth turned up. "I just wanted to see if you had the backbone to die on your feet, rot. Instead of hiding behind a child." Her gaze flicked to the young girl for an instant and their eyes met. Talen didn't see fear or hopelessness. She saw steel.

The girl nodded, barely perceptible.

I'll be damned.

"Have it your way," Talen said and, without looking away, thumbed the left-hand iron's cylinder to a different chamber.

Jack's eyes went wide, and he lifted his iron, leveling it at Talen.

The girl drove her elbow into his crotch.

A ball of greasy black fire belched from Jack's iron, going wide, as he convulsed and howled in pain.

The girl leapt to one side, and Talen pulled the trigger.

A blast of unseen force tore from her left-hand iron, hitting Jack square in the chest. It blew him through the wall and out into open air.

Talen rushed to the hole and looked down.

Jack's twisted and broken body lay still on the dusty road.

She waited. No way would someone that stained go down so easy.

Sure enough, Jack began to move, popping broken bones back into place.

"Run," Talen said to the girl and her mother. "Stay clear of the street."

The mother started to say something, but Talen turned and sprinted back the way she'd come and down the stairs. She took three steps a stride and hit the dirt running.

Jack was on his feet, spell iron up and ready, as she cleared the corner and leapt.

Half a blink later, four mini comets, black as his rotted soul, belched from his iron.

The dark fire passed inches from her body as she tumbled, singeing the tips of her hair.

She rolled to her feet and pushed magic into both irons. Blue light filled the intricate carvings down the length of their barrels and cylinders. Power rushed into the chambers where the waiting components drank the magic.

Three balls of lightning sped from each barrel, spreading out as they flew. Arcs of electricity connected each sphere, forming a wide net.

The crackling web struck and wrapped around Jack, lifting him into the air. His body convulsed, and he hit the ground, smoking and twitching.

Talen rolled the cylinders to fresh chambers as she approached his still-jerking form. She holstered her left-hand iron and drew a bounty crystal from an inside pocket.

Jack stared at her with murder in his eyes but didn't move.

Talen just knelt, tore his shirt away from his chest, and pressed the bounty crystal to a spot over his heart.

The crystal flashed, filled with black, and then Jack slowly turned to ash.

Talen retrieved the full crystal and slipped it back into her duster. Jack's clothing collapsed and his body crumbled and a passing breeze carried him off.

She took the mouthpiece off him and pocketed it, along with a few greenbacks, and his spell iron. On the handle, twenty notches had been carved, each mark done carefully so as to avoid damaging the sigils or the painted spade.

She stood and found dozens of townspeople in the street watching her. They all wore the same conflicted looks on their faces. The mother and daughter from the hotel stepped into view. The mother only gave a stiff nod, but the girl ran forward and threw her arms around Talen's waist, hugging tight.

Talen went rigid at the touch. A part of her she'd almost forgotten existed twinged.

"Thank you," the child said, over and over.

"Laura," the mother called after a couple heartbeats. "Get back over here. Leave the, um, the lady be."

Laura gave Talen a smile, thanked her once more, then turned.

"Wait," Talen said.

The girl looked back.

Talen thought of the women in the saloon and then about Laura's chances. Slim in the best of towns, worse in a place like this. If she got lucky, she'd be little more than a wife spitting out babies. The steel Talen had seen in her eyes would rust.

Unsure why, she held Jack's iron out to the girl. "Don't never let no one define you or what you can be. No man, no woman, no one. You hear me?"

Laura stared with wide eyes at the iron and nodded. "Yes, ma'am."

"Go on, take it," Talen said.

Laura did. It was huge in her small hands. When she gripped it, a faint flicker of blue spell fire danced over the sigils. She smiled up at Talen. "Thank you, ma'am."

"Get on back to your ma now."

Laura did, and her mother drew her close, giving Talen a hard look.

She whispered something Talen couldn't hear, but Talen could read her lips. *Who gives a child a spell iron?*

Talen shrugged. Might be they'd sell the iron. It'd fetch a pretty penny. Then again, she might not. It didn't matter. Laura had given Talen a bit of her soul back, or maybe just a reminder that she wasn't a monster just yet, and no elf ever took without giving back in equal measure, good or bad.

She holstered her right-hand iron and walked back to Gaoth. Some townspeople nodded in thanks, one or two almost smiled. Most only stared dumbly. She didn't know, or much care, what they were thinking. Though she did promise herself the next job would be far from any damned desert—someplace with some green.

When she reached Gaoth, she undid the binding spell on the reins. She climbed into the saddle and noticed the dwarf bartender standing in the saloon's doorway, without the flechette rifle, his expression unreadable.

Her hand drifted to her iron, but when she spotted Laura in the corner of her eye, she just shook her head.

Not today, stump.

He stared for a long moment, his eyes hard. Then, he nodded, took up a knife from his belt, and cut off his beard, damn near to the skin. The dwarf, never looking away, let the beard fall to the ground. The wind took it up and carried it away.

Talen stared, unsure she'd really seen it. She'd never heard of such a thing. To a dwarf, cutting their beard was akin to removing an arm or leg.

She shook her head. "Let's get out of here, Gaoth." She urged the horse into a trot. "Heat is either causing me to see things or the people here to go mad."

Chapter Two

Talen set an easy pace for Gaoth. It was only a day's ride to Santa Fe, but she wasn't in any rush to get to another human city. Around her the rough ground reached to the mountains on the horizon. Scrub brush, mesquite, and other desert trees clung to life in the harsh environ.

She'd never understand why the Pueblo, Apache, Comanche, and Diné people loved this place so well. There was life in the desert, she knew that, and it was strong—it had to be. But it wasn't the lush, verdant life of home. She missed the ferns and the moss, but she missed the redwood and sequoias most of all. When she saw those majestic giants, she saw living history, family, and home.

Humans only saw lumber.

But she didn't have a home or a family anymore. So, who was she now? Her left hand went to the inside duster pocket and the six bounty crystals there. Was that what she'd become: a monster hunting monsters?

She clenched her jaw and pushed back against the emptiness inside that threatened to swallow her whole, though she struggled to think up a compelling reason not to let it drag her down.

Her heart and soul screamed for revenge, but she knew there'd be no solace in it, even if she ever found it. But what else did she have? The few remaining elves had been cloistered together in the Washington territory. Even the tribal nations the elves allied with had been slaughtered or forced onto reservations.

Some days she could convince herself that she was still a Shadow Warden, still defending the magic from corruption and removing those stained by darkness.

"Now I'm doing it for coin instead of honor," she muttered to herself. And at the order of the humans who'd taken everything from her.

Today wasn't one of those days she could lie to herself.

Not a Shadow Warden, not anymore, not even a monster. Just a husk stuffed with the screams and accusations of ghosts.

What of the girl? Laura? her mother's voice asked.

"Like as not, she'll grow up to use that iron against an elf."

Maybe she'll remember the elf who saved her and how it changed her life, the memory of her mother argued.

Talen closed her eyes and drew in a slow breath. She wanted to believe that, but it was hard to trust in good anymore. Hell, it was hard to trust in anything anymore. She stopped herself from questioning if she would've killed the child to get to Jack. She didn't want to know the answer.

She pushed that thought aside and let her mind drift back to better times.

The memory wrapped around her, ragged and threadbare, like the tattered remains of a half-forgotten dream. The gentle roar of the ocean crashing against cliffs enveloped her. She drew in a breath, and it carried the ghost of salty sea air, just beneath the scent of her mother's freshly baked cakes.

The recollection didn't last. They never did.

She wiped her eyes, reminded herself that she deserved it all, and continued on.

Sometime later, she came upon a secluded spot protected by a ring of large rocks and made camp. If she timed it right, she'd reach town early. She could cash in, resupply, find new bounties, and be off before most of the humans were out and about.

Gaoth chewed on a patch of browning grass as Talen laid out her bedroll. She checked and cleaned her irons, then with one in each hand, lay back.

The stars shone like a hundred million sparks in the black of the huge sky.

Maybe the Diné weren't so wrong. She had to admit, the desert did have its beauty.

The tears came then, and her hands started to shake. She didn't fight back, just let the sobs rack her body as she thought of her mother and the countless dead.

In time, the tears ran dry. The soul-hollowing sadness remained, as did the shame and guilt. Not that she ever really let them go. She tried for sleep, continuing the useless hope that tonight she'd dream of home instead of war.

She didn't.

~

By the time the sun rose, she'd been riding for better than an hour.

Santa Fe was the largest city she'd known, which was just one reason that she despised it. Thankfully, the streets were quiet though. Even the churches hadn't begun to stir.

She gave those places a wide berth. Humans of a particular religious conviction viewed the eldar as demons or witches. Given cause—any cause—they'd be glad to burn or lynch her, or worse. As such, Talen tied back her hair, not hiding it per se, but not brandishing it. No need to invite trouble, especially when humans outnumbered her by thousands.

Head down, she made for the courthouse and magistrate's office. Both shared a large, garish stone building in the center of town. She hitched Gaoth to the post but didn't bind the reins. No rustler would get far, though a stained might manage to compel him. But if she had to leave town quick-like—which had happened more than once—

seconds counted. She climbed the stairs and pulled at the heavy wooden doors. They didn't budge.

"*Terisan ut marrin,*" she muttered. "Of course you ain't open yet."

Talen looked around but didn't see anyone, so she found a quiet spot to wait impatiently, trying hard not to be noticed, and head low but still watching the street. As the minutes dragged by, anxiety nibbled at her guts, and her hands began to tremble. She pushed her left into a pocket and rested the other on her belt, inches from her iron.

The minutes passed like the last drops of sap from a dying pine.

Twenty minutes later, the office remained locked tight.

"*Shanzi fetsuian,*" she cursed under her breath and went back to Gaoth.

She'd hoped to be gone by now. Ordinarily, she'd just scrounge for spell components in the wild. Not only were they free, they'd be better quality than any human shop had on offer—or at least would sell to her. But this sun-blasted desert offered precious little, and she needed more than just components.

Her pockets held just over two hundred dollars. A small fortune to most, but since few humans were crafters, those that were could—and did—charge a premium. She ought to have more than triple what she'd need, assuming they charged her something reasonable. Not that anyone ever had.

Despite knowing full well how many spare charges she had for her irons, she checked the saddlebag.

"Still just four."

She closed and warded the pack, chiding herself for waiting so long to resupply. Then she promised—again—not to wait so long next time.

Pulling her hat low, for all the good it would do, she made her way to the main street. It didn't take long to find a dry goods and magical wares shop. Blessed bark, it was open. She pinned her marshal's star to the outside of her coat, so it was in clear view, and stepped inside.

The place was empty, another blessing, save for the shopkeeper.

He was a human of middling years, balding, and sporting a massive moustache. He spotted the star first.

"Morning, Marshal, what can I—" His smile vanished when he took in the rest of her.

Talen kept her eyes down, hands in plain sight and well away from her irons. When she spoke, her tone was soft, deferential, though it wrung her insides. "I need some goods, sir. Couple shirts, canteens, and some components for charges."

"Do you now?"

"Yes, sir, I do." She swallowed her pride and the rising bile both. Humans seemed to delight in the humiliation of those they viewed as less than them.

She studied the labeled glass jars that lined the wall behind him, half hoping he wouldn't have anything worth buying. The selection was surprisingly wide, and the contents seemed good-quality.

Damn it.

That meant they'd cost all the more. A single rune stone—a thieving ward—hung on a string around the neck of each container. The magic would prevent the jars from leaving the shop or anyone but the shopkeep from opening them.

He gave her a long, hard look. "I don't sell to leafers." He turned away. "Get the hell out of my shop."

Talen's hands itched. She wanted to lay out this *juarchian*, take what she needed, and burn the place to the ground. But despite the desolation that ate at her soul, she wasn't in a hurry to die. This wasn't some town taken by a stained, the people cowed into inaction. This city had a population near a hundred thousand. She'd no idea how many were zealots, soldiers, or stalkers, but it was certain to be too many to fight and win. They'd do worse than kill her, and no one would lose a bit of sleep.

Going before her time could mean she wasn't welcomed home by her sisters and mother. So, she drew in a breath and pushed down both her dignity and rage. This was her lot in life now.

"Please, sir, I can pay." She counted a hundred and fifty dollars in her pocket, drew them out, and set the greenbacks on the counter.

He turned back around, looked down at the bills, then at her. "What do you want?"

As ever, human convictions were only as deep as their pockets.

She rattled off a list of components.

He shook his head. "This ain't enough for all that."

She ground her teeth and wrestled back her fury. She pulled out the rest of her greenbacks and added them to stack on the counter. "That's better than two hundred dollars. We both know that's more than enough—"

His eyes went wide. "You telling me how to run my business, leafer?" He jabbed a finger at her. "You listen here. I sell to who I want, and charge what I want. Instead of griping about prices, you oughta be grateful I'm even willing to do business with your kind."

"Yes, sir," she said through clenched teeth, eyes down, but watching him in her peripheral vision. The words tasted like poison. "I apologize."

He nodded. "That's more like it. Your kind needs to learn some goddamned gratitude. We could've wiped you all out, but we didn't. Did we?" He shook his head, his mouth twisting in disgust. "This is what our leniency gets us, uppity leafers."

Talen feared her teeth would crack from clenching her jaw so hard.

"Now, you keep quiet," the shopkeeper said, "or maybe I'll march you down to Father Anderson, let him—"

Talen met his eyes. She didn't say a word. She didn't have to.

If I'm going down, juarchian, I'm not going alone.

The man took half a step back, went a little pale, and swallowed.

Talen pushed her coat clear of her iron.

After a long moment of silence, the shopkeep found his lost bravado, snatched up the dollars, and started putting together her order.

"Don't think of stealing nothing," He made a show of picking out the worst quality stuff and shorted her on the quantity to boot. He nodded to the wall on his right. "You'll find blouses and canteens over there."

She held her tongue and went to collect her goods. The shirts were all cotton, which like as not, came from the southern states. She'd heard tell of some law passed that abolished slavery, but doubted it meant a damned thing. Unfortunately, she didn't have any options.

"Those are men's shirts," the man said when she set them and the canteens on the counter.

She didn't answer.

He muttered something Talen couldn't make out, though she could guess, and bundled up her goods. He shoved the parcel across the counter, making a point of not handing it to her.

She took up her items and turned to leave.

He cursed and spit at her back.

She sidestepped it and though tempted to cut him down, she left the store and the dung heap running it intact.

Once outside, her anger won out and got the best of her good sense. She tore the leather strip from her hair, letting it fall loose and in plain view of the people now filling the street. Some stared, but most looked away, pretending she didn't exist. There wasn't enough pride left in her to care what happened now. Let them come for her. She'd make such end that their great-grand-children would be afraid to even whisper the word "elf."

She made for the magistrate's office, head high, and coat fluttering open, displaying the spell iron on her hip. Those who didn't cross the street stepped well away as she neared. She heard the curses, every one of them, each just feeding the fiery rage inside her.

The office was open when she returned, but three other stalkers were cashing in. The smell coming off them was almost as bad as a stained, though it had nothing to do with magic.

The clerk took two crystals from the obvious leader of the trio and set them, one at a time, in a holder. A ghostly image of the collected bounty floated above the crystal, the reward just below. After checking the last crystal, the clerk dropped them down a brass tube, and turned back to the malodourous collection.

"All right, Jeremiah," he said, setting two fresh crystals down.

"That's one hundred each for Billy Thorn, and the Lincoln kid." He counted out the greenbacks and coins.

Jeremiah collected the crystals and cash then nodded at the clerk. "Pleasure doing business with you, Henry." He smiled at his buddies. "Boys, I think I need me a drink and something sweet on my—" he glanced at Henry and smiled, "arm."

The other two chuckled.

Henry shook his head then spotted Talen. His smile vanished, and he went rigid.

Jeremiah noticed the reaction and turned.

"Well, I'll be," he said and spit to one side, missing the spittoon. "I heard tell of a leafer stalker, but I didn't believe it."

"Ain't right," the stinking heap on his left said. "Paying a leafer to kill humans, even if they are stained. Just ain't right."

"I agree, Thomas," Jeremiah said. "Maybe we ought to relieve her of her crystals and cash them in ourselves. Call it recompass for all those her kind done killed."

It's recompense, you ass.

The shopkeep had used the last of Talen's patience. She let her right hand slip down to her iron. "I don't see things working out that way, *juarchian*," she said with a calm she did not feel.

"Word is," Jeremiah said, hand drifting to his own iron, "that you're a two-gun witch." He looked her up and down, giving her a smile. "I wonder, you got two of anything else?"

His boys chuckled.

"Nah, just the one." She smiled. "And it's lined with teeth."

The smiles vanished.

She glanced at Jeremiah's crotch and shook her head. "Don't worry, little fella, I ain't interested in such a tiny morsel."

Henry whistled, and four soldiers appeared behind him. "I won't have no trouble in here, leafer."

Talen glanced at the man and then the soldiers. "I ain't looking for trouble, just to cash in." Talen looked back at Jeremiah and his friends.

"Well then, get over here and get done," Henry said.

Talen stepped around the stinking crew and up to the counter.

With her left hand—her right still close to her iron—she drew out the six crystals and set them on the counter.

Everyone looked from them to her and back.

"Slow week," she said.

Jeremiah, his friends, and even the soldiers shifted from one foot to another.

Henry cleared his throat and took the crystals to the holder. The first three were low level stained, the standard hundred each. The fourth was a deserter that had been killing his former brothers-in-arms. She'd taken her time tracking him down. The next was an ex-confederate turned highwayman. She'd taken special pleasure in that one. Not because she had any love for the Union. But a willingness to fight, die, and kill to preserve slavery was another matter. Those crystals were two hundred each.

Henry put the last crystal in the holder.

"Holy shit," the third of Jeremiah's trio said, "she done got Black Jack."

The soldiers exchanged a look. They gripped their rifles— mundane shooters—a little tighter.

"She, um, likely got him sleeping or something," said Jeremiah. "Or she killed the stalker what actually took him down."

His friends nodded a little too emphatically.

Henry dropped the crystals down the tube and walked back to Talen. He counted out the bounty in double eagles and greenbacks, setting them in front of her.

"That's twelve hundred all together," he said, setting six clean crystals next to the money.

Talen reached out for them.

"Now don't tell me you forgot about that new leafer tax, Henry," a third soldier, this one an officer, said. He wore a spell iron on his hip and the left side of his face resembled melted wax. It could only be the result of a blast from a spell iron. She knew what came next, and it took every bit of her willpower, but she did nothing.

The soldier reached down and took a full third of the notes from the stack and pocketed them. His gaze met Talen's, daring her to challenge him.

Jeremiah and his boys chuckled.

Talen pocketed the remaining money and crystals, grudgingly nodded at the soldier, and then went to the wall displaying active bounties. One at the top caught her attention right away.

By order of the US Magistrate, Margaret Florence Jameson, aged 24 years, is hereby declared stained by dark magic. A reward of $5,000 is offered for her confirmed bounty crystal.

A woman? That was surprising. Human women didn't tend to take to dark magic. But according to the warrant, Margaret had razed three towns in the Nebraska Territory, leaving no survivors. Talen narrowed her eyes. It wasn't unheard of to post bounties for other states or territories, especially big ones, but she'd never seen one posted so far away. It was a month's ride to the Nebraska Territory.

She stared at the warrant. It would get her out of the desert. Then she read over the rest of the warrant and her blood ran cold.

Last reports had her bound for the Dakota Territory.

Memories of fire and death rose up and threatened to overwhelm her. She clenched her trembling hands and tried to ignore the twisting of her guts.

"You gonna stand there all day, leafer?" Henry asked.

Talen drew in a breath, pushed the anxiety down, and returned to the here and now. It took a moment to get her hands to stop shaking.

"What's this mark mean?" she asked without looking back and pointed to a symbol on the warrant.

"You'll need a special crystal to collect that one," he said, no patience in his tone. "Seems some stained are immune to the regular crystals, but they came up with some new ones that work just fine."

"Immune?" Talen asked, finally turning to look at the clerk. She didn't know much about the crystals; she was a caster, not a crafter. But, as she understood it, they drew out the dark magic.

WANTED
$5,000 REWARD
MARGARET FLORENCE JAMESON
BY ORDER OF THE U.S. MAGISTRATE
MARGARET FLORENCE JAMESON, aged 24 years, is hereby declared stained by dark magic. A reward of $5,000 is offered for her confirmed bounty crystal.
Crimes Include: Destruction by dark magic of Hendricks, Prosperity, and Covenant (all Nebraska Territory)
Last seen bound for the Dakota Territory.

The more corrupt the stained was, the less it left behind. The worst, like Jack, left nothing but ash. Before the crystals, Shadow Wardens had to outright kill the stained, no easy feat. It still wasn't easy, but not like it'd been. Conveniently, the crystals also allowed for bounties. Leave it to humans to profit on the corruption of dark magic.

"Yep," Henry said. "They work same as the old, close to the heart, but you need to get them inside."

"Inside?" Thomas asked. "No thank you. You won't catch me cutting into no stained, much less shoving a crystal into one."

"Reckon that's why only Red Right Hand takes those bounties," Henry said.

Cold fear made its way up Talen's spine, and a tightness gripped her chest.

Most stalkers hunted stained for money, some for glory, but religious zealotry drove the Red Right Hand. All humans, and most elves, could only use magic with their right hand: the left side drew in power, the right pushed it out. The Red Right Hand saw any magic outside what they deemed natural—right hand magic they called it—an abomination. This included any elf, though they had a special animosity for dual casters, or two-gun witches.

When the elven nations fell, some humans had called for the complete extinction of her people. The Red Right Hand had been the loudest voice in the choir. In the end, "compassion" had won out—in the form of a tiny, tightly controlled reservation. But not before The Red Hand had burned hundreds of elves alive, men, women, and even children.

It took a great deal of effort, but Talen kept the disquiet from showing. She hated the Red Hand like nothing and no one else, but she also feared them. She wasn't stupid, and if she took this bounty, she'd damn sure cross paths with the Red Hand at some point, and they never worked alone.

Through the fear and rage, something nibbled at her mind. Desperate to push her thoughts aside, she studied the warrant closer. Something was off, but she couldn't place it. She scanned the poorly drawn picture of Margaret. She hadn't been an outlaw before her corruption. If she had, there'd be a multi-angle magical image of her. That was odd, too. Law abiding humans didn't often turn to dark magic and when they did, not usually bad enough to earn a $5000 bounty.

Lots of oddities adding together.

But it means going back to the Dakota Territory.

She pointedly did not think of Whitestone Hill.

"Ain't got all day, leafer," Henry said.

She didn't like the prospect of returning to where her world ended, nor of crossing paths with Red Hand Stalkers. But, while the Red Hand were cruel to the point of being soulless, she'd know to watch for them.

She smiled a bit, partly at the thought of leaving the desert behind. Mostly though, she liked the notion of snatching a bounty from the Red Hand, and maybe even ending some of the *juarchian* bastards in the process.

"I'll take it," she said and went back to the counter, left hand extended.

Henry just stared at her for several seconds. He gave her a level look as he produced a copy of the warrant and a crystal from under the counter. He started to hand them to her, then thought better of it and set them both in front of her.

She rolled her eyes and picked them up before turning and leaving the office. She made for Gaoth just shy of a jog. Even so, she didn't make it a dozen steps before someone called out from behind her.

"We got us some unfinished business, witch," Jeremiah said.

"*Terisan ut marrin,*" she muttered before turning.

The trio walked toward her, and she weighed her options. She could drop all three, but the soldiers would come running and shooting. Her coat would stop plenty of the mundane slugs, but that officer's spell iron was another matter. She had her knife, but they'd charge her with murder and put a bounty on her head right quick.

She let Jeremiah and his friends draw closer.

"We got no business," she said. "I'm leaving town."

"Oh, we got business," Jeremiah said and nodded at the kid on his left. "Jimmy here had a brother in the army; died up at Stony Lake."

She studied the three and pegged Jeremiah as the biggest threat, Thomas second. Jimmy, the runt of the litter, looked ready to piss his pants. His eyes darted around and sweat beaded on his face. The ammonia-like stench of fear coming off him was strong enough to be noticeable over the stink of sweat, dirt, and shit.

"You killed him," Jeremiah said.

Talen shrugged. "Might've. I killed a lot of blue backs that day."

Jeremiah went for his iron.

Talen lunged forward and seized his wrist before he could reach it. She twisted and the bone snapped, eliciting a growl of pain.

In one motion, she turned, yanked him forward, and drove his face into her knee. A wet crunch was followed by a spray of blood from his nose.

She kicked back with the same foot, driving it into Thomas's gut before he could throw down. The man fell back and tumbled away, gasping for breath.

A blinding pain in her side almost brought Talen to her knees.

"You leafer bitch!" Jimmy yelled, drawing the knife from her side, and made to drive it in again.

Even wounded, Talen could best this *juarchian*. She caught his hand and pivoted, tossing him at Thomas, who was getting to his feet.

She drove her boot heel down on Jeremiah's right hand, breaking several more bones, then turned and hurried to Gaoth, gripping her side.

She got in the saddle as the soldiers emerged from the magistrate's office. They stopped to take in the scene, buying her enough time to turn Gaoth and urge him into a full gallop. By the time they started shooting, she was out of range. She gave Gaoth his head, and they ate up ground at a blinding speed. Renewed pain surged through her every time his hooves touched down, but she stayed conscious. When she finally dared to glance back, the agony almost knocked her from the saddle. But she did get a clear look and didn't see any sign of pursuit.

Chapter Three

asy. We're clear," she said, trying again to convince Gaoth to slow his pace.

He'd been running full out for the better part of five miles. Most horses would be dead, and even Gaoth had reached his limit.

"You won't do me no favors if you die on me, old friend," she said. "Please, slow down."

At last, the horse slowed to a walk.

Talen sighed in relief. She leaned forward, ignoring the twisting pain, and pressed her cheek to his neck. "Thank you," she whispered.

They found a spot near a stream and behind some boulders. With luck, it'd be safe long enough for Talen to heal. She slid from the saddle and about fell on her face.

Gaoth leaned down and nudged her with his nose.

"I'm okay," she said through clenched teeth. After a few sharp breaths, she got the upper hand on the stabbing pain in her side and got to her feet. With effort, she unbuckled the saddle and let it fall to the ground, followed by the blanket.

She motioned to the stream. "Go drink, I'll be fine."

The horse complied, if reluctantly, and began gulping down water.

Talen winced as she gingerly shrugged out of her coat. When the sensation of being ripped in half subsided to merely excruciating, she looked over the ensorcelled jacket. The charms woven into it should've stopped the blade, but there were no marks. It must've come open during the fight. It'd been stupid to underestimate the kid.

She made to sit, but only managed a half graceful fall. She grunted as she peeled off her blood-soaked shirt and turned to look at the wound. Blood still oozed from the inch-long cut. She needed to stop the bleeding, and fast. With cautious haste, she kicked off her boots and stripped out of her clothes. Once nude, she lay back on the bare earth and stretched her arms out to maximize exposure to the sun.

The warmth of the earth seeped into her back then met the heat washing over her from the desert sun. Her muscles relaxed and the agony of the wound faded to mild anguish.

She whispered a prayer to her mother.

With effort, she dug her fingers into the hard-packed dirt to the second knuckle. Focused on the markings that covered her body, she whispered the incantation. The magic spread out from her, a plea for help to the sun, the earth, and all the living creatures nearby. In a forest, even a modest one, there'd be power to spare. In the desert, life guarded its energy with ferocity.

As the invocation continued, her consciousness both expanded and drew in. Her awareness encompassed everything around her as well as the minute details of her own body. She could hear the burbling of the nearby stream, smell the different plants growing around her, and even taste the blood that had soaked into the earth.

The knife had gone deep, but it had missed her guts.

The sun answered first, its power flowing into her. Her body drank in the light, channeling the energy to her wound and encouraging it to close.

The bleeding slowed.

The earth answered next, followed by the trees and brush. Next came the stream, the algae in the water, the insects, even Gaoth heard her plea and answered.

As ever, the outpouring of compassion and generosity humbled her, and left her feeling unworthy.

Life itself flowed into her through the skin in contact with the earth, and that exposed to the sun. She shaped and directed the energy. First, she stopped the bleeding, then she set to knitting the flesh back together.

It was long, mentally exhausting work.

She could've taken all the power offered and healed faster, but she wouldn't repay such generosity with wastefulness. She took only what she needed.

When she opened her eyes, the sun hung low in a sky painted in shades of purple. The air had turned cold, but the sun had been so giving that its heat warmed her still. Her fingers brushed where the wound had been; not even a scar remained. Her head still swam a bit from loss of blood though. She could've used the remaining power to replace it, but she could also do it on her own, given time. She returned the gifted life energy, pouring it back into the earth and to all those who'd given it.

"Thank you," she whispered.

Gaoth whinnied, and she couldn't hold back a smile.

Taking her time, she sat up and then got to her feet. She redressed, using one of the spare shirts in her saddlebag. She submerged the blood-soaked shirt in the stream. Methodically, she rinsed the blood out, gifting it to the small organisms that fed on such things. When done, she pressed the ragged garment down into the soft mud. There, the fabric itself would, in time, return to the earth: a partial repayment for the gift given to her.

After rinsing the blood from the inside of her coat and laying it out to dry, she saw to her faithful friend, brushing Gaoth in slow and loving strokes.

"Sorry I couldn't tend to you sooner," she whispered, running a comb through his mane.

Gaoth, of course, forgave her.

After a grooming that bordered on extravagant, she tended to herself. She drank her three canteens dry. After refilling them, she gathered leaves and bark from nearby trees and scrub, careful not to take too much from any one plant.

Her stomach full and thirst slaked, she set to work on the spell components. Her hands moved by memory, mixing and shaping the components into charges for her spell irons. Some found the work tedious and only bought premade charges. She enjoyed it, finding it meditative. As her hands worked, her mind drifted to calm, and she sank into prayer.

Mother, I miss you, with all I am, all that remains of me. I feel dead and dark inside most times. When I don't, I only feel guilt, shame, sadness, and pain. I'm wandering, lost and without purpose. I tell myself I'm gathering a measure of justice and fighting the corruption still. But I know it's a lie. It's the blackest part of my soul calling out for vengeance. I thank you for looking over me, for the brief moments of peace I find, but it's not enough to stop me dying inside. I'm falling deeper and deeper into despair and I fear I'll fall so far I become what I'm sworn to destroy. Please, bring me peace and light my way through the darkness. Please, just let me leave this world behind and join you and my sisters.

Her mother spoke as she always did, with patience and love tinged in sadness.

My precious, beloved child. Your sisters and I miss you as well. We weep at seeing you struggle alone in such darkness. All the rains could not measure to my endless tears. You survived so much, but your soul bears the scars your body does not. I understand what the promise I asked of you has cost, and I'm so very sorry.

No, my child. It's not your time. So much has been asked of you. It's hard. I know, but I also know your strength. I saw it when you were but a child. I saw it in the Shadow Warden you became, and I see it still in the woman you are now. It isn't clear to you now, but the worry about the darkness in you is precisely what keeps it from consuming you. Your heart hasn't hardened, though you try to convince yourself otherwise. Despite your pain, you still show kindness. This is not weakness but strength. You are still, and forever shall be, my joy and my treasure. I love you.

When the prayer ended, Talen opened her eyes. She didn't wipe away the tears. They were hers, and she'd earned every one of them.

As such, she didn't feel the least bit of shame in them. Oh, she had shame to spare elsewhere though, the same constant disgrace that kept her from praying more often. Her mother's words were a salve to her battered soul, but she still didn't feel worthy of such comfort.

Neither did it do anything to fill the hole in her heart.

Gaoth came over and nuzzled his head against hers. She returned the gesture.

The sky had turned dark by the time she'd finished preparing the last of the charges. She tucked them away and decided to scout the area a bit. She didn't find any signs of pursuit. No surprise really. She busted up those boys but hadn't killed anyone, so no laws broken. Not to say Jeremiah, Thomas, and Jimmy wouldn't come looking. She figured they would, sooner or later. But outside of town, away from the law, it'd end different. Nothing less than they deserved.

By the time she spread out her bedroll, exhaustion had settled over her whole body and seeped into her soul. She lay back and stared at the stars for a long while before sinking into an uneasy sleep, her spell irons close at hand.

As always, death, fire, and shame waited for her.

Talen sat up with a start, irons burning with spell fire and aimed straight ahead. Her eyes moved quick, scanning the darkness. It took almost a full minute to recognize she was awake.

She doused her irons and lowered them, hands shaking so bad she wouldn't hit a cliff side at ten feet. Her heart pounded, and her shirt clung to her with cold sweat. She drew up her knees and buried her tear-soaked face into her arms.

Gaoth lowered his head, resting it on her shoulder, his steady breathing a lifeline. She leaned into him for a long while, trying to breathe as her body quivered.

The countless dead she'd failed—Lakota and elf alike—still drifted behind her closed eyelids. Their screams and unanswered pleas shook her soul so hard it threatened to shatter.

Time passed, though she couldn't say how much, and eventually, the familiar numbness returned.

"Thank you, my friend," she said, kissing Gaoth's cheek. "I'd be lost without you."

Gaoth nuzzled against her and then pulled back to meet her eyes.

She nodded. "It's passed."

He stepped away, though only a couple steps.

Talen lay down once again. The darkness didn't carry even a hint of dawn. She was so tired, weary to her very bones. These moments left her feeling like a tattered whisper, as if the softest breeze would tear her to shreds.

She wanted to pray to her mother, to hear comforting words again, but she didn't.

A distant sound broke the still night, igniting Talen's senses. Everything else melted away. She didn't move, just lay there listening.

Three sets of boots crunched over the hard ground. The footsteps were light but clumsy. Beyond that, three hearts beat: two were steady, one pounded like a drum.

A familiar stench of sweat, dirt, and shit came next.

Sooner it is, then.

She got to her feet, silent as the night, holstered her irons, and drew her knife. She had the charges to drop them with her irons, but she wouldn't waste them on these *juarchian*.

She wrapped herself in shadow and moved through the darkness, her elven eyes not the least hindered by the moonless night. A half a mile from camp she found them. They'd left behind their horses, and —save for Jeremiah—had their spell irons drawn but dark. He gripped a mundane six-shooter in his left hand, his broken right wrapped in a splint.

She smiled as she watched them stumble along. The landscape didn't offer much in terms of obstacles, but the dark could deceive human eyes.

Thomas nearly tripped over a stone and swore in a harsh whisper, "Damn it!"

"Keep quiet," Jerimiah said.

Talen let out a slow breath, reversed the grip on her knife, and sprinted forward.

They didn't hear a thing.

She moved past the bigger two and went for Jimmy. She ended him quick, driving her knife between his ribs and into his heart.

She let his corpse fall.

"What the hell was that?" Thomas asked.

"I don't know," Jeremiah said. "Jimmy, you all right?"

Talen didn't even breathe.

"Shit," Thomas said. "I told you this was a bad idea."

"Shut up!" Jeremiah shouted and spun, his revolver moving from one spot of empty darkness to another.

"I can't see a damned thing," Thomas said.

Talen rolled away from the dead boy, crouched low, then closed her eyes and waited.

"To hell with it," Thomas said and, as expected, ignited his spell iron.

"Damn it!" Jeremiah shouted, blinded by his friend.

Talen opened her eyes and pounced. In a single movement, she grabbed Thomas's forehead and pulled back, exposing his throat. She cut quick, slicing him from ear to ear.

His iron went dark and fell from his hand. He followed it to the ground, gurgling and gasping, hands clutching at the flow of blood.

She dashed to one side.

"Damn you, witch!" Jeremiah shouted and fired into the darkness as he turned in a slow circle.

When his shooter clicked on spent cylinders, Talen came up behind him. She'd make sure this would hurt.

First, she cut across the back of his knees, severing the tendons.

He fell, bellowing like a dying cow, and hurled his spent shooter into the night.

Talen didn't even need to sidestep.

He drew a knife from his boot and spit. "Come on, witch! I ain't scared of—"

Talen stepped from the shadows, kicked the knife from his hand,

and then drove her boot heel down. The small bones in his left hand snapped, and he howled.

"These are the last words you'll hear, so listen hard, filth," she said, cleaning the blood from her knife and then sheathing it. "I could've ended you all in Santa Fe without even breaking a sweat. But I let you live, even after Jimmy stuck me. I was gone and had no mind to ever think of you again."

"Fuck you, leafer whore!" Jeremiah said and then spat at her.

Talen put her full weight on his broken left hand, eliciting another cry.

"But you just couldn't let me be," she said. "All 'cause I had the gall to defend myself?"

He spat more curses, but a sharp kick to the crotch quieted him to a whimper.

"You think you know hate, *juarchian?*" She asked. "You don't. Not like I do. Not the righteous hate of the wronged that eats at your soul and screams for blood." She looked him over, smiled a bit, and nodded. "Well, maybe now you do."

And now I got another reason to hate myself, but then, what's one more?

She drew her right-hand iron, poured magic into it, and took aim at his pelvis. She didn't fire though. The cold, long burning anger in her belly wanted to make him suffer as she had. If she gave into that desire, it might make them even, but it would also made her like him.

He mistook her hesitation for cowardice and started mocking her. His words stopped when the blast of kinetic force crushed his skull, driving blood and brains into the dry earth.

She holstered her dark iron, let out a breath, and then set to looting the bodies. She emptied their irons, helping herself to the charges and the spares on their belts. In Jeremiah's coat, she found two hundred dollars, and pocketed it as well. Lastly, she collected their spell irons, brass stars, and empty bounty crystals. Those she buried near a boulder a couple hundred yards away. The rest, she left for the vultures, coyotes, and other scavengers.

Gaoth waited for her back at camp. His eyes bore no judgment. He never did, though sometimes she wished he would. She packed up, cleaned the site of any sign she'd been there, and saddled Gaoth. In a handful of minutes, they were riding off into the darkness.

It took the better part of a week to get out of the New Mexico Territory and into the Colorado. Gaoth could cover almost thirty miles a day if Talen let him, but she kept him reined in so she could focus on healing.

The next two weeks brought them close to the mountains. She kept a watchful eye out for dwarven scouts but still reveled in being around trees once more, savoring every moment.

All too soon though, they turned northeast into the Nebraska Territory and its flat open plains. What the vast prairie lacked in trees, it made up for in plentiful plant life and other components. By the time she reached her first destination, more than a month after she'd killed Jimmy, she had almost three hundred charges in her saddlebags.

Chapter Four

Talen stood a mile outside of Prosperity, the first of the towns Margaret had destroyed. Her gaze moved along the broad horizon. Tall grass blew in the gentle breeze, an ocean of green and gold. Above her, the sky was a bright blue, painted with billowing white clouds. Despite the beautiful spring day, she grew antsy. The openness of the plains had always made her uneasy since it left nothing to put her back to. Her hands shook and the onslaught of sights, sounds, and smells threatened to overwhelm her. She gripped the reins tighter, gritted her teeth, and beat back the disquiet.

Turning Gaoth in a slow circle, she completed her scan of the wide-open land; nothing for miles and miles but miles and miles. They rounded the town, spiraling closer each time, her—now controlled—senses taking in every detail.

Something felt off.

She slid her right hand closer to her iron.

Then it came to her: no stench of a stained or dark magic, not even a whisper of it. Corruption could've faded in the months since Margaret's attack, but not if she were as stained as the warrant claimed. It'd take seasons—years even—to cleanse that kind of despoilment. The prairie grass had already reclaimed what remained of the town. The tall grass of the plains grew quickly, but it'd take months, not weeks, to grow this tall.

A cold unease settled over Talen for what she knew would be a long stay.

She sat at the edge of town, considering her options. Margaret supposedly was bound for the Indian Territory, but Talen knew warrants got at least as much wrong as right. According to this one, Margaret had been gone for near on two months, but there might be some clues left behind.

Despite her apprehension, Talen nudged Gaoth forward, though she kept a careful measure of her surroundings.

Prosperity hadn't been big, just another popup village on the plains. Near nothing remained of it. The extent of the destruction surprised Talen. Humans tended to exaggerate black magic attacks. Not the case here.

Burnt timbers and the occasional pile of stones—remnants of a fireplace and chimney—were all that hinted anything had ever been there. Some stained, like Jack, fed on fear. They set themselves up as potentate of one town or another and bled it dry. Other stained reveled in carnage and ruin. Margaret appeared to be the latter.

In the absence of humans and their structures, the prairie had moved back in with enthusiasm. Vibrant life pulsed all around Talen. Even in the center of what had been town, the grass had grown tall enough to brush Gaoth's underside.

She dismounted and knelt to examine the vestiges of a building. The fire that had brought the place down had burned long and hot. It had to be magical fire. Mundane flames would've burned out before consuming so much.

She picked up a charred board and sniffed it. Nothing but burnt and the earthy smell of wet wood left out in the elements. She stood and turned, taking in the whole of the destruction. She drew in a slow breath through her nose. She only smelled charred wood, grass, and the earth beneath her feet.

Gaoth made to start chomping the grass, but Talen stopped him.

"I know it smells clean," she said, "but best not risk it."

He snorted and shook his head, unhappy, but complying.

She walked through the ruins of the town, even ventured into the remains of a few buildings. What she found—or rather didn't find—confounded her all the more: no bodies, bones, or remnants of any kind. In fact, aside from the buildings themselves, there was no sign anyone had lived there at all.

"Something sure as hell ain't right here," she whispered.

She pulled out the new bounty crystal and inspected it again. It didn't seem overly strange, just a bit larger and with a different facet pattern.

Could whatever made Margaret immune to bounty crystals also mask the dark residue?

Talen shook her head, pocketed the crystal, and made her way back to Gaoth. As she walked, something else needled her, but she couldn't place the source. With so much wrong about this place, she couldn't see any one thing over another.

"What do you think?" she asked Gaoth, looking around. "Don't feel like a stained rampage, does it?"

He shook his head.

"Maybe I'm wrong, and it was a mundane fire," she said. "A lightning strike could've set the grass aflame." She'd heard tell those fires could turn the plains into a hellscape.

Gaoth just looked at her.

"Nah, too simple," she said. "It also don't explain the lack of dead." She shrugged. "I suppose some could've survived and come back to retrieve the bodies."

Gaoth offered no comment.

"No," she said, "if the attack had been as bad as all that, any survivors would've run and never looked back." She drew out one of the canteens and took a long swallow of water. "Maybe the fire burned up the bodies?"

Gaoth snorted.

She nodded. "You're right. There wouldn't be nothing left of the buildings."

The story of this place was full of holes—or lies. Humans were duplicitous, and the number she trusted to tell her the color of the sky could be counted on a single finger.

"Terisan ut marrin," she swore then took another swallow of water. "There ain't nothing more to be learned here."

As she made to climb back into the saddle, a gentle breeze blew over her. She paused, appreciating the soft touch of the wind, a visceral contrast to everything else around her.

She glanced back one last time and paused. She thought she'd seen something, but now—

The wind blew the grass just enough to expose a dark object. She couldn't make out what it was, but the hard lines and edges stood out against the flowing grass and ruins. Drawing her right-hand iron, she went to investigate.

She found a cross of blackened wood, likely salvaged from the ruins. A dark red handprint—long since dried blood— discolored the wood where the two boards met.

Fear and a slow boiling rage churned inside her. She gripped her iron tighter.

She stared at the bloody handprint as the ghosts of the past threatened to carry her off. She closed her eyes and, instead of turning away the horrific memories, embraced them. The weight of the promise she'd made still tore at her soul.

"No, I won't hide!" she told her mother. "The dwarves and humans are a day behind me, two at most. I didn't push Gaoth near to death just to hide! I'll fight—"

"And you'll die," her mother said.

Heat filled Talen but she kept a civil tone. "And how many will die if I don't?"

Her mother placed a hand on Talen's cheek and met her eyes, the anger and frustration melted away.

"My daughter, they're dead already. We've lost this war, but there is still a chance to save our culture, our history, our identity."

The words were like a physical blow. "But—"

"You can't win this battle, but you can live to fight another." Her mother's hand moved from Talen's cheek to rest over her heart. "Keep me—keep us all—here and we'll live on." Sadness and resignation tempered the strength in her mother's eyes. "Promise me."

Talen put her own hand over her mother's, and though it pained her, she nodded. "Yes, Mother. I promise."

A few fled to neighboring nations, others hid. Some of her sisters had fought, despite the pleas of the mothers. Every one of them died. Her entire family and nation were gunned down or burned alive, either in their trees or on the pyres of the Red Right Hand. The especially savage attackers beat and violated their victims before killing them.

Talen emerged from the memories and stared at the cross through tear-filled eyes and a fire burning where her heart had been.

The fear turned to anger, and she was glad the Red Hand had taken the bounty. More so that they were ahead of her. She had no problem shooting them in the back.

Then, something else occurred to her. The Red Hand left these markers when they brought down a stained. According to the warrant, Margaret had gone on to raze two other towns after Prosperity, so this marker wasn't for her. Did a different stalker leave the marker? Especially unlucky towns might see more than one stained come through, but they were rare. But this cross couldn't have been before the town burned. So why leave it? A message maybe?

Maybe she ought to leave one of her own.

She stood, pouring magic into her iron. The sigils filled with spell fire, and she pulled the trigger. A blast of force splintered the cross and left a small crater in the ground.

"*Shanzi fetsuian,*" she said and spit in the hole.

She returned to Gaoth, saddled up, and headed north to the next town.

Back on the open plain, Talen gave Gaoth his head. He broke into a full gallop, flying across the flat ground. Humans would rarely risk their horses at this pace, but Gaoth wasn't a human-bred horse. He could sense the changing terrain better than Talen, so she didn't worry about him getting tripped up.

She closed her eyes, reveling in the feel of the wind on her face, in her hair, the smell of life all around her, and the delight of her friend. They rode like that for several miles before Gaoth slowed, and they both settled in for a long ride.

Chapter Five

Talen always kept a careful eye out for Red Hand stalkers. But in the days it took to reach Hendricks, she hadn't seen another soul. No settlers or wagon trains, not even a scout or hunting party. The plains were a big place to be sure, so it didn't surprise her. Despite not coming across anyone, her right hand never strayed far from her iron.

Hendricks turned out to be a little homesteader village on the Platte River, smaller even than Prosperity. Nothing remained of it either. In fact, if Talen hadn't been attentive, she might've ridden by without realizing.

The few buildings—a general store and a church from the looks of them—were nothing but blackened timbers and a few surviving pieces hinting at what they'd been: pews in the church, and barrels in the store. Once more, neither the air nor the ruins carried any hint of corruption. The warrant said this town had burned a few weeks after Prosperity, but that didn't fit. This town had died a full two seasons ago, if not three. So, either the warrant was wrong about the date or Margaret hadn't been the one to do it.

Talen gave a cursory search. Once again, no bodies, remains, or any hint as to what the hell had happened. No one had been here in several months at least.

"Wouldn't be the first warrant with the timing wrong," she said to herself, but knew there had to be more to it. The inconsistencies and holes were piling too high.

"No chance this place fell to a stained ravaging."

She almost moved on, but something stopped her. The same sense of wrongness she'd felt in Prosperity nibbled at her brain now. She still couldn't pinpoint the source, but that didn't reduce its insistence.

She followed the nagging unease to the houses scattered around the town proper. They weren't easy to find. The earthen brick homes sat partially below ground with grass on the roofs. No telling if lack of building supplies—wood was scarce on the plains—or a desire to hide had been the deciding factor. Either way, she couldn't deny its effectiveness. Unless you damn near stood on top of them, you'd never see them.

The ceiling of the first house had started to collapse in and the wooden shutters—if there had been any—were gone. Nothing but the four walls remained intact. Talen slid from the saddle, drew her right-hand spell iron, and walked around the structure. Not until she'd circled twice did she realize there were no animal pens.

Human settlers were almost always farmers, but they had to eat while the crops grew. That meant animals: pigs, chickens, even a cow if they could afford it. She walked back around the house a third time and examined the ground. Round holes set in the ground spoke of a long-gone fence. She checked closer to the house and found the earth relatively smooth. Pigs and cows tore up the ground something terrible, especially after rain. Even chickens would leave their mark. The grass grew the same too; it'd be greener or taller where animal manure had been.

She returned to the front and knocked down what remained of the door. The dry-rotted wood splintered under her boot heel. She ducked inside and checked the strength of what remained of the ceiling. She damn sure wouldn't stay the night, but it'd hold for now.

The only light came from the doorway and the gaping hole in the ceiling, leaving a lot of the home in heavy darkness. Talen stepped away from the door and blinked a couple times as her eyes adjusted. The colors of the room vanished, replaced by the shades of gray her night vision allowed.

A single large, and complete empty, room composed the entire home. She saw no bed, no table, no chairs, not even splinters or ashes. Even the poorest humans fashioned something together, a cot, a bench, something.

Talen crouched and examined the dirt floor. She didn't doubt it had rained plenty since the town's destruction, but she might get lucky. In a far corner, she found four small depressions that made a narrow rectangle.

There'd been a bed at one point. So where did it go?

Next to where remnants of the roof had fallen, she found marks suggesting a table and chairs might have been there once. The beams and wreckage blocked the rest of the house off. She stood and left the derelict home, wincing at the bright sun until her day vision returned.

Once she'd recovered, she mounted Gaoth and searched out another home, then a third, and a fourth. Each homestead told the same tale. The destruction had seemingly waited for everyone to pack up all their belongings and go. In her experience, rampaging stained were rarely so polite or accommodating.

She ran a hand through her hair and considered the myriad possibilities. Could be when the destruction started, those outside of town had enough time to flee. But it'd be damn near miraculous there'd be time to pack up all their worldly belongings. Four houses managing such a feat spoke to divine intervention. Someone could've picked over the bones of the town, but the only tracks were from a horse, and those just weeks old. The Red Hand stalkers she presumed.

Tempting as it might be to go back and search some of the houses more thoroughly, she decided against it. No point in going backward, especially if this hunt was now a race.

She climbed onto Gaoth and made an easy pace out of town. No telling how much of a lead the Red Hand had, or how many might be riding together. The ground was too dry to tell if one rider had come through, or half a dozen single file. She kept her eyes open and her iron close at hand as they rode.

A few miles outside town, Talen consulted her map. Covenant, the last town to, supposedly, suffer Margaret's fury sat near the border between the Nebraska and Dakota Territories. Best she could figure, three day's ride and—

Talen spotted a fort between her and Covenant on the map.

"Terisan ut marrin!"

It wouldn't cost more than a day to go around. All the same, she didn't much like being so close to a garrison of blue backs, especially not with Red Hands in the area. Lakota lands weren't far, at least what had been Lakota lands. Her map dated before the war. As such, she didn't know how many—if any—of the Seven Fires Council tribes still roamed free, or even lived. She didn't know if the tribes would be welcoming either, but she doubted they'd be outright hostile. For all their failings—they were still human—the Lakota had always been true.

But that had been before Whitestone Hill. No telling how they viewed elves after she and so many others turned tail and ran.

Dark and terrible memories crashed over her, dragging her back to her failure at Whitestone Hill and the obliteration of her world that followed.

Her hands shook, as the smell of burned flesh assailed her. She tried to push the cries of murdered children and raped women from her mind, but they wouldn't quiet.

Her heart raced, and she struggled to breathe.

She gripped the reins tighter, clenched her jaw, and fought against the onslaught.

It didn't work.

Gaoth stopped and turned to look at her just as she fell from the saddle, gasping for air, her body growing cold.

Mother, please help me!

She looked inside her heart but found only the faces of dead friends and the charred remains of her mother and sisters.

Darkness swallowed her, and she didn't know if she'd ever return.

She didn't know if she wanted to.

In that blackness, she heard the jeers of the soldiers as her people burned.

Anger swelled, wrapping her in a blazing fury that shone brighter than the sun, and cast away the dark.

Gradually, the panic melted away, her breathing slowed, and the rage numbed her. When she opened her eyes, her thoughts centered on those who'd murdered the people she'd loved most. Slowly, she got to her feet and stared at the saddlebag full of charges.

She picked up the map that had fallen to the ground. The fort sat a day and a half's ride away. Without a word, she climbed back onto Gaoth and urged him on.

"Slow and steady, old friend," she said. "Save your speed. We might have need of it."

Gaoth bobbed his head in answer and Talen stroked his neck.

Chapter Six

Heavy clouds obscured the sliver of a moon, making the night especially dark. When the fort's silhouette rose on the horizon, Talen leaned forward and drew the shadows around her. She couldn't completely hide Gaoth, but aided by the night, no human would see them coming. She kept his pace slow. Not only did he have to rely on her night vision, she also didn't want their movement through the prairie grass to give them away.

She couldn't be sure, but guessed the hour neared midnight. Even so, she knew better than to assume the late hour meant fewer sentries. During the war, the blue backs had learned the hard way the dangers of the night. The war might be years gone, but she wasn't going to make stupid assumptions.

As the fort drew closer, she didn't see the familiar faint glow of warding charms. Neither were there any torches, lanterns, or watch fires burning. In fact, no fires burned at all, not even inside the walls.

She stopped and narrowed her eyes.

No guards? Had their victory made the blue backs so arrogant?

She remembered the mistake of underestimating Jimmy.

Could be they don't need watch fires no more.

Humans fashioned new charms and inventions all the time. She wouldn't put it past them to figure some new way to see in the dark.

Mistakes can cost a life, she reminded herself. *Caution don't cost nothing but time.*

She slid from the saddle and led Gaoth to the base of a hillock, too small to hide him completely, but it'd serve better than nothing. They were a quarter mile from the fort, close enough that Gaoth could come running if need be, but far enough away to be safe.

She climbed the hill, crouched low and made for the fort's palisade.

The pointed logs were solid, but pocked from mundane bullets, and scorched by magic. The damage didn't look recent, but she figured months, not years. A few warding charms hung from the wall in regular intervals, but they were all deactivated.

She made to move, but apprehension brought her up short. Something didn't feel right.

The soldiers in Santa Fe knew she'd taken Margaret's bounty. Could that be why they didn't come after her? Or had someone found Jimmy and his friends and figured it had to be her?

Such thoughts might seem obsessive to others, but they'd kept her alive.

Could they have received word at this remote post ahead of her? She'd heard tell of some new device—a telegraph—humans used to send messages over long distances. Unfortunately, she had no way of knowing if they had one here.

She closed her eyes. The smell of old wood, gunpowder, and burned buffalo chips rose above the fresh scent of the plains. But no stench of soldiers in sweat-soaked wool.

Beneath the gentle sigh of prairie grass rustling in the wind, the palisade logs creaked. Beyond that, she found only silence. Nothing stirred inside the fort.

Abandoned?

She opened her eyes and, keeping close to the fortifications, crept to the nearest corner. She peeked around it and found the fort's gate closed. Matching piles of brush and dung sat on either side of the gate, marking where watch fires had burned.

Ignoring the easy way in, she moved back the way she'd come and found a section of wall where the logs had small gaps between them. Slipping her slender hands between the timbers, she pulled herself up, silent as a shadow. At the top of the wall, she peered between the pointed tips and scanned the area.

Like all forts Talen had seen—which hadn't been many—this one was just a walled square with a wall-walk a few feet below the palisade tops. Most of the buildings were built against or near the walls, leaving a wide-open space in the center.

Nothing but darkness and silence filled the courtyard.

She slipped over the top of the wall, crept across the walkway, and dropped to the ground, landing in a crouch.

Still, nothing and no one stirred.

A large, cold fire pit sat in the center of the courtyard, not even glowing embers. Still wrapped in shadows, she followed the wall, paying special attention to the shadows in the spaces between the buildings.

Halfway down the wall she noticed a stable opposite her. The two horses there were well-fed and tended to, which meant someone was here to care for them. The garrison could be out on a night raid or answering the call from a nearby town. In which case, they could return any moment. Humans didn't usually travel at night, but they'd surprised her before.

They would've left guards though.

Talen nudged the shutters open a sliver to peer inside each building she came across. The first couple were store houses. The empty shelves outnumbered the stocked ones by a fair margin. The next held nothing but long tables and benches. She crossed the courtyard, well enough away from the stables to keep from spooking the horses, and peeked through the window of the structure opposite the store houses.

She smiled.

Rows of cots lined the wall. All were empty, save one.

Her hand moved to her spell iron of its own volition, but she did manage to keep from channeling power into it. Excitement and anger rose in equal measure.

She turned away from the window and searched the rest of the fort, just in case. She found a weapons store; nothing but mundane rifles. An office of some kind, presumably for the commanding officer, gave no clue as to where the soldiers had gone. Then, at the very back of the fort, she found an answer in the form of a dozen graves. She crouched and moved her fingers through the soft earth. The oldest couldn't be more than a month old, the freshest a week at most. From the size, she suspected each grave held more than one corpse.

She stood and brushed the dirt from her fingers. Could that sleeping soldier be the only one left? Humans didn't let frontier forts stay empty, but it could take months for replacement soldiers to arrive.

She relished the idea of turning the fort into a pile of splinters and ash, but skepticism warred with a desire for vengeance.

It's too easy. It has to be some kind of trap, her reason argued. *They'd never leave an entire fort to a single soldier, even if only for a short while.*

You're giving the humans too much credit, a dark anger countered. *And even if you aren't, you can still leave a ruined fort and a single corpse for the replacements to find. Remember what they did.*

Anger won out.

She returned to the bunk house, slipped inside, and crossed the room silent as a whispered dream. She leveled her spell iron at the soldier's slowly rising and falling chest, considering how to end him.

Cutting his throat was too quick, too simple.

She could use fire. She didn't care about the fort. In fact, she'd take special pleasure in watching it burn. But it could set the prairie aflame, burning miles of grass.

An arctic charge felt too clean to slake her rage.

She thumbed the cylinder to a force charge. This close, she'd punch a hole straight through him and tear his heart out.

Just like you blue backs did to me.

The soldier stirred, turning his head to her. He blinked a few times and then opened his eyes.

She froze, but her gaze followed the soft lines of a face that had never seen a razor. He couldn't be more than thirteen, if that.

He stared up at her, through her, with a haunted look in his wide eyes. His heart pounded and his breath quickened.

"Wh-wh-who's there?" he asked in a high voice. He looked around the dark room, but he didn't move otherwise.

He's a human! A soldier! the rage inside her screamed. *They slaughtered your mother, your sisters, everyone! Why show mercy? They never did!*

Her finger tightened on the trigger, but she didn't push any magic into the iron. Her body shook and her jaw clenched. Screams of dying elves and Lakota rose from her memory and seized her heart, stoking the rage that'd never stopped burning.

Some of the soldiers that day had been this young, the darkness in her heart whispered. *And you killed plenty this young before.*

Yes, she'd killed soldiers this young, but that had been war, and she hadn't known at the time.

Or had she? Maybe she just hadn't wanted to know?

The boy began trembling so hard he shook the bed. "I-i-is someone there? Please don't hurt me. You can take whatever you want." The fear made him look even younger.

He's a child. A frightened child abandoned to fend for himself in the dark.

She'd been a scared child once, too.

She closed her eyes and thought of her mother. Of the warmth and comfort in her arms.

Talen remembered burying her face in her mother's neck, her skin so soft and smelling of wildflowers.

Would killing this boy do anything but feed the rage, a beast always hungry? It couldn't bring her mother or sisters back nor fill the emptiness inside her. It wouldn't even sate her desire for vengeance. All it would do was make her into what she despised.

The shadows fell away.

The boy whimpered and stared at her.

"Is it just you?" Talen asked in a flat tone.

"Pl-pl-please don't kill me," he said between barely-controlled, shaking sobs. The smell of ammonia filled the air and a wet spot appeared in the bed.

"Are you alone here?" she asked.

He sobbed harder and tried to answer but couldn't get the words out. After a moment he gave up and only nodded.

"What happened?"

"I d-d-don't know. They got s-s-sick, everyone but me and a few others." He swallowed. "They left a week ago maybe, t-t-took off in the night." He looked at her again, his cheeks streaked with tears. "Please, ma'am, d-d-don't kill me."

Human disease didn't worry her. Elves were immune. Not that it'd kept humans from trying various contagions as weapons.

She studied the boy. His brown eyes, though red from crying, were clear. His smooth skin, liberally covered in freckles, showed no pocks, or bruises. He'd chewed his nails to the quick, but they weren't discolored. He didn't show any signs of a sickness, at least none she knew. He could be a carrier, able to spread the illness without showing symptoms. Might be putting this child down would be a mercy.

The spell iron's runes lit with blue spell fire before she could stop herself.

"No, please!" The boy turned away and began bawling like, well, like a child.

Talen bit back the hesitation and slowly squeezed the trigger.

Then, he called out for his mother.

Her heart twisted, and shame crashed over her. The blue light that filled the room vanished as the spell fire went out. She didn't say anything, just holstered her iron.

She might be a monster but there had to be a limit, a line she wouldn't cross. She wanted to look away but didn't let herself. She'd done this, she'd own it, and carry it with her.

After a while, the boy's sobs eased, and he chanced a look at Talen. His eyes darted back and forth. When his saw the iron back in its holster, he stared at her, brow furrowed.

He swallowed. "You're not gonna, um—"

"I'm not going to kill you."

"Truly? Thank you, ma'am." The boy wiped his eyes.

"What's your name?"

"Daniel Carter, ma'am."

"Do you know where Omaha is, Daniel? Do you know how to get there?"

He nodded. "Yes, ma'am."

"Tomorrow, you pack all you can on one of them horses," she said. "You take it, ride the other, and get yourself there, quick as you can. Leave this place behind and don't look back. Hear me?"

He shook his head, eyes still wet. "I can't."

"Why not?"

"They said deserters get shot or hanged," he barely managed to say before breaking into sobs again.

"Terisan ut marrin," she muttered, looking away. Human society seemed to be built upon cruelties like this but wrapped it in words like 'honor' and 'loyalty' to excuse it.

"They won't," she said, calmly as she could. "You leave your soldier's coat behind, and no one will know."

He considered for a moment. "You think?"

She nodded.

"What do I do after?" he asked.

"Where are your parents?"

"Springfield, in Illinois," he said. "Got a small farm outside town."

"Go there," she said. "Go home, hug your mother, and spend the rest of your days treasuring her." She reached into her coat.

The boy flinched back.

She drew out the greenbacks she'd taken off Jeremiah and held them out. "This ought to get you there."

The boy stared at the money as if he expected it to sprout wings and fly away or explode if he touched them.

"Go on. Take it."

He reached out tentatively, staring at her.

She took his hand, put the greenbacks in it, and nodded. Then she turned for the door.

"Thank you, ma'am," he said. "I never killed me an elf, not one. I swear it. Never even fired my rifle."

Talen paused at the door but didn't turn around. She swallowed, forcing steel into her voice.

"I'll be back tomorrow, Daniel. Don't be here."

She left without waiting for a response.

When she got back to Gaoth, she wrapped her arms around the horse's neck and pressed her cheek to him. She held onto him for a long moment, then kissed his forehead, saddled up, and rode off.

Once she'd left the fort several miles to the south, Talen found a collection of trees. There weren't many hours left before dawn, but Gaoth could use the rest. At least, that's what she told herself.

She lay there watching the clouds drift by. She'd tried to sleep, but when she closed her eyes she saw only a terrified, weeping child asking for his mother.

She might've condemned the boy's family and countless others. If he was a carrier for whatever sickness had killed the other soldiers, he could spread it. Had she spared him only so he could watch his family die like the soldiers? It didn't matter. She'd done her part.

Whatever happened, she'd have to hold to the small victory. She'd won out against the darkness in her, and she hadn't become a true monster.

Not today anyway.

Chapter Seven

As the sun reached its zenith, she rode into Covenant, a town two or three times the size of Prosperity. Like the other towns, nothing much remained but burned-out husks of buildings, just more of them.

No surprise, Covenant showed no sign of a stained rampage either. Unlike Hendricks and Prosperity though, she did find leavings from the former residents. In what had likely been a shop were the charred remains of barrels and broken glass shards.

In the ruins of a former bank, a blackened safe remained standing, a stark contrast to the rest of the devastation. Someone had blasted the door open and, presumably, the same had pillaged its contents. If Margaret had cleaned it out before moving on, that would've been a first. Stained didn't care about money. They just took what they wanted. Curiosity getting the better of her, she moved in for a closer look. It'd seen better days: rust covered the exterior, and the hinges were so corroded the door wouldn't budge.

"Steel don't rust like that in weeks," she said. "That's a couple winters in the open at least."

This was supposed to be the last town Margaret leveled, and it'd died well before the other two. Talen added that to the rising list of incongruities and moved on. She found and explored a couple houses on the outskirts of town. They'd been plank built structures, so nothing remained. She picked through the debris and found another Red Hand cross, about the same age as the first one. And like the first one, she destroyed it. Otherwise though, she found nothing.

She couldn't figure why only the barrels and glass jars had been left behind. Surely they'd once held something. But even if they'd been empty, such items didn't come cheap. Why not fill them up with something and take them?

If they hadn't been empty, why did whoever took their contents leave them?

"Maybe to confound whoever came along?"

But why? What reason could there be for such a complicated ruse?

The only thing she could be sure of was that the Red Hand stalker that had left the cross hadn't looted the towns. The timing of the events didn't line up.

The whole place had the feel of a production, a stage set for her, the unwilling player in this drama.

Despite knowing what she'd find, she looked for tracks. As suspected, no sign of wagons or carts, just horses.

"Feels like I'm reading the last few pages of a story," she said to Gaoth between drinks from her canteen. "There's Prosperity, a town no one ever seemed to live in."

Gaoth kept eating grass.

"Could be a decoy town, but that don't make no sense," she said. "Who builds a town just to burn it down?" She shook her head. "There's something we're missing."

She pulled up some of the grass and chewed as she paced.

"Hendricks ain't no less confounding," she said. "Margaret arrives and politely tells everyone to pack their worldly belongs and go? This murderous stained patiently waits for everyone to be on their merry before she set to work?" She gestured around her. "Then there's this place. It burned years ago or I'm a talking otter."

Gaoth nickered.

She nodded. "You're right. Something stinks all right, and it sure as hell ain't no stained."

She spent another hour exploring the town but found nothing illuminating.

"Let it go," she said to herself. "Don't matter none. Knowing the truth might please your curiosity, but it won't bring you no closer to your bounty."

She sighed and kicked at a stone. Too much didn't make sense. One fact did stand true though: this town didn't have nothing else worth finding, so she saddled up and headed north.

Not long after, she spotted horse tracks—fresh ones, less than a week old. She followed until they turned east and vanished in the prairie grass. It had to be the Red Hand stalker. But why'd he turn east? Had he found something? Was he meeting some comrades?

Sioux City lay that way. Stained did tend to keep to cities, but the warrant had specifically said Margaret had been headed into Indian Territory. Had the stalker found something that made him think she'd changed course? Or maybe he found this as confounding as she and set out for a city to get better information. That made sense, though nothing else about this job did. She turned back to the north.

"So, which way? Follow the tracks, or the warrant?"

She spent a long minute considering, looking from north to east and back.

Her gut said north, and she trusted it over any human or warrant.

"North it is then," she said to Gaoth.

A familiar shame wrapped itself around her heart. She had no idea what'd befallen the Lakota after Whitestone Hill. If they survived, did they still think her people an ally? She wouldn't blame them if they didn't.

"Don't go climbing trees that ain't grown yet," she told herself and took out the map.

When she saw the fort marker, she thought of Daniel. Had he listened to her? She pictured him too terrified to leave, holed up and waiting for her to return. If so, maybe he'd find his courage when she didn't appear. Would he make it to Omaha on his own?

Keep Daniel safe. Bring him back to his mother. He might be a human, and a soldier too, but he's a child first.

She thought of her own mother. Talen imagined her smiling at the joy of another mother seeing her child come home. Despite the pain and anger roiling in her tattered soul, Talen smiled too. She'd done the right thing, unquestioningly, for the first time in a long time. It felt like an old friend coming by to visit.

After a moment, she pushed the thoughts aside. She drew in a breath, let it out as a sigh, and then folded the map to cover the fort marker. She had to focus on the task at hand.

She studied the massive Dakota Territory. If Margaret had gone there, she could well be anywhere. Talen traced a line north, equidistance between Prosperity, Hendricks, and Covenant. Continuing the line brought it right through what had been Lakota lands. After a hundred miles or so, the line reached a town called Verdant—ironically—just east of the badlands.

Not many would chance riding through the heart of the Lakota, especially if they were white. A stained though? The tribes might keep their distance. But all this assumed the Lakota still lived and still called those lands home.

"Good a place as any to look I suppose," she said and tucked away the map.

Less than an hour later, she crossed into what had been the Seven Council Fires tribal territory. She'd never fought this far south, but the terrain still felt familiar. Unfortunately, that familiarity compressed the years between now and the slaughter at Whitestone Hill. She broke out into a cold sweat and found herself scanning the horizon not just for Red Hand, but also for dwarven leviathans.

As the sun neared the horizon, she came to a ravine where three small rivers converged. She studied the terrain and shook her head. They'd be vulnerable and have no warning if someone came up on them. But Gaoth needed a rest and water, and none of the rivers came from the north, which meant it could be a ways before they found water again.

She decided to chance it. They wouldn't stay long, and after, they'd push on through darkness and find a better spot to stop for the night.

Gaoth drank, deep and eager. She refilled the canteens, then dunked her head under the water and held it there. She felt the life and power of the cool, clean water as it rinsed the miles of dust and dirt from her face and hair.

The gentle flow reminded Talen of the way her mother would stroke her hair at night. The memory washed over her, comforting and heartbreaking at once. When her lungs started to burn for air, she took long swallows of water, then lifted her head out.

As soon as her ears were clear, she knew they weren't alone. The rustle of footsteps came from the ridge behind her. She froze, head still bowed, as she considered who it might be.

Her heart sped up and her breathing went shallow.

Soldiers? Could Daniel have lied to her?

No, she didn't think so, but replacement soldiers could've arrived and followed her. No one had shot at her yet, but in the shadowy ravine, her wet hair might not look green. No disguising her coat or ears though.

More movement and whispers. But the footfalls were too light, too sure to be soldiers. She had an idea. It was risky, but she needed more information.

Seemingly unaware of her observers, she stood and threw back her head, sending an arc of water through the air. She pushed the wet hair back from her face and listened.

Scrub branches rustled to her right and someone whispered a curse of surprise.

That received a harshly whispered reply, unmistakably, not English.

She strode to Gaoth and stroked his neck as he drank, still playing at being oblivious.

"We got company," she said in a whisper.

Gaoth raised his head and glanced around.

"Dani orin," Talen sighed. "You ain't supposed to look."

Gaoth snorted and eyed her accusingly.

"Suppose there's no point pretending now," she said, loud enough for her visitors to hear. Right hand close to her iron, she went to a nearby tree, pulled some leaves with her left hand, and began eating them. She slowed her breathing in hopes her heart would follow.

Another whispered exchange from the ridge. She couldn't make out everything, but thought she recognized a few words.

She decided to take a gamble. "I'm Talen, of the Western Tree Dwellers," she said in the Oglala dialect of Siouan. If she'd misheard and guessed the tribe wrong, at best she'd offend them. At worst, they weren't Seven Council Fires, and it could end in a fight.

Well, no. At worst, they were Oceti Sakowin, and they hadn't forgiven her for abandoning them.

Swallowing back her disquiet, she put herself between her observers and Gaoth.

Nothing happened.

A good sign. Pawnee would've attacked by now. They'd never been hostile to elves, but that had changed when the elves allied with the Lakota, their longtime enemy.

Talen had no issue with the Pawnee. Some had joined and fought with the Army as scouts. But to her mind, once they'd taken the blue, they were soldiers and—during the war at least—she'd treated them as such. She'd killed more than a few, but she held no grievance against the nation as a whole.

Several long minutes passed, as did more anxious whispers from the ridge. Talen's temperament went from guarded but polite, to downright annoyed.

"I'm not here to fight," she said, again in Siouan. "Our people were friends, and I hope still are. If that's not the case, I'd just as soon we get to it." She drew both spell irons, keeping them pointed at the ground, and pushed power into them. Blue spell fire filled the runes.

"Two-handed witch!" someone on the ridge said in Siouan, the tone a mix of fear and surprise.

"That's right," she said, ignoring the tightness in her chest. "And I know where all four of you are, so no point in hiding. I don't have much, but you're welcome to share in what there is." She shrugged. "Or if you're set on it, we could start shooting and see how that goes."

Of course, if they started shooting, she had no intention of shooting back. Unless they hit Gaoth.

Four Lakota men rose and stepped into view. They were young, and the markings on their faces—if she remembered right—were signs of mourning. They wore a mix of traditional leathers and acquired soldiers' clothing. Two held spell irons—unlit—and two carried mundane rifles, all looked Army issue.

Their expressions were inscrutable.

Talen doused her own irons, holstered them, and showed her empty hands.

The four exchanged a look and lowered their weapons.

"I don't much like leaves," one of the men said, his mouth pulling up at one side.

Talen's shoulders relaxed and she took a breath. "More for me."

The men laughed as they made their way down to join her.

When they drew near, Talen raised her hands, palms out, and then crossed her arms over her chest.

"I welcome you, honored friends," she said. She'd almost forgotten the pleasure of using the old greeting.

The leader of the group copied her gesture. "And I welcome you."

"I'm called Talen." She nodded at Gaoth. "This is Gaoth."

"I'm Bear Heart," the leader said and indicated the others. "This is Iron Crow, Yellow Hawk, and Ancient Fires."

"Your horse is magnificent," Yellow Hawk said.

Gaoth whinnied and bobbed his head.

Yellow Hawk furrowed his brow. "Did he understand me?"

Talen nodded. "And after praise like that, there will be no living with him."

The men laughed again, and some of the shame slipped from Talen's shoulders, but only some. For a moment, she remembered the war wasn't all pain and slaughter. These boys were likely too young to have fought. They'd just know what their elders told them of it. She couldn't help but wonder what those accounts said of the elves and their cowardice.

"I was only a child the last time anyone saw a walker of shadows," Bear Heart said.

"I've only heard the stories," Iron Crow did so while obviously trying not to stare at the markings on her face or her pointed ears.

Talen touched her chest. "It fills me with joy to know you still call these lands home."

Their faces fell, and Talen's blood went cold.

"All we have now is what the *wasicu* let us have," Bear Heart said. "This is the Oglala reservation."

"I'm so sorry. I have no words." Talen swallowed and shook her head. "I didn't know what happened after Whitestone Hill—"

"My father said your people fought well," Iron Crow said. "That after the slaughter, the soldiers and machines chased you back to your home."

Talen could only nod.

"You lost many of your people too?" Ancient Fires asked.

"Yes," Talen said. "But I'm also shamed. We abandoned your people."

The four Lakota exchanged a confused look.

"Your people needed you," Bear Heart said. "What else could you do?"

Talen knew the sincerity of their words. She took comfort—small as it was—in knowing the Oglala didn't see the elves as cowards. Shame and guilt still hung in her chest like a stone though.

Iron Crow pointed to the marks on his face. "We still weep, for your people as well as for our own."

Talen touched her chest. "Thank you."

"Why have you returned?" Bear Heart asked.

"I'm looking for a woman."

"You're seeking a wife?" Yellow Hawk asked.

"No, not like that," Talen said. "I'm hunting someone, a woman stained by dark magic."

Iron Crow cocked his head. "You hunt stained for the *wasicu*?"

Talen nodded.

"Why?" he asked.

"I'm a Shadow Warden," she said. "We're sworn to destroy the corruption of dark magic and those taken by it."

Bear Heart nodded and gave her a knowing smile. He didn't say "and you get to kill humans" out loud, but he might as well have.

"I'll never understand *wasicu*," Ancient Fires said. "Paying an elf to kill their own."

"They were never good at cleaning up their messes," Talen said.

All four nodded.

"The woman," Talen said. "She might've come this way. A month ago, maybe longer. Have you seen any stained *wasicu* travelling alone?"

"Could that have been a woman?" Bear Heart asked the others.

"Maybe," Iron Crow said. "I thought it a small man, but it could've been because the horse was so big."

Talen let herself dare to hope. "When, where?"

"Two weeks ago," Bear Heart said.

"Only two weeks?"

He nodded. "They rode alone, and very slow. The horse was one of those big, strong ones the *wasicu* use to pull heavy wagons. We knew we could catch them and take the horse, but the stench of dark magic was strong. We smelled it a long way off."

"You could smell it?" Talen asked.

"It made my eyes water," Iron Crow said. "I didn't know anyone could be so corrupted, not even *wasicu*."

"Did you attack her?" Talen asked.

Bear Heart shook his head. "Killing *wasicu*, even if they're stained, brings the soldiers. We see enough of them."

Talen considered the fort. Might be the visits would stop for a while.

"What did you do?" she asked.

"Followed her," Bear Heart said. "Made sure she didn't go after any of our villages."

"And did she?"

"No. She kept heading north, so we let her go."

"She's powerful," Ancient Fires said. "I'm not sure we could've stopped her if we wanted to."

The warriors were young, but she'd bet they could hold their own in a fight. If the four of them hesitated, Talen would need to be careful. They'd smelled the corruption though. That meant Margaret—or whoever they'd seen—was in fact stained. Why then hadn't there been any residue in the towns? She'd worry about that later. At least she seemed to be on Margaret's trail.

"Thank you," she said and went to her saddlebag. She drew out two handfuls of spell iron charges and offered them. "Please accept these gifts as a symbol of my gratitude."

"You're very generous," Bear Heart said. "My father said your people walked the true path." He accepted the charges and handed some to his companions. Then he produced a bone handled knife and offered it to Talen.

"No," she said. "You owe me nothing. You gave me valuable information."

"Please," Bear Heart said, "We only told you what we saw."

Reluctantly, Talen accepted the knife and tucked it into her belt. She touched her chest and nodded. "Thank you."

"Would you come with us back to the village?" Iron Crow asked. "I know many would be glad to see a tree dweller again."

"Yes, please," Yellow Hawk said.

Talen wanted to but shook her head. "Thank you, but I can't. I have to find this woman and stop her. She's very dangerous. But I'm happy beyond words to know our people are still friends."

"You fought and died with us," Bear Heart said, "a fight not your own. Our fathers tell stories of your people's courage and skill. You aren't a friend. You're our brothers and sisters."

The other men nodded.

Talen crossed her hands over her chest again and bowed her head. "Then I say to my brothers, when this is done, if I'm able, I'll return and accept your invitation."

"Good hunting, then," Bear Heart said. "If anyone can kill that stained *wasicu*, it's a two-hand witch."

Once they made their goodbyes, the Lakota climbed back up the ravine and were gone.

Talen drew in a deep breath and closed her eyes. A sense of contented warmth settled over her. The Oceti Sakowin seemed… well, not happy. She couldn't imagine how life on a reservation could be happy, but they still had their strength, their pride, and their identity. It was something. She said a silent prayer to her mother that it was enough and would see them through.

When she finished the prayer, she ate the last of the leaves, finding them tastier than they'd been at first. That done, she mounted Gaoth and headed off in pursuit of her quarry.

Chapter Eight

A few hours after nightfall, Talen found a spot on a hill and set camp against a collection of boulders she hoped would keep her and Gaoth hidden. She lay on her bedroll, studying the stars. A hint of excitement kept her mind restless, and she turned over a detail Bear Heart had mentioned. It wasn't unheard of for humans to ride draft horses, and she believed that was what he'd seen. Few humans knew horses like the Oceti Sakowin. But the only tracks she'd seen were for a standard-size horse, and those had turned east to Sioux City.

On the upside, plough horses were built for power, not speed. If Talen pushed hard, she could catch up to Margaret in a few days, a week at the most. This damn bounty had more oddities than any dozen she'd taken before. She'd be glad to have it done. Unfortunately, the more she thought about this confounding job, the more holes and peculiarities she found.

Bear Heart's telling of the rider—she hoped it was Margaret— came to the forefront of her mind. They'd smelled her corruption and from well off. That fit every stained Talen had ever come across; the worse the corruption, the stronger the stench. But she still couldn't fathom why there hadn't been a hint of dark magic in any of the three towns. It didn't make sense Margaret would reek of corruption, but her magic wouldn't. Even supposing it once did, how could it fade so quick?

She pulled out the new bounty crystal and turned it in her fingers, her mental wanderings bringing her back to Prosperity, Covenant, and Hendricks. The pieces still didn't fit. A stained's stench came from dark magic itself. One couldn't stink and not the other. Might be the warrant had one town wrong, but all three?

No, there had to be more to this puzzle. She'd wager her left-hand iron on it. But what the hell could make sense of this mess? In the years since the war's end, Talen had collected one hundred and six stained bounties. In the centuries before that, near a thousand had been put down by her and her Shadow Warden sisters.

"I thought I'd seen every manner of stained, and every level of corruption." She shook her head. "But I ain't never even heard of one like this."

She sighed and looked to Gaoth for wisdom.

If he had any, he didn't share it.

Maybe she had it all wrong. Maybe the humans had the right of it and Margaret was just some new kind of stained. After all, dark magic defied logic and reason by its very nature.

"Would it be all that surprising that humans reached some new level of corruption I ain't never seen, or heard tell of?"

She sighed again.

"Why the hell do I care? What's another stained put down?"

"Because you're eldar," she imagined her mother saying. "Because you're better than all that."

Talen wanted to believe, but what remained of her? Barely enough to keep from killing a child. The war had taken everything, leaving her nothing but a husk that hunted monsters. She told herself she fought to protect the magic, excising the disease of stained souls. Not revenge. While technically true, it was far from the whole truth. She knew that, and pretending otherwise now insulted everything she believed in.

What should I do, mother?

No answer came. She knew prayers weren't always answered, or even heard. But she struggled not to connect the lack of an answer to the ragged shade she'd become.

In time, she managed to put all the pondering aside. Something could explain all this, and she might even discover it someday. Until then, she had a job to do.

Yes, plenty about this job was odd, but in the end, Margaret was just another stained soul—albeit a powerful one—and Talen had to put her down. Doing so wouldn't be easy. Best to suppose the warrant had it right. In that case, she'd have to come at this one sideways, from the shadows.

And what if there's a child in the way again?

She didn't have an answer to that. Least not one she accepted.

Eventually, exhaustion won over, quieting her mind, and she fell into sleep.

She woke to find the sun peeking over the horizon, and Gaoth standing over her.

"We need to do something about your breath." She pushed his head to one side.

He gave an affronted snort and turned away.

"I'm sure mine ain't no better." She got to her feet and stretched.

The sky was painted in shades of blue and purple, the clouds the color of flame. It'd been so long since she'd really looked at a sunrise. She'd nearly forgotten how beautiful they could be.

"Been a long while since I slept past sunup."

Longer still since I felt genuinely rested after.

She pondered the meaning of that but brushed it aside after just a moment. She'd done more than enough thinking last night and thinking wasn't doing.

As she ate a breakfast of leaves and bark, she broke camp and then saddled up Gaoth. In short order they were riding north again. Fear nibbled at the edges of her mind, but never gained ground. If she came across the Red Hand, she'd settle up with them, and one way or another it'd end.

Talen didn't fear death. It would come eventually. No point fretting over it. When it did, she'd finally rest. But first she'd finish this bounty, one way or another.

Gaoth's spirits were brighter, but then he'd always been her constant joy amidst the darkness. Together they ate up the miles in comfortable silence.

A few hours past noon on the second day, she spotted a thin trail of smoke beyond a distant hill. She brought Gaoth to a stop. Had they arrived too late? Was another town burning? Her map didn't show anything here, but that didn't mean something hadn't gone up since the war. She waited and checked the charges in her spell iron, swapping some out.

Twenty minutes later, the single tendril hadn't grown or multiplied. Better to proceed with caution, all the same. She slid out of the saddle and led Gaoth on foot. It slowed their going but let her keep watch on the surroundings. Two hours later, they reached the hill.

"Wait here," she whispered to Gaoth. "If anything happens, run. I'll find you."

The horse shook his head and glared at her.

She sighed. "Sometimes I'd swear you're part mule," she said with genuine affection, and turned back to the hill.

Wrapped in shadows, she started up the rise, not disturbing a leaf or making a sound. As she neared the top, she drew both spell irons. She might be quick on the draw, but there was always someone quicker. She didn't know if a stained this powerful could see through her shadow glamour, so she went slowly, careful to keep behind cover and watch for traps, both magical and mundane.

No stupid chances. Slow and cautious.

She crested the knoll, peeked around a large rock, and let out a breath. A small cabin of wood and stone sat in the shallow valley, a single trail of smoke rising from the chimney. The place had seen better days but seemed structurally sound. Like as not, it belonged to some trapper. No one else would be out this far or so close to the Lakota.

Talen almost turned back but stopped. Just like in the ruined towns, the splinter in her mind nagged at her. Something didn't feel right.

She sniffed the air.

Not a hint of corruption.

Even so, she waited.

The sound of heavy, stomping hooves and a horse's nicker sounded from behind the cabin.

"Easy," a woman's voice said. "Here you go."

There came a crunching sound Talen knew well; a horse chomping on some treat or another, an apple or carrot.

She gripped her irons and slowed her breathing. It might be a trapper, but one—and a woman no less—right where Margaret ought to be? That'd be a hell of a coincidence.

"Good, huh?" the woman asked. "I told you there'd be something nice for you."

Talen narrowed her eyes. Horses were known to remain loyal to a stained, but not often. Rarer still was a stained showing kindness to any creature, even a loyal horse. Everything she knew about stained said nothing fit.

But something else told her to ignore those instincts and attack. It whispered its insistence, and though it felt alien, she couldn't ignore it. It took real effort to keep from pouring magic into her irons.

"Now if you'll excuse me, I must see to my own dinner," the unseen woman said.

Talen crouched lower and took aim, resting her still dark irons on the large rock.

A dark-haired woman stepped in to view, front skirts lifted and filled with vegetables.

Talen tried to make out her face, but the woman kept her head bowed as she shuffled along. Talen narrowed her eyes and fought to reconcile the warring thoughts. She knew, with certainty, this woman was stained. Yet, her gut and every one of her senses said she didn't carry a whisper of corruption. She'd never been so sure of two opposing notions before.

This don't make no damn sense!

Her thumb—without consulting her brain—rotated the cylinder of her right-hand iron to a lightning spell. It had the best range.

As the woman reached the door, the cylinder clicked into place.

When she stopped, Talen held her breath.

The woman turned slowly and glanced around. She stood in plain view, studying the hill for a long while.

Talen's heart beat faster, but she didn't move.

It was Margaret.

The odd certainty urged her to fire, to strike while she could.

And yet, Talen also knew this couldn't be Margaret. She wasn't but a few hundred yards away, and Talen still couldn't sense any corruption. Bear Heart and his scouts had smelled it at more than twice that distance.

The peculiar surety said her senses were wrong, that this woman near on dripped with the fetid corruption of dark magic. The lack of scent could be a trick. Could be some new dark magic ruse aimed at her senses, one her mind managed to see through.

That made sense. Spending too much time around a stained could change a person. Sometimes they'd even give in and turned stained themselves.

She wrapped her finger around the trigger and made to let the magic flow—

No! She held back.

Even if somehow the corruption had fooled her senses, too much didn't add up. What sort of stained paused their rampage to set up somewhere, build a fire, and cook dinner? Stained were monsters, taking what they needed and wanted. They didn't plan or scheme, and they sure as hell didn't settle down in a quiet cabin, alone. Margaret didn't even have a spell iron on her, and no stained would take a step without an iron.

Talen struggled to find the sense in any of this.

The quiet insistence argued that someone else could've called this place home. Margaret might've killed them and taken the cabin.

No, she'd known this place would be here. More than that, she'd known there'd be carrots to give her horse. She'd said as much.

Margaret turned back to the cabin, opened the door, and limped inside.

Again, the surety urged Talen to fire.

I could set the place ablaze and gun Margaret down when she comes out to douse it.

Talen's twitching finger reached out to rotate the cylinder but stopped. She turned, eyes closed, and tapped at her forehead with the irons, hoping to shake some sense loose.

She opened her eyes.

Margaret had been limping. Stained didn't limp. They healed remarkably—often frighteningly—quick, including old wounds from before their corruption.

Still the insistence urged her on. She couldn't risk waiting any longer!

Could it be she'd seen it wrong? Maybe this wasn't her bounty, and she'd just seen Margaret's face where it didn't belong.

And what if Margaret turned out to be a monster after all and Talen didn't end her? Every death that came after would hang on Talen's soul. How many more could she carry? Besides, even if Talen's instincts were right, what was one dead human? They bred like locusts.

"No," she whispered. She might be a killer, but she wasn't a murderer. She did not kill innocents, ever. She hadn't crossed that line. She'd lost damn near everything, but she wouldn't lose the last remnant of her soul. It might cost her life, but the alternative would cost her more.

A sudden realization chilled Talen's blood.

What if that insistence turned out to be some dark magic, working to convince her to ignore her senses? Well, that would sure as hell fit what she'd come to expect from humans.

This thought shone a light on the certainty, revealing the truth of it, and she knew. Someone made to manipulate her. A familiar sense of violation turned her stomach and stoked a long burning rage.

She had no idea what the hell was going on, but she'd sure as hell find out. No way would she let herself be a pawn in some twisted game.

That false certainty still nagged at her, ceaselessly insistent. She'd have to quiet it once and for all. Only one way she could think to do that. She stood, drew in a slow breath, and cleared her mind. One way or another, this would end.

Chapter Nine

Talen moved down the hill, silent as the shadows around her. She kept her eyes on the cabin door and the wooden shutter covering its single window. The woman inside chopped vegetables and hummed a sad tune.

Talen made for the back of the cabin and found a massive draft horse grazing. Not the ideal choice of steed for anyone on the run. No quick getaways on this creature. If things turned bad though, it could still get hurt.

She dispelled her glamour and approached the animal, always keeping a careful ear on the inside of the cabin. Wouldn't do to be caught unaware.

The horse eyed Talen but showed no fear or apprehension. Animals didn't react to elves like they did humans. She drew closer, whispering gentle words. Slowly, she reached out and stroked his neck.

"Yeah, you're a gentle giant, ain't you?" she whispered through a smile.

The horse flicked his ear.

She leaned in close and whispered again, telling him of a nearby herd running free.

The horse's muscles tensed, and he turned in the direction of the fictional herd—in truth just Gaoth—but didn't move.

"It's okay," Talen said in a soft, quiet tone. "Go. Run and be free."

Few humans understood the strong herding instinct in horses, or that it never went away.

"Go, friend," Talen whispered a third time. "They're waiting for you."

The horse turned and hurried off, probably faster than he'd run in years. He headed for a trail that led around the hill, the soft earth muffling his heavy hoof beats.

Talen smiled at the sublime beauty and obvious joy. She hated lying to such a gentle beast, and her heart ached at the thought of his disappointment when he didn't find the promised herd. But he'd be safer away from here.

Talen drew in another breath, pushed her emotions down, and stepped back into the shadows. Crouched low, and keeping close to the structure, she made her way to the front of the cabin. Her heart beat slow and steady.

She listened at the door, painting a mental image of the inside of the cabin. Margaret stood facing the wall to Talen's left. The sounds of chopping and humming continued.

Talen whispered a silent prayer.

Then, she dropped her shadow veil and poured magic into her irons, filling the runes and sigils with blue spell fire. She stood, kicked open the door, and stepped in, both irons levelled at the woman's back.

Margaret went silent and stopped chopping.

"Don't move," Talen said. "Twitch, and I'll cut you down."

"I understand," the woman said. Her tone was calm but tinged with fear and something else: resignation?

The dark certainty rose up, but Talen slapped it back down.

"Are you Margaret Jameson?"

"I am." Now the acquiescence in her voice was plain.

"Show me your hands. Slow."

Margaret's right hand inched into view, holding a large knife.

Talen opened her mouth, but Margaret had already set the knife down. She slowly pushed it across the old counter—well out of reach—then raised both hands.

"You've been declared stained by order of the US Magistrate," Talen said. "As a duly sworn—"

"I know." Margaret bowed her head. "I've been expecting this for some time now. I have to say, I didn't think it would be a woman. It's a relief really. Thoughts of what a stalker might do before killing me kept me up most nights."

"You don't deny you're stained?" Not that any ever had, but neither had one ever been so passive.

"No." Margaret drew in a long breath. "I know what I am and what comes next. I only ask that you make it quick. If it helps, I ask as one woman to another."

Talen stared. She'd imagined this going down in a lot of different ways but not like this. Margaret should be insisting her innocence or doing her best to tear Talen to pieces. Further complicating things, she confessed. That made the bounty legal.

Talen's fingers twitched, but she didn't fire.

Margaret started to tremble. "Please don't draw this out. I don't know how much longer I can keep my composure. Let me at least die with dignity."

Talen didn't move. For the first time in a long time, she didn't know what to do.

"What are you waiting for?" Margaret asked, and a sob broke through her resolve.

"Turn around," Talen finally said. "I ain't shooting you in the back."

When Margaret did, her mouth fell open.

Talen searched her dark, wet eyes. She found desperation, fear, and oceans of sadness, but no trace of dark magic.

"You're an elf," Margaret said.

"And you ain't stained," Talen said, lowering her spell irons.

"What?" Margaret asked, brows drawing together. "But the smell. Sometimes it's so bad it makes me sick to my stomach."

Talen narrowed her eyes. She kept her irons lowered but lit. "You smell it? Right now?"

Margaret nodded. "Of course. You don't?"

"No." Talen glanced around the room. "Where's your iron?"

"Behind you." Margaret said, hands still up and gesturing with her head.

A mundane repeating rifle leaned against the wall next to the door. "No, your spell iron," Talen said.

Margaret frowned, her head tilting to one side. "I don't have one. Never had need, or the money, even if I did."

Talen clenched her jaw. This whole thing stank, and it had nothing to do with corruption. "Mind if I look around?"

Margaret frowned. "You're asking my permission?"

Talen nodded.

"Go right ahead."

"Stay put. Don't make no sudden movements."

"Of course."

Right-hand iron pointed at Margaret, Talen glanced around the sparse cabin. It held nothing but an old cot in a corner and a small table with a couple of rickety chairs. The kitchen area boasted a counter, a sink complete with hand pump for water, and some cupboards. A small bundle of cloth lay spread out on the bed, but no spell iron.

She looked Margaret over. Unlike mundane shooters, spell irons weren't small, they couldn't be and still work. Margaret couldn't be hiding one in that close-fitting blouse, and Talen didn't see any bulges in her skirts.

Talen went to the cot and looked through the bundle of cloth. She found spare clothes, a carved cameo brooch, a framed photograph of Margaret and a man, and nothing else. Not even charges for a spell iron. There were other spell throwers: staves, wands, and the like, but they were harder to hide than an iron, and you still needed charges for them.

She pushed the cot to one side with her boot, revealing only bare floor. She stepped on a few of the planks, but none gave.

Margaret could've tossed her iron, but that notion seemed so unlikely as to be laughable. Spell irons weren't cheap or easy to come by and stained didn't go unarmed, ever.

The nagging certainty screamed for her to finish Margaret. Talen wrestled it into silence and prepared to kill it once and for all.

"You admit to your crimes?" she asked again, carefully studying Margaret's reaction.

She swallowed and nodded. "Yes."

"How'd you do it without an iron?"

Margaret tilted her head to one side and narrowed her eyes. "I don't understand. What does a spell iron have to do with it?"

"I'm just a bit curious as to how you burned those towns without one."

Margaret's face paled and her eyes went wide. "What? No! I didn't —dear God—what towns?"

Talen lifted her irons and pointed them at Margaret's heart. "Prosperity, Hendricks, and Covenant in the Nebraska Territory, all burned to the ground."

"What? No, I didn't burn anything!"

"You just said—"

"I admit I'm stained! But I didn't—oh God, is that what they're saying?"

The shock and surprise appeared genuine, but to be sure, Talen had to push her over the edge.

She nodded. "Warrant says you're a cold-blooded stained. A monster of dark magic what razed three towns and murdered more than a hundred, including women and children."

Margaret put her hands to her face and shook her head. "No, I swear, I didn't—"

"Don't you lie to me, rot!" Talen pushed more magic into her irons, causing the sigils to burn brighter. "You ain't fooling me so stop pretending! I saw the corpses! Whole families huddled together, burned alive!"

Margaret turned a little green, and her knees buckled. "I'm going to be—" She turned and wretched into the sink.

A wave of relief washed over Talen, joined by guilt and shame. She doused and holstered her irons, then went to the sink and worked the pump, washing the vomit down the drain.

"There weren't no bodies," Talen said.

Margaret looked up at her. "What?"

"The towns were gone but no bodies."

Margaret gave her a horrified look. "But why—"

"I had to be sure," Talen said. "Now I am. You're no more a stained than me."

Margaret looked as if she wanted to say something, but nothing came out.

"Drink some water," Talen said and worked the pump again.

Margaret rinsed out her mouth and then drank a few handfuls.

Talen helped her to one of the chairs and took the other. Her right hand rested near the handle of her iron. As she waited for Margaret to compose herself, she put together what she knew. Someone wanted this woman dead, and they were putting up a $5000 bounty to get it done. She'd bet her left-hand iron that was why a special crystal was needed. Bounty crystals only worked on stained. What about the stench? And why couldn't Talen smell it?

"I don't understand," Margaret said, face in her hands.

"You ain't alone. How long have you smelled the corruption?"

"It started a month after George passed away. Three months now."

"Who's George?" Talen asked.

"He's my husband." She shook her head. "Was my husband."

"How'd he die?"

"Pneumonia."

"That him in the picture?"

Margaret nodded. "The irony is, we moved to Kansas to get away from the diseases in the cities back east." She turned and lifted her skirt, exposing her bare legs. The left seemed normal enough, but the right looked underdeveloped and small.

"What happened?"

Margaret lowered her skirts. "Infantile paralysis. I caught it as a child."

"You know stained don't suffer from deformities or ailments?"

"Of course, I've heard all the stories." Margaret shrugged. "But, as I said, this happened when I was a child."

"Don't matter. I've seen stained that lost limbs years before grow them back once they turned. Hell, some turn for that very reason."

Margaret rubbed her leg. "I understand the temptation."

Talen felt genuine sympathy for this woman. It was strange and familiar all at once. Unfortunately, she still needed information.

"You said you noticed the corruption after your husband died?" she asked. "Any signs beyond the smell?"

"What do you mean?"

"Overwhelming urges to murder, rape, or otherwise destroy?"

Margaret's mouth twisted. "No! Of course not!"

"A stained does. Those urges are about all they are."

"But I can smell it. Others did too."

"I don't."

"Do elves sense corruption the same as humans?"

"More so," Talen said. "As bad as you think it smells, it's worse for me. And I find the fact I don't smell nothing a mite peculiar. Let's say you're right, when did it happen?"

Margaret shrugged. "I don't know the specific date. Like I said, sometime after George passed away. It started faint but grew stronger quickly. For the first weeks I assumed something in the house had gone bad, but it followed me. Then, others smelled it too, and I'd get looks when I went outside. One night a friend told me I needed to leave town. She said others were talking about putting a mob together and coming after me."

"Where was this?"

"City of Kansas," Margaret said. "We had a dry goods store there."

"And you left."

"That very night. I packed up what I could into our little wagon and headed north."

Talen narrowed her eyes. "The Nebraska Territory?"

"I was terrified and didn't really have a destination in mind," Margaret said. "I found a little town south of Omaha. Some Mormons took pity on me and gave me food, but their charity didn't last. It wasn't even a week before I had to sell the wagon and anything that Joseph—our old horse—couldn't carry."

Talen arched an eyebrow. "Someone bought your things despite you reeking of corruption?"

Margaret scowled. "Closer to theft. He didn't even pay me half what it was worth." She shrugged. "But what choice did I have? I found a hotel and managed to keep the smell hidden under perfume. That didn't last either, and one day a lawman came calling."

Talen furrowed her brow. She'd hoped things would've started making some kind of sense, but it just kept getting more bizarre. Margaret had been in the Nebraska Territory, but on the wrong side of it. She somehow just turned stained like she caught a damned cold? That didn't happen.

"You mean a stalker, right?"

"No, he was the local sheriff. Said I hadn't technically broken any laws yet and since the corruption hadn't taken me wholly, he'd give me a chance to leave. He said an old trapper had died recently and, for a small fee of course, he'd provide me with the location of his cabin." She motioned around. "This cabin."

Talen shook her head. Lawmen didn't deal in stained unless they had to. It didn't surprise her though that this one decided to fleece Margaret on her way out of town. Probably figured her for a dead woman.

"And you're sure you ain't never been to Prosperity, Hendricks, or Covenant? Not even before all this happened?"

"Never. I hadn't even heard of them before you mentioned them." She let out a breath and slumped her shoulders. "I don't understand. Why is someone saying I burned them?"

Talen shrugged. "Could be someone, maybe that lawman, knew about the towns, heard about you, and connected the two. I'd bet that lawman reported you to the Magistrate not long after talking to you. Even offered up the general direction of this cabin for a nice payout."

"But you said I'm not stained."

"You ain't. Apart from your leg, there ain't no polite conversations with stained." She scoffed. "When it comes to stained, lawmen don't know a damned thing. Corruption takes hours, not days, and sure as hell not weeks. It takes time to grow in power, but it ain't long before the corruption takes control."

"Then where is the smell coming from?"

Talen frowned and shrugged. "That there is the question. One of them anyhow."

Margaret narrowed her eyes. "One of them? What are the others?"

Talen studied Margaret, unsure how much to reveal. It didn't take long to decide. Someone had set this woman up to die, and Talen figured that earned her the truth, at least as much as Talen knew.

"I ain't got anywhere near a full picture here, but here's what I think," she said. "This ain't happenstance. Someone put a bounty on your head, complete with crimes of sufficient evil to back it. Those towns don't fit the warrant though, but that's down a different path."

Margaret just listened.

"As to the stench? Well, I don't smell no corruption on you. But soon as I saw you, something in my head told me you were a stained all the same. It almost had me convinced to ignore my own senses and take you down."

Margaret's brows went up a little. "Something in your head?"

Talen nodded. "I think it's the same thing that tells you there's a stench. Never heard of nothing like it, but I suspect it's dark magic of some sort."

"Who would do this?"

"I don't know, but they want you in a crystal," Talen said. "Your bounty is $5000."

Margaret's eyes went wide. "Holy shit." She looked away. "Pardon my language."

Talen smiled a little. "Only the worst get a reward that size. You should've gotten a hundred, five hundred if they wanted you bad. A bounty that big, only the best, or craziest stalkers would take it up." She met Margaret's gaze. "Or the most zealous."

Margaret swallowed. "Red Right Hand?"

Talen pulled two bounty crystals—one old, one new—from her pocket.

Margaret cringed back.

"I ain't going to hurt you," Talen said and held up the first. "This here is a bounty crystal. I've been using them for years and they don't do a damned thing if you ain't stained. If you are, just touching it sets it off, though it works best placed over the heart." She set it on the table and pushed it toward Margaret. "Pick it up."

Margaret hesitantly reached out for the crystal.

"It's fine," Talen said.

"Easy for you to say. It's not your—"

Talen grabbed Margaret's hand and slapped the crystal into it.

Margaret startled, but otherwise nothing happened.

"See?"

"That wasn't very nice." Margaret examined the crystal.

Talen smirked. "Now, warrant says you're some new kind of stained, immune to bounty crystals." She held up the new crystal. "This one is new, and it's supposed to work just fine on you, only it don't work by just touch. You got to get in inside the stained."

Margaret drew her hands out of Talen's reach. "So, the bounty is high because I'm supposed to be this new kind of stained?"

Talen nodded. "Ain't exactly easy even making skin contact with a stained. They tend to resist such efforts."

Margaret gave Talen a flat look.

"But I suspect it served to keep anyone but Red Hand stalkers from taking the bounty." Talen sighed. "They didn't plan for a damned fool elf though."

Margaret opened her mouth, but Talen shook her head and Margaret stayed quiet.

Talen had been a damned fool, for years, and she knew it. But she'd lied to herself so often she'd come to believe her own bullshit. Her life hadn't been about defending magic, not really. Sure, she took down stained, but only those the humans told her she should, or could.

She knew damned well that if she ever took down a stained without a warrant, they'd have strung her up real quick. It might not have ever been said, but it didn't need to be. She'd been so lost in her own anger, shame, and self-pity that she hadn't cared. They'd not only gotten the last of her, she'd handed it over willingly.

Talen looked at Margaret. Once, she'd hidden in the shadows while her people were massacred. It might not have been just the Red Right Hand, but they'd led the way. Now they were doing it again, and she refused to believe Margaret was the only one in this situation. This time, she wouldn't just watch it happen.

When Talen came back to herself, Margaret was watching her warily.

"Are you okay?" Margaret asked.

"Not even a little." Talen looked at the new bounty crystal, then at Margaret, and back again.

I wonder.

She picked up the crystal and got to her feet.

"You're going?"

"No," Talen said. "Stand up."

Margaret eyed her but didn't move.

Talen gestured at her face. "What you're seeing is anger. But it ain't for you. It's reserved for those who brought this situation about. You ain't got nothing to fear from me. I swear it."

Margaret nodded and, after a moment's hesitation, stood.

Talen stepped close and lifted the bounty crystal. "Hold real still."

"What're you going to do with that?" Margaret asked, stepping back until she was against the counter. "You said—"

"I ain't going to hurt you. I'm just going to test a theory."

Margaret pursed her lips. "I don't know—"

Talen drew her right-hand iron, spun it, and offered it to Margaret, handle first.

Margaret stared at it, then at Talen with wide eyes, her mouth open.

"I don't know what the hell is going on here," Talen said. "But I'm going to learn the truth of it. I'm going to stop it. Then I'm going to send every Red Right Hand son of a bitch to hell."

Margaret's brows drew together.

"To do that, I need some answers," Talen said, "which I hope this here crystal can give me. But I can't do nothing if you don't trust me. So, I figure I best lead by example and trust you first."

Margaret looked at the offered weapon. "How do you know I won't use it to kill you?"

"I don't. Like I said, I'm trusting you first."

Margaret pushed the iron back, drew in a breath, and nodded. "Go on."

Talen crouched down, and slowly moved the crystal over Margaret's body, careful it didn't touch her. She'd handled enough crystals to know they were drawn to dark magic.

First, she moved the crystal over the shriveled leg.

Nothing happened.

She moved to the other leg and again, nothing. Then she stood and held the crystal near Margaret's face.

Margaret flinched a little, but that was all.

"Keep still," Talen said. "I need to get close."

Margaret closed her eyes tight and nodded.

Talen passed the crystal over Margaret's hair and face. When it neared her chin, something in the crystal changed; a familiar thrum and gentle tugging so subtle Talen doubted a human would've noticed. As the crystal moved down Margaret's neck, the reaction grew and then faded when Talen moved it along her shoulders. Near the center of Margaret's chest, the tugging grew more insistent, the thrumming almost a buzz. Talen touched the spot with her free hand.

Something lay under Margaret's blouse.

"What's that?" Talen asked.

Margaret made to touch the spot but stopped short. "It's just a warming talisman. George gave it to me for Christmas."

"Why is it under your blouse?"

"It has to touch my skin to work."

"Take it off," Talen said and stepped back.

Margaret hesitated, placing her hand over the charm. "Are you sure?"

Talen nodded.

Margaret removed the necklace and offered it to Talen.

She took it by the leather cord, careful not to touch the talisman. As soon as Margaret let go, the alien certainty that had been berating Talen since she arrived, abruptly vanished.

Well, that's something.

The amulet was a red stone carved into the shape of a flame. Talen didn't know enough to identify it, but it seemed well made. She brought it close and studied it. The magic was obvious, a simple charm to keep frostbite or hypothermia away.

Carefully, Talen touched the crystal to the stone. The two clicked together like magnets.

"What does that mean?" Margaret asked.

Talen narrowed her eyes. "Don't know for sure. But I'd say it means this charm and crystal are connected." She pulled the two apart, pocketed the bounty crystal, and after steadying herself, put a bare fingertip to the stone.

Nothing happened for a long moment. Then, a warm and sweet taste filled her mouth. It reminded Talen of the cinnamon honey her mother would drizzle over leaf cakes.

"If it's dark, I don't sense—"

The taste turned, quickly going from sickly sweet to rancid and foul. In a few seconds, Talen had to fight to keep from gagging. She turned away and handed the talisman back.

"What happened," Margaret asked.

"It ain't like any dark magic I ever seen," Talen said. "But something ain't right about it. It's deep, hidden behind the warming charm." She spit to one side. "I'd bet my left-hand iron that thing is what's causing you to smell stained." She looked at Margaret. "You said your husband gave it to you?"

Margaret nodded. "I always complained about the cold. I'd been eyeing warming charms since we moved to Kansas. He surprised me with it this past Christmas." She smiled wistfully. "He said the crafter filled it with his love for me. I told him we couldn't afford it, but he insisted. He was always so thoughtful."

"When was this?"

Margaret gave her a look. "Christmas, like I said."

"Is that the one in December?"

Margaret wiped her eyes. "Yes."

Talen scratched her neck. "That don't make no sense. Your warrant was only issued a couple months ago. Why'd it take so long?"

"I don't know. I used it all winter. This is the first time I've taken it off." Margaret let out a sigh and looked from the charm to Talen. "Do you think I'll be okay so long as I don't wear it? Apart from the picture, it's all I have left of George."

Talen shrugged. "Might be. I don't feel the certainty no more, but then I ain't no crafter."

"Does this mean I can have my life back?"

"It don't make the warrant go away."

"Can't I go to the Magistrate. Or a judge and show them?"

"You're supposing this is a regular warrant," Talen said. "I don't think it is. I suspect this only ends in one of two ways. You in a crystal, or the Red Hand in the ground. I'm sorry."

Margaret wiped at her eyes again. "Why would someone want me dead? I'm no one! I—"

The sound of approaching hoofbeats drew Talen up short. She stood and drew both spell irons.

"What is it?" Margaret asked.

"Trouble."

Chapter Ten

As Talen opened the door, Gaoth came into view, Margaret's big draft horse close behind. When they reached the cabin, Gaoth, his eyes wide, whinnied and turned in circles.

"Which way?" Talen asked.

He motioned with his head to the east.

"You're sure?"

He nodded a few times in answer.

"Are you talking to your horse?" Margaret asked from behind Talen. "And is he answering?"

Talen didn't respond. She just glanced at Margaret and then away. Talen had a decision to make. If she left now, she could get clear, but that meant leaving Margaret to die. The idea left Talen feeling indecent. Margaret might be human, but she was innocent.

If I stay...well, that's a whole other tangle of ivy.

Margaret stared with wide, panicked eyes, but didn't say anything.

Talen knew that she didn't really have a choice, not if she meant to salvage what remained of her ragged soul. The fact she'd even debated doing anything else would shame her mother.

"Get out of here," Talen said to Gaoth. "Find some place out of sight."

He snorted, shook his head, and stomped at the ground with his front hooves.

"Don't argue. Just do it." Talen pointed at Joseph. "You need to keep him safe."

Gaoth snorted once then led Joseph to the northwest, where they vanished into the trees.

"Terisan ut marrin." Talen turned and bowed her head, trying to form a plan. "The *juarchian* must've turned east to go around the reservation."

"The who?" Margaret stepped into Talen's view. "I don't understand. What's happening?"

"Another stalker," Talen said. "One of the Red Right Hand."

The color drained from Margaret's face. "Dear God."

Talen bit back a comment about Margaret's choice of words. She nodded at the mundane repeater. "How good are you with that?"

"Decent enough I suppose. I hunt with it and sometimes I hit something." Margaret swallowed. "I've never shot a person though."

"Stay here and keep an eye out. If you see anyone that ain't me, shoot them."

"But—"

"I got no time to argue," Talen said. "If you want to live, shoot. You might not get a chance, but if you do and don't take it, you're dead. Understand?"

Margaret nodded and picked up the rifle. "What are you going to do?"

Talen didn't answer. Instead, she drew the shadows around her and hurried off to the east. The soft earth kept her footfalls silent. But, if the Red Hand stalker knew to look, her footprints would give her away. Hopefully, he'd be dead before he got the chance.

The promise of revenge quieted her mind and fueled her muscles. She wasn't out of breath when she topped the hill, but her heart pounded in anticipation. Peeking around a tree, she studied the sparse woods, but didn't see anything. She closed her eyes and focused. Sure enough she heard the heavy footfalls of two—no, three—humans.

"Terisan ut marrin," she whispered. She might be able to take them

if she had the drop on them. Jeremiah and his boys had been amateurs. The Red Right Hand were skilled, and they had experience killing elves.

Just like the war. Be quick and keep moving.

She put her back to the tree and rolled the cylinders of her irons to new spells.

The humans were on foot and moving slow, probably silent to their own dull ears.

With each of their heavy steps, she painted a more complete mental image of the approaching stalkers. They walked single file, a few feet between them. They were big, over two hundred pounds, and one wheezed. Could be he was old or sick, or just fond of tobacco.

Talen wrinkled her nose and turned her head to one side. The air tasted foul, stinking of sweat and heavy with the rancid, coppery tang of blood-soaked leather. She resisted the urge to spit.

Now sure of the group's location, she opened her eyes and made her way down the hill, going wide to get behind them.

She froze.

A fourth stalker hurried after the other three, smaller and less confident in his movements. Twigs broke under his footfalls, but his breathing came slow and steady. He lacked skill, not vigor. He stank less than the others too, though he did reek of old blood and leather.

The Red Right Hand had brought a child to battle.

Again.

Talen gritted her teeth. She couldn't hesitate.

Don't think about it. You don't have a choice, so you'll just have to live with pulling the trigger.

She pushed the thought aside and crouched low behind a tree, readying her irons. She'd only get a couple well-aimed shots off before they returned fire. She'd start at the end of the line and move up. It might work if she was fast enough.

Her hands shook, and her heart pounded. She gripped her irons tighter and drew in slow breaths. She needed to focus on the threat and what needed doing.

"Show them why they fear the dark," the Warden Masters had said. "Flow from shadows, strike fast and hard, then vanish."

The disquiet faded to numbness as time dragged, seconds seemingly becoming minutes, then hours. But she waited with the patience of the earth in the embrace of her shadow glamour.

The group drew closer – thirty yards, then twenty, ten, then five.

Her heart beat slow and steady as they passed her. She didn't breathe or move, not even her eyes, just watched them with her peripheral vision.

They kept walking, none the wiser to her existence. The older three were huge and grizzled as bears. They all held battered spell irons in their red-gloved right hands, white spell fire dancing in the runes and sigils. A smooth-faced boy brought up the rear, spell iron massive in his small hand, likewise clad in a blood-soaked, leather glove.

Still she didn't move, and she didn't allow herself to consider the boy's age.

A couple more yards—

One of the men turned his head.

A blue gem covered in etched symbols sat in place of his left eye.

He turned full toward her, and his face twisted into a hateful sneer.

"Witch!" he roared, leveling his iron.

The others spun and took aim, but too slowly.

In the time it took to blink, Talen rolled to the side, ending in a low crouch, her legs ready. She released her shadows, poured magic into her irons, and pulled both triggers. Three spheres of bright blue power leapt from each barrel.

She didn't wait to see if her aim had been true. She pushed off from the ground, leaping back the way she'd come and rolled her cylinders to fresh chambers.

Fire, lightning, and acid spells spat from the Red Hand stalker's irons, their magic pulverizing the boulder that had been behind Talen.

Her starburst spells struck the two outermost stalkers. One took shots to the face, chest, and stomach, the other in the chest, stomach, and thigh. The magic exploded, sending the stalkers twisting and tumbling back. Sparks rained and smoke filled the air, forcing the others to turn away.

Talen kept moving, putting a tree between her and the stalkers. A blast of magical force splintered the trunk, sending debris into her face.

She tumbled forward into a roll, blinking shrapnel from her eyes.

A trio of small comets came at her, and she rolled again. One of the fireballs struck her shoulder, sending her spinning. The enchanted leather of her coat didn't catch fire, but the heat soaked through and seared her skin.

She ignored the pain and redirected her tumble.

"You're dead, witch!"

The taunt gave away his location. Talen took aim and fired. Three crackling balls of lightning flew from her right-hand iron, a lance of kinetic force from the left.

A stalker shrieked and then went silent.

She kept moving, finally ducking behind a rock. She rolled her cylinders and waited, wiping at her eyes with the back of her hand, and listening.

Soft weeping and wet, ragged breaths.

"Pa," the boy said between sobs. "Pa!"

When Talen's vision cleared, she chanced a quick look over the edge of the stone. All four humans were down, none of them moving.

After a long ten-count, Talen—with effort—wrapped the shadows around her and darted out. She leapt, planted her foot on the trunk of a tree, and bounded again, taking cover behind a large oak.

No one shot at her.

Still draped in shadow, she peered around the tree.

The stalkers hadn't moved.

She dropped her glamour and stepped out, irons leveled at the men on the ground.

Two were dead. A pool of blood collected on and around the rock one of their skulls had collided with. The other's body bent in a way that could only mean his spine had snapped.

That's for my mother and sisters, juarchian.

Taking aim at the remaining two, she approached, cautious and careful to keep her distance.

The lightning blast had dropped the stalker with the magic stone for an eye. Smoke drifted from his blackened chest and burnt shirt. His breathing came wet and heavy. She guessed his lungs had cooked and were filling with blood. He'd be dead in minutes.

Better than you and yours deserve.

The force blast had struck the boy, but her aim had been poor. It'd crushed his right leg and pelvis. The angle of the pulverized limb twisted Talen's guts and she felt more than a little ashamed at delighting moments before. He wept, but his eyes were filled with pure loathing. His spell iron lay in the dirt a few feet away.

"You killed my pa, witch!" he spat.

"I did." She didn't look away from his hateful glare.

"I'll kill you!" He tried for his iron, clawing and dragging his ruined body.

What remained of her heart broke for the boy. Humans bestowed hatred upon their young like an heirloom. She hated, but hers was her own, no one else's.

"I'll kill her, PaPa," the boy said, his fingers touching the handle of his iron.

"No, you won't," Talen said softly.

She took aim and fired.

The boy went still.

She said a silent prayer for the hate-filled child.

Then, she set to the ghoulish work of searching the bodies. She collected their spell irons, never touching the bloodstained handles, and what charges they had.

Aside from a little coin, she found a dozen severed elf ears. They were old, flesh turned near to leather. The boy's father had them strung on a necklace.

Talen almost shot the *shanzi fetsuian* again. Instead, she tore the anathema from his neck, and—without a trace of shame or guilt—watched as the last stalker drowned in his own blood. Once he'd drawn his last breath, she headed back to the cabin, leaving the bodies to feed the crows.

Chapter Eleven

It's me. Don't shoot," Talen shouted to the cabin as she stepped into view. Every movement caused her coat to rub again her burned flesh and without the distraction of battle, her shoulder screamed its discontent. The front door opened, and after a long pause, Margaret emerged, repeater up and ready.

"Did you…I mean to say…"

"They're dead." Talen tried to bite back the pain, using her anger as an anesthetic. Even so, she winced with every step.

"Oh my, you're hurt!"

"Glancing shot. Burnt skin and a bruised shoulder is all." She held the empty Red Hand spell irons out to Margaret. "Take these, but don't touch the handles."

Margaret looked at the iron and then at Talen. "Why? Are they poisoned?"

"Poisoned with blood magic," Talen said, biting back her impatience. "Now take 'em."

Margaret shifted the rifle under her arm and took the irons.

"Put them on the table. I'll see to them later." Talen gave a high whistle and waited.

Moments later, Gaoth came running, the big draft horse following close behind.

When he came to her, she retrieved some leather pouches and her last spare shirt from his saddlebags.

Margaret disappeared into the cabin, gripping the irons by the barrel.

Gaoth gave Talen a concerned look.

She stroked the horse's neck. "You know I've had worse."

He nuzzled her good shoulder and chuffed.

Talen looked at the cabin, sighed, and pressed her forehead into his cheek. With the fighting done, her mind was free to consider the consequences of her actions. The weight of it crashed into her like a mudslide.

"What the hell have I done?"

Gaoth chuffed again.

"You know damned well I ain't talking about the Red Hand." She let out a breath. "But I ain't so sure about what comes next. Binding myself to this woman might not be the best thing. For either of us."

Gaoth sighed.

"I hope to hell you're right," she said, stroking his forehead. "Not like I can do anything about it."

Gaoth leaned into her touch. After a moment, he snorted.

"I'm going, damn it," Talen said and then went inside to find Margaret standing by the table.

"I put the irons there," Margaret said, nodding at the mantle. "I didn't think it would be a good idea to put them on the bed, or the table. I was careful not to touch the handles."

Talen nodded. "That's fine. Would you fetch me some water?" She tossed the shirt and pouches on the table and then fell into the chair.

Margaret filled a bowl from the hand pump, brought it over, and set it down.

Talen clenched her jaw and mentally braced herself. She tried pulling off her coat, but the pain hit her like a stampeding herd of feral horses and brought her up short.

She winced and bit back a curse.

Margaret reached out. "Let me help—"

"I got it," Talen said, through clenched teeth.

Margaret drew back.

"Just give me a moment." That was as close to an apology as Talen could muster just now.

After taking a steadying breath, she peeled back the edge of her coat and looked over the damage. The protective magic had stopped the impact of the fireball, but not the heat. Her shirt had burned away and seared her flesh, which stuck to the leather of the coat.

No point in putting it off any longer.

Talen took another breath and set to work. Inch by inch she managed, through gritted teeth and a barely contained scream, to peel the jacket away from the burned flesh.

When it was done, she leaned back, closed her eyes, and slowed her breathing, trying not to pass out as the cold, agonizing pain faded to something near bearable.

Margaret reached for the coat.

Talen opened her eyes and held tight to the jacket.

Margaret flinched and lifted her hands. "I wasn't going to go through it or anything, just set on the bed, I swear."

Talen sighed, chided herself, and released her grip. "Much obliged."

Margaret took the coat and laid it out on her bed. "I just want to help if I can. You did save my life, after all. Thank you for that, by the way."

Talen didn't answer. She needed to tend to her shoulder first. Once that was done, then she could regret doing the right thing. Not killing the Red Hand stalkers, even the boy. The only other way that could've ended was with them standing over Talen's corpse. But by helping Margaret, or rather by saving her life, Talen had accepted a responsibility.

Later.

She looked over her shoulder. The wound wasn't great, but it could've been worse. There wasn't any muscle damage or dislocation. It'd heal with a prayer or two. Unfortunately, she had no idea when she'd get a chance to do that.

"I need to make a poultice," Talen said and tore the remnants of her left sleeve free. "But I'll need your help. The ingredients are in those pouches."

"Just tell me what to do."

Talen drank what she wouldn't need from the bowl. Then, she talked Margaret through the mixing of plants and minerals into the remaining water.

Talen tested the mixture's thickness. "It's ready."

Margaret applied the paste to the shirt sleeve and wrapped it over Talen's shoulder.

The pain faded almost immediately. Talen closed her eyes, savoring the euphoric absence of pain, and soothing touch of the wet plaster.

"You should eat," Margaret said.

Talen opened her eyes as Margaret set down a cup of water and a bowl of steaming vegetable stew. It smelled good, and her stomach rumbled, but she shook her head.

"Ain't time for that," Talen said and had every intention of standing, but her legs didn't listen. "You need to pack up and go."

"Why?" Margaret asked, sitting down with her own cup and bowl. "You killed them, didn't you?"

"They'll be more. The Red Hand don't give up. And for a bounty big as yours, they'll have set a mess of their boys after you. I got no notion how far behind the next crew is, but I do know we best be gone before then."

"But you're hurt. You need to eat something. Surely the matter of a few minutes to eat won't make a difference."

Talen opened her mouth to object, but her stomach overruled her. She nodded, picked up the spoon, and started eating. It tasted even better than it smelled.

"There's no meat in it," Margaret said, between bites. "Though only because I didn't have any."

"We eat meat," Talen said between mouthfuls. "We just prefer plants."

"I'm sorry. I'd heard—"

Talen didn't look up from her bowl. "Assumptions made by humans who never bothered to learn the truth?"

Margaret stiffened. "You're right of course." She refilled their cups with water and then resumed eating her stew in silence.

Talen could practically hear her mother's admonishment. *After she helped tend to your wounds, offered food—which you accepted—you repay her kindness with a rebuke?*

"I apologize," Talen said. "I violated the rules of hospitality. A guest ought not speak to their host in such a way."

"From bounty to host." Margaret smiled a little. "Seems I've progressed greatly in a short period of time."

Talen almost smiled herself. "Well, it has been that kind of day."

"As your host then, I say you owe me no apologies," Margaret said. "In your position, I imagine I'd feel the same about humans. I don't know if it matters to you, but George and I never approved of the war. The only fighting should've been protecting settlers from Indian raids."

Talen drew in a slow breath. When she spoke, it took focus to keep her tone civil. "Them raiders are the ones protecting their homes from invaders. They offered to share the land, signed treaties in good faith even. Your kind—" Talen winced. "I apologize again. The government wasn't content with that and broke treaties whenever they got inconvenient."

Margaret nodded. "As you say, but as I said, I bear no ill will toward elf or Indian."

Talen fought back another surge of anger. "They ain't a single people," she said, gripping her spoon so tight it nearly snapped. "The tribes are as varied and different as the states of your union. More so, in fact. The Diné are as different from the Lakota as you are from a Russian."

Margaret considered for a moment. "I always thought of them like Americans," she said without a trace of anger. "The tribes are like the states, minor differences but all the same in the end."

"And the states never had any disagreements over culture or tradition?" Talen fought to keep the acid from her words. "So alike, they fought over the freedom to keep slaves."

Margaret bristled, just for an instant. It happened so quick, Talen wasn't entirely sure she'd seen it right.

"That's a fair point," Margaret said. "We do seem a species bent on murder and cruelty. At times, I'm amazed we've survived so long. Or if we even deserve to."

Talen's anger evaporated. She stared, mouth agape, unsure how to respond. She wondered if Margaret wasn't being insincere, using some subtle mockery. But the earnestness in her eyes said otherwise.

"I'm a cripple and a woman," Margaret said, as if reading Talen's thoughts. "I know quite well what it's like for those who know nothing about you to prejudge. I've dealt with it my entire life. As such, I work very hard not to be that way." She shrugged. "But we're all bound by the limits of our own experiences and the biases of our society."

Talen stared, utterly lost for a response. She didn't often come across humans so ready to admit their own failings and shortcomings. After a moment, she just gave up and resumed eating.

"Would you like seconds?" Margaret asked.

Talen nodded and offered over her bowl. "Thank you kindly."

Margaret filled it, handed it back, then refilled her own.

"I do appreciate you saving my life," she said, sitting back down. "But I'm going to stay. I have nowhere else to go and, frankly, I'm weary of running."

"They'll keep coming. They won't stop till you're in a crystal."

"I know. I'm resigned to that."

Talen furrowed her brow. "I don't know why, but they sold that charm to your husband, and in so doing, took your life away. How can you be content to just give them what little you got left without a fight?"

Margaret shrugged. "I'm not like you. I'm not a fighter. I never was. I don't have the courage for it. I never did."

"Like hell," Talen said. "You traveled all this way on your own and set up in a cabin you'd never seen before. What did it take you, a month, to get here?"

"Nearly two I think," Margaret said. "Truth to tell, I've sort of lost track of time."

"Few could make that journey. Fewer still would even try," Talen said. "You did. Don't give up now. Can't you see someone is making you a pawn?"

"What are you talking about?"

"There's got to be a connection between these new bounty stones and that charm of yours," Talen said. "I'm sure of it. Sure as I am that you might be the first, but damn sure won't be last."

Margaret shook her head. "Please don't take this as lack of appreciation for what you've done, but why do you care?"

Why indeed?

Talen set down her spoon and met Margaret's eyes. "I saved your life, freely and by my own will. I'm now honor-bound to protect that life."

"Wouldn't they have killed you, too?"

"Maybe, but I could've left you and gotten clear."

"Again, I don't mean to sound unappreciative, but it seems to me that saving my life saved your own."

"I don't play with technicalities," Talen said. "Especially not in matters like this."

"Then I release you from your obligation."

If only.

"I made the choice," Talen said. "Ain't for you to undo it. Besides—" She closed her mouth. "Never mind."

"What?"

"Nothing."

"Please, Miss—" Margaret shook her head. "Good heavens, I don't even know your name."

"Talen. No Miss. Just Talen."

"Talen," Margaret said "Please, finish your thought."

Talen hesitated. Did she really want to share something so personal? And with a human no less?

But you've done it before.

She let out a long sigh and looked away. "There's a personal side for me as well."

"And that is?"

"For years, I collected bounties and was okay with it," Talen said. "They used me, no mistake, but to kill stained—monsters that are an anathema to the magic." She gestured at Margaret. "You ain't a monster and, well, I seen plenty of injustice. I ain't gonna be a part of any if I can help it."

Margaret listened without looking away.

"You're right. I do hate humans. In part for what you did to my people, but also cause of what it made me into." She sat forward in the chair. "The truth is, I made myself this way. Might be I never agreed, but I never said no. I want—I need—to say no now. If I'm gonna salvage any part of me worth saving, I need to make a stand for what I know is right."

Margaret didn't say anything, and Talen didn't push. Talen had made her choice when she'd gone to face the Red Hand stalkers. Now Margaret had to choose.

If Margaret decided to stay, Talen would too, and she'd fight whoever came along. And like as not, they'd both die. Sooner or later, someone would get lucky, or Talen would just run out of charges. But at least she'd die on her own terms, by her own choosing, and doing something that felt right. That sort of certainty had become a rare commodity of late.

They both went back to eating their cooling stew in silence.

"What do you suggest?" Margaret asked, after a long while.

"We got to learn more about that charm and the crystal. That means we'll need us a crafter."

"Where do we find one who won't turn me in for the bounty?"

"I know someone," Talen said. "A friend."

Margaret's eyebrows went up.

"There ain't many humans I trust, but I do him, with my life."

"And mine as well?"

Talen nodded.

"Where is he?"

"Lawrence, Kansas. It'll be a hard ride but—"

Margaret's face went pale.

"What?" Talen asked.

"There was an attack some months ago," Margaret said. "I heard about it before... Well... Well, before all this started."

"Another? Ain't the war over?"

"It is, but some Missourians still hold a grudge. I only know what I read in the papers: that it wasn't as bad as Quantrill's raid, but more than a hundred people died. There's a full garrison stationed there now."

The image of Wilfred's murdered body, lying ignored in the street, broke what remained of Talen's heart. It'd been years since she'd last seen him. For all she knew, he'd been dead a while, but still...

"Ain't no one else I trust. It'll take three weeks to get there, and that's a long way for a dead end, but—"

"Then we'll pray he survived."

"You made your choice then?"

"Yes." Margaret gestured at the Red Hand stalker's spell irons. "What do you plan to do with those?"

"Destroy the cursed things."

"What do you mean cursed?"

"You know why they're called the Red Right Hand?"

Margaret shrugged. "I presume it's because of the red glove they wear on their right hands."

"The gloves are red because they soak them in blood." Even just explaining it left a foul taste in Talen's mouth. She wanted to spit, but she was still a guest, so she swallowed it. "They think the blood makes their magic stronger and purer, but they're wrong. It's nothing but an affront to magic. Add to that, too many of them killed my sisters. So, I plan on reducing them, and their damned charges, to ash."

"Oh, I see."

Talen stood, went to her coat, and fetched the collection of ears from the pocket. "And I'm also gonna lay these to rest."

Margaret swallowed and looked away. "Merciful God. Sometimes I'm shamed to call myself human."

"Gather up your belongings. You can't never come back here." Talen grimaced as she pulled on her coat, careful not to displace the poultice. "We should get some distance from here before nightfall."

Chapter Twelve

s Margaret packed her meager possessions, Talen loaded wood in the fire. She stoked the flames high and hot. When it was ready, she tossed in the Red Hand spell irons and their charges.

"Is the fire enough to destroy them?" Margaret asked.

"The charges will help, but I plan on adding some heat to the flames," Talen said. "Load up your horse. I need me some privacy for this part."

Margaret left to secure her belongs to the old draft horse.

Talen found a quiet spot away from the cabin, fell to her knees, and dug a hole with her hands. It took some time and left her fingers raw and bloody, but it was nothing compared to the pain in her heart. She set the ears into the foot-deep hole, wiped at her eyes, and then, very gently, filled the makeshift grave. As her hands worked, she began a prayer for her unknown sisters.

"In the embrace of the earth, may you find peace," she said in Elven. "With this last link to pain and fear returned to the earth, may you find solace and comfort with the mothers. I don't know your names, your clans, or nations, but you are my sisters, and I love you. I'll mourn the loss of your light in this darkening world."

She bowed her head and let a few tears fall onto the small graves. After a moment, she wiped her eyes and went back to the cabin.

Margaret led Joseph to a rock and, with some obvious effort, hauled herself up onto it, favoring her good leg. She caught her breath and then started pulling herself into the saddle.

Talen didn't know what to do. Look away? Offer to help? She didn't want to take any of the woman's dignity or insult her.

With a final grunt, Margaret got herself settled in. "I'm ready when you are," she said, her breathing a little heavy.

Talen led Gaoth well away from the cabin and motioned for Margaret to follow.

"Wait here," she said. She went back to the open door and drew both spell irons. She poured magic into them, igniting the runes, and pulled the triggers.

Six balls of flame streaked out and hit home in the fireplace. In the space of a couple heartbeats, the wood, and even the stone, blazed white hot. The magic woven into the spell irons would protect them for a time, but this fire would burn long and hot. There'd be little left but slag and ash.

She replaced her spent charges and glanced back at the fire. She wondered if she oughtn't have taken the charges, but only for an instant. They were as foul and blood-tainted as the weapons.

Let it all burn.

She went to Gaoth and whispered instructions into his ear. He nodded and then made for a rocky path to the southwest. Talen led Margaret and Joseph due north, leaving an obvious trail in the soft earth. When they reached tougher terrain, she pointed.

"Head on over to where Gaoth is waiting. I'll follow behind and mask the tracks.

"You think it'll work?"

Talen shrugged. "Might, might not. Depends on who's doing the tracking. It don't cost nothing but a handful of minutes though."

Margaret nodded.

When she returned to Gaoth, Talen saddled up and led the way, slow and steady, along the rock-strewn path. She steered them well away from the corpses. Carrion birds already circled above, and the darker part of Talen's soul wished she'd let the last live long enough for the crows to set to work on his eyes.

And she hated herself for it.

Joseph set a ponderous pace, but his endurance made up for it a bit. The days passed slow, the miles even slower. Margaret kept on without complaint. Though visibly in pain and stiff every time they stopped, she never once grumbled.

Their chosen path rarely provided a rock or stump to assist Margaret in climbing into the saddle. When needed, Talen mounted Joseph and then pulled Margaret up behind her. Every time, Margaret would thank her. Talen would nod in reply as she slid off and climbed onto Gaoth.

How many miles had Margaret walked on her trek to the cabin? There had to have been long stretches with no means for her to mount the big horse. It made her journey all the more impressive.

"Can I ask you something?" Margaret asked on the fourth night.

They'd spoken little as they rode during the day. At night, Margaret was usually so tired that she'd be asleep within seconds of lying down. Tonight, they camped near a rocky outcropping. It provided enough cover for a small fire, their first since leaving the cabin.

"You can," Talen said, her back to a boulder as she cleaned her irons. She fought hard to ignore the dancing flames and to not hear the screams of the dying. "Don't mean I'll answer."

"I apologize in advance, but I can't think of a way to ask without sounding rude," Margaret said. "I can only plead an honest ignorance when it comes to elves."

Talen looked up and arched an eyebrow. "Go on then."

Margaret nodded at the pristine spell irons in Talen's hands. "How do you make them? They're strikingly beautiful and, I'm assuming, aren't human-made?"

Talen furrowed her brow. "We got crafters, same as you."

"No. I mean, where do you get the metal? I'm guessing the image most humans have of elves living in trees isn't accurate."

"Actually, that much is true. We do live in trees, but it don't mean we ain't got metal or a means to shape it. Hell, we were working metal when humans were just learning to sharpen stones."

"So, you have mines. I didn't know that."

"No, not like humans do." Talen swallowed back the rising bile. "We used to do some trade with the dwarves." She spit. "Before they decided slaughtering us held more profit."

"I'm sorry. I didn't mean to—"

Talen waved her off. "For the metal we use to craft our irons and magical wares, well, we coax it from the earth."

"I don't understand."

"We treat with elementals. Make them offerings for materials of sufficient purity to forge our wares."

Margaret's eyes went wide. "They're real? Elementals, I mean."

"Of course," Talen said, returning her attention to her irons but still watching Margaret in her peripheral vision.

Margaret opened her mouth and then closed it.

"I suspect you're curious as to why they didn't fight with us when the dwarves and humans came a calling."

"I confess that I am, but—".

"The affairs of us mere mortals are outside their concern. They don't involve themselves. Even the life of an elf ain't nothing but a flash of lightning to them."

"So it's true that you live for centuries?"

Talen nodded. "Though our life expectancy has grown rather shorter as of late."

Margaret winced. "I'm sorry. I don't mean to be disrespectful. I only want to know the truth about you and your people. Seems the least I can do since you're helping me. I'm sorry if I broached a tender subject. Thank you for answering."

"Thank you for asking," Talen said without looking up. "Not many have enough care to ask."

Margaret rolled over, pulled her blanket high and settled in.

When her breathing slowed and sleep took her, Talen stowed her irons and stripped down. She lay down on the bare earth and said her silent incantation. The moon offered what it had in place of the sun, and though not as powerful as her sister, it was still more than enough.

Talen began processing the moonlight, channeling the energy to her burned shoulder. The earth, trees, grasses, and many of the animals answered her plea, including—as ever—Gaoth. Even Joseph made an offering to her. The massive horse's generosity touched Talen deeply. She promised him to protect his human companion with her life.

When Margaret woke the next morning, Talen sat tending to a small rabbit cooking over the coals.

"Do you sleep?" Margaret asked, wiping her eyes and getting to her feet. She took a step and stumbled toward the waning fire.

Talen caught her. "Easy."

Margaret stared at her, eyes wide and mouth open. "Goodness, you're fast."

"I am." Talen helped her back down. "Take your time. You eat. I'll see to packing up Joseph."

"Thank you, but I can manage."

"No point in pushing yourself when there ain't no need. We still got a long ride ahead of us." She met Margaret's eyes. "You got nothing to prove to me."

Margaret's smile vanished, and she stiffened. "I don't have anything to prove to anyone."

"Of course, you're right." Talen bowed her head. "I'm sorry. I meant no offense."

Margaret let out a breath. "No, I'm sorry. I've gotten used to being condescended to, as if everything I do is some sort of miracle." She rolled her eyes and let out a sigh. "I've gotten by my entire life, and I might need help at times, but I'm far from helpless."

"I can see that plain."

"Thank you." Margaret carefully took the spit off the fire and, after giving the rabbit a moment to cool, began eating.

Talen collected the bedroll and secured it to Joseph. When Margaret finished breakfast, Talen doused the fire and covered it in dirt. Before long they were riding in silence once more.

They avoided every town and fort they knew of. When they stumbled onto one, they swung wide around it. It cost days, but then, so did the long overnight stops. Margaret needed twice as much sleep as Talen, and Joseph couldn't navigate in the dark like Gaoth.

Luckily, food wasn't so much of an issue. Since Margaret couldn't subsist on leaves and grasses, they hunted and fished. Every meal Margaret offered some, and Talen always refused. The weather even held for most of the ride. It rained a couple of days but not hard or for long. Talen used the extra time at night to continue her healing rites. After near on a week, she'd completely healed.

On the third week they set camp in a cave outside Lincoln. Talen prepared some charges for her irons while Margaret cooked a fish over the fire.

"How did you know about this place?" Margaret asked, looking around.

"Pawnee used to use it for rituals," Talen said. "So be respectful. I learned about it from the Underground Railroad."

Margaret stared with wide eyes. "You worked with the Underground Railroad?"

"For a time. It worked in secret, especially during the war, and I tend to stand out." She shrugged. "I did what I could for as long as I could. Don't know if it's still running. I like to think there ain't a need no more, what with the war over. But I suspect there's still more than a few that need help getting away. The conductors I knew, including the crafter we're going to see, they weren't the kind to turn away when needed."

Margaret studied the cave with what seemed a kind of reverence, but deeper, more personal somehow. "I wonder how many passed through here."

"Not nearly enough."

Margaret furrowed her brow. "Wait, we don't need to worry about the town?"

"Nah." Talen chewed on some leaves. "Lincoln is close—closer than I'd like these days—but few knew about this place. Can't imagine too many have found it since."

"Would you like some fish?" Margaret asked, as she turned it.

"No, thank you."

"May I ask you something?"

Talen didn't look up. "Go on."

"You say you eat meat, but I've never seen you do it. Is my offering it an offense?"

"Not at all. I get by just fine on leaves and bark. You can't, so no need to waste it on me when I got other options."

A long moment passed in silence.

"Um," Margaret said.

Talen sighed. "Just ask your question. If it's rude, I'll tell you."

"Is it true only women elves are warriors, or soldiers, or whatever you call them?"

"Yes and no. Like you, our crafters can make items, but not use them. Among humans, crafters are a small percentage."

"About one in twenty are born a crafter as I understand it."

Talen looked up. "Well, with elves, it tended to divide almost exclusively by sex. So, Shadow Wardens tended to be women because most casters were women. But we didn't have gender roles like you do. If a man were born a caster and trained to be a Shadow Warden, we'd have treated him same as anyone. We were free to pursue whatever life we wished, with whomever we wished."

Margaret looked at her. "With whomever? You mean—"

Talen nodded and set back to work. "We loved without shame or reproach. Like I said, gender didn't play as significant a role as it does with humans."

Margaret's cheeks flushed. "Oh, I see."

"I don't expect you to understand."

"What about two-gun witches?" Margaret asked.

"What about us?"

"Can men be two-gun witches?" Margaret frowned and looked away. "Would they be called witches?"

"Don't know 'cause there ain't never been a male dual caster. It weren't prohibited, just never happened."

"Should I call you a dual caster instead?"

Talen shrugged. "It's what we called ourselves. Humans came up with 'two-gun witch,' as much from fear as hate, I reckon." She smiled. "I've grown rather fond of it, and the way so many piss themselves when they recognize me as one."

Margaret went quiet for a bit, pulled her fish off the fire, and set it aside to cool.

"I told you," Talen said, keeping her eyes on her work. "If you got questions, just ask 'em."

"It's not important, I just—" Margaret shook her head. "No. Never mind."

Talen stopped working and looked up again, but Margaret wouldn't meet her eyes. "Well, now you got me intrigued."

Margaret let out a breath and turned to Talen. "I noticed everything you said was past tense."

It took a moment for Talen to realize it hadn't been a conscious choice. The thought left her feeling like the last leaf on a dead tree: dried out and crumbling a little more with each passing breeze. Except her tree hadn't just died, it'd burned.

She swallowed and cleared her throat. "Did I?" She tried to go back to her work, but her hands wouldn't be still.

Margaret moved a little closer. "Please tell me you're not the last."

For a long while, the only sounds were the buzzing insects outside the cave and the crackling fire inside.

Margaret put a hand over Talen's.

Talen flinched away, and Margaret drew back. "No, I ain't the last."

In truth, she had no idea how many of her people remained. Probably less than five thousand in the whole world, but she couldn't bring herself to say it aloud. "But I am the last of my clan, and almost certainly my nation."

Margaret made to reach out again but seemed to change her mind. "I'm so very sorry."

Talen bit back the rising bile. "Is that an offer of condolence or an apology?"

"Both, I suppose." Margaret moved closer to the fire, looked at the fish, and then pushed it away. "I'm going to get some sleep. I sort of lost my appetite." She stretched out on her bedroll and rubbed at her hindered leg.

In a matter of minutes, Margaret had slipped into sleep. Talen stared at the peculiar woman. Aside from Wilfred, no human had ever cared enough to bother asking about her people. Maybe Wilfred wasn't entirely unique after all.

Chapter Thirteen

The next three days passed in near silence. Late on the third night, they set camp some miles outside of Lawrence. The flat land and sparse trees meant no fire. However, they did find a low spot that offered some cover.

"What's the plan?" Margaret asked, as she laid out her bedroll. "Do we go to see your friend at first light?"

"That's no good. This town might've been loyal to abolition, but I'd draw a lot of unwelcome attention. Being anti-slavery is a long way from being pro-elf. Besides, you might still reek of stained to other humans. Give me the charm; I'll take it to him."

"Tonight?"

"Right now, in fact. I can make my way unseen. You can't."

"You're sure the charm won't give you away?"

Talen paused. She hadn't considered that. She didn't sense any stain on Margaret, and hadn't since she'd taken off the talisman, but Talen wasn't a human. No telling how it might affect her.

"After the last raid, the garrison is likely on edge," Margaret said. "If you're spotted sneaking into town—"

"It might get ugly." Talen nodded. "All right then, you stay here with the charm, and I'll fetch Wilfred back here."

"What if something goes wrong?"

Talen climbed into the saddle. "Bury the charm deep as you can and head north. Keep away from others as long as you can. With luck, by the time you're desperate, the effects will have worn off, and maybe you can find a new life."

"I meant in the short term. Like if someone finds me here alone."

"You got that repeater, don't you?"

Margaret nodded and produced the rifle.

"Shoot them."

Margaret paled, and her eyes widened. "What? No, really, what should I do?"

Talen turned Gaoth toward town and urged him on.

He took off, delighting in running again after weeks of slow plodding. Once they were clear of the camp, Talen drew the shadows around them both. It wouldn't make them invisible; a bright moon hung amid a sea of stars with nary a cloud in sight. But she hoped the late hour meant fewer eyes to spot them.

She slowed when they neared town and dismounted amid a copse of trees.

"Wait here," she whispered. "If anything happens, get on back to Margaret. She'll tend to you."

Gaoth shook his head and pawed at the ground.

"Don't argue with me." Talen whispered harshly but stroked the horse's nose. "I'm counting on you to live up to my obligation. Get her to the Oglala. I don't know if they'll help her, but it's the only option."

Gaoth nodded, peered at her, and snorted.

"I will," she said and hugged his neck. "I love you, old friend."

He pushed her with his forequarters and chuffed.

She rolled her eyes. "Yeah, if I come across any apples, I'll bring you one."

Gaoth gave her a toothy smile.

"Sometimes I wish I had a dog," she muttered and turned.

Gaoth bumped her with his head.

She wrapped herself in shadow, her footsteps light, and careful not to make a sound. She scanned for patrols. They might not be able to see, or even hear her, but on occasion some could sense her. After two raids, the soldiers were likely to shoot first and ask questions later. A lucky shot would kill her as sure as an aimed one.

She kept to the darkness and off the main road, moving between unfamiliar buildings. The town had changed quite a bit.

Hope to hell Wilfred is still here.

From the cover of a shadow-drenched alleyway, she scanned the main street. She spotted five humans, a hundred yards off and getting closer. Her stomach knotted at the sight of blue uniforms. Her hands went to her irons.

If the soldiers were on patrol, they didn't take it too seriously; a bottle passed among them as they laughed. They all carried mundane rifles, not a spell iron in sight. Her hands drifted from her irons to the bone handled knife Bear Heart had given her, and to her own.

She gripped them tight and slowed her breathing.

She could do it. Even with that many, it'd be easy, especially since they were liquored up. Step from the shadows, cut them down, and be back in darkness before the last body hit the ground.

They drew closer, even stumbled toward her side of the street as if tempting her.

She drew the blades and crouched. She thought of Margaret then, and her pledge. Her own words sounded in her head, "I need to do what I know is right if I'm going to salvage any part of me worth saving."

No reason I can't do both.

If she stashed the bodies in the alley, it'd be morning before anyone noticed them missing. Hell, she'd have Wilfred back to his home long before then.

And what if you're wrong? her mother's voice asked. *You can't hide from an entire town, not with Wilfred or Margaret, let alone both. You made a promise, child. The promise.*

The soldiers were a dozen feet away now. The air reeked of cheap rot gut and the stench of unwashed human. She gripped the knives so tight that her fingers ached.

She stared into the eyes of each one as they passed, so close she could almost reach out and touch them. Not a one had a clue that death lurked in the darkness.

When the last passed her by, she moved, fast as lightning and silent as the night.

The soldier didn't even feel the blade.

It took some time, but she found Wilfred's house, smaller and plainer than those around it, and set well away. Thoughts of equality only went so far. A weathered crafter's shingle hung from the porch awning.

Either he still lives there, or another crafter has moved in.

Like all the neighboring houses, the windows were dark, and nothing stirred. Talen made for the back, mindful of the passing seconds but careful not to make a sound. She didn't bother with the door or even the windows. Instead, she made for a spot some fifty feet from the house. There, she found the old stone still in place. She knelt, pressed her hand to the stone and poured magic into it.

"The wheel will keep turning," she whispered.

The stone slid to one side, revealing a staircase roughly cut into the earth. Talen glanced around and then descended into darkness.

The safehold appeared to still be in use. Jars of preserved food and canteens sat on wooden shelves, boxes of fruits and root vegetables lined the wall. The musty air had the smell of earth soaked from too much blood, sweat, and desperation. The only occupants of the small room were the ghosts of the countless souls who'd passed through over the years.

She should've done more, much more. It warmed her heart to see the Railroad still running, but she seethed that it had to be.

Pushing aside the regrets, and after pocketing an apple, Talen crossed the room and down the short, narrow passage. Her night vision did little in the utter darkness, but her memories served well enough. She found the old stairs and headed up. She unlocked the magic door with another passcode and stepped into the kitchen of

Wilfred's home. The secret door closed and locked behind her. The seams vanished, making it indistinguishable from the surrounding walls.

The scents of cornbread, beans, and wood smoke greeted her. Beneath that, she smelled Wilfred. Vaguely sharp and clean, like the air after a thunderstorm. And yet, like nothing she'd ever known before or since.

Enough light leaked in from the windows to let her night vision cut through the dark. She went to Wilfred's workshop but didn't find him there.

She collected his kit bag from a table and went to the bedroom. When she touched the door handle, memories rose from the darkness of her mind. She ignored them, set the kit bag at her feet, and pushed the door open.

She smiled at the sight of him sleeping soundly. He'd grown older and grayer—the curse of humanity—but just as beautiful as she remembered. Talen tended to favor the feminine, but there'd been something about Wilfred. His gentle vulnerability added to his strength, and he didn't hide it like most human men. His bare arms and shoulders were above the blanket. She glanced at the strong hands and nimble fingers she'd known so intimately. Her gaze drifted up his arm, following the lines of muscle and the scars that marked his dark skin.

She approached the bed and knelt beside it, studying his face. New lines—born from joy and despair—marked his visage but took nothing from it.

He still smiles in his sleep.

Like the countless times she'd watched him, she wondered what he dreamt of. Her hand reached out to touch his cheek. She stopped herself so close the warmth of his skin reached her fingertips. She closed her eyes, steeled her will, and pushed the memories away. Those days were behind them, and they both knew it'd been for the best.

She opened her eyes and pressed her hand to his mouth.

His eyes snapped open, and he let out a muffled cry. He tried to sit up, but she held him down.

"It's me," she whispered.

He blinked a few times before recognition made its way through the haze. He nodded.

She withdrew her hand.

"Sweet Jesus, Talen," he said, sitting up. "That really you?"

She nodded. "I need your help."

"Of course."

"Get dressed. I'll fill you in on the way." She stood and left the room, closing the door behind her.

She picked up the kit bag and started a silent count. At seventy-six, the door opened and he stepped out. They looked at each other for a bit.

Perhaps a few bits.

She handed him his kit bag. "Gaoth is waiting on the west side of town."

"It's good to see you." He took the bag and their fingers brushed.

"You too," she said, savoring the touch for a couple heartbeats.

She turned and drew up the shadows, wrapping them both in the magical veil. They moved as one, and without a word, out the front door. Talen led the way with Wilfred on her heels, offering guidance with a gentle touch to one shoulder or the other. When they reached the main street, Talen tensed and paused, listening.

Only silence.

She waited a full minute more. Still no sound.

Wilfred waited patiently behind her, his presence a nearly forgotten comfort. She smiled inside at how easily they fell back into their old ways.

They crossed the street and stepped into the alley where Talen had laid in wait. The shadows held no bodies, and Talen felt more than a little regret about it. But she cheered herself imaging the soldier finding a long, clean cut up the back of his coat and being unable to explain it.

They reached Gaoth who waited, less than patiently.

"Long time, Gaoth," Wilfred approached him. "Good to see you again, my friend."

The horse bobbed his head and neighed.

Wilfred stroked the horse's nose.

"As promised," Talen said and held out the apple she'd pilfered from the safe hold room.

Gaoth chomped the fruit, his reunion with Wilfred forgotten.

"I see where I stand." He climbed on to Gaoth and slid back.

"He's still got his favorites," Talen said. "Apples chief among them." She climbed up and settled into the saddle in front of Wilfred.

He slid his arms around her waist and held her close. The heat from his body and the clean, stormy smell of him washed over her.

Her thoughts turned to rough sheets, and soft grass.

Talen urged Gaoth forward and they sped off.

She let herself enjoy the contentment of being close to Wilfred again. It'd been years, ended by mutual consent and on good terms, but she'd missed this familiarity. She couldn't help but wonder if he did as well. There was no going back, she knew that, but it didn't mean they couldn't have a moment together.

"I ought to warn you," Talen said. "I'm helping a human woman. She might smell stained, but I swear to you she isn't."

"How's that possible?"

"I'm hoping you'll be able to tell me," she said. "Something near had me convinced she was stained, but too many things didn't add up. Once she took off this bauble of hers, whatever had tried to convince me went away, quick as that."

"Well, shit."

Under the circumstances, Talen reckoned that as a rather eloquent summation.

Talen slowed Gaoth to a walk when they neared camp. "It's me. Don't shoot," she said and slid from the saddle.

Wilfred did the same, and they walked into the camp.

Margaret stood with her repeater rifle ready but pointed to the ground.

"This is Margaret," Talen said to Wilfred and then turned to Margaret. "This is Wilfred."

"Pleasure to meet you, ma'am." He doffed his hat and bowed his head.

Margaret stared, blinking back her surprise. She recovered quickly and smiled. "Thank you."

"I take it she failed to say I was Black," Wilfred said to Margaret.

"What? No! Well, yes," Margaret said. "But it's of no concern. I'm simply grateful for your help."

"It's okay," he said. "White folk—even the kindly ones—don't tend to think of Black folk as crafters or casters, for that matter." He smiled. "It sure did catch my former master by surprise when he done got shot down by that makeshift spell iron I made. Course, a fellow slave had to use it on my behalf."

Margaret swallowed, bowed her head a bit, and began smoothing out her skirts. "You were a slave?"

Her tone made Talen think back to the cave when the topic had turned to the Railroad. Could be Margaret had just been an abolitionist, but Talen suspected there was something more there.

"And you escaped?"

Wilfred nodded. "A few of us did. I heard tell word spread and after that, slave holders got a might more cautious about their slaves' possessions."

"Do you smell any stain on her?" Talen asked, eager to get to the matter at hand.

Wilfred narrowed his eyes. "Matter of fact, I do a bit. Not strong as it should be. Like as not, I'd have missed it if you hadn't asked."

"That means it's fading." Margaret closed her eyes and clasped her hands together. "Thank the Lord."

"Show him the charm," Talen said.

Margaret opened her eyes. "Yes, of course." She went to a spot near the tree, moved some freshly turned earth, and pulled the charm from the ground. "Be careful."

"Much obliged if you'd take this?" Wilfred said to Talen, offering his bag.

She took it and held it out for him.

He removed his hat, pulled some goggles fitted with various eyepieces from the bag, and slid them on. Next, he pulled on a pair of thin leather gloves, took the charm by the cord, and began looking it over.

"Red jasper," he said. "A well-fashioned stone. Mind if I ask where you came across it?"

"City of Kansas," Margaret said. "My husband bought it from a local crafter."

Wilfred adjusted some of the lenses. "A warming charm?"

"Yes," Margaret said.

He shook his head. "I don't see nothing peculiar." He tweaked the lenses again and held the charm up into the moonlight. "It looks like a nor—what the hell?"

Talen and Margaret exchanged a glance.

Wilfred moved so the moonlight shone unobstructed on the charm. "I'll be damned."

"What do you see?" Talen asked.

"I had it wrong, and mightily so," Wilfred said. "Whoever done crafted this was a genius."

"What do you mean?" Talen asked.

"There's magic woven around the stone, as you'd expect," Wilfred said. "But there's a second layer. It looks woven right into the stone itself. I ain't never seen such a thing."

"Ain't that how you craft charms with multiple functions?" Talen asked.

"It is not," Wilfred said. "If you're making something like that, the spells are woven together at the edges. They're distinct, but connected, and they're a single layer." He shook his head. "This here is damned clever."

"Could you do it?" Talen asked.

He sighed and pursed his lips. "I wouldn't even know where to begin."

Talen gave him an even look.

He glanced at her, and one corner of his mouth turned up. "But I reckon I could figure it out in time."

"Can you tell what the second spell is?" Talen asked.

"I expect I can. Would you mind, ma'am?" he asked Margaret, offering the charm to her.

"Of course." She took the amulet by the cord and held it up.

Wilfred pulled off his gloves, returned them to the bag, and drew out a different pair. These had fine copper wire woven over them in a delicate spider web pattern. He tuned the lenses yet again and examined the charm from different angles.

"Could you lift it a bit higher, please?" he asked.

Margaret did so.

"Much obliged, ma'am." He held his hands out around the charm. "Now, let's see what you're hiding."

"Be careful," Talen said. "Whatever it is feels dark as anything I've come across."

He nodded, moving his fingers as if manipulating unseen threads, pulling them apart and reweaving them. "Whoever made this sure didn't want no one finding it." His chewed his lower lip. "I wonder…" He worked the unseen filaments some more and then smiled. "I'll be. Now that is something!"

"What?" Talen asked.

"It's the moonlight," he said. "It's only visible in moonlight."

"Am I right?" Talen asked. "Does it create an illusion of corruption?"

Wilfred shook his head. "No, you are incorrect."

"That doesn't make sense," Margaret said. "When I took it off—"

"It ain't no illusion," Wilfred said. He removed the goggles and gloves and returned them to his bag. "It *is* dark magic."

"What?" Talen narrowed her eyes. "You're saying it stains the wearer? But that ain't possible. You got to willingly embrace the dark magic. It can't get in if you don't invite it."

"I didn't say I knew how it worked," Wilfred said. "Just that it does. I know what I saw. The core of that thing"—he pointed to the charm dangling from Margaret's now lowered arm—"it is dark magic, and no mistake."

Margaret dropped the charm and stepped away.

Talen joined her, right hand drifting to her iron.

"If I had to guess," Wilfred said, "I'd wager the crafter is a stained."

"I didn't know crafters could be," Talen said.

"Sure, we work magic, same as you." He shrugged. "Except of course we use it to make charms rather than use them. But we're as ripe for corruption as any caster. Mind, you wouldn't hear much about it. Ain't no stalker needed to bring down a crafter. Without any charms, we'd be no more dangerous than a nasty tempered, unarmed, drunk."

"Apart from the ability to heal," Talen said.

Wilfred smiled and chuckled. "Sure, if we lived long enough to get that corrupted."

Talen drew the new bounty crystal from her inside pocket and held it out. "They said I had to use this to collect Margaret. That I had to place it under the skin."

Wilfred's face scrunched up. "Well, that don't make a lick of sense. A bounty crystal ain't but a positive resonance to dark magic, like a magnet. It draws the corruption in. But if you ain't stained, it won't do nothing to you." He put his goggles back on and studied the crystal.

"If you're right and the charm corrupts the wearer," Talen said, "why wouldn't a normal bounty crystal work?"

"And why did the corruption stop when I took off the charm?" Margaret asked.

"I never said it corrupted the wearer," Wilfred said. "I said the core was dark magic." He handed the crystal back to Talen and once more removed his goggles.

"I can't speak for her," Margaret said, "but I don't understand at all."

"You go right ahead and speak for me," Talen said and then looked to Wilfred. "Care to try explaining that again?"

"Mind, what I'm about to say ain't nothing but my best guess," Wilfred said. "I ain't had but a quick look at the thing. Without some serious studying of both items, I can't be certain of nothing. And I'm talking days, maybe weeks of study."

Talen narrowed her eyes. "Did you become a lawyer? Or just take up talking like one?"

He smiled. "Bounty crystals draw out corruption, but only corruption. That's why newly stained sometimes survive."

"If the stalker don't kill them," Talen said.

"What I seen makes me think the charm don't corrupt the wearer, rather it binds dark magic to them." He pointed to the new crystal. "Unlike regular bounty crystals, that one looks to work only with a certain kind of dark magic." He looked at Talen. "And anything it's bound to."

Talen's blood ran cold at the thought of how such a thing could be used.

"So," Margaret asked, her face pale, "the crystal would see anyone wearing the charm as stained?"

"Saturated with corruption, in fact," Wilfred said. "It'd take every bit of essence from you." He looked at Talen, his face grave. "There wouldn't be nothing left. I reckon the need to get it under the skin is a design limitation. Like as not, the crystal needs more direct contact to the wearer's essence."

"Their blood," Talen said, her own starting to boil.

"That's my guess, and like I said, only a guess."

"Merciful God," Margaret said. "Who'd make such a terrible thing? And why?"

Talen wasn't sure who, but she did know whoever it was needed killing. "It's a damned weapon," she said through clenched teeth. "Of course, they found a way to turn bounty crystals into weapons."

Wilfred winced. "A nasty and effective one at that," he said. "The wearer would look and smell like a stained. The crystal would prove it."

"And if whoever put them down took the charm," Talen said, fists clenched so hard her knuckles cracked. "Soon enough they'd reek of corruption too."

"And on, and on, and on," Wilfred said. "A chain of justified killings."

"Self-genocide," Talen said.

"A fine term for it," Wilfred said.

Margaret looked from Talen to Wilfred and back. "What do you mean self-genocide?"

"Stalkers only go after the worst stained," Talen said. "Plenty get put down by local lawmen—or even regular townsfolk—before they get that far. Imagine seeding a population with charms like that. Pick a group: a tribal nation, an unruly state—"

Margaret paled. "You wouldn't have to kill them. They'd kill each other out of a misguided sense of self-preservation."

"Yes ma'am." Wilfred turned to Talen. "Good news is, based on what you said, they don't seem to work on elves."

"Not yet," Talen said. "But I'm sure they'll figure it out. In the meantime, there are reservations full of humans it would work on."

"Or any group of undesirables," Margaret said. "You wouldn't need a trial or anything. Slip someone a charm then sit back and wait. It could even be used to wipe out stalkers."

Talen shrugged. "It could, but once you do, who's there to kill stained? Besides, you could just shoot us. Stalkers turn up shot all the time. Nah, I reckon this is for something bigger."

"What the hell have you stumbled upon?" Wilfred asked Talen.

"No idea," Talen said. "But I'm damn sure going to find out."

"Well—"

"I ain't pulling you into this," Talen said. "This ain't your fight."

Wilfred smiled and opened his mouth again.

"Don't you argue with me," she said. "I came in through the safehold room. I know you're still working the rails. What you're doing is important. If the wrong type gets wind of this, you'll have your hands full. You take care of them. Leave this to me."

"To us," Margaret said.

Talen turned to her. "No—"

"This isn't just about me anymore," Margaret said. "Even if I wanted to, I don't think I get to say no."

Wilfred smiled and let out a chuckle. "You're sure in the right company."

Talen ignored him and opened her mouth to argue against Margaret—insist she stay here where it was safe. But she stopped herself.

You can't win against them both.

"We can do this," Talen said, turning back to Wilfred and stepping close. She just barely stopped herself from reaching out to him. "You keep getting people to sanctuary. Keep the wheel turning."

He just looked at her for a long moment before sighing and nodding. "I know I don't need to say it, but I will anyway. You be careful."

"Of course." Talen glanced at the sky. "If we leave now, you can still get some sleep before dawn."

"Oh, I'm sure to sleep like a baby after learning this," Wilfred said. "You know, ain't no reason to camp here. Y'all are welcome to stay the night at my house or in the safehold room."

"You might be able to hide us, but the horses will be harder," Talen said, staring hard into Wilfred's eyes. "But thank you for the offer." *It's too dangerous,* she added silently. She didn't want the Red Right Hand tracking them to Wilfred.

He studied Talen for a moment. He nodded at Joseph. "Yeah, I reckon that big fella would stick out." He turned to Margaret. "Ma'am, it has been a pleasure making your acquaintance. Though I wish it were in better times."

"As do I." Margaret offered her hand. "Thank you very much for your help."

He shook it. "You're quite welcome." He nodded at Talen. "You take care of her, we'll call it even."

Margaret laughed. "I'm sure that's how it'll work out."

"You might be surprised," he said and climbed on behind the saddle.

"Try and get some sleep," Talen said to Margaret, pulling herself onto Gaoth's back. "We need to be riding before dawn."

"Where are we going?"

"City of Kansas," Talen said. "We're going to meet with the crafter who made that charm."

"I can make it from here on my own," Wilfred said after sliding off Gaoth when they reached the edge of town.

"What about the sentries?" Talen asked, still in the saddle.

"I live here. I'm one of the people they're meant to protect. Without an elf following me around, I got no reason to hide."

"Thank you."

"Of course." Wilfred smiled, looked to his feet and then up again. "I know there ain't no going back to what we had, but that don't mean you can't visit. It's been a long time, but it was still mighty fine to see you again."

"I'll try. I promise. Meantime, I got a favor to ask."

"Name it."

"There's still a bounty on Margaret. Plenty of stalkers won't care about lack of signs. If it goes bad and I send her back to you—"

"I'll get her someplace safe. I promise."

"Thank you. Again."

"You take care of yourself, hear?" He turned and started toward town.

Talen watched him for a second and then rode up next to him.

"Did you forget some—"

Talen leaned down, grabbed his shirt, and pulled him into a kiss. It wasn't like it had been, but the touch and taste of his lips pushed away some of the darkness and cold.

When the kiss ended, she smiled. "For luck."

"Mine or yours?"

"Bit of both," Talen said and then turned Gaoth and rode back to camp.

Talen returned to find Margaret still awake. No surprise there. Talen didn't say anything, just set to work removing Gaoth's saddle and brushing him down. After tending to him, she checked on Joseph, and then settled onto her bedroll.

"If it's none of my business," Margaret said, "you can tell me—"

"Ain't we done this dance before?"

"Yes, I suppose we did, but—"

"Ask your question," Talen said. She checked her spell irons and then settled back and closed her eyes.

"Why did the elves get involved with, well, any of this?"

"We didn't live separate from the larger world."

"I didn't think that," Margaret said and reconsidered. "Okay, I suppose I did."

"We heard tell of the forced relocations," Talen said. "Too late to help the Cherokee but soon enough for other tribes, so some of us decided to do something. Those of us who wandered kept to the shadows." She let out a sigh, as the old memories settled over her. "I stumbled across an Underground Railroad waypoint. Wilfred, the conductor, was leading a group north."

"In a slave state?" Margaret asked.

"Kentucky."

"You're well-traveled," Margaret said.

"I decided to help out how I could. I scouted ahead, led pursuers off, or provided protection when possible. If my people wouldn't act as a nation, I would as an individual."

"Why?" Margaret winced. "That didn't come out right."

"Why would an elf get involved in human affairs?"

Margaret held up her hands. "Please, forget I asked. Obviously, it being the right thing to do and you being a good person, you helped them."

"I almost didn't," Talen said. "Damn near packed up and moved on. I'd seen slavery before. It turned my stomach, but anything I could do felt pointless. Like going against a forest fire with water in my hands and spit in my mouth."

"What changed your mind?"

"The children." She could see every face even now. "The terror in their eyes. The scars on their flesh. No walking away from that. I knew I couldn't make a difference when it came to slavery." She let out a breath. "But to those children and their parents—if they had any —I could make all the difference in the world."

Margaret chuckled.

"Something funny?"

"For someone with every reason to hate humans, you don't seem able to stop yourself from helping us."

Talen didn't know what to say to that. Humanity might be capable of nightmarish deeds, and excelled at rationalizing away their atrocities, but maybe there was a difference between humans and humanity.

"Remember, child, we aren't pure and innocent either," her mother had said. *"Darkness and evil mark our own past. If we can claim to be virtuous, it's only in the recognition of our darkness and our desire to do better. There are kind humans, just as there are cruel eldar."*

"What's the plan for the City of Kansas?" Margaret asked, after a long silence.

"If Wilfred is right and a stained crafter is behind that charm, we need to find them." She opened her eyes, but the memories remained clear in her mind. "And put them down."

"You think the new crystals and the charm are part of some bigger plan?"

"Be one hell of a coincidence if they're not."

Neither of them said anything after that.

Before long, Margaret's breathing changed, and she slipped into sleep. Eventually, Talen joined her. For the first time in a long time, her dreams weren't of war. Neither were they of home. Rather, she dreamt of quiet, tender, loving moments between a good human and an eldar who recognized the darkness in herself.

Chapter Fourteen

Well before dawn, Talen's eyes snapped open. Someone was approaching. On instinct, she rolled to her feet and wrapped herself in shadow. As she lifted her irons and took aim at the still unseen stranger, she remembered Margaret.

She still slept, the repeater next to her bedroll.

Talen nudged her with a boot, never taking her eyes or irons from the nearing visitor.

"Wha—"

"Shh," Talen whispered. "Someone is coming. Grab your rifle and get behind a tree."

Margaret blinked a few times, but after a heartbeat, recognition set in, and she did as Talen asked.

"If you value your life, stranger," Talen said from the shadows, "you best turn back."

"I ain't no stranger," Wilfred said and stepped into view leading a horse, his hands raised.

"*Dani orin!*" Talen swore, lowering her irons. "What in the nine hells are you doing back here? I told you—"

"I know what you told me, but I aim to help."

Talen crossed the distance between them and spoke in a harsh whisper. "And I told you how you could. Who's going to get her to safety if things go bad?"

"I sent word along—"

"Would you put your damned hands down? What about the railroad? People are counting on you."

Wilfred smiled and lowered his hands. "Things ain't so busy since the war ended. Plenty figure our job is done, but I done sent word along the line anyhow. They know my station is closed for a time. I also arranged for passage if Margaret needs it."

Talen opened her mouth.

"*Sans shulla*," he said, stepping close.

The familiar words rung her heart like a bell. She closed her mouth and tried to glare but knew she failed.

"You gave up years to help me and my cause," he said. "I aim to repay you in kind. I seem to recall that sort of thing being important to your people."

"Anyone ever tell you that you pay too much attention?"

He smiled. "I also reckon you might have need of a crafter down the line."

"He's right," Margaret said, no longer behind her tree but still a respectful distance away.

"You don't know what you're agreeing to," Talen whispered and holstered her irons.

"Did you when you agreed to help her?" Wilfred whispered back.

"Red Hand," she mouthed, pleading silently.

His eyes answered for him.

Talen sighed. "All right then. Let's saddle up and head out."

Wilfred just smiled.

"Your accent is still terrible," she whispered to him, the hint of a smile on her own face.

What should've been a single—albeit hard—day's ride from Lawrence to The City of Kansas took double that, thanks to Joseph's pace and keeping well away from the main roads. They stopped for the night near the Missouri River with a few hours of riding to go. Despite being well south of Fort Leavenworth, Talen remained vigilant. The next morning, they agreed on a plan and rode out before the sun had cleared the horizon.

"Are you sure this is safe?" Margaret asked Talen, as they approached town. She turned to Wilfred. "Can you smell any corruption on me?"

"A bit," he said. "But I know it's there. I don't expect no one else will notice. Not once we get into the city proper."

Talen nodded. The wretched stench of the city already threatened to overwhelm her. She worried more about someone recognizing Margaret, especially Red Hand stalkers. For most humans, the stained and outlaws lived in dime store novels or were something lawmen and stalkers tended to.

"I'm nervous," Margaret said.

"You're smart," Talen replied. "But in this case, the best place to hide you is in the city. A woman outside of town on her own would raise suspicion."

"Yes, almost as much as a white woman traveling with a Black man."

"I don't think anyone is going to notice with an elf right here," Talen said. They weren't even on Main Street, and people were already staring and whispering.

"Is it always like this for you?" Margaret asked.

"I think maybe us riding together is drawing extra attention," Talen said. She put some distance between them.

Talen reached the Magistrate's office ahead of Margaret and Wilfred. She slid off Gaoth and looped his reins around the hitching post. Down the block, Margaret and Wilfred stopped at the general store. Talen didn't turn, just watched them with her peripheral vision. They tied off their horses and approached the store. Wilfred held the door and followed after, eyes on the ground.

The sight of him playing the dutiful servant knotted her guts. It might be an effective ruse, but she still hated it. She didn't like splitting up either, but they needed supplies, especially now. Margaret wouldn't get charged an "elf tax" or face the derision and hostility Wilfred would, if they'd sell to him at all.

Talen made her way up the long stairs to the government building. Her right hand never strayed far from her spell iron, and she kept a close eye—or the corner of one—on the storefront. If anything happened, from the smell or someone recognizing Margaret, it'd happen quick. Wilfred had a mundane revolver hidden at his back, and he could use it, but he'd only draw if he had to.

Talen reached the main doors and paused. She turned and surveyed the area, going through her pockets, as if looking for something. As she affixed the brass star to her coat, a woman and a girl came out of the store. Neither were running or screaming, and no gunshots or cries for help either.

So far so good.

She said a silent prayer, opened the doors, and went inside.

This magistrate's office was twice the size of the one in Santa Fe and had twice the number of soldiers. Everyone turned as she entered. A line of stalkers waited to cash in but no Red Right Hand. Then the whispering started. Near everyone eyed her with suspicion, curiosity, loathing, or a mix of all three. She pushed back the familiar urge to bathe and walked to the wall displaying the bounties.

"You lost, leafer?" one of the stalkers asked. "Let me help. Your reservation is that way. What's left of it anyhow." He laughed and a couple others joined him.

Talen ignored them and examined the posted bounties. Most of them she'd never seen before. She expected that. All but the largest and most dangerous bounties stayed local. What she hadn't expected was the lack of a poster for Margaret—not even an empty spot where it might've been.

That didn't make no sense. If they were posting her bounty as far away as Arizona, they'd damn sure have it listed here.

She checked again, slower this time, and careful to read each name. She hadn't missed it, but she did spot two bounties posted for stained:

one in New Mexico and the other in Arizona. She'd never seen either before.

Like Margaret, they were high-dollar, $5000 each, and bore the symbol marking them as needing the new crystals. Also like Margaret, their pictures were hand-drawn. The dates on the bounties were from before she'd left Arizona and no way would she have missed them. Hell, Margaret had stood out like a selkie in a pack of wolves.

She glanced over the list of charges, and her heart stuttered. They were each charged with destroying three towns, and Talen knew them all. Five had been "cleansed" by the Red Right Hand almost three years ago. The last had been the bounty Talen had bagged after she arrived in the Arizona Territory. It might be coincidence for the towns to be different but share a common name. Six of them, though? No chance in the nine hells.

"Is this all there is?" Talen asked the clerk without turning from the wall.

"Not enough for you, leafer?" one of the stalkers asked.

"Nothing worth my time," she said. "Not close by, anyway."

"That's all I got," the clerk spat. "I guess that means you'll be making your way to Arizona or New Mexico, eh?"

"Suppose so," she said.

"Good riddance," another stalker said. "Do be sure you let that door hit your ass on the way out."

This earned a round of laughter.

Talen turned and gave the line of smiling, laughing men a hard look. Some of the laughter stopped, and some just leered back. More than a few hands drifted to holstered irons.

"Time you were on your way," one of the soldiers said, his hand going to his own iron.

Talen waited a good five count before nodding and leaving the stinking room.

Her mind turned as she walked back to Gaoth. Why would someone pick towns already wiped out and pin them on innocents as fresh crimes? The more she considered it, the more strange-kind of sense it made. Posting the bounties well away meant few, if any, would see through the lie.

What she'd found in Hendricks, Prosperity, and Covenant made a lot more sense now. Unfortunately, if she were right, it wasn't some random crafter behind this. It'd take a lot of power, money, or both to arrange those sham warrants and get them posted so far away. The upside was odds were slim anyone would be looking for Margaret here, much less recognize her. Hell, if she picked the right place, she might have a life again.

Talen took her time unhitching Gaoth and waited for Margaret and Wilfred. After a short while, they emerged from the general store. She strode empty-handed, save for the new cane she leaned on. Wilfred followed two steps behind carrying a collection of parcels. A young man walked between carrying another package. Wilfred secured the lot to Joseph and his own horse before helping Margaret up. She took the cane, fit it into the saddle and then dismissed the young man with a wave of her hand. They rode down the street, Wilfred to the left and just behind Margaret.

Talen bit back her anger and saddled up. She headed back to the main street, following them at a reasonable distance. To her credit, Margaret never looked back. Wilfred knew the game and played it well. No one gave them so much as a second glance. Any attention they did draw Talen immediately stole as she came into view.

She ignored the stares, glares, and whispered derision, much of it anyway. She focused on figuring out where these new pieces she'd found fit in the bigger picture. Plenty made more sense now, but she still had no idea why anyone would do it. A personal vendetta might explain a single warrant but not three. Besides, Margaret didn't seem the sort to make well-connected enemies.

Ahead, Margaret and Wilfred turned down a side street. Talen kept riding, watching them from the corner of her eye. Margaret glanced back and motioned to the right with her head. Talen gave an almost imperceptible nod and continued for another block before turning. She made the next left and met the pair in an alley. They were alone, but Talen kept a watchful eye all the same.

"I told you, don't fret on it," Wilfred said. "We was just playing a part."

"I appreciate that, but it doesn't make me feel any better about it," Margaret said.

"Well, I surely do appreciate *that*," Wilfred said.

Me too.

"We found everything," Margaret said to Talen when she pulled up next to them. "No one recognized me, and if they could smell anything, no one reacted."

"That's good," Talen said.

"You find anything?" Wilfred asked.

Talen filled them in.

"You really think I have a life again?" Margaret asked, the hint of a smile emerging.

"Maybe," Talen said. "I don't know where else that warrant got posted. I do know the Red Right Hand is hunting for you, and they don't give up easy."

Her smile faded, and she nodded.

"I still plan on getting you clear of this," Talen said. "I just need more time. You're free to go whenever you like, I won't stop you. But I need to figure out for sure what's going on, who's behind it, and what the reason for it all is."

Margaret nodded again. "I'm staying."

Wilfred smiled. "When you're ready, I'll see to you personally. We'll get set some place, even get you a new name if needs be."

"Thank you," Margaret said.

"I see you picked up a cane," Talen said.

"Yes." Margaret pulled a handful of bills from a pocket in her skirts and offered them to Talen. "Here's the change. I hope you don't mind. It didn't cost much and—"

"You don't need to explain to me. You needed it, that's enough." She pointed at the wad of greenbacks. "You go on and hold on to that. If we need supplies again, you'll be buying anyhow."

Margaret tucked the money away and then nodded at the building behind them. "This is the crafter's shop, by the way."

Talen turned and looked over the two-story brick and wood block. It had a single window at the back and a wooden staircase wound down from a door on the second level.

"Do you have a plan?" Wilfred asked Talen.

Talen eyed the second floor. "Does the crafter live above the shop?"

"I don't know, but we did," Margaret said. "The landlord gave us a better rate to rent the shop and the apartment upstairs together."

Talen nodded. "Wait here. I'll be right back."

"Where are you going?" Wilfred asked.

"To ask him." Talen slid from the saddle.

"You're going to what?" Margaret asked. "No. Let me go with you!"

"Or me," Wilfred said.

"You suppose an elf and a Black man might prove less conspicuous?" Talen asked then turned to Margaret. "And we can't risk him recognizing you. Even without the warrant, he might remember who he sold the charm to." She started walking around the building to the entrance.

"George bought it, not me!"

"Best to save your breath for cooling your soup," Wilfred said.

Talen wound around to the front and looked it over. The shop had large windows with plenty of charms and talismans on display. She eyed the crafter's shingle hanging from the awning—Weaver's Wares—and couldn't help but think of Wilfred. Like as not, he worked twice as hard for half as much.

She pushed the rising anger down and stepped inside the shop. She perused the wares like a fancy lady shopping for a new charm to show off.

"Can I help you?" a man asked, his tone less than cordial.

"You Weaver?"

"I'm Edwin Weaver, yes. And as this is my shop, I can refuse to serve anyone I—"

"Just looking over your wares," Talen said, without looking up. The stuff looked pretty, but she judged the quality wasn't near as good as what Wilfred could produce.

"If you're not buying, I'll have to ask you to leave," Weaver said, his tone even less cordial.

Talen looked up. Weaver was more of a dandy than she'd expected. He wore a gray suit and sported a massive handlebar moustache so heavily waxed it could serve as a candle.

He eyed the star pinned to her coat, but his stony look of disapproval didn't budge.

"I'm new to the area," Talen said, putting on a friendly smile. "And in need of a place to stay—"

"We have a fine collection of boarding houses," he said, through clenched teeth. "Some of those on the other end of town might even agree to rent to you. Now good day—"

"Is that an apartment above your shop?" she asked, looking at the ceiling and then back at Weaver. "Is it for rent?"

The look of shock and revulsion almost made Talen smile.

"It most certainly is not!"

"You sure, Edwin?" Talen asked. "I'd prefer to ask the landlord directly. Nothing personal, mind. I'm willing to pay well for fair accommodations."

"I own this building, thank you very much!" he said, his cheeks flushed. "So, yes, I'm quite certain about the availability of my own apartment!" He looked to the door as a couple of human women came inside, and he struggled to put on a genial smile.

The two glanced at Talen and, seeming to recall an urgent appointment elsewhere, left abruptly.

Weaver took a step toward her, hate pouring from his eyes. "You cost me customers, leafer bitch. Get the hell out of my shop before I have you thrown—"

"That's not a very nice word." Talen moved her coat, showing her right-hand iron. "I've been nothing but polite to you, Edwin." She leaned in closer, her hand resting on the grip of her iron. "Up till now."

His bravado held, but his hand wandered to his waistcoat. He caught himself before his he reached the pocket.

So, you're heeled then? Good to know.

Talen almost pushed him again—she enjoyed watching him sweat —but stopped herself. She couldn't risk him calling for a lawman or soldiers.

"I apologize," he said, looking as if he'd swallowed something rotten. "But as you're not buying, and the apartment is unavailable, I bid you good day." He motioned to the door.

Talen nodded, turned, and walked out. In case he watched her, she went down a couple blocks before heading back to the alleyway.

"Well?" Margaret asked.

"He lives there," Talen said.

"All right then, what now?" Wilfred asked. "Don't reckon it's a good idea to just wait around for him to close up shop. We ain't what you'd call inconspicuous."

Talen glanced at the stairs. "I think we ought to get out of the sun and sit for a spell."

Chapter Fifteen

Hours later, the door to the apartment opened, and Weaver stepped inside. He hung his coat on the rack near the door, and lit a lamp, filling the dim room with light. He turned and froze, staring at Margaret. She sat in a plush chair, her withered leg resting on a footrest.

"What the hell are you doing in my home? I'm sending for the law!"

Talen released the shadows that hid her and Wilfred, took a silent step forward, and put the barrel of her right-hand iron to the back of his head. "Don't reckon you'll get far." Wilfred went to the door and checked the hallway. "He's alone."

"Take whatever you want." Weaver's right arm moved slowly along his waistcoat. "Just don't—"

Talen kicked the back of his knees, sending him to the ground. As he fell, she clubbed him with the barrel of her iron. He fell hard but stayed conscious. Before he could regain his senses, she rolled him onto his back with her foot. She planted a boot on his right hand—an old habit—and reached into the pocket of his waistcoat. She found a four-barrel Derringer.

"Fine piece of work," she said, examining the mundane shooter. "Silver plated. And is the engraving custom?"

"Surely looks it," Wilfred said.

Weaver gave Wilfred a look of unapologetic loathing and then glanced at Talen. "You're hurting my hand, elf. Do you mind?"

Talen aimed her iron at his face and poured magic into it. Blue spell fire filled the runes and sigils, casting dancing lights on the walls.

"As a matter of fact, I do, Edwin."

"What do you want?" His tone had the confident indignation of someone with money and power. Even neck-deep in the shit, he still saw them as beneath his contempt.

"Do you recognize me?" Margaret asked from the chair.

Weaver rolled his eyes. "I'm afraid I didn't get a good look, and the elf on my hand prevents me from turning now."

Faster than a blink, Talen bent down, seized the front of his shirt, hauled him to his feet, and slammed him against a wall. She held him there, a few inches clear of the floor.

He stared at her with wide eyes.

She smiled. "Humans, especially men, are always surprised by how strong we are." She set him down but didn't let go. "Now, do answer the lady's question."

Weaver spared barely a glance over at Margaret before smirking at Talen. "No, I don't recognize—"

Talen pressed the barrel of her iron—still burning with spell fire—against his cheek. "Maybe you ought to take a longer look."

He swallowed and turned his head, narrowing his eyes.

Margaret stood but struggled some and had to use her cane. She took a few steps forward and Weaver sneered, his eyes burning with revulsion.

"So, you do recognize her," Talen said.

"I—uh, what? No." He looked from Margaret to Talen and back.

"I do believe he's surprised to see you alive," Talen said to Margaret.

"What did you sell my husband?" Margaret asked.

"You're mistaken," he said. "I don't know—"

Talen, keeping her right-hand iron at his chin, drew the left, and held it high so Weaver could get a good look as she poured magic into it.

The color drained from his face and sweat beaded at his forehead.

Talen gave her best malevolent smile. She had no idea what stories he'd heard—humans told plenty. That sort of ignorance, often a source of aggravation, did have its uses.

"I reckon I'm playing this wrong," she said. "You don't seem to value your neck. What might you value more, I wonder?"

She shoved the barrel of her left-hand iron into his crotch, eliciting a whimper.

"Now, Edwin," Talen said. "We're going to ask you some questions. Every time you lie, or hold back even a little, I take something you value. Understand?" She pressed her iron into his balls to emphasize the point.

He grunted and bent a bit but nodded.

Talen eased off the pressure but didn't move her iron.

"Do you recognize me?" Margaret asked again.

"Oh yes," he said, no longer trying to hide the contempt.

"And you recognize this?" Margaret asked, holding up the charm.

"Of course."

"Where'd you get it?" Talen asked.

"Did you craft it?" Wilfred asked.

Weaver glared at Talen. "I don't answer to nigg—"

Talen jammed the barrel of her right-hand iron under his chin, knocking his head against the wall and closing his mouth.

"I will say this only once," Talen said. "I have a strong dislike for that word. Do not use it again. Now, you answer the man with respect."

"Yes, I made it," Weaver said, his jaw still held closed by the iron at his chin.

She glanced at Wilfred who shook his head.

"I done told you not to lie!" She poured more magic into her left-hand iron, causing it to burn brighter, and pressed it hard into his balls. "Tell me, you fancy the left or the right one more?"

"Please, I'm not lying! I swear!" he said, trying to turn his head away.

She, Margaret, and Wilfred all exchanged a look. They knew he wasn't lying, but that didn't make sense. He might be nine kinds of a bastard, but he wasn't a stained. To be certain, Talen holstered her left-hand iron, and pulled out one of the old-style bounty crystals.

"What are you doing with that?" he asked more in confusion than fear.

Talen held the crystal out. "Take it."

He did but nothing happened.

Talen took it back and pocketed it. She took a step back, the barrel of her right-hand iron leveled at his heart.

His brow furrowed, fear giving way to confusion.

Talen's brain churned. She couldn't let much time pass or she'd lose the upper hand.

She motioned to the chair with her iron. "Sit your ass down."

He did so, skeptically glancing at Margaret and Wilfred, the fear from moments ago fading.

"Why would you make such a terrible thing?" Margaret asked.

"What are you talking about?" he asked. "It's a damn warming charm. Your husband commissioned it."

"That ain't all it is, and you know it," Talen said. "It's got dark magic in it."

"What?" He laughed.

Talen drew the stolen Derringer with her left hand and pressed it against the back of Weaver's right hand.

"Wait, no, please—"

Talen pulled the trigger.

It clicked but nothing else happened.

Weaver gasped, his hands shaking so hard the chair trembled.

Talen glanced at the gun then passed it to Wilfred. He took it, staring at Talen with wide eyes and raised eyebrows.

"Misfire." She turned back to Weaver. "Not such a fine piece after all. That's why I stick with spell irons." She pressed the barrel of it to the back of his right hand. "They don't never misfire."

"No, please! What do you want from me?"

"Why were you surprised to see her alive?"

"Because I remember her," he said. "She went stained a few months back and left town. I figured she wouldn't last a week before some stalker had her in a crystal."

Talen slammed the barrel of her iron onto his hand, breaking some of the small bones.

He screamed and reached for his broken hand, but Talen caught it and held it to the arm rest. To be safe, she also stepped on the toes of his shoes so he couldn't kick at her.

"That little bobble is chock-full of dark magic, Edwin," Talen said. "And I'm a stalker, understand?"

"Charms can't have dark magic in them," he said through gritted teeth. "It doesn't work that way."

Talen glanced at Wilfred.

"He might believe that," Wilfred said. "But he ain't saying everything."

Talen held out her hand to Margaret. "Give it here."

Margaret draped the leather cord over Talen's hand.

Talen held it inches from Weaver's face. "Time for you to recognize something. You got precious little chance to walk out this with all your parts intact."

He glared at her, his boldness returned. "None of you know what the hell you're talking about! Not that I expect your sort to comprehend the complexities of charm creation."

Wilfred chuckled.

Weaver gave him a caustic look. "What do you know about it, boy?"

Talen smashed the barrel of her iron down on his hand again, breaking more bones.

He bellowed. "Leafer bitch!" He tried again to grab at his broken hand.

Talen smacked his hand away with her iron and pressed the barrel into his forehead so hard the chair tilted back. "I do not care for the tone you are taking with my friends. You got five seconds to save your life. One."

"You wouldn't—"

She poured more magic into the iron and stared hard into his eyes. "Four."

His eyes went wide. "What? What happened to—"

"Fi—"

"All right, Goddamn it," Weaver said. "A man came into my shop six months ago. He perused my wares and asked some basic questions. I figured he's just wasting my time."

"I know the feeling," Talen said. "Get to the point, and quick."

"He said he had a business proposition."

"What sort?" Wilfred asked.

"He showed me a collection of stones, including that one," Weaver said, nodding at the charm. "Said he worked for a supply company looking to get into the market, that they used new materials and could cut way back on costs. Offered me a hundred dollars to take the stone and use it in something. Then said he'd pay another hundred when I told him who I sold it to."

"He offered you two hundred dollars to take something that might cost you forty?" Wilfred asked. "That didn't seem queer to you?"

"Of course, it did," Weaver said, not looking at Wilfred. "That's why I asked what the catch was. He said these new materials hadn't been fully tested as yet. As such, there could be side effects."

"They were looking for test subjects," Wilfred said.

Talen looked from him to Margaret then back to Weaver. "And you just went along?"

"I'm a businessman," he said. "I won't apologize for making a profit."

Talen resisted the urge to knock his teeth out.

"George commissioned the charm," Margaret said. "That means you chose that stone specifically. Why?"

Weaver stared at Talen.

"You best answer the lady," Talen said.

He turned and gave Margaret a smile saturated with hate and

loathing. "Because I knew it was for you." Margaret stumbled back a step, as if Weaver's words had been a physical blow. Her mouth worked, but no words came.

"She's not just a cripple, you know," Weaver said to Talen then turned back to Margaret.

Margaret's face paled, and her eyes went wide.

"Oh yes, I know your secret. We all did, the whole town, and it made us sick. I figured anything happened to you it would be God's own righteous judgment."

Margaret's eyes hardened, she clenched her jaw tight, and took a couple steps toward him. "No—"

"Thought you were so clever," Weaver said. "You uppity nigg—"

Margaret punched him.

Not a hard or solid blow as they went, but she didn't have much practice.

Weaver laughed. "That all you got, whore?"

Talen punched him.

The chair spun and slid almost a foot as his head snapped to one side. Bloody teeth clattered to the floor.

"I warned you about that word," Talen said. "Apologize."

"Go to hell, leafer," Weaver said, and spit blood at her feet.

In one quick motion, Talen drew her knife and hammered it into his left hand, pinning it to the chair.

He screamed and tried for the blade with his broken hand.

Talen batted it aside with her iron, eliciting another pained cry. She leaned in and spoke softly. "When we're done, you'll either be in need of a doctor, or an undertaker. Which, is up to you."

She yanked the knife out, and he grunted. Blood dripped from his mouth and onto his very fine waistcoat.

Talen wiped the blade clean on his pants and sheathed it. "Now, the hole in the ground might look awful tempting about now, being an end to the pain and all." She leaned in closer and stared into his eyes so he could see the depth of the fury burning in them. "But believe me it'll be a loooong time in coming. You got no idea the terrible things a person can live through." She let a long moment pass.

"So please, do call either of my friends that word, or just tell me to go to hell again. Then we'll get started."

"I—I'm sorry," he said through tears, snot, and a mouthful of blood as he soaked his trousers.

"Better," Talen said. "Now, this man?"

"I don't recall his name. That's the truth."

Talen reached for the knife again.

"But he left a calling card!"

"Where?" Wilfred asked.

"There." Weaver nodded to an expensive wooden desk.

Wilfred went to it.

"Top left drawer," Weaver said, casting a quick glance at Talen.

Wilfred reached for it.

Talen lifted her hand. "Wait." She eyed Weaver.

He swallowed and turned his eyes away. "Top right drawer."

Talen aimed her still-burning spell iron at his crotch again. "Anything happens and I make you a gelding, understand? And unless you accounted for an elf in whatever trap you set, rest assured I'll manage it."

He nodded.

"Go on, but slow," Talen said.

"Wait. Use this," Margaret said and offered her cane to Wilfred.

He took a few steps away, used the cane to hook the handle, and pulled the drawer open.

Nothing happened.

Wilfred rummaged through the drawer. A moment later, he held up a small white card. "This it?"

Weaver nodded.

"If you're lying, I'll be back," Talen said, staring hard into his eyes. "If you run, I'll find you." She lowered her voice. "And your nightmares will seem like heavenly dreams compared to what I'll do when I find you."

"I believe you, witch."

He spit the last word, but it was all he could do. She'd broken him.

"We're done here," she said. "You two go on, leave out the back."

Margaret and Wilfred started for the door.

Talen put the spell iron's barrel between Weaver's eyes. At this range, the force charge would turn his skull and its contents to mist.

"Best make peace with your—"

"Wait, I told you! I gave you what you wanted!" he said.

"What are you doing?" Margaret asked.

"We can't just leave him," Talen said. "He knows you. And while he don't know me, there ain't many elven stalkers about. We'll have the law on us before sunrise, army too. We can't risk it." She didn't mention how much she would enjoy it.

"You can't just kill him!" Margaret said. "It's murder!"

"And?"

"I don't like it neither," Wilfred said to Margaret. "But she's right."

"I won't say anything," Weaver said, starting to bawl. "I swear. I'll—"

Talen clubbed him with her iron again. This time he went out cold.

Margaret put a hand on Talen's shoulder. "Please don't do this. He said he wouldn't tell."

"You can't possibly believe this sack of shit?" Talen asked.

"No. But I don't want the weight of his murder on my soul. Or yours."

"Thank you kindly, but mine is plenty heavy already."

"No, it isn't." Margaret tried to push the spell iron down, but Talen's arm didn't budge.

"I'm trying to spare you," Talen said. "Some people need killing, some deserve it. Sometimes"—she pointed to Weaver—"it's both." She looked to Wilfred. "Get her out of here. And get the horses ready. We'll need to get scarce and don't got much daylight left to do it."

"Come along now," Wilfred said, putting a hand on Margaret's shoulder.

She pulled away. "No, there has to be another way!"

"Why the hell do you care? He took everything from you!"

"No, he didn't. Not everything. And what little I have left I won't give away in anger. Not to the likes of him."

Talen stared at Margaret. Shame settled over her like a cold, wet blanket. She hadn't noticed when it had gone, but it was back in earnest now. Had she slid so far?

The spell iron went dark, and Talen holstered it. "So, what do you reckon we do? I wasn't exaggerating about who will come after us. We'll have the Red Right Hand, stalkers, and soldiers too. Hell, we might get our own damn regiment."

"Afraid even the Railroad won't be able to hide us from all that," Wilfred said.

"Too bad we can't make him forget we were here," Margaret said.

A memory clicked and Talen looked at Wilfred. "Something to forget?"

"You don't suppose?" he asked.

Talen gestured at Weaver. "Him? Oh, hell yes I do."

"What? Are you saying that's possible?" Margaret asked.

"Not as such," Talen said. "But—"

"When we worked the Railroad, we heard stories," Wilfred said. "Some passengers said they'd seen compulsion charms used on other slaves. Never saw it myself, but they swore to it."

"Dear God," Margaret said. "I didn't know such things existed."

"Slaver wares," Talen said. "Not technically dark magic, but near enough for my tastes." She studied Weaver. "I'd bet my left-hand iron Mr. Businessman here traffics in such goods."

"Do you know what to look for?" Margaret asked.

"Maybe," Talen said.

"I'll know if we find them," Wilfred said.

"We can't leave him here while we're hunting through his stock," Talen said.

"I don't expect he has rope lying around," Margaret said.

"No, but I think we can make do," Talen said, spotting the coat on the rack. She took more than a little pleasure in turning the—almost certainly—very expensive jacket into strips of cloth.

Weaver came to just as they finished securing him to the chair.

"What?" He tried to move but cried out when he drew up short. He glanced at his bandaged left hand and then at Talen.

Talen nodded at Margaret. "I was content to let you bleed out. Still am, in point of fact, so I suggest you behave."

"Did you cut up my coat? Do you know how much it cost? It's from—"

Talen shoved another piece of cloth into his open mouth and secured it with a final strip tied around his head.

"Much better." Talen and turned to Margaret and Wilfred. "Come on. Let's be quick."

"What's it look like?" Margaret asked, after they descended the stairs and reached the shop's backroom.

"It'll be a talisman," Wilfred said. "Not jewelry. Just a carved stone or the like."

Talen peeked into the store front. "Street looks clear, but we ought to be mindful no one spots us. We don't much look like customers."

"They won't be out for everyone to see," Wilfred said. "He'll have them tucked away someplace secret."

They searched through drawers and cabinets but after several minutes, turned up nothing.

"Maybe he doesn't have anything," Margaret said, leaning on a counter and rubbing her bad leg.

"I don't believe it," Talen said. "There's something here. We just ain't found it. Even if he don't have any geas stones, he'll have some special stock."

"Geas?" Margaret asked.

"Eldar word," Talen said.

"Then we keep looking." Wilfred and turned to Margaret. "You stay put and rest your leg."

"I'm fine. Besides, I want to help," Margaret said. She grimaced as she made to push herself up. As she did, something clicked in the counter, and a cabinet on the wall came away an inch or two.

"I most assuredly meant to do that," Margaret said.

"Of course." Talen went to the cabinet, opening it all the way. "Well done."

"Thank you. Why isn't it warded though?"

"Ain't no better way to tell folks you got something worth taking than to put a ward on it," Wilfred said, as Talen retrieved a box from the hidey-hole.

"That makes sense in a counterintuitive way," Margaret said.

Talen set the box on the counter, opened it, and looked inside. Her stomach turned.

"That son of a bitch," Wilfred said.

"Dear, God, what are those?" Margaret asked.

Talen stared at the half dozen iron manacles, each covered in sigils. Rows of metal thorns lined the inside of each shackle.

Talen looked to Wilfred who rubbed at the wicked scars around his wrists. At that moment, she wanted nothing more than to spend several weeks killing Weaver in ways that'd shame her mother.

"They're called pain shackles," Wilfred said.

"Slaver wares?" Margaret asked.

Talen nodded and picked up a leather bag sitting on top of the shackles. She poured the contents into her hand. The collection of onyx tear drops seemed familiar, but she couldn't explain why.

Wilfred took one and studied it. She examined another.

The fury in her heart died beneath a wave of soul-numbing cold.

Wilfred said something, but Talen didn't hear him. She could only stare in disbelief. Humans might've crafted the talisman, but the design was eldar, and hadn't been seen since the Eldar War.

It had ended thousands of years before Talen had been born, but the shame of it was so great that every elven child was taught about it. Ogres, trolls, kelpies, and countless other eldar were wiped out in the centuries-long war. It was that shame which finally drove the elves to step in and try to stop humanity from making the same genocidal mistakes.

Geas stones were used by some of the goblin tribes in the war, but the elves eradicated them and forbade the crafting of such terrible charms.

But then where did the humans learn how to craft them?

"Talen?" Wilfred put a hand on her shoulder.

She blinked and turned to him. "What?"

"I said these are them."

"What's wrong?" Margaret asked.

"I don't know," Talen said. "But I'm sure as hell going to find out." She poured all but a single stone back into the bag, returned it to the box, and carried it all back upstairs.

Margaret followed, her pace slowed by her leg. Seeing her struggle in strength and silence tempered Talen's anger, though not much.

"Do you need help?" Wilfred asked.

"Thank you, but I'll manage."

Together they went back into the apartment.

Weaver saw the crate under Talen's arm, and the color drained from his face.

She set the box down and tore the gag from his mouth.

"Now, don't do anything rash," he said, looking at each of them in turn. "I'm just a business—"

"You craft this?" Talen held up the geas stone.

He didn't answer.

"Where did you learn it?"

He hesitated.

"Margaret, kindly pass me a set of them shackles."

"I bought one on a trip to Georgia last year," Weaver said. "Took me a couple months of study and experimentation, but I managed to recreate it."

"Bought from who?" Talen asked. "A human?"

He looked at her as if she'd grown a second head. "What? Of course."

"Where'd he learn it?"

"How should I know? I'm not even certain where I bought it. Outside Savannah perhaps?"

Talen drew a deep breath and let it out slow. She hated the very notion, but this mystery would have to wait. There were more pressing matters to tend to. She stepped close, looming over Weaver and eyeing the stone.

"What are you going to do with that?" he asked.

Talen motioned to Margaret. "You ought to thank her again. I'm inclined to kill you in a most slow and terrible fashion. Lucky for you, she's a good and decent soul."

"Which you certainly are not," Margaret said. "Those shackles are horrifying."

"Not too late to change your mind," Talen said.

Margaret stared at Weaver for a moment then shook her head. "No."

"You're a better person than me," Wilfred said.

"Than either of us." Talen turned back to Weaver. "Damn, you are one lucky *juarchian*."

Talen ripped the bandage from his left hand. Weaver opened his mouth, but before he could start spouting shit, she shoved the stone into the open wound. Skin contact like as not would've sufficed, but she wanted him to feel it.

He grunted through clenched teeth as she poured magic into the talisman. The power spread out as the stone broke down, flowing through him and drifting up to his head.

After a moment, his face went slack, and he stared off into the middle distance.

"You're no longer in the business of slaver wares," Talen said. "We were never here, and your injuries resulted from an unfortunate crafting accident. Say it."

"I had an unfortunate accident," he said, in a dreamy voice.

"Does that mean it worked?" Margaret asked.

Talen looked to Wilfred.

He nodded. "Oh, it worked alright."

"How long will he be like that?" Margaret asked.

"Not long," Wilfred said. "We best be going, right now."

"Shouldn't we untie him?" Margaret asked. "Being tied up works against the story."

Talen nodded, cut the bonds away, and tossed the fabric strips into the pilfered box. Then, she went downstairs and fired a force shot into the counter of the backroom, turning it to splinters. When she returned, Margaret and Wilfred gave her a look.

"Needs to be some sign of an accident," she said. "Let's go."

Wilfred hefted the box then followed her and Margaret to the back door.

He went down the stairs first. Talen trailed, keeping in front of Margaret in case her weakening leg gave out. Margaret leaned on her shoulder on the way down.

"I'll carry those," Talen said and took the box from Wilfred. "Help Margaret into the saddle."

Reluctantly, he passed the box off and went to Margaret.

Gaoth wanted nothing to do with the shackles. Every time she tried to climb on, box under one arm, he turned away.

"I know," she whispered, after the fourth failed attempt. "We're going to destroy them, I promise, but we need to get away from here first."

Gaoth held steady while she mounted up.

"Thank you, old friend." She stroked his neck with her free hand.

They rode out of town, keeping to back streets. Talen held some distance from Wilfred and Margaret so as not to raise any suspicion. As it happened, few people were about.

They rode for better than an hour after sunset. They set up camp in a copse of trees, well away from anyone, or any road anyone might travel down. They did build a fire, two actually. Wilfred made a dinner of the freshly bought provisions—beans and bacon from the smell—over one fire. Away from camp, Talen sat at the other. She watched with satisfaction as the pain shackles, and all but one geas stone, died in the magically assisted flames.

After she settled the business at hand, she'd be making a trip south to find the source of the geas stones and shackles. Humans could've figured the crafting on their own, but she wouldn't bet on it.

Could some goblins have survived all these centuries?

She'd find no answers tonight, so she settled her mind, closing her eyes and whispering a quiet—and long overdue—prayer to her mother.

Chapter Sixteen

Talen ended her prayer and opened her eyes. The fire had died to glowing coals, the shackles turned to slag. She stood and stretched, doused the coals with dry earth, and returned to camp. Wilfred and Margaret had settled in for the night. She lay on her bedroll, and he sat with his back to a tree, puffing on his pipe.

Talen smiled at the familiar aroma, tobacco with a vaguely sweet hint of sage. She took a seat next to Wilfred and started in on her own dinner of leaves and grass.

"Is it done?" he asked without looking at her.

She nodded and eyed Margaret. "You told her we don't give a damn about her parentage."

"I did. A few times during the course of our supper, as I recall."

"I'm guessing it didn't help?"

"It isn't about the secret," Margaret said, turning but not looking at them. "Not really. I suppose I'm more ashamed of being ashamed of who I am." She sighed. "Even George didn't know. He wanted children, and I did as well, but..."

"You were afraid they wouldn't pass for white," Wilfred said.

"I'd be lying if I said that didn't play a part. What terrified me most was what it would mean for them and for George." Now she did look at them. "Does that make me a terrible person?"

"You were born free, weren't you?" he asked.

She nodded.

"I spent most of my life in chains. I'm telling you there ain't no shame in being afraid. Whatever stories you might've heard, they couldn't come close to the truth. Crops might grow on the plantation, but hope dies there. Even if you managed to cultivate some and keep it hidden, one day, they'd find it and take it away." He puffed his pipe. "I swore to die before they took me back, and I full planned to take some with me when I went, no mistake."

Talen kept quiet. But she did silently thank her mother that Wilfred had insisted on coming along. Without looking from the fire, she reached over and took his hand in hers.

"But the war ended," Margaret said. "They passed the Thirteenth Amendment and abolished slavery. I know I shouldn't be afraid anymore, but..."

Wilfred chuckled. "You don't know them southerners. They got all kinds of laws to make us slaves by another name."

"What do you mean?" Margaret asked.

"They'll toss you in jail for any reason they like," Wilfred said. "Call them Black codes. If you ain't got a job, or one they approve of. If you ain't got a place to live, or they don't like where your home is. Hell, any reason they can think of serves. They'll arrest you and lay a fine on you. You won't be able to pay, so they'll lease you out to former slaveholders to work off your debt. You never will, of course." He took another puff on his pipe. "Nah, Old King Cotton ain't done with us yet. It's why the Railroad still runs."

Talen squeezed his hand. He squeezed back.

"I didn't know about any of that," Margaret said. "But I should've. I was too afraid to look into much, and I let my light skin shelter me from it all."

"Ain't no shame in that neither," Wilfred said. "You can't help the color of your skin any more than I can. It's a cruel life, and if you can avoid it, I say good for you. I'd wish the same for my children."

"You have children?"

His jaw quivered, and he looked away. "I do, but none I made willingly. They forced us on the women, you see. Bred us like cattle. Most children got pulled from their mamas and sold off to other plantations when they were old enough." He took in a breath through his nose, wiped at his eyes, and looked back to Margaret. "So don't you dare feel shame for fearing that life. Anyone with a bit of sense would. Hell, I find it a might satisfying that some of us live right next to white folk, and they don't know."

Talen held his shaking hand. She knew all this, but she also knew how hard it was for him to talk about.

He just stared off into the middle distance.

"My mother never spoke of it," Margaret said. "I can see why."

"She escaped?" Wilfred asked.

"From a plantation in Alabama." She sat up and poked at the fire with a stick. "The slave master raped her whenever the notion took him. She never said those words, but that's what he did. His wife found out. Of course, she couldn't do anything to him, so, she beat my mama almost to death, scarred her face up, too." Margaret sighed. "When mama turned up pregnant with me, she knew what would happen."

"How'd she get out? If you don't mind me asking."

"A local preacher arranged to get her out." She beamed at them. "The Underground Railroad took her to Boston with me in her belly. That's where I was born."

Talen smiled a bit. Margaret's reaction in the cave made more sense now.

"We saw too many women like your mama. Still do on occasion."

"Mama worked as a housekeeper for a young couple, also supporters of the cause. They put us up in their servants' quarters and got her a new name. When I got old enough I helped out, but..." Her face turned sad. "Mama got the consumption when I was six, and she didn't last long. The damp air did her in. But she died smiling. Told me she'd breathed free and knew I had a chance at a good life. The Flemings, the couple we worked for, they took me as their own and raised me. Told everyone they adopted me. I passed for white, so I just went along."

"I'm sorry about your mother," Talen said. "She sounds like a brave and remarkable woman."

"Thank you. I've never met anyone braver, or kinder. The Flemings told me about her and made sure I knew the truth of it all. I always appreciated that, but I lived my whole life afraid. Law said I belonged to that bastard and his harpy. I woke every day sure it'd be the one they'd come for me." She let out a breath and rubbed her bad leg. "Not long after I turned nine, I got sick. I thought God meant to punish me for the monstrous sin of my existence." She smiled. "Then I met George and dared to believe otherwise. I never thought anyone would ever love me, but he did."

Wilfred smiled. "Love does tend to surprise us."

Talen thought of her own mother and the great sacrifice she, and so many others, made. They died in fire, but never said where Talen was hiding. Her heart broke again, and she saw the faces of lost friends, family, and loves. When she looked at Margaret, into her eyes, she saw a bit of herself.

"I always meant to tell him the truth," Margaret said, still staring into the fire. "When the war ended, I didn't think I had anything to lose. I knew in my heart he wouldn't care, but I just kept saying 'tomorrow,' and every day it got harder." She winced and drew in a breath. "And now he's gone."

"It's a hard thing," Wilfred said. "White folk learn early how to see Negroes, and even the good ones got a hard time seeing past that learning. But you're still here, and if he was the man you say, that'd make him happy."

"That doesn't make it any easier though." She shrugged. "At first, that's the only reason I kept going, because I figured that's what he and my mother would want. She suffered through so much so I could live free." She looked up at Wilfred. "But I'm so tired of being afraid, and tired of being ashamed of being afraid. I try not to be, but I can't help it." She narrowed her eyes. "Now, I look at my life and feel like nothing I did—or could ever do, if I'm honest about it—will be enough to honor her sacrifices."

"I saw what happened to your mother done to dozens of others," Wilfred said, barely contained anger behind his words. "Lord knows I ain't never gonna be able to imagine what it's like. Some women it broke clean through, and I reckon they died inside. Others lived but turned to stone. Your mother found a way through, and I'm guessing that's 'cause of you. It's a hell of a thing to find something good in a world of nightmares." He shrugged and let out a breath. "Mind, I'm just a fool old man, but it seems like the light your mother had inside her, she passed on to you. Ain't no shame in wanting to protect that, protect what your mama risked so much to save."

Margaret looked up and smiled at him.

"I ain't known you but for a short spell," he said. "But even I can see you done made your mother's sacrifice mean something already. I'd be mighty proud if you were my daughter, and I suspect your mama is as well."

Margaret wiped at her eyes. "Thank you."

"I know that shame," Talen said, the faces of the dead still churning in her mind. "I know it well. When the dwarves and soldiers came, my sisters and I stood ready to die if it came to it. My mother knew there'd be no surviving that fight. She told to us all to hide and keep hidden no matter what happened. Some did, plenty didn't. My mother made me promise; swear on her name even."

Wilfred turned to her, but she couldn't bear to look at him.

"Ain't been a day in the last three years I don't regret making that promise," Talen said. "But I did as I promised. I hid, wrapped in shadows and shame while some of my sisters fought. Everyone died. I watched as my mother, my sisters, and those I'd loved were butchered and worse." She nodded. "Yeah, I know that guilt, that shame, and that fear. Yours is a different burden to be sure, and you've walked with it longer than me, but we walk the same path." Talen looked at Margaret with wet eyes. "And, well, that makes us sisters of a sort."

For the first time in years, Talen felt almost whole. She felt lighter too, as if the weight of all her guilt and shame had been set aside, if even for a moment. Those feelings were still there of course, but they weren't all she was, or had, anymore.

Margaret blinked some tears away, wiped her checks, and swallowed. "I don't know what to say to that."

"I've walked in complete darkness for so long, I fear the darkness has soaked into me," Talen said. "I see in myself the very things I despise in others. You"—she nodded again at Margaret—"you reminded me there's light, of what matters most. Thank you for that."

"I always wanted a sister," Margaret said, wiping at her eyes but smiling.

"I'm proud to have another," Talen said.

"Oh, for the love of mercy," Wilfred said and pushed Talen to her feet. "Go hug her already, would you?"

Talen went to Margaret, helped her to her feet, and hugged her new sister. Something broke loose inside, something that she'd almost forgotten was there, and she wept without shame.

"Thank you for saving my life," Margaret said.

"I suspect you're saving mine right back."

When the moment passed, they both sat back down.

"I'm sorry about your mother and your people," Wilfred said. "I heard stories, but you don't know what's true and what ain't." He shook his head. "I got no words."

"A true friend can say more in silence than with words."

"I suspect getting to the bottom of this would make both our mothers proud," Margaret said to Talen. "So, what do we do now? I confess, I've no idea."

"Pass me that card we got from Weaver, if you would?" Talen said to Wilfred.

He did so.

"Franklin & Tuller Company. Crafter supplies and sundries." When she read the city name, Chicago, a block of cold stone settled in her stomach.

"You can read that by the firelight?" Margaret asked.

"She could read it by starlight," Wilfred said and chuckled. "She sees better in darkness than plenty of folk do in full daylight." He turned to Talen. "Does it say where they're at?"

"Chicago."

Wilfred furrowed his brow and opened his mouth.

"Wait, did you say Franklin & Tuller?" Margaret asked.

"You know it?" Wilfred asked.

"The company no, but"—she looked at them—"you don't know who Franklin Tuller is?"

"Should I?" Wilfred asked.

"He's one of the richest men in the country. A railroad magnate. He landed a big part of the intercontinental railroad contract." Margaret grimaced. "But why would someone rich as him bother with some little crafting supply company?"

"Could be just happenstance?" Wilfred asked. "Or using the name to seem more important?"

"I suppose," Margaret said. "But I don't think Mr. Tuller would tolerate his name being used, even indirectly."

"Could be he don't know," Wilfred said.

Talen heard everything they'd said, but the lead weight in her chest made it hard to speak. She stared at her feet and after an effort of will, managed to say, "We'll find out when we get there."

"What is it?" Wilfred asked.

"What?" Talen glanced up. Both Margaret and Wilfred were staring at her. She looked away again. "It ain't nothing."

"Like hell," he said. "It's been a while, but I still know you."

Talen looked from Wilfred to Margaret and sighed. "It's the Eldar Treaty."

"What's that?" Margaret asked.

"When the killing ended," Talen said, "the remaining elven nations signed a treaty with the US Government." She swallowed back some rising bile. "Unconditional surrender is more like it. It set up the reservation in the Washington Territory. The last elven nations were already there, and it's also the furthest corner of the US."

"I'm sorry. I still don't understand."

"When I took the star," Talen said, "became a stalker I mean, I had to agree to the terms of the treaty."

"I think I remember reading about it in a paper," Wilfred said. "Forbids any elf from crossing the Mississippi or some such."

Talen nodded.

"What happens if you do?" Margaret asked.

"Treaty stipulates any violation without writ is punishable by death," Talen said flatly. "On sight and without trial."

"What? How can they do that?" Margaret asked.

Talen clenched her jaw tight. "They won. They get to do whatever they want." She sucked in a breath and straightened. "Don't matter though. We're still going."

"Like hell you are," Wilfred said.

"He's right," Margaret said. "It's too dangerous. We'll find another way."

"That's where the answers are. I don't see as we got any other choice."

"Then you two can camp at the river's edge," Wilfred said. "I'll go and see what I can learn."

Talen gave him a level look. "You really believe you'd be able to stop me?"

Wilfred smiled. "I can be quite charming when I want to be."

"Not that charming," Talen said flatly.

"What about the shadows?" Wilfred asked. "I've seen you stay hidden for a long while."

"I can for a few hours, longer if I push myself. But a city that size will have Red Hand about, maybe a lot. I ran into some back where I found Margaret, and one had an eyepiece that could see through the shadows." She shook her head. "Besides that, a keen eye could spot the footprints or some other sign. When there ain't but a few humans I can be wary and cautious, but there'll be people everywhere."

Wilfred shrugged. "So we're back to where we started."

"I'll go on my own," Margaret said. "You've done enough. It's my turn."

"No, ma'am. I'll go with you," Wilfred said. "There's plenty of Black folk in Chicago. I'll be okay."

"You might be a fair hand with a mundane shooter," Talen said, "but you ain't ready for a fight against a spell slinger. Red Hand or otherwise."

"You've risked so much for me already," Margaret said. "I've been relying on others my whole life. It's time for me to do something for myself. I won't let you—"

"Let me?"

"Oh, bad choice of words," Wilfred said to Margaret.

"There ain't no letting or not letting me," Talen said. "Neither one of you can stop me."

Each made their arguments, which only frustrated Talen. Finally, she sighed and gave up on the notion of keeping the secret any longer. These were her friends. They were worthy of her trust. "I got something I ain't told you about."

"What?" Wilfred and Margaret asked in unison.

"Glamour charms," Talen said and pulled a pouch from her belt. She emptied the half-dozen stones into her hand. "They'll make me look human for a couple hours each."

"I never even heard of such a thing," Wilfred said.

"You wouldn't have. We don't—didn't—tell anyone about them." She eyed them both. "Understand?"

Both nodded.

"We all got six when we went to war," Talen said, "in case we needed to hide among the humans for a time." She stared at the stones and thought back to that day.

"You never used any?" Margaret asked.

"No," Talen said, still eyeing the charms.

"Why not?" Margaret asked.

Fire filled her belly, and she looked at Margaret. "Because I shouldn't have to hide! I lost near on everything. I wasn't about to give up who I am as well! Using them might've saved me some coin or some trouble over the years, but the cost was too high."

Margaret stiffened. "I understand. I'm sorry." She turned away. "I can't imagine what you must think of me."

"What? No. One ain't got nothing to do with the other. I don't judge you for what you did to stay alive or out of chains."

Margaret fretted her lower lip. "I suppose you're right."

Talen knew she wasn't convinced. She stepped over and put a hand on Margaret's shoulder. "You didn't hide who you were, just the color of your mother's skin. You were always you." She sighed. "Hell, I know I ain't explaining it well—"

"No, I understand," Margaret said. "I think."

Talen let it go. "Problem is, these are all I got. There ain't getting more, least without going to the reservation."

Wilfred leaned forward. "Maybe if you let me study them—"

Talen gave him a look that could've turned rain to snow in August. "No."

He lifted his hands and bowed his head. "All right then. Between them glamour charms and your shadows, you ought to be able to get around all right for a time."

"We still don't have a plan for getting into the city," Margaret said. "It's what? A month's ride from here?"

"If we stick to stage roads and push that big horse of yours harder than we should," Talen said, "I'd wager closer to two. But it is what it is."

"How long after we cross the river 'til we get to the city?" Margaret asked.

Talen scratched at her neck. "Not sure. A week? I'm thinking it's well over a hundred miles at the closest point."

"And that ain't accounting for actually crossing the thing," Wilfred said. "Not like you can ford it on horseback."

"You could use your magic to take a ferry or a bridge," Margaret said. "But that means sticking to roads. If we run into a lot of people, you could use all the stones before we even get to the city. If we're unlucky enough, you'll exhaust yourself hiding in shadows. too. Too bad we can't take a train."

"We'll figure it out," Talen said. "We got the time." She retrieved her map from Gaoth's saddlebags, unrolled it, and followed the line of the river. "I think the best bet is to head due north, get above the city and come down—"

"I might know of another way," Wilfred said. "In getting there, I mean."

Talen and Margaret both turned to him.

He didn't look at them.

Talen narrowed her eyes. "What is it?"

"I know someone with a ship. "Good man, supports the cause. He helps move passengers when there's need."

"A riverboat pilot?" Margaret asked.

"Not a riverboat," Wilfred said. "It's an airship."

"A real airship?" Margaret asked, her eyes wide, and smiling like a child. "I saw them flying in and out of Boston, but I didn't think any came this far west."

Talen knew of airships, though she'd never seen one. As she understood it, they'd cover in an hour what would take a horse a day or more. She glanced at Wilfred, but he wouldn't look at her.

"What aren't you saying?"

"Some do when the occasion warrants," Wilfred said to Margaret, ignoring Talen. "This one does more than most. He's kind of a specialized sort, not always exactly legal you understand, but—"

"What...else?"

Wilfred let out a breath. "I don't reckon you're going to like it."

"I figured as much. Spill it."

"The pilot...well, he's a dwarf."

Talen let loose a line of curses—in Elven—that would've earned her a slap from her mother.

"Did you understand any of that?" Margaret asked Wilfred.

"Not much. But I suspect she ain't happy about my suggestion."

Talen glared, fighting back the rising tide of anger and bile.

Chapter Seventeen

I don't care," Talen said. "Ain't no way in any of the nine hells I'm stepping foot on a dwarven vessel. I'd sooner dig and fill my own grave."

"It's the only real option," Wilfred said, yet again.

His patience, which Talen had always thought near eternal, had started to wear at the edges. He'd been countering every argument for the last hour with that same line. It being true only served to frustrate Talen all the more.

"Then you two go," she said. "I'll take Gaoth and meet you in Chicago. We'll make good time on our own. We could be there in a couple weeks, maybe less." She'd used this argument before too, but she wasn't giving in.

"Fine," Wilfred said. "If that's what you want."

Talen opened her mouth to argue but stopped herself. She narrowed her eyes and nodded skeptically at him. "Good."

"Really?" Margaret asked in a low tone, clearly suspicious as well.

"Sure," Wilfred said. "We'll have plenty of time to sort this business out and meet her on our way back south."

"Like hell!" Talen said. "You got no idea what kind of trouble might be waiting for you. What if the Red Right Hand shows up?"

"We'll manage," Wilfred said, his tone genial, and his patience exhausted. "You go on and do what you feel is right. We'll do the same, which means taking the airship." He turned to Margaret.

She nodded, unsure.

Talen swore under her breath. "I can't believe you expect me to trust a dwarf."

"I don't," Wilfred said, turning and meeting her eyes. "I expect you to trust me."

Talen tried to speak but she couldn't think of any words. What could she say that would counter that simple statement?

"You go on and decide what you're doing," Wilfred said. "I'm going to reach out to see when and where my friend can collect us." He stood, went to his horse, and began untying something from the pack.

Talen's stomach knotted at the idea of floating through the air at the mercy of a dwarf. "Do you trust him?"

"I do," Wilfred said. "And he earned it several times over. I ain't met no other dwarves, but this one has put himself in danger when there weren't no reason to do so."

Talen sighed. "You got any notion what you're asking of me?"

"Likely not," Wilfred said. He removed a leather-covered box from his horse's pack, returned to sit next to her, and set the box on his lap. "I imagine it'd be like you asking me to trust some southern aristocrat. And I would, if you were wondering."

Talen half smiled. "Only 'cause you know how I feel about most humans."

Wilfred smiled back. "I do not deny that would play a part."

"Isn't it possible he isn't like other dwarves?" Margaret asked.

Talen glanced her way.

Margaret's face scrunched up. "You don't care much for humans either, but there are a couple of us sitting here you seem to trust."

Talen put her face in her hands and let out a long breath. The anger in her had lost its heat, but the unease knotting her insides hadn't let up at all. Even so, she knew they were right. She didn't have to like it though.

"How do you reach him?" Talen asked Wilfred.

"With this." He opened the box. He removed a brass handle, inserted it into a hole on one side, and began turning. "Takes a bit to power up."

"What is it?" Margaret asked.

There were four rows of four buttons, each faintly lit from below. As Wilfred turned the crank, the lights grew brighter.

Talen stared in silent bewilderment. In the last few weeks, she'd seen a number of things that shouldn't be possible—magically speaking—but this contraption didn't make any sense at all.

"Wireless telegraphy," Wilfred said, smiling.

Margaret's eyes went wide. "Wireless?"

Wilfred nodded, still cranking away. "Invention of my friend."

"How the hell are you working it?" Talen asked, peering at the queer contraption. "You're a crafter."

"Ain't magic," Wilfred said. "It's science. 'Magic of the masses' they call it. Now don't ask me how it works. It uses electricity and crystals or some such. I only know how to work it. It uses a code to send messages to other machines."

"Where's the code?" Talen asked.

Wilfred tapped his head. "We had to memorize it. That's part of how they decided who got one. The buttons work in pairs to make letters or some words. But first you have to set what machine you want to talk to." He hit a series of buttons, and as he did, the light beneath each lit briefly. "Now we wait."

A few seconds later all the lights blinked twice.

"What's that mean?" Talen asked.

"Means it's ready."

Talen stared in wonder as, using two fingers, he began tapping some kind of message.

"I don't like it," she said. "Don't seem natural."

Wilfred chuckled and smiled, still tapping away. "Ain't no stranger than a mundane shooter. We crafters ain't got the options y'all do. We can't use charms, so devices like this are all we got."

"I suppose that makes sense." Talen still didn't like the thing. Apart from being dwarven-made, it felt too artificial. The polished hardwood had no markings or sigils. A thin copper wire wrapped around it so many times the sides were completely covered.

"Now we wait for an answer."

"What did you tell him?" Talen asked.

"Where we are, and that we need an express special."

"How long before he answers?" Margaret moved closer and peered at the contraption in wide eyed wonder.

"Hope it ain't long." Wilfred started cranking again. "Need to keep the charge up."

Long minutes passed, and Talen felt like a damn fool for staring at the thing. Then the lights flashed twice.

"Answer incoming," Wilfred said.

The buttons blinked in pairs, over and over, a short pause between each.

Wilfred watched, his lips moving as he decoded the message. Talen couldn't see any discernable pattern, which likely made it a good code.

A single light came on, held for a long moment, then the box went dark.

"End of message," Wilfred said.

"That's amazing." Margaret looked from the box to Wilfred. "And you understood those flashing lights?"

"I did. Draven—that's his name—says he's unloading in St. Louis, but he'll make his way to us when he's done."

"Where do we meet him?" Margaret asked.

"There's a bend in the river a few hours north of here. He'll meet us there around noontime."

"All the way from St. Louis by noon?" Margaret asked.

"That ship of his can cover more than twenty miles in an hour," Wilfred said.

Talen's chest tightened, and her knotted insides started quivering, but nothing could be done about either. "I'm turning in for the night." She went to her bedroll and laid back, spell irons close by.

"Probably a good idea," Wilfred said.

"Goodnight," Margaret said.

They both also settled in without saying another word.

Talen stared at the stars. Before long, the sounds of steady breathing told her Margaret and Wilfred were asleep. The heavy dread hanging over her would keep sleep away tonight. Instead of trying, she closed her eyes and spoke a silent prayer.

Mother, I'm so lost. For a moment I found joy in a sister who walks a true path. I know what's right, but I don't know how to proceed. I'm afraid: afraid of failure, of success, even of being afraid. How can I trust a dwarf? And what do I do when this is at an end?

I thought I knew myself, my place is this new and wasted world, but now I'm not sure. It isn't death I fear but the living. I pray you hear me. I need you—your wisdom and insight.

I know I've been a terrible daughter these years of wandering. I'm sorry I don't pray more. You must know the shame I carry for my countless failures, and how comforting the embrace of darkness has become.

With all the hope she could muster, she sent her plea out into the magic of the world.

My child, her mother's voice said in her mind. *You cling to the darkness inside you because it's been your only companion for so long. Being lost is not a failure. There is no shame in it, nor in fearing the light after so long in the dark.*

But the darkness is not you. You see only the anger, pain, and death in your wake. You forget too easily the mercies. Even now, a mother weeps with joy because her son came home to her. A young girl studies a gifted spell iron and dreams of being the fearless elf that saved her and her mother. Perhaps most surprising, a beardless dwarf tends bar in a town once ruled by a monster and cuffs any man who speaks ill of the eldar.

You are not a failure, my beautiful daughter. You walk in darkness, surrounded by pain and grief, but still you hold to the light. You carry too much burden that isn't yours. Until you lay that load aside, the light cannot shine on the path before you.

She wanted so much to believe her mother's words, but her heart wouldn't allow it. The memories, filled with ignored pleas for mercy and screams of the dying, wouldn't allow it. Her body shook from the warring. Talen ached for her mother. For the magical way a mother's embrace and kind words could banish every worry and fear from a child's heart.

Her mother didn't speak again but she did sing, the same song she'd sing when as a child, Talen couldn't sleep. The song lifted some of the stones hanging from Talen's heart—not all, but some—and she slid into sleep.

~

Her eyes opened at the sound of the shop door. A tall, broad-chested man with a massive brown mustache stepped in. He smiled and tipped his bowler hat to Talen.

"Good day, sir," he said.

She nodded. "And to you. Can I help you find something?"

"Thank you, no," the man said. "If I may, I'd like to peruse your wares for a moment."

"Of course," Talen said in a voice not her own. "I'm Edwin Weaver, at your service. This is my shop, and I crafted everything you see. I have a wide selection of charms and talismans. I also do commission work if you're looking for something more personal."

"Thank you, Mr. Weaver." The man offered his hand. "I'm Chester Pratt."

Talen shook. "A pleasure, Mr. Pratt."

Pratt looked over the amulets. "Do you do the metal working and jewel crafting yourself?"

"I do," Talen said, an alien sense of pride swelling inside her. "I apprenticed with some of the most gifted smiths and jewelers before opening this shop."

"It does show."

Talen studied the man. He wore a well-tailored suit and carried himself as someone of means. There could be a nice profit here if she played it right.

"I can tell you're not only a skilled crafter but also a shrewd businessman." Pratt turned and approached Talen, producing a calling card from inside his jacket. "Perhaps I can interest you in a bit of business?"

Talen managed to hide her disappointment and took the card. She looked it over and couldn't hold back a sigh before handing it back.

"Thank you, Mr. Pratt, but I'm quite content with my supplier."

"Of course you are, Mr. Weaver. I can see they provide you quality goods. However, if you'd indulge me, I promise to make it worth your while."

She sighed again and nodded. "Very well." She had no other customers to tend to and nothing pressing. Besides, she could always dismiss the man if a real customer came along.

He produced a small case, set it on the counter in front of Talen, and opened it. A collection of stones, all polished and in fine condition, sat on black velvet.

"We're a new company attempting to break into the market. Our goal is to provide quality goods at an exceptional discount."

Talen nodded politely, already bored.

"What would you say," Pratt said, smiling as all salesmen do, "if I told you, that you could have any one of these stones less than free of charge?"

"I'd ask what less than free means."

"It means I'll pay you one hundred dollars."

Talen narrowed her eyes. "You'll pay me one hundred dollars to take one of your stones?"

Pratt nodded. "Indeed, Mr. Weaver. You must only promise to use it in some form of craftwork."

"What's the catch?"

Mr. Pratt smiled more. "Just as I said, shrewd."

Talen rolled her eyes. "You'll forgive my frankness, sir. But in matters of business, I prefer plain talk. Kindly cease your attempts to blow sunshine up my ass."

Mr. Pratt laughed and held up his hands. "Fair enough, Mr. Weaver. Here's how it is. Our methods of preparing crafting goods are new. Revolutionary, I dare say. It permits us to sell our wares at a fraction of the cost our competitors charge."

"But…?"

"But we need a broader sampling to test our methods. Of course, we've tested extensively in our laboratories, but we believe in an abundance of caution."

"You expect me to use untested wares and put my reputation on the line for a mere hundred dollars?"

Pratt leaned in. "You say you prefer plain talk, Mr. Weaver?"

Talen nodded.

"Very well," Pratt said. "I've done my research. I know this town has precious few crafters, and you are the best regarded. You're a smart man. Surely you can fashion our stone into a trinket for, shall we say, someone less inclined to be a repeat customer? Someone undesirable perhaps? Collect your hundred dollars and your profit off the charm. We both know they'll never know the difference."

Talen pursed her lips, considering. She did have occasional customers of a lower quality than she preferred, but their coin spent as well as any. She could craft some trinket for a whore or Negro looking for a bit of pretty. They'd pay top dollar thinking they had a bit of finery, and every penny would be profit. "All right then. It's a deal."

"Excellent," Pratt said and offered his hand.

Talen shook it and looked over the stones.

"If you're interested in adding to your profit margin," Pratt said. "I'll pay another hundred if you let us know who you sold it to."

Talen saw the red jasper and smiled. She remembered the man and his half-breed cripple of a wife whispering about warming charms. Talen had been in this business long enough to know when someone would be back, and the husband would be. The fool didn't even seem to be aware of what he bedded down with every night. The thought turned her stomach. Well, she'd give that mongrel what it had coming.

Chapter Eighteen

Talen's eyes snapped open, and she sat up with a gasp, both irons up and lit with spell fire. A moment later, she came to her senses. She doused and lowered her irons and then glanced around. Thankfully, Wilfred and Margret still slept.

She let out a breath, set down her irons, and put her face in her hands. She'd had her share of nightmares and then some, but this had been different. Something about this one felt wrong, as if the dream hadn't even been hers. Every vivid detail clung to her mind and turned her stomach.

As the scene played in her head, over and over, she shivered in spite of the warmth of the night. Her heart lurched, and she lifted her head as realization set in.

Not a dream, memories. Weaver's memories, but how—

Her mouth went dry.

The geas stone?

No. They didn't work that way—at least, not eldar-crafted stones. Could Weaver have botched the crafting? Or had it been intentional? Or could this all just be her imagination running wild? It damned sure didn't feel that way. Even now she could picture the mustachioed man, clear as if he stood before her.

She debated telling Wilfred and Margaret but decided to keep it to herself for now. She'd tell them if it turned out to be more than just a dream. She had no idea how she'd figure that out, but that gave her an excuse to keep from admitting she just didn't want to say anything yet.

And if it was more? What did that mean for the countless others who'd had the stones used on them? Had the slave masters gotten a glimpse into their heads? She shuddered at the idea and ran her fingers through her hair, trying to smooth out her frayed nerves.

By the time she'd finally calmed, the sky had turned to purple, slivers of orange and red on the horizon. No point in trying to rest with dawn quick approaching. She got to her feet, holstered her irons, and moved so as not to disturb her friends. She gathered up and secured her bedroll to Gaoth and collected some leaves and bark. The dream left a lingering bad taste in her mouth, making the bright, healthy foliage taste of ash.

The hairs on the back of her neck stood on end. She froze mid-chew, hands going to irons but not drawing.

Half an instant later, hoofbeats, faint still, and whispers she couldn't make out, sounded through the trees.

They'd set camp better than a mile off the nearest road. The river wasn't far, but she'd checked it. No one had been there in a long time. She closed her eyes and fashioned a map from the sounds around her: three horses and at least that many men led them on foot. They were south, the direction of the city, and moved slow, playing at stealth and failing.

The copper-tinged scent of old blood reached her nose.

She opened her eyes and moved, quick and silent. She put her hand to Wilfred's mouth, and he woke with a start, but didn't make a sound.

She leaned in close, whispering in his ear, "Red Right Hand."

"How close?"

"Five minutes maybe."

He took up his revolver and nodded.

She shook her head and pointed at Margaret. "You two get away."

He opened his mouth, but she cut him off with a look. He nodded once.

Talen crept to Margaret's side and roused her, a hand over her mouth as well.

Margaret stirred slowly and then jolted awake.

"Someone's coming. You need to hide," Talen whispered.

Margaret nodded, and Talen helped her to her feet.

Wilfred retrieved the repeater from Joseph's saddle and handed it to Margaret. He gave Talen one last look and helped Margaret down the path. After a hundred yards, they took cover behind some trees and readied their shooters.

Talen glanced at Gaoth, Joseph, and Wilfred's mare, Elise. No way to move them, especially heavy-hoofed Joseph, without making a ruckus. She'd planned on lying in wait to ambush the Red Hands but that would put the horses at risk.

She let out a breath and drew her irons, keeping them dark. After wrapping herself in shadow, she sprinted in the direction of the Red Hand stalkers. Even at a dead run she made almost no sound. Unfortunately, she had no idea if any of them had those eyepieces. Even if they did though, if she moved fast enough, she might still catch them unawares.

She darted between the trees, heart pounding so loud it drowned all other sound. The rancid taste of blood on the air grew stronger though.

A minute later she came on them: three men, spell irons drawn, walking in a line, and leading their horses.

Still veiled in shadow, she launched herself at the stalker in the middle, driving an elbow up under his chin. His jaw snapped with a heavy crack, and he toppled back.

As he fell, she stepped from the shadows, irons raised, and poured magic into them. As the last rune lit with spell fire, she pulled both triggers, one aimed at each of the remaining men.

A force blast hit the one on her right, striking his left side. The impact pulverized his arm, crushed his rib cage, and sent him barreling into a tree. His head smacked the trunk with a wet thud.

The other stalker vanished in a ball of flame, making the predawn as bright as noon.

Her vision went white, and she cursed herself for not being mindful of her charges. She couldn't see but heard the panicked screams of the burning man.

Still blind, she rotated the cylinders, aimed where the first stalker had fallen, and fired. Another bright flash of light followed by a clap of thunder erupted from her iron and rang her ears.

Talen dropped and rolled to one side, hoping if she'd missed, the stalker was as blind as her.

Her vision returned enough to make out the three bodies on the ground. The smell of charged air, charred flesh, and old blood twisted her guts. She approached the lead stalker, rotating the cylinder on her right-hand iron.

Margaret screamed, and three gunshots split the air.

Talen turned and sprinted back to camp, desperately trying to blink her vision back as she ran. More gunshots rang out, and Margaret's angry shout ended abruptly.

A cold fist gripped Talen's heart, but she fought it back. She poured so much magic into her irons that the spell fire flickered like a pyre of mundane flame.

She pushed herself faster.

"Marcus? Randall?" someone shouted from ahead. "Jed? What happened?"

"You'll be seeing them soon enough!" Talen shouted back.

"Whoever you are, we got the woman and the Negro!" came the reply.

Talen slid to a stop. Burning rage melted away the ice that had gripped her heart, and her hands shook. "Turn them loose and run. You might even make it."

"We're here on a lawful bounty," the man said. "Let us take it, and we'll be on our merry." The words would've carried more weight if the voice hadn't wavered.

Talen gritted her teeth. Even right in front of them, the jackasses couldn't see Margaret wasn't stained. Or, more likely, they didn't care.

"You ain't taking nothing." Talen walked toward the sound of the voice, quickly, but still walking. She didn't bother with the shadow veil. Fury wrapped her instead. Even so enraged, she still caught the word 'we.'

Talen wanted to sprint but held back. It wouldn't do to barrel into a trap. Also, depending on how many there were, one could kill Margaret or Wilfred while Talen ended the others. She prayed her friends weren't dead and imagined the hell she'd rain down if they were.

"You boys best run now," Wilfred said. "She's out cold but still breathing. That might earn you a bit of mercy or at least a head start."

Talen sighed in relief and silently thanked Wilfred.

"You best keep your mouth shut, boy," the stalker said. "I got no problem killing a Negro."

"Besides," said another stalker. "We got the drop on you easy enough."

"I ain't no two-gun witch," Wilfred said.

Silence.

With her friends alive, for now at least, Talen got the upper hand on her wrath. She holstered her irons, drew her knives, and stepped into shadow. She ran, going wide to come up behind the Red Hands.

When she reached Wilfred, Margaret, and the three stalkers, Talen went to a crouch.

One stalker stood behind Wilfred, an arm around his neck, and a lit spell iron pressed into his ribs. The second stalker hunched over Margaret, knife in one hand, bounty crystal in the other. The third stood apart, brandishing his burning iron and scanning for a target.

All three had their backs to her.

"Damn it, Charlie, just cut her and get the crystal in," the man holding Wilfred said in a harsh whisper.

"She don't stink," said the one kneeling over Margaret. "You sure this is her?"

"Use the damned crystal, and we'll know, won't we?" said the third. "You want in the Hand? Do as you're told."

"What about the witch?" Charlie asked.

"I'll see to her," the stalker on guard said.

Charlie nodded and moved his knife toward Margaret.

Talen crossed the distance between them before his blade got within an inch of her. She put her left hand over the man's mouth and pulled him off Margaret. As he came back, his chin lifted, and Talen opened his throat.

"Holy shit!" The man moved his iron from Wilfred's ribs to where the dead stalker had fallen.

Talen crouched next to the corpse, still as a stone but ready to move in an instant. Her gaze followed the spell iron as the stalker jerked it from one spot of empty air after another in hopes of finding a target.

Wilfred drove his elbow into the man's gut.

The stalker stumbled back and doubled over, gasping for air. A heartbeat later, he regained enough of his senses to lift his iron and take aim.

Wilfred threw himself at Margaret, covering her body with his own.

Talen, still wrapped in shadows, stepped under the stalker's arm, pushing it to one side as he pulled the trigger. Fire belched forth, lighting the twilight.

Talen's hands screamed in pain from the fire, but her rage strangled the agony in an instant.

I'll hurt when the killing is done.

She drove her knife up, under his rib cage and yanked it hard to one side. As he crumpled, she shoved him back into his lone remaining companion.

Fire leapt from the barrel of the third stalker's iron. The flames swallowed the dying man and rushed at Talen.

She turned her back to the fireball, bent low, and covered her head with her hands. Her coat absorbed much of the blast and while intense, the heat was short-lived. When it passed, she stood and turned, glaring at the final stalker.

The soon to be dead man stared with wide eyes and took aim to fire again.

Talen stepped to one side, grabbed his wrist, and twisted. Bone snapped, and the stalker dropped his iron with a scream of pain.

"Wait," he said. "I surrend—"

Talen drove her knife between his ribs and into his heart.

"Not after hurting my sister, you don't." She stared into his eyes. The life left him, and something inside her, something dark and terrible, sang in delight. With effort, she pushed that darkness aside and went to check on her friends.

Wilfred knelt over Margaret's still form, his lithe fingers brushing her hair aside.

Talen crouched beside him. "Is she okay?"

"Looks it," he said. "Son of a bitch distracted me while his friend pistol whipped her. Thank the Lord he didn't just cut her down."

"They need her alive to collect the bounty," Talen said. Though that didn't explain why they spared Wilfred, not that she minded in the least. Could be the *shanzi fetsuian* had some kind of honor after all, at least when it came to other humans.

He looked at Talen. "I'm sorry. I should've—"

She drew him close and kissed his cheek. "You did all you could. This is on me. I knew they'd come after us, but I let my emotions get the best of me. I ought've set a watch."

"Seems there's plenty blame to go—good Lord!"

Talen looked down. The skin on her hands had burned away, leaving bright red flesh. The sight of her injury was enough for the previously strangled pain to return to life. It slammed into her like a falling sequoia. The blinding, indescribable intensity of it almost dropped her.

"I'll be fine," she said, through gritted teeth. "We need to get gone, right now."

"You reckon they got friends?"

"Might be. That fight made a hell of a ruckus. Anyone within a couple miles would've seen the light show." She moved on shaky legs to pick up Margaret, but Wilfred beat her to it.

"I got her." He stood, cradling Margaret in his arms. "Mind your hands."

"I said I'll be—"

"My revolver is empty," he said. "And you're a better shot anyhow."

Talen collected Margaret's repeater and cane and followed Wilfred. When they got to camp, he set Margaret down with her back to a tree and set to packing their campsite.

"What happened?" Margaret asked and tried to get up.

"No, you stay put," Wilfred said. "You took a hit to the head."

"Did I break whatever hit me?"

Wilfred chuckled.

"No." Talen forced a smile and demanded her knees not give out as she knelt. "But you did put a hell of a bend in that spell iron's barrel."

"Sorry."

"We took care of them, but we need to hightail out of here."

"That's the last of it," Wilfred said, securing a pack to Joseph.

"Can you ride?" Talen asked.

"Think so," she said and held out her hands. "Help me."

Talen took Margaret's wrists and hauled her up. The pain intensified, and it took all Talen had not to scream.

Margaret started to wobble, but Talen caught her.

Focus on them. The pain doesn't matter.

"You take Elise and lead Gaoth," Talen said to Wilfred. "I'll ride double with her on Joseph."

Wilfred shook his head. "Let her ride with me. Your hands—"

"We'll fit better on Joseph," Talen said, through a jaw clenched so tight she genuinely worried about breaking teeth. "I can hold on to her just fine and still shoot."

Margaret looked down. "What about your—merciful God! What happened?"

"Caught some flame is all," she said, leading Margaret toward Joseph. "I'll be fine."

In truth, she wanted to scream, or fall to the ground and weep, or both, but she didn't have that luxury right now. She climbed onto Joseph's back and hauled Margaret up, setting her in front.

For a moment, she thought the remaining flesh might've sloughed off her hands, but it only felt that way.

They headed off. Thankfully, Joseph's slow and ponderous pace made for a gentle ride, but his broad back strained Talen's long legs. She couldn't wait to get back onto Gaoth.

They rode in silence as the sun climbed into the sky. After a short while, Margaret slumped back against Talen. Doing so gave Talen a clear view of the large, angry bump on Margaret's forehead. Hopefully the bastard hadn't hit her too hard. Talen added her concerns to the growing pile. She could tend to Margaret's injuries properly once they got on the airship.

Can't believe the day came that I'm eager to see a dwarf.

Margaret stayed conscious the whole time, a good sign. A few very long hours later, they reached the spot where the river turned. Talen's hands wouldn't stop shaking. The pain had her soaked in sweat and fighting not to pass out. Her jaw ached from the clenching.

"No dwarf," Talen said, with more venom than she'd intended.

"He'll be here," Wilfred said, without a trace of impatience. "It's hours till noon yet." He helped Margaret from the saddle and over to some trees away from the river.

Talen near fell off Joseph but caught herself at the last moment. Wilfred eased Margaret down, and Talen looked her over again. The blow hadn't broken the skin, but there'd be an ugly bruise. She probed gently around Margaret's skull but didn't feel any give.

Margaret winced.

"I don't feel no cracks or breaks," Talen said.

"I showed that spell iron."

Wilfred chuckled. "You surely did."

"You dizzy or sick at all?" Talen asked. "Sleepy? Confused?"

Margaret shook her head, but only a little. "No, nothing. Save for the splitting headache."

"Good." Talen forced a smile. "You sit tight. I'll fetch you some water and a wet cloth."

"Thank you." Margaret closed her eyes.

Talen motioned with her head for Wilfred to follow.

"We need to watch her," Talen whispered, as they walked. "She ain't showing no symptoms but if there's a brain bleed…"

"Anything we can do?" He retrieved some canteens from Joseph's pack.

"I'll brew up something that might help." Talen pulled the pouches of herbs, the mortar and pestle, and the leftover rags of her old shirt from Gaoth's bags. "But healing ain't never been my area of expertise. I do better with the hurting."

"You'll do fine," he said, as they walked to the river. He began filling canteens. "Just don't forget to tend to yourself. Those burns look bad."

"I'll see to them once we get Margaret settled," Talen said, soaking the rags. The cool river water felt damn near euphoric on her burned hands.

"I'm holding you to that."

One corner of Talen's mouth pulled up. "Just not by the hand."

Wilfred gaped. "Did you just make a joke? That's two in as many days. I'll need to mark a calendar."

Talen narrowed her eyes, but her half-smile remained. "You recall I just mentioned being good at hurting, right?"

Wilfred chuckled. He collected the rifle as well as some fresh loads for his revolver and Talen's irons.

Talen set the wet cloth on Margaret's head right over the lump.

She sighed and smiled. "Oh, that's nice."

"I'll make you up something even nicer. It ought to take care of the pain." Talen sat and made to add herbs to the mortar, but her own pain wouldn't be ignored. Even these small movements sent ever-growing waves of agony through her hands and arms. Talen tried to wall it back up, but her willpower had crumbled without the rage to reinforce it. Her hands trembled, and she almost dropped the mortar.

"Let me," Wilfred said, taking the supplies. "Tell me what to do."

Talen closed her eyes, working hard to push back the insistent agony. It took everything she had, and a few tears spilled down her cheeks, but Talen managed to talk Wilfred through the steps. When the mixture was ready, he filled the mortar with water, and Margaret drank half.

"You take the rest," she said and pushed the stone to Talen.

Talen opened her eyes, and a couple more tears broke free. She shook her head and opened her mouth to protest.

"Did you hear a question in that?" Margaret gave Talen a hard look. "Drink."

Talen reached for it, but her hands had gone from merely quivering to spasm-like jerking.

Wilfred took the makeshift cup and held it up for Talen to drink.

She did, swallowing it all and even chewing the dregs. The pain eased, not much, but enough to let her get the upper hand. Talen sighed and after a moment, guided Wilfred through the steps to a second mixture.

"This one here is just for you," Talen said to Margaret, when Wilfred had finished. "It'll help with swelling."

"Smells terrible," Margaret said and then took a drink. "Ugh, it tastes worse."

"I know, but you need to drink it all." Talen glanced at the sky and figured she had a couple hours till noon, and she needed to heal if she wanted to be at all useful. Carefully, she drew her irons and passed them to Wilfred. "Reload those for me, will you?"

"Any preference?"

"Anything but fire," she said and stood.

As he set to work, she slowly slipped off her coat and kicked off her boots.

"What are you doing?" Margaret asked.

"I aim to get some healing in." Talen started unbuttoning her shirt.

"And you need to strip down for that?" Margaret's cheeks turned pink. She motioned at Wilfred with her head. "Right here?"

Talen sighed and shook her head. "I suppose not." Human modesty mystified her. She didn't understand their issue with nudity. But neither was she in the mood to debate it, so she went behind the trees and resumed undressing.

"Better?" she asked.

"Yes, thank you," Margaret said.

"No," Wilfred muttered.

Talen pulled off her shirt, sucking in a breath as the sleeves brushed her hands.

"Eyes on your work, mister," Margaret said to Wilfred.

Wilfred chuckled. "Yes, ma'am."

Once nude, Talen lay down in a patch of warm sun and began her silent incantation. Burns were hard to heal, and she didn't have a lot of time, but maybe she could do enough to function at least. It took effort to clear her mind and focus on the prayer, though not just because of the pain. She kept thinking of her friends and fretting over someone tracking them. Of course, she wouldn't be any good in this shape. She cleared her mind and slowed her breathing.

If someone does come, I can get to my irons quick enough, she told herself. *And being naked might serve to distract, or terrify, or cause a moment of confusion, at the least.*

Her mind eased. She drew in long, slow breaths and let them out, focused on the abundant life around her. Power flowed in from all around. Cool relief spread over the back of her burned hands and the skin begin to heal as her conscious mind drifted.

Her eyes opened at the sound of the shop door. A tall, broad-chested man with a massive brown mustache stepped in. He smiled and tipped his bowler hat to Talen.

"Good day, sir," he said.

She nodded. "And to you. Can I help you find something?"

Chapter Nineteen

The scene played out exactly the same as before, and once more, it left Talen feeling sullied. No denying it now, these visions had to be a side effect of the geas stone. She had no notion if the memory transfer had been an intentional consequence or not. Either way, it left her disquieted.

She shook off the mental wanderings and flexed her hands. They hadn't fully healed—the skin was tender and tight—but the pain had faded to something manageable. It'd have to serve while she healed unaided. She didn't foresee a chance to do this again any time soon.

She returned the surplus energy gifted to her, opened her eyes, and checked the sun. No more than a couple hours had passed. She stood and got dressed.

"How you feeling?" Wilfred asked, from the other side of the trees.

"Well enough," Talen said. "How about you, Margaret?"

"I'm okay. Whatever you gave me seemed to help. Do I want to know the ingredients?"

"No, you do not." Talen pulled on the last of her clothes and her boots. She stepped around the trees and saw all three horses grazing happily.

"Thirsty?" Margaret offered a canteen.

Talen sat and drank deep. This close to the city, the water tasted a bit foul, but not undrinkable.

Wilfred handed over her irons. "Arctic, kinetic, and starburst loads."

Talen looked them over. "Did you clean them too?"

He nodded. "I recall you being a might particular about that."

She smiled and holstered the irons. "Any sign of your dwarf?"

"All quiet."

Talen glanced at the sun and back at him.

"He'll be here," Wilfred said.

"Have you eaten?" Talen reached behind her to pull some bark from the tree and started to chew.

"Cold beans and bread," Margaret said.

"Sounds delicious." Talen turned her head a little. A faint sound in the distance caught her attention.

"It wasn't," Wilfred said, "but it did the job. Plenty times in my life I'd have been happy for cold beans and bread."

"Amen to that," Margaret said.

Talen stood and scanned the distance. She didn't draw her irons, but her right hand did rest on the handle.

"Trouble?" Wilfred stood as well, revolver in hand.

"I don't know," Talen said. "I hear something."

Margaret grabbed her rifle.

Wilfred came up beside her. "Horses?"

"No." She tried to place the queer sound but couldn't. "Closer to an insect swam."

"Locusts?" Margaret asked.

"No." The sound resolved into a clear buzzing hum, a deep droning sound.

"What direction?" Wilfred asked.

Talen pointed to the east.

"Is it a humming sound?" he asked.

She turned to him. "You can hear it?"

He smiled. "No, but I reckon it's our ride." He holstered his shooter and walked down to the river.

"Wait here," Talen told Margaret and followed.

The buzzing grew louder and deeper. Then she saw it.

"*Terisan ut marrin,*" she whispered.

The airship could only be dwarven-made. It seemed a cross between a sailing ship and a flat bottom river boat but covered in as much brass as wood. It hung suspended by dozens of cables from a giant, grey egg-shaped thing of woven metal. It had no sails or paddle wheels. Instead, four metal rings—two on each side—stuck out of the ship, narrow windmill blades spinning in each one.

This ship bore a distant likeness to the leviathans in her memories. A cold dread crawled down her spine and settled in her stomach. Her hands shook and her heart pounded so hard she feared it might burst out. She wanted to run, or to hide, or to blast the thing from the sky. Instead, she looked over the outside of the craft, but found no weapons—none visible anyway.

"I know this ain't going to be easy for you," Wilfred said. "But I swear to you on my very soul, he's a good man."

Talen swallowed but found her mouth dry.

Wilfred reached out and touched her arms.

Talen wrestled back the fear and nodded at him. "I trust you," she said. "You. And I swear I won't do nothing untoward." She drew in a slow breath. "But you know I won't stand by if things go bad."

"If things go bad," he said, "I hope you know I'll be right there with you."

She nodded.

The airship drew closer, and the four rings pivoted, slowing and steering the vessel until it floated above the river. The craft descended slowly and settled on the water so gently it scarcely made a ripple. It crept forward and ran aground fifty feet away.

"It sure is something, isn't it?" Margaret asked from beside Talen.

Talen turned and damned near drew down. "I told you to stay put."

"No, you didn't."

"Well, I meant to." Fear and panic rose up again, but Talen managed to beat them back down. Mostly.

The front of the ship opened. A wide brass and wood gangplank extended and settled on the riverbank. A barrel-chested dwarf, clad in a—relatively—long leather coat, goggles, and heavy boots, stepped into view. Talen didn't see any weapons but kept hold of her right-hand iron all the same.

The dwarf marched down the gangway and turned to them.

Talen narrowed her eyes.

The dwarf sported a long, dark moustache, replete with gold and silver bands. And an entirely bare chin.

"Draven." Wilfred stepped forward. "It's good to see you again, my friend."

"And you, Wilfred," Draven said in a low, grumbly voice, closing the distance before exchanging a fierce handshake with Wilfred.

"Are you okay?" Margaret asked in a whisper, touching Talen's arm.

"I'm fine. Why?" Talen asked, through teeth she hadn't realized were clenched.

"Because you're gripping your iron awful tight."

Talen glanced down. The iron remained dark, thankfully, but she held it in a white-knuckled grip. She eased up her hold, but left her hand resting on it, and nodded her thanks to Margaret.

She only smiled and patted Talen's arm.

Draven studied Talen. "This must be the elf you ran with, aye?"

Talen looked the dwarf over. Could it be?

"This here is Talen." Wilfred gestured at her and then to Margaret. "And this is Margaret Jameson."

Draven gave them a polite nod, attention lingering on Talen's spell iron.

"Captain." Margaret offered a small curtsey.

Talen looked from Wilfred to the dwarf and returned the nod. "Madame."

The color drained from Margaret's face, and Wilfred stared at her in wide-eyed silence.

Draven erupted into a deep belly laugh then gave Talen a wide smile and a deep bow. "Sure, but it's a Shadow Warden who sees truest."

"I, um," Wilfred began, looking from Draven to Talen and back. "Is there a joke I ain't understanding?"

"No joke." Talen nodded at the dwarf. "She's a woman."

Draven smiled and arched an eyebrow.

"But she has a moustache," Margaret whispered. "A rather large one."

"Thank you, ma'am," Draven said, stroking the moustache.

"All dwarves have facial hair," Talen said. "Usually beards, too."

Draven stiffened a little but lifted her bare chin proudly and met Talen's eyes. "There are things I don't suspect you're aware of, happenings with my people since the Great Dishonoring."

"The great dishonoring?" Talen asked.

Draven nodded. "What we call the day some sold their souls and honor for gold. It caused a schism in the kingdom. Those of us that saw the truth of it, we cut our beards and refuse to grow them back until the Dolomite King comes to his senses. What my people did to yours is a stain that'll mark us for generations. And it damn well should. Tell you true, I'm not sure it'll ever wash away." She bowed her head. "Serve us right if it didn't."

Talen was utterly dumbstruck. It took several moments to wrap her head around it all. "The dwarven kingdom split?"

"Like the states?" Margaret asked.

"Much like that, aye," Draven said to Margaret and then turned to Talen. "Split us damn near down the middle. There's been some brawls, but no direct fighting, not yet. The Granite Lord of the east broke away and invited all the beardless to join him. What the humans call the Rockies still belongs to the Dolomite clans and the King. The Appalachians are the Granite clans and beardless. Only the wide plains keep the peace now, though no telling for how long."

Talen thought back to the dwarven bartender in Agua Fria. Had he become a convert to the beardless cause? She'd been so close to cutting him down.

Mother, what have I become?

"Not all of us value gold over honor," Draven said and went to her knees. "It's little, and far too late I know, but I offer to you my deepest and truest apologies on behalf of my people. I'd offer you my beard as well, but it's as I said."

Talen stared and, after a moment, realized her mouth had fallen open. She'd never felt so humbled, shamed, and confounded all at once. It took her a few heartbeats to put any words together. "Thank you, Draven." She offered her hand. "I accept your gracious apology. I see why Wilfred speaks so well of you."

Draven took the offered hand and Talen pulled her to her feet. "Much obliged." Draven turned to Wilfred. "Now, your message said express run. We'd best get you loaded up and head out. Where are the passengers?"

"Just us," Wilfred said and gestured to the horses. "And them."

Draven narrowed her eyes. "So, this ain't a Railroad run?"

"Uh, no. You see, we're—"

Draven lifted a hand. "You owe me no explanations, old friend." She turned to Talen and put a fist to her heart. "My ship is at your disposal, Shadow Warden."

Talen was grateful for the lack of a breeze. Surely it would've knocked her over. "You honor me." She offered a deep bow.

"Right then," Draven said. "I got stabling quarters down below. That big fella might feel a bit confined, but I got oats, apples, and carrots to placate him if need be. I give you free run of the ship, save for the locked section at the rear. It's for your own safety. There's shielding around the reactor core, but exposure to earth fire is deadly to humans. Best to keep away."

"What's a reactor?" Margaret asked.

"Dwarven furnace," Draven said. "It's how we generate the steam for powering our machines. The burning of earth fire also creates the helium I use to keep the Cumulus—that's my ship—in the air."

"You use helium?" Margaret asked.

"Safer than hydrogen. Also, more reliable than hot air and readily available." She turned to Talen. "I don't know for sure about elves and earth fire, but you best stay clear as well. I'd just as soon err on the side of caution."

"Agreed," Talen said. "Will the horses be okay?"

"Stables are well away," Draven said. "No worry there."

"And the flying won't spook them?" Talen asked.

"No windows down there," Draven said, "and not by accident. No, unless we hit a nasty storm, my Cumulus flies smooth as a lazy river."

"You all right?" Wilfred asked Talen.

She drew in a breath and nodded. "We've been here too long already."

"Right this way then," Draven said.

"We'll get Joseph," Talen said to Margaret. "You go on ahead."

Margaret nodded.

Draven offered her arm, and Margaret took it after a brief hesitation.

Talen and Wilfred went to collect the horses.

"Damned if you don't find the queerest company," Talen said, shaking her head. "A two-gun witch, a stained human who ain't, and a rebel dwarf airship pilot."

Wilfred laughed, taking Elise's and Joseph's reins. "Let's call it refined."

Talen smiled a little. "Did you know about the dwarves?"

Wilfred shook his head. "Draven don't speak much of his people, and it ain't my place to ask."

"Her people."

"Right," he said. "Gonna take me a bit to change that in my head."

They led the horses onto the ship and got them settled in the stables. The stalls were roomy—less so for Joseph—and lined with fresh hay. Gaoth neighed, snorted, and stomped his hooves in protest. At least, until Draven returned with the apples.

After Gaoth charmed a second apple from Draven, Talen left him to chomp his beloved fruit. Wilfred followed her up the stairs. The buzzing started, and the ship lurched once as it lifted from the river. They stumbled, but the Cumulus held steady after that, and they reached the top deck with ease. Talen gaped.

They were a hundred feet above the river and rising. The view took her breath away, and she went to the railing, eyes wide. Her heart sang and a smile, or the ghost of one, settled on her lips.

"I missed that smile," Wilfred said, coming to her side. "Quite a sight, ain't it?"

"It reminds me of home." Talen couldn't look away. It was too beautiful. "Of the view from the trees. I'd almost forgotten how the world looked from up high." She gave herself a long five count to take in the scene and then nodded. "Let's go."

"Draven will be on the bridge," Wilfred said.

"Bridge? On a ship?"

"It's what she calls it. Ain't got no notion as to why."

Wilfred led the way. A few small, spider-like brass machines skittered across their path on the deck. Talen drew her iron and took aim.

"Easy now," Wilfred said and gently pushed her hand down. "Draven calls them spindles. They do repairs and work the ship so she can fly without a crew."

Talen holstered her iron and noticed more of the contraptions in the rigging. She watched the bizarre creatures go about their work. She recognized the skill and artistry that must've gone into them, but they still made her uneasy.

Wilfred nudged her along and up to the bridge, which bore no resemblance to a bridge at all.

"I never grow tired of it," Draven said to Margaret as Talen and Wilfred stepped inside.

The room, though not large, held the four of them comfortably. A massive window—with perfectly smooth glass—took up most of the front wall. A large ship's wheel faced the window, a collection of gauges, dials, buttons, and levers on either side. Metal tubes and tendrils were strung along the ceiling like spider webs.

Talen ignored them and stared out the window, not sure which impressed her more, the glass or the view. An azure sky, speckled with white clouds, stretched out before them. The wide-open plains ran for what had to be a hundred miles, maybe more—a grass version of her beloved Pacific Ocean.

"Isn't it amazing?" Margaret said.

"I'd be happy to spend every one of my remaining days up here," Draven said.

Talen nodded in appreciation.

"So, where we headed?" Draven asked.

"Chicago," Talen said.

"Chicago?"

Talen turned to face Draven. "That's right."

"You know what you're asking?" Draven asked. "You know the risks? I ain't judging, just making certain you understand?"

"I do," Talen said. "It's important."

"Aye, it'd have to be, wouldn't it?" Draven said. "All right, Chicago it is."

She went to the table in the middle of the room. She shuffled through the collection of maps on it until she found the one she wanted. Using tools that Talen had never seen and an abacus, Draven made some calculations.

"Four hundred and twenty miles as the crow flies," Draven said. "Which just so happens to be how we travel." She glanced outside. "Winds up here are working a bit against us, but we ought to keep to about fifteen miles an hour. That's twenty-eight hours, give or take."

"Incredible," Margaret said.

"I caught a powerful tailwind once that got me up to more than forty," Draven said and walked over to the wheel. She climbed onto a raised platform in front of it and began working levers and dials. "But speed is only half of it. Not having to work around rivers and the like can shrink the distance more than you'd imagine. That and we don't need to stop. Not even for sleep."

Talen watched the rings pivot and drive the ship forward. "I've lived a long time," she said, watching the dwarf work the controls. "I've known my share of dwarves, but never one like you."

Draven laughed. "Aye."

"That's meant as a compliment."

"Oh, I took it as one. You're not wrong though. I'm an oddity even among my people." She grinned. "And not just 'cause I like engineering and got lady parts."

"What do you mean?" Margaret asked.

"We're born from the earth," Draven said. "We're tied to it, connected in a way impossible to explain. Most want to keep close to her. It's why we live underground, deep in our mother's bosom, mining and digging for her treasures."

"But not you?" Talen asked.

"Not me," Draven said, straightening and smiling broader. "Even as a child I'd stare up into the sky. Odd enough I had a mind to be an engineer, but wanting to fly?" She chuckled. "Hell, my parents didn't know what to think."

"What did they do?" Talen asked.

Draven turned. "They taught me right and wrong, and supported me in what I wanted to be."

"Wait. You built this ship?" Margaret asked.

"With my own two hands." Draven said and laughed. "Though sometimes the hands worked a crane or some heavy machinery." She lowered a metal hook that held the wheel fast and turned to her passengers. "I didn't have many friends. Fewer still once I built this." She let out a breath. "Dolomite sure got interested though when the humans came calling with their gold."

"He wanted your ship for the fight," Talen said.

"He did at that. And I told him what he could do with that notion." She shrugged. "Maybe not in those words, mind, but I made my thoughts clear enough. Not long after he signed the contract with the humans. That's when those of a like mind made our way east. I carried many of my brothers and sisters to the Granite halls, and well, I've been flying ever since. Whatever else happens, can't no one take the sky from me."

"What happened to your parents?" Margaret asked.

"They left, too. Bare chinned as the rest of us, I'm proud to say."

"You're lucky," Talen said.

"Aye, the King and his supporters showed more charity and compassion to us than they ever did to others." She let out a breath. "But I've gone on enough. You should get yourselves settled in the cabins below. Take any berth you like. Wilfred knows the way. Galley is on the same deck when you're of a mind to eat. I keep it stocked well enough with goods that'll last, canned and jarred."

"You should rest," Talen said to Margaret.

"I'm fine."

"Didn't say you weren't. But the more rest you get now, the less I'll worry in Chicago."

"So, you won't argue about me coming with you?"

"I will not." Talen cracked a slight smile. "Not like it would do any good."

Margaret practically beamed. "It's a deal then." She turned to Draven. "Thank you again, Captain."

"Yes, thank you." Talen offered her hand.

Draven took it and nodded once. "I'll like as not be here if you need anything. You can also reach me through any of the speaking trumpets you see. They all connect up here."

Wilfred led the way out, Margaret in the middle with Talen close behind. They got Margaret settled before choosing their own rooms. Talen considered bunking with Wilfred but decided against it. Too much churned in her heart and mind right now. She didn't need any complications. He chose his room, she hers, and Wilfred, to his credit, didn't bat an eye.

Talen's room, with only a couple of small windows, felt like a coffin in no time at all. The hum of the engines had faded to background noise, but she felt the subtle vibrations in her bones. After less than an hour, she couldn't take it anymore and went back top side.

She leaned on a polished brass rail and watched the world drift by. It reminded her of home, though views like this were only found atop the tallest sequoias. Her favorites were those nearest the cliffs, offering a view of coastline and deep blue ocean. She missed the taste of salt in the air and the rumble of the waves crashing against the rocks. Hell, she just missed home.

As the sun made its way across the sky, her mind turned and wound back on itself. She thought back to Draven's revelations about the Dwarves.

She'd been a damned fool, guilty of the same prejudices she claimed to despise in humans. Not to say she hadn't come by her biases honestly, but it still wasn't right. Humans and dwarves were far more complicated and varied than she'd ever given them credit for.

She might never be quick to trust a human or dwarf, least not those she didn't know. She'd seen plenty of cruel or selfish humans—the Red Right Hand, Weaver, slave holders, soldiers—but she couldn't judge humanity for the crimes of their worst.

She thought of the dwarves who'd broken from their king and their damned beards. That meant there had to be more humans like Wilfred and Margaret. The darker part of her mind said they were few and far between, but maybe that was enough? Weren't rare things all the more precious?

It wasn't an easy task to change beliefs, especially if they're hard won, but she'd try. Sure, she'd fail plenty, but she'd keep trying. If she hoped to save the worn tatters of her soul, she had to. All else aside, it's what her mother would want.

Chapter Twenty

Talen spent the rest of the day at the rail, alone with her thoughts and watching the world go by. In time, her fear and dread melted away, as if left behind on the passing landscape. A new feeling arose, one that had been a stranger for years: freedom. More than merely the lack of restraints or impediments, she felt the freedom to choose a new path.

A familiar thumping came up the stairs.

"If you aim to invite me to dinner," Talen said, not looking away from the sunset that painted the sky. "I ain't much in the mood."

"You sure? There's vegetables, even some fresh fruit," Margaret said, coming to stand beside her and taking in the view. "It's beautiful."

"Ain't it just?"

"I feel as though I should offer a sisterly reproach for not eating. But truth is I don't know how much you need to eat. I'd starve if I ate what you did, but you're strong as five of me."

"I eat when I'm hungry."

"Are you doing all right?" Margaret asked. "It seems something is turning in your head. I just want you to know I'm open to listen if you want to talk."

The sun dipped below the horizon, shifting the sky from fiery red and orange, to a deep blue and purple.

"I'm trying to sort through things," Talen said. "Reconsidering my past judgments."

"Draven's story was a powerful one."

"That's a fact. It started me thinking, but it ain't the whole of my considering." Talen sighed. "Hell of a thing to find you been wrong about so much. Can't help but make me look back on my life, and inside myself. Truth to tell, I'm not much liking what I see."

Margaret chuckled and shook her head.

"Something about that seem funny?"

"I don't know who set this standard you hold to, but you need to go easier on yourself."

Talen stared at her.

"You have no idea what I'm talking about, do you?"

"No."

Margaret put a hand on hers. "Not to say as I'd approve, but I'd understand if you set out to gun down every human or dwarf you set eyes on. Considering what you've been through and all." She shrugged. "If someone offered to go after the man who raped my mama or the woman who beat her, I can't say as I'd refuse. I'd sure consider for longer than I should." She squeezed Talen's hand. "You might have gruff words and little patience for humans and dwarves, but you aren't bent on murder."

"You so sure?"

"You could've killed me before I'd even known you were there. You had no reason not to. In fact, you had a legal warrant from the US Magistrate saying you should." She smiled and it reached her eyes. "But you didn't. More than that, you put yourself between me and those who would've killed me."

"You ain't stained. And I'm not fond of being used to kill innocents."

"That doesn't explain why you took on those Red Hands back at the cabin. You could've saddled up and been gone before they got close."

Talen shrugged. "I reckon, but it wouldn't have been right."

"That's precisely my point. You did the same with Draven. You could've killed her before she set a boot on the dirt."

Talen stared at Margaret slack-jawed, eyes wide. "I promised Wilfred—"

"A human," Margaret said. "You promised a human you wouldn't kill a dwarf. Do you understand what I'm saying?"

"I suppose."

"You're not just a good person," Margaret said. "After seeing nine kinds of hell, you're still one of the kindest, most selfless people I've ever known. So, when you tell me you don't like what you see inside, I find it more than a little funny."

Talen chuckled, and the sound was a bit unfamiliar. "I suspect Edwin Weaver would offer some dispute to your argument in regards to my kindness."

Margaret scowled. "The son of bitch had it coming." She bumped Talen's shoulder and chuckled. "And I said you were good and kind, not a saint."

Talen outright laughed. It felt nice, if a little strange. She purposely didn't think about the last time it had happened. "Appreciate the clarification."

"You're welcome."

They stood in companionable silence for a bit, and Talen decided she needed to tell Margaret and Wilfred about her visions.

She sighed. "I suppose I should eat. Besides, I need to talk to you and Wilfred."

Margaret led the way below deck to the galley. Wilfred stood in front of a large pot, filling a bowl with what smelled like stew. He offered Talen the steaming dish as if he'd been expecting her. She accepted it and another for Margaret, who'd sat herself at a sizeable table in the middle of the room. Wilfred joined them soon after, and they ate in easy silence.

"There's something I need to tell you," Talen said, pushing her empty bowl away. "I held off on the telling till I was sure it was more than my imagining. Now I am."

Wilfred and Margaret exchanged a look.

"Must be important," Wilfred said.

"Something happened when I used the geas stone on Weaver," she said. "Something unexpected."

"Unexpected?" Wilfred asked.

"Last night I had a dream. Except it wasn't a dream."

"I don't understand," Margaret said. "How is a dream not a dream?"

"When it's a memory. Except, it weren't mine. It was Weaver's."

"Beg pardon?" Wilfred said.

"I saw Weaver meeting the Franklin & Tuller man. The whole of the encounter, through Weaver's eyes no less. Thought his thoughts, felt his feelings."

Margaret's face twisted. "In his head? I can't imagine a more appalling place to be."

"You ain't wrong. Left me feeling a mite soiled."

"Not saying I don't believe you," he said. "But how are you sure it wasn't just a dream?"

"I saw it again during my healing sleep," she said. "Exactly the same, start to finish."

"So, you saw this fella?" Wilfred asked.

Talen nodded. "Pratt. His name is Chester Pratt. Not like to forget him."

Wilfred leaned back in his seat and crossed his arms. "I ain't never heard of nothing like this." His eyebrows lifted. "Of course, before a few days ago, I'd never heard of a charm made with dark magic, neither."

"I wish to hell it were just a dream," Talen said. "I don't much care for having that bastard's memories in my head. They were unpleasant, to say the least."

"How is that possible?" Margaret asked.

Talen lifted her hand. "I don't know crafting well enough to answer. But those stones... Well... Well, I've seen their like before." She explained about recognizing them.

"You reckon Weaver botched his crafting?" Wilfred asked. "Or you suppose he planned it to work that way?"

"And could he have gotten any of your memories?" Margaret asked.

"If he did, I hope he got the worst of them. It'd serve him right if they give him nightmares for the rest of his days—" She looked at Wilfred.

It took him a moment, but he furrowed his brow. "You reckon?"

"Might be."

"You realize I can't hear what you're thinking," Margaret said.

"She compelled him to forget us," Wilfred said. "Might be the stone gave the memories to her in response."

"But that isn't what you saw," Margaret said.

"Could be I got what he'd been focusing on at the time," Talen said. "He'd just told us the tale." She sighed and scratched her head. "Or I got what I did 'cause he did botch the crafting. Not sure the how matters so much as the what."

"I see why it troubled you," Margaret said. "I can't imagine being in his head. I'd need a hot bath, a stiff brush, and ten pounds of lye soap to feel clean again."

"That about sums up my feelings on it."

"Knowing what this Pratt fella looks like could be helpful," Wilfred said. "If we spot him, we'll know we're on the right track."

"I ain't likely to forget a moustache like that."

"Mind if I join you?" Draven asked from the doorway.

"It is your ship," Talen said.

"And your food," Wilfred said, standing to get a bowl.

Draven waved him off as she stepped inside. "And I'm more than capable of serving myself, thank you very much." She set a map on the table and got herself some stew before sitting, taking a spoonful, and nodding. "Needs some meat, but it ain't bad."

"If you're here, who's steering this thing?" Talen asked.

"Ain't like piloting a riverboat," Draven said. "We're flying straight and true with nothing in our way. I checked all around before coming down. Sky is clear and open as far as my glass showed, better than thirty miles."

"What do you do when you need to sleep?" Margaret asked.

"Dwarves don't need much," Draven said between mouthfuls. "When I do, it's only for an hour or two. If the sky is clear, I let the ship sail on. If not, I set down, or find a spot to float till I'm rested." She unrolled the map with one hand as she put another spoonful in her mouth with the other.

"Is that Chicago?" Talen asked, standing to get a better look, and stared. She'd known it was a big city, but she never imagined it would be this big. She'd figured maybe three times the size of Santa Fe, but it had to be a hundred times bigger, if not more.

Draven nodded.

Talen's gaze moved over the vast city drawn out before her, still in disbelief. "How many people live there?"

"Over a million last I heard."

Talen couldn't put any words together. At their most populous, the elves never neared a million in total. For humans that was a single city? She struggled, and failed, to imagine what that many people would look like. The thought of what the world would look like in just a few decades made her blood run cold.

How long would it take for humans to fill the entire continent? And what would become of her people?

"It's so detailed," Margaret said.

"And accurate," Draven said. "I made it myself, though I started with a human map." She nodded at Wilfred and Margaret. "No offense to you two, but I don't trust no one for calculations I can do on my own. I had to make some adjustments to get it accurate and to proper scale."

"How do we find this one shop in all that?" Talen asked, her heart struggling to beat normal again. "It'd be like searching for a single needle in a pine forest."

"Didn't the card list an address?" Margaret asked.

"What's an address?" Talen asked.

"Let me see it," Margaret asked.

Talen passed it over.

"131 W. Madison," Margaret said and passed the card back. "It's a number and a street name to help you find a place in the city."

Draven scanned the map and pointed to a spot. "That should be about here." She traced a river line that came in from the lake and turned south. "This is the Chicago River. Lots of traffic on it. Factories, mills, and the like line the riverside. Unfortunately, the river ain't designed to take an airship. We can move along the water easy enough, but the gas bladder is the problem. Lots of bridges and such we can't get under."

"What about here?" Talen asked, pointing to a spot in green.

"That's Lake Park," Draven said. "City wouldn't look kindly on us pulling up there, nor would those out enjoying the day."

"If we land during the day."

Draven shrugged. "We'll get there about four in the afternoon. I figured you wanted to get in as soon as possible."

"We'll have less consideration at night," Margaret said. "But we'll also draw more suspicion. Odds are, the offices won't be open, and poking around could draw unwanted attention from the law."

"Chicago police are corrupt as all get out," Draven said. "You pass some coin to one and unless you're gutting someone, they'll leave you to your business. If you are, it'll cost you two coins."

"Police?" Talen asked. She didn't much care for being this ignorant.

"City lawmen," Margaret said. "Like deputies."

Talen nodded.

"They got an ordinance against weapons inside the city as well," Draven said. "They don't mind a pistol so much, so long as it's kept out of sight. They are pretty strict about spell irons though. Best you don't have yours visible."

"Cities are like a whole other world," Talen said.

"That's the plain truth." Draven eyed the map for a bit and then pointed to a spot on the lake shore. "This here, it's a sort of private docking system. Not legal as it were, but the man who runs it keeps the police paid up. Means you'd have to make your way through the city though."

"How far is it?" Talen asked.

"Mile and a half." Draven traced a route with her finger.

"That's nothing. Even without the horses." Talen glanced around. "I'm guessing we need to leave them behind?"

Margaret nodded. "Gaoth and Elise might do well enough, but Joseph wouldn't."

"We'll head out over the lake then," Draven said. "Float about out of sight till nightfall, then we tie up, and you can see to your business."

"I'd like to draw up a copy of this to have with us," Talen said. "Do you have any paper and pen?"

"I'll see to the copying myself," Draven said. "Matter of pride, you understand. Nothing personal."

"Much obliged," Talen said, eyeing the map again.

"What you thinking?" Wilfred said.

"It don't make no sense," Talen said. "With so many people, why go through all the trouble of sending their wares out and about? Why not test on locals?"

"Lots of eyes," Margaret said. "If people started going missing, it'd raise questions. Even corrupt officials have a point where they can't ignore something anymore."

"And in my experience," Wilfred said. "The worse a person is, the more they value everyone thinking them a good, respectable sort."

Talen just nodded. Her friends knew humans a damn sight better than she did, so she'd trust in them.

Casual conversation started up, but Talen only half-listened. Draven explained to a rapt and attentive Margaret the workings of the ship. Talen caught something about it not really being steam powered. A device called a generator made the electricity that powered the ship. She didn't really understand it, so instead, she turned her attention to the map. How many humans must there be in the world if more than a million filled this single city?

Her thoughts drifted back to the talks she and her sisters had with the Lakota elders. They'd said for every white man killed, a dozen would return. They saw it as unstoppable as a rising river, one that would eventually wash everything else away. She'd dismissed the notion as dramatic exaggeration.

How wrong she'd been.

Every year, things happened faster. She'd seen more change in the last thirty years than in the last four hundred. Since the destruction of her nation, she'd never much pondered on the future. Not hers or her people's. Now, she wasn't sure any of them even had a future. Would her people join the countless tribes of humans wiped from existence?

"I'm going back up," she said, getting to her feet. Wilfred eyed her, but she shook her head and gave him a half-smile. She didn't want company just now.

He turned back to Margaret and Draven's conversation.

The chill night air served as a balm to her worn soul. The stars, those not hidden by the huge gas bladder, twinkled bright and serene.

Some hours later, Draven came topside.

"Your friends have bedded down for the night," she said as she joined Talen at the rail.

Talen closed her eyes and savored the feeling of the wind on her face.

"You'll forgive me saying, but you look a might weary."

"And then some," Talen said.

"Soul or body weary?"

Talen opened her eyes. "A bit of both." She and sighed. "A lot of both."

"I know the feeling well." Draven shared the view for a little while then made to go. "I'll let you be. If you need anything, I'll be on the bridge."

Talen turned to her. "You said the plains were all that kept the dwarves from going to war. Is that really true?"

"Most of us believed—hoped at the least—it wouldn't ever come to outright war. Not with how easily the Dolomite let us leave."

"And now?"

Draven stared off into the distance. "Aye, it's coming, one way or another. The bearded just keep working for the humans. I even heard tell they considered joining in the war between the states."

"For which side?" Talen asked but then caught herself. "I'm sorry, that was uncalled for."

"No, it wasn't." Draven deflated a little. "Truth of it? They'd likely join the side that offered the most gold." She worked her jaw a moment and then spit into the open air. "Knots my guts right up, I tell you. And I'm not the only one. Word is, more and more are going bare-chinned, and more of them ain't content to just stand aside."

"Do you think the Dolomite's people would come east? Seems a good way to find nothing but trouble."

Draven shrugged. "I don't reckon the King sees us as a threat. I suspect he, and those loyal to him, think we broke off because we didn't want to fight. Not because we didn't believe in the fight."

"It'll go badly, won't it?"

"Terrible bad. For everyone. A war the world hasn't seen."

"I'm sorry," Talen said. "Sincerely, for your people."

"Don't take no offense to this, 'cause I know the truth of your words, but you ain't nearly as sorry as I am."

"Fair enough."

They stood for a long while, sharing the silence and watching the sky. In time, Draven went to the bridge and Talen, much later still, went down to her cabin and tried for sleep. The visions didn't return, but it might've been because the nightmares that did, scared them off.

Talen managed a few hours of broken, and hardly restful, sleep. She'd grown accustomed to exhaustion though. She spent much of the night turning over things in her mind. She knew nothing would come of it, no answers or insights, but she couldn't stop herself.

After a few hours' sleep, Talen stood on deck once more, watching the sun rise in an explosion of color that spread across the sky like water. Wilfred stirred not long after—he always did—but Margaret slept a few hours past sunrise. Talen let her. The more rest she got, the more she'd heal.

"Penny for your thoughts," Wilfred said when he came to Talen's spot at the rail. "Course I ain't got no penny, so you'll need to lend me one. But I'll give it straight back."

Talen chuckled at the familiar joke. "Churning dark thoughts. Hoping to get them out of my head, though I know better."

"Darkness." He nodded "It only whispers. It don't never shout."

"What?"

"Something I heard a while back," he said. "Means when we get to thinking dark thoughts, they're quiet and patient, not loud or sudden. They haunt the silence, always there, always whispering. We don't block it out cause it ain't but a whisper. Most times, we don't even notice. But like water on rock, over time, it does change the shape of things."

"First you talk like a lawyer. Now, you're a poet."

"Impressed?"

She smiled. "I am. But not surprised. You always had a poet's soul, even if you didn't always have the words."

"Might be the nicest thing anyone, including you, ever said to me."

"That's a damn shame." She turned back to the sky. "Am I making a mistake going into the city? Or taking Margaret along?"

"I don't rightly think you got much say in the second part. And not just 'cause she wouldn't listen."

"True enough."

"It's risky. Things go bad, they're likely to go real bad." He shrugged. "But no, it ain't no mistake. You're doing what you know is right, like you always done, and I suspect always will."

"What if I'm wrong?"

He reached over and took her hand without looking.

His hands were warm, and the warmth spread into Talen, like it always had. Her heart ached a bit, longing for what they'd had before. But she also appreciated what they had now. She squeezed his hand and leaned against him.

"Then you're wrong, and you face what comes next," he said. "But I reckon we both know you ain't."

"We need to plan," Talen said. "Figure some escape routes at the least. And I don't like that we'll be a gun short."

"We will?"

"We won't have but my irons and your six-shooter. If Draven has the right of it, Margaret can't be toting that repeater around town. Not without stirring up trouble."

"That is a fact. Suppose you could give her one of your irons."

She looked at him. "She's a good person, but she's got no experience with one."

He narrowed his eyes for a moment. "Reckon we could cut the repeater down. I seen a few like that in my days. Draven could likely do it proper while we're waiting for sunset."

"That's not a bad idea. She ain't a crack shot, but I like the idea of her heeled. Also, a shorter barrel and stock might prove easier for her to manage. Let's go ask Draven. Then we'll go and see if Margaret minds us cutting up her rifle."

Draven said she'd be more than happy to assist, even offered to make some improvements as well. Talen left that decision to Margaret, who was quite taken with the idea.

Within an hour, Draven provided them with a copy of her map and a rather meticulous design proposal for the repeater. Margaret gave her enthusiastic consent, and Draven set to work.

The three of them turned their attention to the map, figuring various routes in case things went to hell. Even with multiple options, depending on how deep into hell things went. Then they set to memorizing street names. Margaret assured Talen there'd be signs.

A few hours after lunch, Draven called through the speaking tube for them to come up on deck. The vast city of Chicago sat in the distance, a sprawling urban mass on the edge of a lake that reached the horizon.

"Oh my," Margaret said, a little breathlessly.

"Sweet Mother of God," Wilfred said. "I ain't never seen nothing like it."

"Reminds me of Boston," Margaret said and turned to Talen. "Incredible, isn't it?"

"It's…horrible," Talen said.

She couldn't fathom what Margaret found so incredible. Farms at the distant edges of the city were the only hint of green. The massive sprawl, all filthy brown and gray, stretched for what had to be a dozen miles.

The smell made Talen want to up her chuck. It wasn't the city smells she'd come to expect, though she reckoned they'd come as the airship drew nearer. This foul stench—like wood smoke, but dirtier, and mixed with what she could only describe as unnatural—came from the tall brick stacks and rail engines belching thick black smoke.

Talen did find it all impressive—horrifyingly so. Some buildings had half a dozen or more floors, all packed close together. If a fire ever broke out, she couldn't imagine how it wouldn't consume the whole city.

Ships of all shapes and sizes crowded near the shore or sailed up the river into the city; the steam ships vomiting their own plumes of heavy coal smoke. The sickly yellow and gray of the lake broke Talen's heart. Thankfully, it did eventually turn a deep and beautifully clean blue farther out.

How could anyone stand to live in such a place? Besides the filth, it had no trees and only sparse grass. It had no life. *Is this what the whole world would one day come to?*

She didn't know if she wanted to live in such a world.

"I never thought about it before," Margaret said, breaking Talen from her stupefaction. "But I see what you're saying. I grew up in a city, so I never noticed the soot or foul air." She turned to Talen. "But there is beauty, too. I'm sorry you can't see it."

"It's a sight to behold, and no mistake," Wilfred said. "But I reckon it's a mite too big for the likes of me."

Talen looked again, but she couldn't see past the dull colors, black smoke, and filthy water. She spotted a few other airships, of varying design, but only a few.

"Bumpkin," Margaret said, giving him a playful grin.

The airship turned away from the city and ventured over the lake. That view took Talen's breath away. The water, too calm to be the

Pacific, did remind her a bit of home. "I understand," she said to Margaret. "You see home, and home is always beautiful."

"I suppose you're right."

The Cumulus came to a stop above the lake, miles from the city. The stench of coal smoke vanished, dispersed or blown away on the strong winds. So strong that the engines didn't stop running. They slowed but had to keep working to hold the airship in one place.

Draven left the bridge and led everyone below. While Talen and the others went to the galley, Draven set to work on Margaret's repeater. In less than an hour, she'd cut down the barrel and removed the stock, making it look more a large pistol than a rifle. The remaining improvements took a few hours. They included a refining of the barrel to improve accuracy and range. Draven also expanded the magazine, doubling the capacity, and rebalanced it accordingly. When done, she revealed she did have weapons on board. In point of fact, she had a small arsenal. The armory held a dwarven rifle she called a rail gun, more than a dozen mundane shooters—rifles and pistols—and enough ammunition to fire them all for days on end.

Talen took the revelation in stride. On the outside anyway. Inside, she fought hard to not consider what Draven and her airship could've done to the elves and the Oceti Sakowin at Whitestone Hill. She gave a silent, profound thanks to the mothers that Draven was someone of character and honor.

When the sky turned dark, Draven piloted them back to the city. As she did, Talen, Margaret, and Wilfred geared up and readied themselves. Wilfred offered Margaret his coat. Thought several sizes too big, it would serve to hide her shortened repeater.

Not an hour later, the Cumulus descended. The craft settled on the lake as gently as it did the river in Kansas the previous day. A sudden lurch told them the ship had reached shore.

Minutes later, Draven joined them belowdecks, now sporting a pistol on each hip.

"Let me do the talking," she said. "If questioned, you're my crew and anything more than that ain't anyone's business, aye? You're going into town to see to the goods we're picking up. If anyone protests, follow my lead."

Everyone nodded.

"Wait," Talen said, when Draven went to open the hatch and lower the deck.

The dwarf held the lever but did not pull it.

Talen took one of the glamour stones from the pouch, closed her eyes, and drew a deep breath. She set the talisman in her mouth next to her cheek and poured magic into the stone. It tasted sweetly familiar, reminiscent of her mother's honeyed cakes. The charm's flowing power spread over her body, settling into a constricting warmth. She focused on shaping it, choosing basic details. When the glamour had resolved, she opened her eyes.

Margaret and Wilfred gawked. Draven gave a half-smile and nodded.

"How do I look?" Talen asked, pitching her voice lower.

"You make a rather handsome man," Margaret said. "If you don't mind me saying."

Wilfred cleared his throat and furrowed his brow. "I admit, I'm feeling a might confused about a great many things just now."

Talen pushed all her fear and anxiety into a tight ball, shoved it down deep inside, then nodded at Draven.

Chapter Twenty-One

The hatch opened and the gangplank descended. The stench of the city hit Talen like a herd of stampeding horses. Coal and wood smoke mixed with a foulness she didn't want to consider. It took an effort of will not to cough or gag. Draven gave one last look back before heading down the gangway, Talen, Margaret, and Wilfred following behind.

"Captain Draven," a pasty, but filthy and rough-looking, man said, offering his hand. "Been a while since you've graced our fair city."

"Billy," Draven said, taking the man's hand and shaking. "Good to see you, boy."

"Got yourself a crew now?" Billy asked, eyeing Talen, Margaret, and especially Wilfred. "Colorful bunch."

Draven shot him a look and passed over a small stack of folded greenbacks.

"None of my business, of course," he said, giving a wide smile riddled with gaps, and pocketing the money. "How long will you need the spot?"

"We should be gone before dawn." Draven turned to Talen and motioned for them to go.

Talen led Margaret and Wilfred past the man.

"Our nightlife is mighty popular," Billy said to them as they walked by, and then he turned back to Draven. "You got any more of that dwarven belly burner?"

They crossed the short strip of shore to the road. Talen gaped at it, paved with an uncountable number of stones, but only for a moment. She eyed the metal rails—too narrow for a train—that ran down the middle of the street.

"Horsecars," Margaret said. "Like big stagecoaches that run on rails. We had them in Boston. You need to watch for them. They'll run you down if you're not paying attention. Come on."

Margaret led them to a sidewalk at the far side of the road and took in her surroundings, getting her bearings. As she did, Talen tried to comprehend the immensity around her. Even at the edge of the city, the closeness of everything bore down on her. A cold sweat began to soak her shirt, and her heart pounded. The buildings loomed all around, closing in on her, and the air seemed unbreathable.

All the noise and movement overwhelmed her senses.

Her vision tunneled, and her stomach tightened.

Every breath felt like it was all filth and no air.

She stumbled and fell against a wall. "I can't breathe."

"Easy now," Wilfred whispered to her.

"Is she okay?" Margaret asked.

"She'll be fine. Just needs a minute is all."

Talen closed her eyes tight, her heart stuttering and threatening to give out.

Her whole body shook, and she struggled through the fear and panic. A wave of frigid darkness crashed over her, howling with the rage of the restless dead. It slammed into her, pushing her down. Drowning her with its emptiness.

She couldn't see a way clear.

In growing desperation, she thought of her mother. Talen pictured her serene face, dark kind eyes, and ever-present smile. As she did, she quietly hummed the song her mother sang to her as a child.

Each verse, each word, was like a whisper of breath; barely enough to keep her alive. But each whisper built on the one before, and inch by inch, she clawed her way out of the darkness.

Her heart slowed, and she at last managed to draw in a breath, barely noting the foulness to it. When the terror had passed, she opened her eyes. Margaret and Wilfred both stood with their backs to her, putting themselves between her and the passersby. She still saw them though, people in carriages or on foot. She especially noticed the hard look most gave Wilfred.

She reached out and touched her friends' shoulders. "I'm okay."

They turned.

"You sure?" Wilfred said.

"It's okay if you need another minute," Margaret said.

Talen shook her head and straightened. "No, I'm okay."

Margaret and Wilfred exchanged a look but said nothing more. He motioned for Margaret to lead the way. The oppressive panic in Talen's chest didn't go away, but she was able to push it back.

They got plenty of odd looks as they walked, at least Wilfred did. No one so much as gave Talen a second glance.

"I ain't used to being the one overlooked," she said, keenly aware of the dissolving glamour stone in her cheek.

"What's it like?" Wilfred asked.

"Oddly unsettling."

"We need to cross here," Margaret said. She checked up and down the street before crossing, quicker than Talen expected.

Talen and Wilfred followed.

As Talen stepped onto the sidewalk, one of the horsecars—a small and open rail car pulled by a large draft horse—trundled by. Talen's heart broke for the miserable animal, head bowed as it plodded along.

They ventured deeper into the city, and each block seemed to close in more and more. At least it felt that way. Talen couldn't believe how many people there were. In these twenty minutes, she'd seen more than in the last five months.

"You all right?" Wilfred asked as they walked.

She nodded. "I'm okay. Just feeling a mite confined."

"Me too. They pack them in tight here, no mistake."

"It ain't natural. And it don't seem safe."

A man ahead of them used a long pole to light some kind of lantern atop a decorated metal post. It cast a weak yellow glow and gave off a terrible smell.

"Street lanterns?" Talen asked.

"Gas lamps," Margaret said. "They pipe coal gas to them."

Wilfred's mouth fell open. "Gas? Ain't that tempting fate? Seems like crafter lights would serve better and be safer."

Margaret gestured around. "I suspect this section of town has neither the money nor influence to get them."

The streets and sidewalks grew more crowded the farther along they went. At times, Talen had to wind her way past people. She tried to draw herself in, will herself smaller, but every few steps someone pushed by, often knocking her into someone else.

Her hands trembled again, but she fought back the rising panic, and found her steel. Instead of making herself smaller, she did the opposite. She stood straighter, going to her full height. When a man jostled her, she didn't give, he did. He made to glare at her but met her eyes and thought better of it.

Wilfred had no issue. The crowd opened for him, most not wanting to get too close.

Margaret, for her part, made her way like a salmon swimming upstream.

They crossed a bridge, likewise crowded with people, carriages, carts, and odd conveyances. The river water smelled as foul as the air and Talen made it a point to not look down. Soon the crowds thinned out and after a couple more turns, the three of them were the only ones on the street.

"Where the hell did everyone go?" Talen asked.

Margaret scanned the building signage. "I think this is the industrial section. These are all factories and mills. Everyone is either home or working the night shift."

"A bit unsettling after them crowds," Wilfred said.

Talen noticed how many buildings had their entrance below street level. Some had half the first floor visible, others sat so low there were doorways on the second floor.

"Why do some buildings have doors on different levels that others?" Wilfred asked.

"I don't know. It's not uniform though." Margaret narrowed her eyes. "I think they're sinking."

"Sinking?" Talen couldn't hold back a smile. Apparently, the earth wasn't giving up without a fight. *Give 'em hell.*

Margaret pointed to a nearby street sign that read 'W. Madison.' "This is it. We're almost there."

They continued until they came to a plain brick building, six stories tall. A polished brass '131' sat above the entrance at the center of the ground floor. Unlike some of the other buildings, this one had no signage to mark its purpose or residents.

"Well, we're here," Margaret said. "What now?"

Talen surveyed the building. The windows were dark, save for one at the corner of the second floor that flickered with lamplight.

"Reckon someone is home," Talen said. "Let's go have a chat."

They made their way down roughly-made wooden steps that led to the entrance—several feet below the street—and found the door unlocked. After a quick scan about for watching eyes, they stepped inside. A set of stairs sat opposite the door, and a sign on the wall listed a series of names, a number next to each. Otherwise, the lobby was dark and bare.

Margaret went to the sign and read it over. "Franklin & Tuller Co.," she whispered. "Number 220."

"They got addresses inside buildings, too?" Talen asked.

"Of a sort. It's where the offices are in the building. First number tells you the floor."

Talen moved to take the lead up the stairs, but a heavy door thudded shut on the floor above. She froze and listened intently. The click of a lock working was soon followed by brisk footsteps heading their way.

"Someone's coming," she whispered.

They pressed themselves into a dark corner next to the stairs. Talen gripped her right-hand iron but didn't draw. She considered wrapping them all in shadow but decided against it. With the glamour and there being three of them, it'd be a wasted effort. She positioned herself in front of the others and waited.

The footsteps grew louder and then descended the stairs. Moments later, a large man reached the lobby. He didn't so much as glance back as he left the building.

Talen narrowed her eyes and watched him intently.

Once outside, he turned. Talen recognized his face, and the massive, heavily waxed, brown moustache.

"It's Pratt," she whispered.

He checked a pocket watch and then hurried up the stairs to the street.

"Come on. We got to follow him," Talen said.

Wilfred and Margaret hurried after.

When they reached the door, Talen crept up the stairs and scanned for Pratt.

He'd made it halfway down the block.

She motioned for Wilfred and Margaret to follow.

"No way will I be able to keep pace," Margaret said. "You go on, and I'll follow best I can."

"I can carry you," Wilfred said.

"A large Black man carrying a white woman down the street?" Margaret shook her head and then turned to Talen. "When he gets where he's going you can double back and meet up with me."

"I'll stay with her," Wilfred said. "Go on."

"You sure?" Talen asked.

Wilfred nodded, his right hand patting the pocket that held his revolver.

"Go," Margaret said in a harsh whisper.

Despite her misgivings, Talen hurried after Pratt. She kept a reasonable distance and noted every turn. She might not be at ease in the city, but she knew stalking and hunting.

Not being able to veil herself—what with the glamour—did make it harder, but she managed, not making a sound as she followed. A few times he grew suspicious, but she ducked out of sight before he looked back.

At the corners, she listened for his footsteps to be sure he hadn't set an ambush. It only got harder as the noise of the city grew. Before long, the cacophony around her entirely masked his passing. However, the increasing crowds did mean she wouldn't stand out—a strange new way to hide. She closed the distance, careful to keep plenty of others between her and her quarry.

The streets got cleaner, the buildings fancier. The dim, foul-smelling gas lamps gave way to crafter lights. The shining crystals floated in glass globes set atop elaborately shaped metal posts. Even the humans had more shine here. The worn, dingy clothes vanished. In their place were pristine suits, lavish dresses, and all manner of finery. Talen didn't pay it any mind.

Pratt stopped at a large house with an ornate stone front and went up the stairs.

Talen slowed.

He knocked on the door. It opened, letting laughter and music spill out, and then he stepped inside. She walked past the home, casting a casual glance at it. Finely dressed men and women stepped in and out of view, glasses in hand.

He curses people then goes to a party?

It took some effort not to kick down the door and drag the bastard out by his collar. Instead, she hurried back the way she came to find Margaret and Wilfred.

It didn't take long for the urban landmarks to look the same. She grew increasingly uncertain about the street names and reached for the map. The empty pocket reminded her she'd given it to Margaret before they'd left. She cursed her own arrogance and moved in a slow circle. There weren't a lot of people on the street, but them that were gave her a wide berth. That, as it happened, offered a comfortable familiarity.

"You lost there, boyo?" someone asked in a heavy Irish brogue.

Talen turned and her blood ran cold. A man of middle years with a bushy red moustache eyed her. He wore a dark blue uniform and sported a tall, rounded helmet. It took a couple of heartbeats to realize it wasn't a soldier's uniform. Unfortunately, she'd already reached for her right-hand iron.

Before she could draw her hand back, the wide-eyed policeman reached for his pocket.

No turning back now.

Even if the hammer of his mundane shooter hadn't caught on his pocket, she still would've beaten him to the draw. He hadn't even cleared the barrel by the time she had her spell iron leveled at his chest. She did maintain enough presence of mind to keep it dark.

The man froze, let the gun slip back into his pocket, and slowly raised his hands. "Easy there, lad. No need for things to go that way."

Talen holstered her iron and glanced around, but no one appeared to have seen.

"I apologize." She pitched her voice low and matched his brogue. "You caught me by surprise, is all."

The man lowered his hands and eyed her. "Do I hear a bit of the old country there?"

"Aye, my parents."

"The famine, yeah? My own tried to last it out, but in the end, we all boarded a coffin ship and made our way here." He checked for onlookers and then leaned in. "Not sure you know, but them spell irons ain't allowed in the city. I'm supposed to confiscate those I come across and take the owners into custody."

Talen covered the iron with her coat. "I didn't know."

"I ain't takin' nothing from a fellow Irishman. That thing must've cost you plenty, and our people suffered enough. Just be sure you keep it out of sight, yeah?"

"Aye, I'll do that. Thank you."

He smiled and nodded. "It's nothing, lad."

Talen smiled back, going along with the fiction he'd be anything but dead if she hadn't held back. *Cheaper than paying him off with coin.*

"Have yourself a pleasant evening now," he said and made to walk past Talen.

She stepped to one side and let him go. He turned down the next street and vanished from view. Talen scolded herself for being so jumpy and drawing down. After a long moment, she went to the corner and checked. No sign of the man. With luck, he'd just hurried off and hadn't gone to find any fellow lawmen. She couldn't risk waiting around to find out though.

She closed her eyes and drew in several breaths, smoothing her nerves and calming her heart. She thought back, trying to remember details of her pursuit, and which of the countless streets she'd followed him down. Bit by bit, it came back to her. She opened her eyes, went down two more streets, and went left. She hoped the lawman had gone right.

She found Wilfred and Margaret a few minutes later. They waited at a corner, trying not to look desperate as they glanced around. When they spotted Talen, it took a second for them to recognize her beneath the glamour. They both visibly relaxed.

"Thank God," Margaret said.

"We lost you and weren't sure as to which way you went," Wilfred said.

"Figured it best to let you come to us rather than risk getting lost," Margaret said.

"Sorry for the delay," Talen said. "I got turned around and had a run-in with a police deputy."

"What happened?" Wilfred asked.

"Do we need to get back to the Cumulus?" Margaret asked.

"No, I reckon we're okay, but we best get moving in case I'm wrong. I ought to change my look first though."

"Can you do that?" Margaret asked.

"Means burning another stone," Talen said, "and I need someplace out of sight to do it."

"There's an alley back that way," Wilfred said. "We can watch out while you change."

Talen stepped into the alley, a narrow space between two buildings, barely wide enough for Wilfred. He and Margaret waited at the entrance. Talen found a dark spot, spit out the old glamour stone, and crushed it under her boot. She took a moment to enjoy being herself again, then took out a new stone and put it in her mouth. Once more she shaped the magic as it settled over her. They didn't have the luxury of time, so she kept the same face, but aged it several years, as well as shifting the hair and eye color.

Shrouded once more in glamour, she led Margaret and Wilfred back to the house. When they reached it, they walked past and kept going to the far corner.

"Looks like a dinner party," Margaret said, rubbing at her leg.

She didn't say anything, but Talen could read the pain on her face.

All this walking must be taking a toll even with the cane.

"I didn't see Pratt inside," Talen said. "Hopefully he hasn't left."

"This is a fancy neighborhood," Margaret said, looking around. "His clothes weren't near nice enough for that dinner party."

"You reckon maybe that's Tuller's house?" Wilfred asked.

"I don't know," Margaret said. "These are some fine homes, but they'd be like servant quarters next to his place in Boston."

"If they sent Pratt as far as Kansas City," Talen said, "I don't reckon he's too terribly important."

Margaret nodded. "Maybe the house belongs to Tuller's local man?"

"All this assumes the name ain't just a coincidence," Wilfred said.

"Let's stick with what we know," Talen said. "It was Pratt that gave the stone to Weaver. We start with him."

"Do we wait for him to come out?" Margaret asked.

"How long do these things last?" Talen asked.

Margaret shrugged. "It could be just dinner and some drinks after, or it could last all night. Depends on the type of party and the host."

"We're here, and it don't seem to cost nothing to wait," Wilfred said.

"Not yet," Margaret said. "We don't look like vagrants, but we clearly don't belong, especially in the middle of the night."

As if on cue, footsteps and whistling filled the quiet night.

Moments later, a lawman—not the one Talen met earlier—came around the corner. He glanced up and down the street and spotted them immediately. He drew the truncheon at his side and headed their way.

Talen wanted to kick herself for not thinking to shape the glamour to look like a policeman.

"Let me guess," the man said as he approached, tapping the cudgel against his leg. "Locked yourself out, have you?"

"We simply got turned around," Margaret said, leaning dramatically on her cane. "We tried to find a carriage, but I got tired, so we stopped to rest for a bit."

The man eyed her, his gaze lingering on her ill-fitting coat. Then he turned his attention to Talen, completely ignoring Wilfred. "That so?"

Talen nodded, and her muscles tightened. There wasn't anyone else on the street. If she was quick and quiet about it—

"Well, I'm afraid there's an ordinance," the man said, a half-smile settling on his face as he finally turned to Wilfred. "Twenty dollar fine for loitering and vagrancy."

Bile rose in Talen, contempt riding along, but she pushed it back. Best to cater to greed and self-serving, especially not knowing how long they'd have to wait for Pratt.

"Of course," Talen said, stepping forward and reaching into a pocket. She drew out two double eagle coins and held them out. "I fear we might be here a while, so best to pay a second fine right now. Don't you think?"

The policeman's smile widened, and he nodded. He took the coins, pocketed them, and tipped his helmet at Margaret.

"You have yourself a pleasant evening, Miss," he said and then turned and headed back the way he came. He vanished around the corner.

"Can't afford many of those fines," Talen said.

"Wouldn't be one if I weren't here," Wilfred said.

"I'd hand over every greenback I got and use every charge in my irons before I let anyone take you to jail."

"Let's leave that as a backup plan," Margaret said. "First, we'll try a spot less obvious."

They found a house that looked empty, or at least it didn't have any lamps burning. Like most of the homes, it sat below street level, but not so far that the view from the front door was blocked.

They settled in just outside the front door, Wilfred and Talen taking turns keeping an eye on the house. Time passed slowly, and Talen knew it'd be a hard wait. The persistent fear eating at her guts told her such. If anyone saw past her glamour, one of them would be dead in short order.

She looked to Margaret, sitting with her back to the empty house, eyes closed and sleeping quietly. She'd lived with this sort of fear her whole life. And she did it without shadow glamour or spell irons.

You are one hell of a woman, Margaret Jameson.

"How you holding up?" Wilfred asked, his voice low.

"I'm fine." Talen nodded at Margaret. "Just wondering what's next for her. What kind of future she can have after this."

Wilfred smiled and chuckled softly.

"Why the hell am I so funny all of a sudden?"

"Most folk would be wondering about their own future. I mean, I reckon you'll not be going back to stalking."

"Hell no."

"Then what?"

"I don't know, but I'll figure it out. I did before, and I reckon I will again."

"And so will she. So will I when the time comes."

Talen looked at him. "I'm sorry there ain't no going back for us. We're both different now."

He nodded. "I know that, and I'm sorry too. Those were some mighty good years." He let out a sigh. "But I'm old enough now to appreciate good times, even if they're done. Don't mean something new can't be good, though."

"I hope you're right," Talen said, watching Margaret sleep, serene and lovely.

"I know that look. You used to look at me that way."

"I still do on occasion." Talen smiled. "Just not when you're looking."

Wilfred gave her that familiar, knowing grin. It boasted of wisdom far beyond his years, even with more years behind him.

Talen shook her head. "Nah, even if she were so inclined, and we were on the other side of this mess, it wouldn't be right. Her heart's still grieving, and I reckon will be for a while yet."

Wilfred opened his mouth to reply, but the echoing of clopping hooves and carriage wheels brought him up short.

Half a dozen coaches rolled up the street and stopped in front of the house.

"Might be time to get moving," Talen said. "Best wake her up."

As he did, the partygoers began exiting the home. They climbed into their respective carriages and, one by one, disappeared into the night.

Margaret, still wiping at her eyes, joined Talen scrutinizing the procession. "Sorry, I didn't mean to doze off. Any sign of Pratt?"

"Not yet."

They watched the house until a young couple took the last carriage, and it rolled away.

"*Terisan ut marrin,*" Talen muttered. "He must've left while I was getting lost."

"Wait," Margaret said. "Look at the top floor."

Talen followed her gaze to a lit window, one that had been dark. Two figures, silhouetted against the curtains, moved in and out of sight. Talen closed her eyes and focused on listening, hoping to pick up something from the room. But she couldn't make anything out, so she opened her eyes and waited.

The minutes dragged by and the glamour stone, half the size of a tooth, continued to shrink.

"If that's Pratt," Talen said. "I'll follow him on my own. You two get on back to the Cumulus. If it ain't him, I'll meet you there."

Margaret and Wilfred both opened their mouths to protest.

"The glamour stone is almost done."

"You have four more," Margaret said.

"I do, but I'd like to not use them if I don't need to. We got no idea what'll come after this. Besides, I can see your leg is paining you."

Margaret looked as if she meant to object but stopped when she caught herself rubbing her leg.

"There ain't no nice way to put it, but you'd be more hindrance than help." Talen turned to Wilfred. "And it ain't smart for her to make her way back alone."

Wilfred nodded, if grudgingly.

Margaret clenched her teeth and glared.

"You know I'm right," Talen said. "You both do. Believe me, I'd like nothing more than having you both at my back, but that ain't going to happen. This here is the best of our few options."

Wilfred and Margaret traded glances. He shrugged and shook his head.

Margaret let out a heavy sigh. "We're not leaving without you."

"Who the hell said you should?" Talen asked. "If I ain't back by dawn, I expect you to come get me. And bring Draven."

"How do you reckon we'll find you?" Wilfred asked.

Talen pointed at the house. "Start right there. After that, head to the office."

The glamour collapsed, and it was like taking a deep breath of cool air on a hot night.

"I don't like it," Margaret said.

"I don't expect you to," Talen said. "Just get moving. Sooner you're back on the Cumulus, the better I'll feel about it. You got the map?"

Margaret pulled it from Wilfred's coat pocket.

"Go on then," Talen said.

Wilfred gave her a long, pleading look.

"See you soon," she said, hoping he heard the promise behind the words.

He helped Margaret up to the street, and they made their way back to the waiting airship. Talen watched them round a corner and vanish from view.

Being on her own felt familiar, though not as satisfying or comforting as she'd expected. Pushing aside the dark whispers rising up, Talen opened her coat, putting both irons in easy reach, and watched the house.

Before long, the front door opened. Pratt stepped out and onto the cobblestones. He checked the street and then headed back the way he'd come.

Talen wrapped herself in shadow and followed.

Chapter Twenty-Two

Pratt set a brisk pace, and it didn't take long to see he was bound for the Madison building. Every couple of blocks he'd stop, check his surroundings, and listen. Could be caution, paranoia, or him sensing her presence. Talen didn't know. He didn't have one of those eyepieces like the Red Hand used back at Margaret's cabin, but she played it safe, keeping her distance and stepping out of sight when he stopped. It felt mighty fine to be in her element again.

No mistakes tonight.

As he rounded onto Madison, Pratt checked his watch, cursed, and quickened his pace.

She matched him, silent as the shadows that hid her.

He reached the building, yanked open the door, and hurried up the stairs. Talen waited, listening at the door until his footsteps had faded. She cracked the door enough to slip inside and closed it behind her, careful to not make a sound. She reached the stairs and stopped, waiting, still as a statue.

A door closed on the floor above her.

She crept up the stairs, watching the upper floor as it came into view. No one and nothing waited for her. She checked the landing before stepping on it, but found no wards or traps.

A single long hallway ran the length of the building, doors on either side all the way down. Nothing stirred, and the silence gave her pause. Even with the door closed, she ought to hear something. With the building empty, she should be able to hear him breathing or even his heartbeat echoing.

Nothing.

The hairs on the back of her neck stood on end, and her right hand drifted to her iron.

It could be he lived here and went straight to bed. That didn't fit though; after checking his watch, he'd hurried right along. He'd moved like a man late for an appointment, and not with a bed, not even if someone were in it and waiting.

She inched down the hallway, all her senses on edge.

Midway down, the fetid, coppery smell of old blood and leather reached her nose.

She drew both irons but kept them dark. She wrapped the shadows tighter and waited.

Her heart beat slow and steady.

One beat.

Two beats.

Three.

Beyond the steady thump of her heart, she could hear voices. Something distorted the sounds, making them too muffled to make out words. The back and forth told her Pratt wasn't talking with himself.

She crept down the long hall, each step slow and deliberate. She noted numbers on the doors and kept her back to the odd numbered side. She didn't even risk blinking as she moved, watching the doors across from her.

212

214

The voices grew louder, but still impossible to understand. Did she hear a third person? Hard to be sure. The smell of old blood grew strong enough that she could taste copper, and her stomach turned.

She gripped her irons tighter and kept moving.

216

218

The door lay just ahead. It stood apart from the others in the hall-way. They were all cedar planked, a frosted glass pane bearing the number and name of the business filling the top third. The last door, Pratt's, had been made from a single piece of old white oak, solid as iron. More than that, her skin tingled from the magic pouring off it from more than ten feet away.

She leveled both spell irons—still dark—at the door, right at chest level, and examined it. Intricate sigils, remarkably small, ringed the outside edge. She'd come across charmed doors before—enchanted to lock, or warded with protective magics, sometimes both. Never one of this sort though. The carving of the sigils alone would take months. Being a single piece of wood, one mistake meant starting over on a new piece. She had no notion what spells had been woven into it. A privacy charm had to be at work though; even this close she couldn't make out any words. There were sure to be wards too, and powerful ones, on a door like this.

She might not be able to make out the words, but the tone of the conversation came through clear as day. Someone was unhappy and seemed disinclined to accept the other party's explanation. If Pratt—or his boss—had put the warrant out on Margaret, the Red Hand failing to bring her in would be cause for discontent.

Talen crouched low on the far side of the doorway, back to the hallway's dead end. With luck, anyone coming out wouldn't even look her way. If they did, and they saw through her shadows, they wouldn't see her right away. It could buy her a second or two. That'd give her time to get at least two shots with each iron, maybe three.

She waited again, irons at the ready, each minute taking months to pass.

The pulsing, humming power from the door vanished abruptly, causing Talen to flinch back in surprise.

It opened and four men stepped into the hall. Each had a spell iron on their hip and leather gloves on their hands, the right, the dark red of old blood.

Talen took aim at the first and last men out.

Pratt cleared his throat. "Aren't you forgetting something?" he asked from inside the room.

"We'll get it done just fine without your accursed weapons," the last man said. "We never failed to bring in a bounty, and we ain't starting now."

"Suit yourself," Pratt said. "But I don't care about promises, only results. No more goddamned mistakes."

"We don't take to blasphemy," the Red Hand leader said. "I don't care who you are or how much you're paying."

The door closed on the man's face.

He spit at the door, turned, and then led the other three to the stairs.

Talen kept her irons aimed at the men as they continued down the hall.

"Pass the word," he said as they walked, never even glancing back. "I'll pay fifty dollars for anyone what brings me that witch's head."

So, the Red Hand knew she'd been helping Margaret. Before long, she'd have an official bounty on her head alongside Margaret's. It didn't matter none though; she'd become an outlaw the moment she crossed the Mississippi. The star in her pocket might've made her a stalker, but she'd been a Shadow Warden for centuries. Ain't no one could take that from her.

She didn't waste much worry on the Red Right Hand. They didn't need no bounty to want her dead. She did have to resist shooting the leader out of principle though. Fifty dollars was downright insulting.

Their heavy boots thudded down the stairs. Shortly thereafter, the front door slammed. Talen turned her attention back to the office and narrowed her eyes. Pratt hadn't reactivated the charm. Could it be a trap, or in his anger, had it slipped his mind?

Could I be that lucky?

"I hate dealing with those damned fanatics," Pratt said, his words clear as a bell.

He uncorked a bottle and poured himself a drink, a stiff one from the length of the pour, and by the smell, not a high-quality spirit.

"That's why I pay you so well, Mr. Pratt," Pratt said in a mocking, affected tone.

She stared at the door, putting pieces together, and considering what to do next. If she had the right of it, Pratt, or his boss, was seeding the country with them stones. The crafters would report back on who bought the stained charms, and then came the bounties. If they meant the Red Hand to be the ones collecting, setting the payout high and posting them well away would do it. She had to admit, someone had thought this out, and no mistake. It kept things tidy and technically legal.

Of course, she didn't know none of this for sure, and had no clue as to the why. And something this complicated had to have one hell of a why.

Perhaps Mr. Pratt could enlighten me.

She touched a fingertip to the wood. Nothing, not even the faintest vibration of magic. That meant no wards or charms, unless whoever crafted the door also knew a charm that masked other charms. She brought that line of thinking to a stop, right quick. No time for second guessing choices she hadn't made yet.

She turned her attention to the mundane aspects of the door. She'd been right: solid white oak, and well-aged at that. She might be able to kick it in without breaking her leg, but it'd take a while. Not likely Pratt would patiently wait for her to get inside.

Blowing it off its hinges seemed the surest bet and had a certain appeal to it. It'd cause one hell of a ruckus, but with luck, the late hour meant no one would hear.

She closed her eyes and listened, drawing a mental map from the sounds.

Pratt paced in a small circle, pausing only to drink some of his turpentine. The pitch of his echoing footsteps gave her an idea as to the size of the room. Something—several somethings—were against the wall, bulky and soft based on how they absorbed sound. Wood crates, if she had to guess.

Pratt walked to a window. He let out a long sigh and took another swallow of rotgut. He had his back to her, and like as not, the glass in his dominant hand.

Ain't like to get any prettier than that.

She drew in a breath and made to pour magic into her irons when her gaze settled on the doorknob again.

No. There ain't no way in all the nine hells.

She holstered her left-hand iron and tried the doorknob, turning it real slow.

Not locked.

She nudged the door open, just enough to clear the bolt. To her further amazement, the hinges were well oiled and didn't make a sound.

I'll be damned.

She redrew her left-hand iron and let the magic flow, igniting both it and its twin with spell fire.

She kicked the door wide and took aim at Pratt's back.

In the heartbeat it took for the door to hit the wall, she took in the room.

Pratt was alone, and he stood at a tall window near one end of the long, narrow room. Two wooden crates were set against the wall opposite where he stood. He carried no arms, but what looked to be a flechette rifle leaned against the wall, a foot from where he stood.

"You so much as twitch and I'll paint that window with your insides," she said.

Pratt didn't move, he just stood there, seemingly unperturbed. His heart wasn't racing, he breathed slow and easy. Hell, he hadn't even flinched when the door smacked the wall.

That both impressed and worried Talen. She'd hoped for a brainless, if muscled, henchman. Pratt had brains and battlefield experience.

She tightened the grip on her irons and focused her attention on his shoulders, ready to drop him at the first sudden movement.

"I presume you're the elf that's been such a pain in my ass," Pratt said. "Shame you didn't arrive sooner. I had some friends here mighty eager to make your acquaintance."

"I saw them. Don't fret none. I'm sure we'll cross paths soon enough. I'll send them to meet those I left to rot in the Dakota Territory."

"Seeing as I'm still breathing," he said, his tone calm, "I take it you want something from me?"

Yeah, to blow a hole clean through you and bury you with your Red Hand lackeys.

"I do. Answers."

"Then I propose a trade. I'm curious about a few things myself."

He was playing for time, and she knew it. No way were both of them walking away from this, but maybe she could learn something before the shooting started. He might have experience, but so did she.

"All right then."

"May I turn around? It seems terribly rude not to talk face-to-face."

His smug confidence just made her want to shoot him more, which was, of course, his intention. Get her riled up, angry or nervous, and give him an opening. The lingering scent of blood-soaked leather wasn't helping.

"That suits me just fine. And keep your hands where I can see them."

"Of course," he said, far too calmly. "I'll ask first. Why would you risk a rather prolific career as a stalker to help some gimpy, half-breed widow? Certainly not out of fondness for humans. Is it pity? Or do you have a liking for human women?"

She didn't take the bait. "I hunt stained. We both know she ain't one. So, here's my question: what do you want with bounty crystals from non-stained?"

He straightened ever so slightly. "So, she didn't appear stained to you? How interesting. We never considered the effect might not work on elves. Not as though we could test that though. Your kind aren't exactly cooperative when it comes to that."

"That ain't an answer," Talen said.

"No, it isn't," he said. "But I'm afraid the answer is what we call proprietary information."

Talen opened her mouth, but before she could speak, he spun and hurled his glass at her. He moved faster than she would've expected a human could.

She dodged the glass easy enough, though some of the whiskey splashed her face, but he hadn't meant it to do any damage. It did, however, serve to give him time to move and caused her aim to drift. She compensated and pulled the trigger on her left-hand iron. A blast of force blew the window—and the wall around it—out into the street.

Pratt dived and rolled to one side, grabbing the rifle as he tumbled.

He came up on one knee and fired.

Talen just managed to pivot before a writhing black mass belched from the rifle. It missed her by less than an inch and slammed into the far wall, turning the brick into powdery ash.

Before she could even consider what the hell had just happened, he fired again. And again, and again.

She tumbled back out the door and into the hall. As soon as she was clear, she doused her irons, wrapped herself in shadow, and went prone.

For half a heartbeat, all was quiet. The whole world shrank to just Talen, the falling ash, the adrenaline rush, and the overwhelming smell of whiskey.

Sections of the wall, a foot across, vaporized above her.

She rolled away from the door to the end of the hallway, keeping low as more of the wall turned to ash.

She lost count of how many times he fired, but it seemed like a lot. She hoped that rifle didn't have many shots left.

When the shooting finally stopped, she held her breath and listened.

He got to his feet, and though the holes gave her a clear view into the room, she couldn't see him. She waited for some snide comment or curse, but none came. He must've fought against elves before and knew it'd give away his position.

It seemed her luck had reached its limit.

She didn't dare move, not even to brush away stray ash that fell on her. However, she did finally let herself breathe. The foul stench of corruption hit her like a runaway stage. It near reached down her throat and tried to turn her stomach inside out.

Could that thing be some kind of stained spell iron?

Pratt took a couple steps back, his footsteps light. So light, they'd be silent to human ears.

Got you, you son of a bitch.

Talen vaulted through an opening in the wall. As she cleared the partition, she spotted Pratt. His eyes were down, focused on the task of inserting something into the rear of the rifle. She hit the floor in a roll, released the shadows, poured power into her irons, and fired both barrels.

A kinetic blast caught his left thigh. His leg snapped and twisted back on itself, dislocating the hip with a wet pop. At the same time, the arctic charge hit the right leg, sheathing it and the floor in several inches of ice.

Pratt twisted and fell forward. The rifle slipped from his hands as his right knee snapped from the torsion. He flailed and screamed as he fought like hell to get himself upright.

Talen kicked the rifle away and rolled the cylinders of her irons.

Pratt grunted, hefted himself upright, and produced a Peacemaker from seemingly nowhere.

"Shit," she said and made to turn away, putting her ensorcelled coat between the coming hail of fire and her body.

He fanned the shooter at her, which, apart from being hard on the piece, didn't allow for much accuracy. But he was so close it didn't much matter.

A couple of shots hit the brick wall behind her, a couple more smacked against her coat and bounced off.

One grazed her leg, a burning bug bite just above her knee.

The last one got lucky, tearing into and through the outside edge of her abdomen.

Thanks to the adrenaline, there was almost no pain, just a dull, warm thud that made her wobble a bit, about like a hard punch to the side. On reflex, she grabbed at her side and fired her right-hand iron at his chest.

The kinetic spell crushed his rib cage and toppled him back so hard, his frozen leg broke from the ice. But not before his spine snapped.

He fell to the floor, gasping wetly.

More than a little delight surged through Talen. Still gripping her side, she holstered her iron, drew her knife, and knelt over him, blade to his throat.

"Answer my question," she said through gritted teeth, "and I'll end it quick. Otherwise, I let you go slow. Drowning on your own lifeblood ain't pleasant, Pratt."

Part of her really wanted him not to answer.

He coughed blood and stared at her with unbridled hatred. "I'm... sorry," he gasped.

"You're gonna need to be more specific."

He could only gasp, so each word took its own shallow breath. "I... won't... see... your kind... wiped... away..."

He tried to spit at her but only spattered his own face.

Talen stood, sheathed her knife, and stepped back. She watched him for a few moments. That was all the time it took for her to become disgusted and angry at herself for delighting in the pain and misery of another.

She put a boot to his chest and crushed his heart. It might've been better and quicker than he deserved, but she wasn't ready to become a full monster just yet. She also didn't have the time to watch him die.

His labored breathing stopped, and she set to ransacking the room. She didn't know how long she had before the adrenaline rush faded and the pain really hit her, but it wasn't long. There was also the risk of bleeding out.

She ripped the top off the first crate and found six rifles, each a match to the one he'd fired at her. Half a dozen bounty crystals, all full, sat in the straw beneath the rifles.

Her heart near turned to ice when it dawned on her.

"Ammunition."

They'd done made stained weapons—something so foul even the Red Right Hand wouldn't touch them. The human skill at reaching new lows was almost impressive.

She tore open the other crate. It held the same as the first.

The world spun, and she had to brace against the wall.

Never once had she considered what happened to the crystals after turning them in. She'd assumed, somehow, they got purged and reused. Or barring that, destroyed. After all, that's what elves would've done.

I was so naïve.

How many hundreds had she filled over the years?

A fiery rage filled her. It threatened to burst out and reduce the city to ash. The darkness in her howled to set the city alight, to burn all the wretched inhabitants. No, they weren't all Pratt, but they were all poisoning the land and the lake. They were all defiling the natural beauty without even pausing to think about it.

They actually see it as progress.

But, she reminded herself, that would make her the monster they said she was. While part of her didn't care, more of her did.

After a long moment, and a considerable effort of will, she brought the fury under control. There was work to do and not much time. The police could be along any minute. Hell, even if no one had seen the fight, they'd notice the blown-out window or debris in the street.

She straightened and winced at the sharp stab of pain at her side.

"Of course, it won't matter none if I bleed out first."

Gritting her teeth, she bent to check the wound. The bullet went straight through and looked to have missed anything vital. It bled but slow and steady. There was time, though not much.

When she pressed on the wound to slow the bleeding, a wave of near blinding pain slammed through her. Every muscle tensed hard, and she damn near passed out.

When her vision cleared, and she was able to breathe again, she glanced around for anything that might buy her more time. She spotted a makeshift bedroom, little more than a cot and a small table, at the far end of the office. She tore a length of blanket and tied it tight around her midsection. It kept her from taking too deep a breath —which wasn't entirely a bad thing—but it should serve long enough to get back to the Cumulus. She grabbed the bottle of whiskey and used it to wash the blood from her left hand. No way would she handle either of her irons with bloodied hands.

Talen spotted a haversack on a desk near the cot and rifled through it. It held a mess of papers, a book, and a box she recognized as the stone sample case. Next, she went through the desk drawers, shoving any papers she found into the satchel without even looking them over. She could do that when death wasn't standing at her shoulder. After adding the bounty crystals from the crates, she closed the bag and slung it over her shoulder.

She checked her irons and the spare charges in her pockets. Too bad she'd told Wilfred not to include fire charges. It would've been worth the risk to the building to slag the rifles.

Nothing for it. She'd just have to make do with what she had.

Talen rotated the cylinders and fired and then rotated and fired again. The arctic magic turned the crates into blocks of ice.

Sure hope this works.

Stepping back, she rotated her cylinders to the force charges, covered her face with the sleeve of her coat, and fired. The crates shattered into icy chunks: crates, rifles, and all. She fired again and again, emptying her irons, and pulverizing the chunks into smaller and smaller bits.

After reloading, she holstered her irons. On her way to the door, she grabbed the rifle Pratt had used, wrapped herself in shadows, and left.

Each step down the stairs sent a fresh wave of sharp pain through her, almost breaking her concentration and collapsing her veil. More than once, her knees buckled, but she caught herself. Leaning hard on the railing, she made it to the ground floor, and onto the street, still in shadow. The empty road seemed even longer and darker than it had on the way here. Powered by a sheer refusal to die in this city, she began the long trek back to the shore, hoping like hell she remembered the way.

Time and distance lost all meaning. She kept herself focused on taking the next step and then the next. She passed a few police, but none were hurrying off in the direction she'd come. She didn't imagine that would last. She tried to quicken her steps but had no idea if she accomplished it or not. A bone-deep cold settled over her and set her to shivering.

After what felt like weeks, the lake came into view, if distantly. Her head swam, and everything seemed to get darker. Part of her wanted to embrace the cold and darkness. Beyond it, maybe her mother and sisters waited for her in a place without pain.

The outline of the Cumulus's gas bladder was visible now, but it might as well have been on the other side of the world. She wanted to rest, to sleep and never wake. That noiseless, peaceful dark with the promise of no more pain or worry called to her in soft, welcoming whispers.

A building slammed into her, or she into it, she couldn't be sure. Gasping for breath, she slid to the ground. The strength and will to continue had left her, and darkness rose to meet her like an old friend.

"Good lord," someone said.

She knew the voice but couldn't place it, and her eyes wouldn't open. It didn't matter. She was done. No one could do anything more to her or take anything else from her.

"Talen, don't you leave me," Wilfred said. "You hear me? Don't you dare give up!"

With the sound of his voice came a flood of memories. She remembered countless nights of passionate lovemaking and gentle embraces, a thousand kisses, and hours spent in comfortable silence.

And she remembered a promise made to a sister.

She opened her eyes. "Help me."

"I got you, *sans shulla.*" He lifted her from the ground.

Her cheek fell against his broad, warm chest, and the steady beat of his strong heart pushed back the rising darkness.

Chapter Twenty-Three

Talen had no sense of the world around her, slipping in and out of awareness, if not actual consciousness. One moment, Wilfred carried her through a darkening city. The next, she lay on a table, fighting Draven and Margaret as they tried to pry the stained rifle from her hands.

"Let it go," Draven said softly. "We can't get to your side with you holding to it."

"Dangerous," Talen said. "Don't touch."

"As you say. We won't handle it; just turn it loose."

Talen did and slipped away again.

Searing pain jerked her back to consciousness and she screamed.

Wilfred and Margaret struggled to hold her as Draven pressed a glowing red piece of steel to her side a second time.

Talen cried out again and gritted her teeth so hard she thought they might crack.

"Keep her still!" Draven bellowed. "I don't want to sear the good flesh."

"We're trying." Wilfred leaned on Talen with all his weight.

Draven lifted the smoking metal from Talen's side. The pain didn't vanish entirely, but the difference was so massive, it might as well have. The sudden disappearance of an agony that had been all-consuming left Talen feeling weightless. It seemed the whole world had simply gone away, and she floated in a vast, delightful, euphoric nothingness.

"That's one side done. Turn her over, easy now."

Talen tried to hold to the bliss as long as she could, knowing that in moments she'd come crashing down to the cold, hard rocks below.

Wilfred helped her roll onto her side.

She gripped the wooden table, priming herself for what came next.

"You ready?" Draven asked.

Talen nodded.

She wasn't ready.

Where there had been nothing, now there was only pain. A renewed agony that burned but didn't consume her. It would never consume her.

Talen didn't bother fighting against it. She screamed. A section of the table broke away in her hand, and this time, when Draven lifted the cauterizing brand, she did pass out.

She woke to find Margaret applying a damp cloth to her face. Her body tingled numbly, as if her nerves had been exhausted and now could only just acknowledge the world around her indifferently.

"Welcome back. Just relax. Draven got the wound closed but said you lost a lot of blood."

"We have to leave the city," Talen said, her throat raw and burning. Her voice little more than a dry rasp.

Margaret handed her a cup of water.

Never had water, or anything else, tasted so sweet. Talen gulped it down, coughing up the last half, and the pain in her side flared.

"Easy." Margaret took the cup away.

"We need to go, right now. Tell Draven we need to leave Chicago."

"We did," Margaret said. "Two days ago."

It took a moment for Talen's mind to comprehend and another couple to believe it. "Two days?"

Margaret nodded. "Draven said you'd made it through the worst, but I confess, I worried something terrible." She forced a smile and let out a breath. "But you pulled through."

"Where are we?"

"Near Wisconsin. Draven said you'd want to heal and would need a safe place full of life to do it. We're on an island in the lake, a couple hundred miles from Chicago."

The weight of the world lifted from her, and Talen took a deep breath. Half a heartbeat later, she put the burden to one side and focused on what had to be done.

"Help me up."

Margaret hesitated for a second before taking Talen's hand and helping her upright.

Talen's side screamed in protest, and her head swam, but after a moment, the world stopped spinning. She looked around, not recognizing the room. There were a couple low tables, cabinets, and a brazier—now cold ash—with half a dozen metal rods in it.

"We still on the Cumulus?" Talen asked.

Margaret nodded. "Draven calls it the hospital, though she admits to not being any kind of doctor."

"Where is she? And Wilfred?"

"Draven is where she always is: on the bridge. I sent Wilfred to bed a few hours ago. We've been taking turns staying with you."

Talen reached over, took Margaret's hand, and squeezed. "Thank you."

Margaret smiled and squeezed back. "Of course."

Talen glanced around again but didn't see any windows. "Is it day or night?"

"Nearly morning. I think it's an hour or two off yet."

"Where's the rifle you and Draven took off me?"

"She put it in the armory," Margaret said. "No one has touched it since. What is it?"

"Something terrible. We need to get Wilfred and Draven."

"I'll get them." Margaret turned to go.

"I'm coming too," Talen said, getting to her feet. "I've been on my back long enough." The room shifted, and she had to steady herself on the table.

"I don't think you should be out of bed yet," Margaret said, rushing back to her side.

"I'll be okay. I'm weak and need to heal, but I ain't going to fall over dead." The room settled into place, and Talen could finally stand up without feeling like she'd fall over dead.

"I'll call Draven down, and she can collect Wilfred on the way." Margaret went to the speaking tube on the wall. "Draven?"

"Is she awake?" Draven's voice asked.

"She is, and she's trying to leave. Can you please get Wilfred and come down?"

"On my way. And tell her if she tries to go anywhere, I'll drag her back and tie her ass down."

Talen chuckled, but the pain in her side turned it into a grunt.

Margaret looked to her, but Talen held up a hand. "I think you changed her mind," she said into the tube.

"Good. We'll be right down."

Margaret brought Talen a fresh cup of water and a bowl filled with leaves and grasses. "I wasn't sure what you liked, so I tried to pick a variety."

Talen's heart twitched as she accepted the bowl. It'd been a long time since anyone looked out for her. She set the bowl aside and gave Margaret a long hug.

She hugged back, careful to avoid Talen's wounded side.

Talen ate and sighed, or it could've been a moan. The leaves were fresh and clean, the grass wild and full of life. After the first swallow, she felt a little better.

A few minutes later, Wilfred and Draven came in through the room's only door.

"You scared near ten years off my life." Wilfred went to her and started to lift his arms but hesitated. "And I ain't got many to spare no more."

Talen pulled him into a hug, biting back the pain. "If you hadn't found me, I'd have died on that street."

"The instant we got onboard, he insisted on going after you," Margaret said.

"I said I'd escort Margaret to the ship. Never said I wouldn't leave once I got there."

"*Sans shulla*," Talen whispered and kissed his cheek. She turned to Draven and nodded. "And I reckon you kept me from dying on the table."

Draven shrugged. "I just stuck you with a hot brand. You got plenty healing left to do."

"I'll be getting to it right soon. But I got things you need to hear. Where's the bag I had with me?"

Wilfred grabbed it from under the table and set it beside her.

She told them everything, every detail she could remember.

All three stared at her.

"Gaia's everlasting teat," Draven said. "You don't do by half, do you?"

"Explains why you didn't want us touching that thing," Wilfred said.

Margaret looked away and opened her mouth.

"Don't you dare apologize. This ain't on you."

"If my leg—"

"We might all be dead," Talen said. "I don't know as more guns would've helped none. I'm damn sure I couldn't have hid the three of us in that hallway."

Margaret shrugged. "I suppose, but I'm the reason any of you are involved at all."

"Reckon you're right." Wilfred nodded. "Wouldn't know nothing about this neither. Lord only knows how many other folk would've found themselves in the same spot as you before anyone reasoned the truth out."

"If they ever did," Talen said. "Don't matter how we got here. We're in this together, and we're all going to see it through." She glanced at Draven, not wanting to volunteer the dwarf.

She lifted her bare chin. "I'm in, as well. They might not be looking to use those guns on my kind yet, but sooner or later someone will find an excuse."

"So, what do we do?" Margaret asked.

"Chicago wasn't the factory," Talen said. She emptied the contents of the bag on the table. "We need to go through these and see if we can learn where they're making them stones."

"And wipe it off the map, yeah?" Draven asked.

"And then some," Talen said.

"I'll go through them," Margaret said, picking up the papers. "I handled all the books for our shop. I'm used to paperwork."

"While she's doing that, could you look over the rifle?" Talen asked Wilfred.

"I can and will."

"Don't touch it with bare skin," she said. "I got no idea if—"

He arched an eyebrow and pinned her in place with a look. "You telling me my craft now?"

"Never. See if you can figure out how the damn thing works, and if there's any way to protect against it." She handed the sample case to Draven.

"What's this?" She took the case and opened it.

"Don't touch them neither. That's a sampling of the stones."

"And what do you want me to do with it?"

"You think seeing them would change any dwarven minds? If they see that humans aren't just turning stained, they're causing it—of a sort—and experimenting with dark magic, might they rethink their alliance?"

"Aye, they might at that. Not sure it would sway the Dolomite, but it might some of those under him. It sure as hell will be of interest to the Granite Lord though." She looked at Wilfred and Margaret and then back to Talen. "I think they have things well in hand and that it's time for you to do some healing."

Talen shook her head. "I'm fine for now. I—"

"Don't argue," Wilfred said, giving her a look. "Go."

Talen turned to Margaret but found a look to match Wilfred's.

"I'll keep watch over you," Draven said, patting the dwarven pistols on her hips.

Talen opened her mouth.

"You've done enough," Margaret said, as if reading her mind. "It's like you said back in the city." Her mouth turned up at one side and she narrowed her eyes. "You'd be more hindrance than help. We need you healed up and ready for whatever comes next."

"Damn," Wilfred said through a chuckle. "I've been waiting years to use her words against her, and here you done beat me to it."

Margaret winked. "Next one is yours."

Talen sighed, shook her head, and turned to Draven. "Let's get the horses out as well. Let them graze and exercise."

"If you want some time with Gaoth, just say so," Wilfred said.

She smiled, shook her head, and motioned for Draven to lead the way. She did, and offered to help Talen down the stairs. Talen refused but changed her mind when her legs nearly gave out after the first step. She put a hand on the dwarf's broad shoulder, and it felt like leaning on a boulder.

When Gaoth saw her, he bobbed his head and chuffed, shifting about in his stall.

She hugged his neck and stroked his mane. "I missed you, too," she whispered.

Draven took Joseph and Elise's leads. Talen, despite Draven's protest and her injured side, pulled herself up onto Gaoth's back and rode him out. She had to lay flat against him—which hurt like nine kinds of hell— to avoid the beams, but she didn't care. It felt damned good to be with him again.

Outside, the eastern horizon showed the first hints of dawn. Talen looked around the small island. The grass soft and thick, the trees large. If she climbed one, she could probably see one side of the island from the other.

The lake, a placid dark blue, reached out to the horizon. Nothing and no one for as far as she could see. She slid off Gaoth and let him graze. She closed her eyes and took a deep breath. After the foul city air, it felt like breathing for the first time. Birds sang in the trees and small animals moved through the brush. The only better place to heal would've been home, under her mother's care.

Talen started to strip down, but found she needed help. Thankfully, dwarves had no more shame about nudity than elves. Draven helped her out of her clothes and then to the water.

The moment she stepped into the water, some of the pain and a lot of her tension faded. Though cold, the lake felt alive and most importantly, clean. Talen, on the other hand, did not.

She let out a sigh as she settled onto the soft sand, her body half submerged in the cold water. Even as she began the healing prayer, and though the sun hadn't risen, staggering amounts of energy flowed to her. She drew it in, humbled as ever by the generosity, and felt an unfamiliar power. She opened her eyes and looked at Draven.

"Use it to replace your lost blood," Draven whispered. "That's all I ask in return."

Talen swallowed and nodded. You didn't say no to a gift like that. She closed her eyes, sinking into the incantation with a grateful heart.

Surrounded by life and its compassion, Talen set to work healing. She examined the gunshot wound, surprised to find she hadn't healed in the past two days. Not at all. While she didn't expect much, she should've at least started to mend.

How close to death had she been? How close was she still?

She pushed the question aside and set to work, starting at the deepest part of the wound, knitting the flesh back together.

It resisted her.

The shock nearly brought her out of the trance. Her body had never resisted healing before. She hadn't even known such a thing could happen. Even wounds suffered at the hands of a stained didn't resist curing magic.

She narrowed her focus, examining the injury in more detail. She found traces of something at the edges of her wound, infinitesimal but unmistakable. Corruption.

Her mind went first to her soul. Had the darkness finally won out and started to manifest?

No.

She might have dark thoughts and done terrible things, but she'd never invited dark magic into her. It couldn't have been the stained rifle. She hadn't been hit. Besides, that whole ordeal had happened before Pratt shot her.

A shiver ran down her spine, and her heart nearly stopped.

Could Pratt have coated his bullets in dark magic? Seemed a small step from the stones.

Fear found its way through the serenity of the prayer and nibbled at her guts. With effort, she pushed the notion aside and refocused, this time on excising the foulness.

She had no idea how much time passed when she finally gave up. Nothing worked. No matter how much power she drew on or how fine an edge she made of it, the darkness resisted.

Even the flesh around the corruption proved impervious to her efforts. It had spread so far that even if she cut away the healthy flesh around, what she'd have to remove would likely kill her. Worse still, the corruption seemed to be growing. Could it actually be feeding on the healing magic?

The fear grew, wrapping itself around her insides and twisting them into knots. In desperation, she tried again and again, but every effort failed, except in proving her dread well-founded. The corruption did grow as she worked against it and only slowed when she stopped.

Panic set in.

Hope drained away.

What if she couldn't stop it? Would it consume her, make her into a true monster and servant of the darkness?

She couldn't let that happen. A stained Shadow Warden would be a terror this world hadn't seen. Draven might get lucky and put her down, but Wilfred and Margaret would die, and die at her hands.

But what could she do? She felt like a child again, small and helpless. Over the centuries she'd been so confident. No matter the opponent, she'd always found a way through. This path had only one destination, and she couldn't let herself reach it.

Draven had to end her now, stop her before she became the monster.

Part of her screamed that these thoughts were only the dark infestation's whispers. Another part, more persuasive, said she was only admitting to a truth she'd long denied. She'd known one day it would end like this. Hadn't she?

She pushed back. All the anger and grief she'd been carrying now served to feed what meant to destroy her. She would fail, the persuasive darkness whispered. The Red Hand would claim Margaret, likely killing Wilfred and Draven in the process. Her people would vanish, as would the Lakota and countless other nations. She'd become a raving monster, finally claiming the vengeance so long denied her. The allure of vengeance, of a reckoning, intoxicated her.

Stop it! It's all lies!

She wanted to fight, tried to, but the maelstrom of hopelessness threatened to drown her. She could no sooner stop the darkness than she could the rain. Her future held nothing but more pain, more loss, more death, and a monster's skin.

The shame, guilt, and self-loathing rose and seized her.

End it now. That's the only option. Margaret and Wilfred will understand.

No, they won't!

With one last effort of will, she drove it all from her mind: the doubt and fear, the hopelessness and dread. She dug for, and then clung to, the love she felt for her lost mother and sisters, for Margaret, Wilfred, even for Draven.

Mother, I need you now as never before. This corruption is not the dark magic we fought before. This is new, stronger, and I can't beat it. My greatest fear has come to pass. I can feel the corruption inside me, devouring me. I need you. I know I've let sorrow and anger drive me, but I need you now. Please, help me. Show me a path, and I will follow. Please, I can't do this alone!

Silence.

Hope evaporated, and the dark storm surged forward to swallow her.

And something stopped it. Something as powerful and resolute as time itself.

She had only an instant to wonder before power, more than she'd ever felt, flowed into her from all around. The immensity of it took her breath away. It took a moment for her to realize the source. The lake, not the countless lifeforms that called it home, but the lake itself. She knew natural formations—mountains, oceans, forests—could develop a resident elemental, but she'd never encountered one before.

Unwelcome corruption, it said, but used no words. *Invasion of inviolate protector.*

The mere impression of the magnificent entity nearly overwhelmed her. The awe-inspiring power grew, and grew, and kept growing. Only then did Talen realize what she'd sensed before hadn't been the elemental itself, just its presence, its aura. Its inconceivable power flowed not just into her, but through her. In the face of such a being, she felt so very small, but—quite strangely—not at all insignificant.

The light and life surging through her surrounded the darkness and built an intricate lattice work around it. She twisted in pain—undefinable and indescribable in its intensity—as the crystalline pattern grew, capturing and binding the foulness.

It's making a damned bounty crystal.

She'd never known where they'd come from. They were relatively new, less than a century old. Prior to their creation, there was no drawing out the dark magic, only destroying the stained. The Shadow Wardens had been created specifically for this dangerous task.

The crystals were nothing short of a miracle, even to the eldar. But someone should've questioned how the humans had created, or discovered, such a marvel. She doubted any human could bind an elemental, but maybe one had found a way to manipulate them.

She tried to ask but had no notion as to how. Elementals weren't like any mortal being. They experienced time not in centuries or even millennia, but epochs. To the most powerful of them, the rise and fall of mountains passed as seasons did to her.

Another spike of intense, blinding pain tore her from her ruminations. The incantation—which should've collapsed when her focus faltered—didn't even waver. The elemental must've been holding it together for her. The ancient being, either unconcerned or unaware of Talen's agony, continued its work. She could feel the crystal forming inside her, and her body healing around it.

Then, she was whole again, more than whole actually.

After a moment, she managed to gather her wits. She did her best to express profuse and sincere gratitude. Then she asked, or tried to, why it had helped her. Elementals did, on rare occasions, offer aid but never so focused an effort, and never one so powerful.

Time passed, and she presumed her attempt had failed.

Then it answered, clearly, as if it had spoken the words: *a mother's request.*

Chapter Twenty-Four

When the elemental withdrew, Talen ended her prayer and opened her eyes. The sun hung directly overhead. She looked down at her body. No trace of the scarred flesh from Draven's searing remained, just a single facet of the crystal visible in its place. The flesh, warm to the touch, had returned to a normal, healthy brown. She touched the facet and found the crystal as warm as the flesh around it.

Ain't this just the damnedest thing?

She got to her feet, hesitant and slow at first, but didn't feel a bit of pain or tightness, not even an ache. In fact, she felt more rested and energized than she had in years. As she moved, she could feel that her muscles had shifted around the crystal. It felt damn strange, but oddly comforting at the same time.

She turned to find Draven staring in silent, unmasked awe.

"You drew out one of the old ones," she said.

"What? No," Talen said. "It ain't like that. It just answered a call for help is all."

"Old ones don't do that. How did you get it to answer you?"

Talen looked away, unsure how much to share. Prayers, including the healing sort, were exceedingly personal.

"Somehow, my wound had corruption in it," Talen said. "I reckon Pratt had bullets crafted like the stones. I tried to remove it, but nothing worked. More I did, the stronger it got. I didn't know what to do. I feared it might turn me stained, so I asked for help, and the elemental answered." She touched the facet. "It made this to trap the corruption."

Draven's face went slack, and her eyes widened. "An old one answered your plea. Do you realize how rare that is?"

"Dwarves always knew elementals better than us. I never heard of old ones before now. They some sort of king?"

"Closer to a god," Draven said. "They were there when the world got forged. One of them helped you, saved you. It had to be for a reason." She went to one knee, putting her fist to her heart, and bowed her head. "Through fire or rain, joy or pain, I'll fight by your side for as long as you'll have me."

Talen opened her mouth to reply but couldn't think of what to say. She didn't know what that oath precisely meant, but she could guess. "That ain't necessary, you already said—"

Draven stood. "You misunderstand. I'm asking you, entreating even. It might be once in a millennium that an old one even communicates to a mortal, much less bestows a gift on one. To walk, fight, or even die beside one so blessed..." She shook her head. "There's no greater honor in life."

Talen's head spun. She opened her mouth to protest but decided against it. She damn sure wasn't a hero, but that elemental had given her a great gift. If it came with a cost, she'd pay. If it came with a purpose, well, having a purpose again sounded mighty fine. She had her doubts, but they were hers alone.

She held out her hand to Draven. "It'd be my honor to have you by my side and call you friend."

Draven accepted the gesture, gripping tight and smiling.

After several moments, Talen glanced down and then back up. "I need the hand back to get dressed."

Draven chuckled and let go. "Aye, sorry about that. This is new to me."

"Me too," Talen said, picking up her trousers.

As she dressed, her mind churned something fierce. How had her mother convinced an ancient elemental to come to her aid? What exactly waited beyond the veil of death? Her people had stories of course, but they were just that, stories. They could speak with the dead—their own mothers anyway—but as far as she knew, no mother had ever revealed anything of the world beyond.

"There've been three dwarven heroes that have spoken with and been bestowed a gift by an old one," Draven said. "Three, in all our history."

"How many elves?" Talen pulled on her coat.

"None I ever heard of." Draven's brow furrowed. "How do you not know about the old ones? I thought your people got their iron and steel from elementals."

"We do, minor ones," Talen said. "But our knowledge of even them ain't nothing compared to yours."

Draven nodded. "When there's time, and if you'll permit me, I'll tell you all you care to know."

"I'd like that."

Now dressed, she checked on Gaoth, Joseph, and Elise. The horses were content, so she let them enjoy the open air a while longer. Gaoth would lead the others back inside if anything happened.

Talen and Draven returned to the ship. They found Wilfred and Margaret in the galley, both going over the papers.

"And here's another one." Margaret pointed to a spot on the page in front of her.

"What's the date?" Wilfred made a note on a page with a pencil.

"Two months ago. How many is that?"

"Eleven."

"Eleven what?" Talen asked.

Wilfred smiled wide. "You're looking a mite better."

Margaret looked up from her papers. "I'll say." She looked out the window furrowed her brow. "How long has it been?"

"It's about noon," Talen said.

"That's all?" Margaret rubbed her eyes then leaned back and stretched. "I figured you'd be at it all day."

"I had some, uh, unexpected help."

Draven didn't say anything. She just cast a glance at Talen and chuckled.

Wilfred narrowed his eyes. "There's something more to the telling."

"So, eleven what?" Talen asked Margaret.

Wilfred's eyebrows lifted. "Okay, another time then?"

"Tell her about the rifle," Margaret said to Wilfred.

He leaned back and folded his hands. "It ain't magic. Least not wholly so."

Talen and Draven exchanged a look.

Draven furrowed her brow. "What the hell does that mean?"

"Ain't something either magic or not?" Talen asked.

Wilfred chuckled. "Yeah, well, it's sort of been a week of shattered assumptions, ain't it? The crystals are magic, and no mistake. They are, to a one, full bounty crystals and where they fit into the rifle is in fact magic, but that's about it."

"Just the one piece?" Talen asked.

"Oh, it gets better," Wilfred said. "You ain't got to be a caster to make it work."

"Every charm needs magic to power it," Talen said. "And you got to be a caster to do it."

"Outside magic, you mean."

Talen narrowed her eyes and then it came to her. "It uses the magic in the goddamned crystal."

"Got it in one," he said, pointing at Talen. "Near as I can figure, the rifle takes the power from the crystal and changes it into, well, something. I don't rightly know what. Damnedest part is, I don't think it shoots what it makes."

"What the hell does it do with it then?" Talen asked.

"No idea," he said. "But it ain't connected to the barrel. It feeds into some sort of mechanism, and I ain't no engineer or gunsmith."

"Well, I'm both," Draven said. "I'll take a look at the thing and see if I can figure out the workings of it."

"Sort of hoping you'd say that." Wilfred pointed to the corner. "It's right over there, with my gloves."

Draven collected the rifle and set it on another table. After taking some tools from her belt, she started breaking the weapon down.

"Is that safe?" Talen asked no one in particular.

"Pretty sure I already know what it is," Draven said, removing a plate from the side of weapon. "But I aim to make sure."

Talen watched the dwarf work for a minute, impressed at her dexterity, despite the gloves and large fingers. "How long you reckon—"

"Those thieving sons of bitches!" Draven slammed a tool on the table. "I knew it."

"What?" Talen asked.

"It's a damned rail gun!"

"What's a rail gun?" Margaret asked.

"Dwarven rifle," Talen said.

"Powderless," Draven said. "And no moving parts, save for the trigger."

"How is that possible?" Margaret asked.

"You know how a magnet attracts metal?" Draven asked.

"Sure," Margaret said. "Ferrous metals anyway."

Draven nodded. "Imagine lining a barrel with magnets you can switch on and off. Power them up and down just right, and you can shoot a solid slug of iron alloy with more power than a cannon." She turned the rifle and pointed to some component. "This here connects the crystal socket to the magnetic control. I'd bet my mother's beard, if she still had one, that the bastards based this design on our rifles."

Talen ran a hand through her hair. "I'm confused. I saw it shoot dark magic, smelled the corruption after, too."

Draven shrugged. "Well, I'll need Wilfred's help to know for sure, but I suspect the crystal powers the rifle and makes the ammunition."

"So, it ain't quite a spell iron," Talen said. "And ain't quite a mundane shooter. Sort of a cross between the two?"

Draven nodded. "I suspect so."

"And since it don't need no outside magic," Wilfred said, "anyone can shoot it."

"And if you ain't channeling magic, you won't never get tired," Talen said.

"Not from the shooting anyhow," Wilfred said.

"What have you got to drink?" Talen asked Draven.

Draven gestured at a cupboard. "Whiskey."

Talen fetched the bottle, uncorked it, and took a long pull. The liquor slid down her gullet like burning silk, settling in her belly like a welcome campfire on a cold, rainy night. It beat the hell out of the rotgut she'd gotten used to on her travels. She took another drink.

"You mind?" Wilfred asked.

She passed him the bottle.

A weapon like that would change everything. No cocking between shots, no rotating to a fresh chamber, and shoot the thing as fast as you can pull the trigger. How many shots had Pratt got off before he had to reload? A dozen? They'd come so quick she couldn't keep track. It could've been twice that many. No loading single bullets like a repeater. Just swap out the crystal and you got another dozen shots. She let out a breath. The only reason Pratt hadn't killed her was he didn't have a fresh crystal at hand. Like as not, without that pause she never could've taken him down.

She shuddered, imagining armies of soldiers with those things, turning everything in their path to ash. Her coat might stop a single shot, maybe. Pratt had the right of it. Those things could wipe out every elf, dwarf, or human they wanted. But Talen knew how it'd play out. Sooner or later, another army would get their hands on the rifles. Then there'd be wars fought with them, if you could even call them wars. Wouldn't be no winners there, just a world turned to ash, reeking of corruption.

Rage and fear wrestled for dominance, but her insides felt so vast and empty at the thought that it could've been happening to someone else.

She grabbed the bottle back from Wilfred and took another drink.

"I got cups, you know," Draven said, back to working on the rifle.

Wilfred joined Draven at her table.

Talen offered the bottle to Margaret.

She accepted it, drank too much, and damned near coughed a lung up on the table.

"Good stuff." She handed the bottle back. "So, the book you found is a ledger. Whatever else they're doing, they're running a legitimate business, too. Have been for near on a year now." She tapped the book. "And a profitable one at that."

"Imagine my relief." Talen sat down. "Any clue as to where they're making those stones? I reckon they'll be making the rifles there, too."

Margaret nodded. "So far, I've got it down to three possibilities." She pointed to the top of one of the pages. "Boston, New York, or San Francisco."

"You got more whiskey?" Talen asked Draven.

"Aye." Draven pointed, not looking up from her work.

"I reckon I'm going to need it." Talen took another drink and looked at Margaret. "Tell me what you learned."

She gestured at the three stacks of papers in front of her. "What I've gotten through so far are either order forms." She pointed to the stack on the right. "Or manifests for goods sent or received." She tapped the pile on the left. "Neither reveals much, but there is something odd about them."

"Start with the order forms."

Margaret slid the stack in front of her and leafed through them. "At first glance, they look like generic forms. What any run-of-the-mill crafting supplier would use." She pulled one of the pages out and showed it to Talen. "But in nine instances, it doesn't show a balance. It shows receipt of some kind of wares, but with a credit, not a charge."

"Paying them to take the stone," Talen said. "Just like Weaver."

"It isn't written that plain, so I can't be certain, but that's sure what it looks like."

"Only nine?" Talen asked, both horrified and relieved. While she'd hoped Margaret and the two bounties in Kansas were the only ones, she'd feared there'd be dozens more.

"So far. I've still got about a third of them left. Thing is, though, not all the forms are in the same handwriting."

"So, Weaver ain't the only one peddling the stones," Talen said.

"Right. Chicago seems to be a central office. Everything routes through them. I've seen orders from just about everywhere, California to Maine."

Talen thought on that. "Reckon they want them used in remote towns."

"San Francisco ain't what I'd call remote," Wilfred said, still looking over the rifle.

"No," Talen said. "But lots of folks bound for the Yukon start there. And it don't get much more remote than that."

Margaret grimaced. "I don't want to think about one of those charms showing up in some Alaskan mining camp. People would keep arriving, but no one would be able to get word back to warn others."

Talen didn't either. "Pratt offered payment for the name of the person who got the tainted charm. You find any names?"

Margaret shook her head. "No, and I looked. The ledger does show secondary payments to eight of the nine. But if they listed the name anywhere, I haven't found it yet."

"Reckon they sent it on to get the bounty started," Talen said. "What about the manifests?"

Margaret slid the second stack over. "There are two regular shipments every week, one coming in, one going out."

"If the stones and rifles ain't made in Chicago, why are they shipping out from there?"

Margaret shrugged. "Like I said, Chicago seems to be the wheel's hub. Everything got shipped to him, and he just sent it on from there."

"So wouldn't we be looking for where he didn't ship to?" Talen asked. "No need to send nothing to the place making the goods, right?"

Margaret lifted a finger. "Actually, there is. He'd be sending back anything damaged or destroyed *en route*. Trust me, by rail or stage, something always breaks. Every shipment we got to our store had at least one thing that had to go back."

"And it don't say where it ships to?" Talen asked.

"Oh, it does. That's my point. He ships to all three."

Talen leaned back in her chair, let out a long sigh, and rubbed at her eyes. She'd much rather be following a trail or kicking in a door somewhere.

Wilfred chuckled. "That's the same look I had for the last two days."

"Huh?" Margaret said, studying one of the manifests. "That's interesting."

Talen looked at her. "What is?"

"How did I not see this before?" She flipped through the stack of papers.

"See what?" Talen asked again, her patience slipping.

Margaret held up a hand, still reading. "Give me a minute."

Talen finished off the whiskey and waited. Then waited some more, her fingers drumming the tabletop.

"That's not helping."

Talen sighed, crossed her arms, and scrounged for patience.

"I can't believe I missed that!" Margaret finally said, smiling and sitting upright.

"Am I allowed to ask what you're talking about now?"

Wilfred laughed again. "Yup, just like the last two days."

Margaret turned some pages for Talen to see.

Talen didn't even glance at them. "If you didn't see it, I damn sure won't."

"You see this line for insurance."

"I do now. What's it mean?"

"In case something breaks, gets stolen, or is damaged, the transport company pays out the value of the item."

Talen gave her a level look. "I do know what insurance is."

Margaret ignored her. "For almost every shipment leaving Chicago, the insurance is less than five hundred dollars. That's about what I'd expect."

"You said almost?" Talen leaned forward.

Margaret tapped some spots on the page. "On five occasions, there were shipments to Boston insured for five *thousand* dollars."

"Holy shit. Reckon that ain't just a big order."

"No way. It has to be those new crystals. I can't think of any other crafting supplies worth that much. At that price, those shipments would get handled with kid gloves, and have their own armed guard all the way."

"So, it's Boston." Noxious unease settled over Talen at the notion of another big city, and one even farther east. But she didn't have a choice, not if she wanted to see this to the end, and she did.

"I still don't understand what they need the new crystals for, though," Margaret said. "The old ones seem to work fine."

"Better ammunition maybe? I don't get why they ship them to Boston. Seems simpler to get the Red Hand to deliver them direct."

"I can't speak to the second part," Wilfred said. "As to the first, it don't look like the new crystals would fit."

Talen and Margaret both looked over.

"The socket is mighty precise in its size," he said. "It makes contact with every facet. They'd need to fashion a different socket to use the new crystals."

"And change the rifle design for the new power source," Draven said.

"So, you were right about its workings?" Talen asked.

"I think so," Draven said.

"You think?" Talen asked. "You need more time?"

"No, it's just—and it pains me to say it—this is beyond anything I've ever seen before."

"Lots of that going around," Wilfred said. "I ain't never even heard of such a thing, and I'm mindful for whispers of anything new."

Draven patted the rifle. "Whoever designed this is a genius. It's terrible, but remarkable at the same time. A blend of science and magic."

Wilfred nodded. "It takes the power in the crystal and shapes it into a new type of energy. One that works as both power and ammunition." He let out a breath. "It's dark, and no mistake. If I had to name it, I'd call it distilled corruption, odd as that sounds."

"And the magnets, for lack of a better term, that launch the projectile aren't typical either," Draven said. "They use positive and negative forces, but not magnetic. I don't know what it is, but the principles seem the same as electromagnetism."

"We got to destroy it all," Talen said. "Root to branch."

"Couldn't they just make more?" Margaret asked. "Even if we find the designs and destroy them, someone could—" Her face paled. "Oh, you mean the designers as well."

"Whoever came up with this," Talen said. "They're dealing with dark magic. To my mind, that makes them the same as any stained, worse even."

Margaret and Wilfred exchanged a look but didn't say anything. Talen understood. They weren't killers. Wilfred had killed a few, but only when he had to, and it still ate him up inside. Margaret never killed anything not meant for dinner.

"How long to get to Boston?" Talen asked Draven.

She furrowed her brow, considering. "I'd need to check the maps, but I'm guessing it's about 900 miles. Right around two days if the weather don't work against us."

Talen shook her head. The idea of covering that kind of distance in such a short period of time still boggled her mind. "We need to leave now. Odds are word of Pratt's untimely demise already reached Boston."

"It's a long way past the Mississippi river," Margaret said.

"The treaty sees one step the same as a thousand miles," Talen said. "I got four glamour stones and a purpose. I'm troubled. I'd be a fool not to be, but I aim to see this through."

Margaret shook her head. "I know you made a vow, but—"

Talen touched Margaret's hand. "Sister, this ain't about that vow no more. Shadow Wardens exist to fight and destroy dark magic and all its corruption." She pointed to the rifle. "That there ain't but a new manifestation of the darkness. Might be I've only been a stalker a few years, but I've been a Shadow Warden for centuries. Ain't no human law or treaty going to stop me from being one again."

Margaret nodded.

"Aye, it's settled then," Draven said. "Once the horses are back on, I'll get us underway."

"Let's get to it then," Talen said to Wilfred.

"I want to go, too," Margaret said, standing and collecting her cane. "I want to walk on grass and smell the fresh air."

"I'll be on the bridge," Draven said. "Let me know when it's time."

Wilfred, Margaret, and Talen left the Cumulus. As they strode across the soft grass, Talen turned over all the facts, trying to make sense of the parts that didn't. The pieces still didn't fit into a clear picture, no matter how she turned them.

"I know that look," Wilfred said. "What are you thinking?"

Talen sighed and shook her head. "It don't square. Mind, I don't expect everything to, but seems like there's been too much planning and conspiring for this not to."

"You mean about shipping the crystals to Boston?" Margaret asked.

Talen nodded. "And why is Pratt collecting them in Chicago? I don't know it for sure, but as I understood it, the collected crystals get sent back to Washington."

"Reckon we just ain't seeing enough of the whole yet," Wilfred said.

"You said Pratt met with the Red Hand, right?" Margaret asked.

Talen turned to find Margaret had stopped walking. "He did. You see something in it?"

"I'm just thinking out loud, and I'm probably wrong but—"

"You're plenty smart," Wilfred said. "What do you reckon?"

"What if they didn't want the new crystals in the official system? A new, harder-to-kill stained could send waves of fear through people. Might be they'd have to send in the army."

"Go on," Talen said.

"You can't use a crystal on a dead stained, right?" Margaret asked.

"No, they got to be alive. Not that killing them is exactly easy."

"I sure would've been," Margaret said. "So too, I imagine, would the others like me."

"You're thinking they never meant for no one to collect them bounties," Talen said.

"Not officially, no," Margaret said. "Think about it. Whatever the reason, you want these new crystals. But you don't have many, again for whatever the reason. Each one is precious, so precious you insure them for a small fortune."

"Meaning you damn sure don't want none killed instead of collected," Wilfred said.

"Exactly," Margaret said. "So, what would you do?"

Pieces fell into place in Talen's mind. "You only post bounties in regions far away," she said, "which combined with an almost unheard-of high payout keeps most stalkers away."

"Except the ones you want," Wilfred said.

"The Red Right Hand collects the crystals and delivers them to Pratt," Talen said. "He pays them the posted bounty and sends the crystals on to Boston."

"I don't think it's just Pratt," Margaret said. "We only found manifests for the Chicago office. I'd bet there's a Pratt in San Francisco and New York too. Might be Pratts scattered all over."

"That's an unpleasant notion, but it does make sense," Talen said. "It wouldn't take much to convince the Red Hand to help. Hell, they'd hardly need the promise of the bounty. Just the chance to take down some new devilish creature would be enough for most of them."

"We still don't know what they want the crystals for," Margaret said. "If it's just better ammunition for the rifles, why make so few of them?"

"Might be testing them still," Wilfred said. "They ain't ready for production."

"I'm not sure being a test subject makes me feel any better," Margaret said and then looked at Talen. "We're going to run up against the Red Hand, aren't we?"

"I'd bet my left-hand iron on it." Talen almost asked if Wilfred and Margaret still wanted in, but she didn't. Aside from being a stupid question, asking would be an insult to her friends. If they wanted out, they'd say so and know Talen wouldn't judge them for it.

"Well then," Wilfred said. "We best get a move on then."

Chapter Twenty-Five

S queeze the trigger, don't pull," Talen said.

"I know how to shoot," Margaret said, aiming down the barrel of her modified repeater.

"Rabbits and the like. You ain't never shot nothing that shoots back. You got to aim and fire, sometimes from the hip. Shoot, move, shoot, move. If you ain't moving, you're an easy target."

Margaret lowered the sawed-off rifle and fired. The shot nicked the very edge of the makeshift target sitting atop the railing.

She let out an exasperated sigh. "The rocking of the ship isn't helping."

"Nah, that wasn't bad at all. You got to account for the shifting though. You ain't always standing or on even ground. Don't get distracted by what's around you, focus on the target and your body's positioning."

"I'm very aware of my body. It's always telling me how unhappy it is."

"Use that then," Talen said. "Think about how you're standing, holding your arms. When you get a hit, let your body ease back into that same position. You'll move some working the lever, when it fires, and just plain moving around. Think of it a bit like a dance: fire, move and work the lever, then back into position and fire again."

"You imagine I did a lot of dancing?" Margaret asked.

Talen opened her mouth to apologize.

"You can laugh. It was a joke," Margaret said. "I understand what you're saying though." She took aim and fired again. On the third shot, she got inside the roughly drawn circle.

"Well done!" Talen said. "Now do it again."

Margaret emptied the repeater, but only landed one more hit. She reloaded and started up again.

Talen watched Margaret empty the rifle a fourth time. "How you feeling?"

"I'm getting sore," Margaret said. "And tired."

"I meant about your shooting."

She shrugged. "I suppose I'm getting better, but that isn't saying much."

"I don't expect you to knock cones from a pine," Talen said. "I just need you comfortable enough with that shooter to keep firing. If you can put lead in the same general area, even if you ain't hitting much, it'll damn sure keep heads down. That can make one hell of a difference."

Margaret nodded. "I think I can do that much. Could still use more practice though."

"You've got a few hours of daylight yet, and part of tomorrow, when we're not over towns that is. Don't want no one getting spooked and shooting at us. Otherwise, practice all you like."

"Isn't that a waste of bullets?"

Talen chuckled. "You seen the stores in that armory? Draven's got enough to supply a small army, and she said to help ourselves. Don't worry none. I aim to pay something for what we use."

"I don't think she'll take it."

"Ain't going to stop me from trying." She looked at the sky, checking the time. "We've been at this a while, take a break. Get yourself something to eat."

Margaret rubbed her leg. "I believe I will."

Talen pointed at the rifle. "Be sure to clean that thing. Make it a habit. Better you take care of it—"

"The better it will take care of me." Margaret smiled a little sadly. "George said the same thing whenever I commented on how often he cleaned it."

Talen offered Margaret her cane. "Sounds like a good and wise man."

"And then some."

Shifting the rifle to her left hand, she took the cane and followed Talen below. In the galley, Wilfred sat working at one of the smaller tables. He had a dozen spell loads broken down, adjusting the component mixtures.

Talen tensed as heat rushed through her. "Are those my charges? What the hell are you doing to them? They ain't some shoddy mix. I did them myself."

Wilfred grinned at her. "They say it's better to ask for forgiveness than permission."

Talen bit back her anger again. Most of it anyway. "Well, they ain't never messed with a Shadow Warden's charges."

"I reckon you'll see things different when I tell you what I'm doing." He finished up one of the loads.

"You best tell me quick then," she said.

"I'll just be over here." Margaret took a seat at one of the other tables and began breaking down her rifle to clean it.

"It's a new type of load," he said, prepping another and setting it next to the first.

"New load?" Talen stepped closer, her lingering irritation eclipsed by interest.

Wilfred finished a third charge. "I would've asked you, but you seemed otherwise occupied."

Talen picked one up and looked it over. "What is it?"

"Call it a basilisk load." He finished a fourth.

"As in the extinct creature that turned people to stone?" Margaret asked.

"They ain't extinct," Talen said. "Least not last I heard. Few still wander the remote parts of South America and Siberia."

"But that's the one, yes," Wilfred said.

"You saying they turn people to stone?" Talen eyed the charge. "What made you even think to craft such a thing?"

"They do," Wilfred said. "Specifically, to whatever kind of stone is closest. In answer to your second question, I didn't. Army asked me to look into it during the war."

"Don't much like the idea of them having these," Talen said.

"They don't and won't. I told them I couldn't get them to work."

"I don't expect they'll stop trying."

"I don't reckon they'll get far. Ground palladium filings are a key part. It's rare and awful expensive. Most crafters don't bother with it at all." He shrugged. "Even supposing they figure it out, I don't reckon the army would much care for the cost to make them."

"You flush in precious metals now?"

"Hardly," Wilfred said, chuckling. "I only used it 'cause my eyesight ain't so good no more. I was working on a fire charge and took it for ground aluminum. Afraid these four used the last of what I had. You ain't getting no more till I do, and I don't reckon that'll be anytime soon."

Talen looked at him, unable to find the words. Wilfred hadn't ever been well off. Hell, most times he just scraped by. He damn sure couldn't afford to toss away precious crafting ingredients. "Thank you."

He smiled, and she knew he understood all those two words held.

"You think we'll run into a stained for you to use them on?" Margaret asked, cleaning the barrel of her rifle.

"I'm hoping not," Talen said. "Course hoping never made something so. If we do though, I ain't wasting these. Transmutation magic don't work so well on stained. The corruption resists it." She flashed Wilfred a fierce grin. "Reckon they'll work just fine on Red Right Hand, though."

"Make them last," he said. "Like I said, four is all you get."

Talen nodded and tucked them into her jacket. "I take it the dozen you pulled apart ain't useful no more?"

"Sorry to say. My bag don't hold much so I ran short on components. It's why I had to borrow some of your charges. I'll get you replacements when I'm able, or at least pay for—"

"Like hell you will. You done paid for them and more already. If anything, I owe you."

"You don't owe me nothing," he said. *Except to live through this,* his eyes added.

Talen nodded again and then went to the cupboard. Least she could do was fetch him and Margaret something to eat. She filled a couple bowls with bread, some dried meat, and cold beans. She took the remaining leaves and grass for herself.

"How's the shooting going?" Wilfred asked Margaret.

"I'm hitting the target on occasion," Margaret said. "So, improving."

"Reckon I could do with a bit of practice myself." Wilfred got up and joined Margaret at her table as Talen set the food down. "Never much took to shooting, but my aim was fair."

"Yeah, you could hit the broad side of a barn near every time," Talen said, chewing on some leaves. "At noon, if the wind weren't blowing too hard."

Wilfred a put hand to his heart and made a pained face but chuckled.

As they ate, Margaret told them about growing up in Boston and of George. She smiled when she talked about him, though her eyes were sad. No mistaking how much she loved him.

Talen's heart ached in empathy. Her own loss still haunted her. In fact, as three years was barely a blink to an elf, it still hurt like nine kinds of hell. Margaret's grieving had just begun, but it seemed as if talking about George did ease her heart some. Not much, but some.

A while later, Draven came down, a roll of something under one arm. "Did I miss supper?"

"Not at all," Wilfred said. "Lots of beans and bread left. I'll even warm them up."

"No need." Draven set what looked to be some kind of document on the table and went to get herself some food.

"What's this?" Margaret asked, unrolling the paper.

"Map of Boston." Draven scooped some beans into a bowl.

Margaret looked it over. "How old is it?"

Draven sat and started eating. "Sixty years. I've updated it as I had the time and the city in view. Not as good as my others, but it might serve well enough."

"I haven't been back in years," Margaret said. "But I think I can fill in some details." She pointed to a peninsula south of the city. "This is Fort Point Channel. According to the manifests, it's where the crystals went. Makes sense, too. Lots of factories and mills there."

"Hiding in plain sight," Talen said.

"Is that a pier?" Wilfred said.

Draven nodded. "A big one. Boston is a deep-water port."

"With a lot of ships coming and going," Margaret said. "It's busy day and night. I'm not sure that's the best place to start."

"If Tuller is our man, would he live nearby?" Talen asked.

Margaret laughed. "No chance." She pointed to a spot to the northwest. "His house is in Beacon Hill, South Slope. About here."

"You know where he lives?" Talen asked.

"Everyone in Boston does," Margaret said. "He's a Boston Brahmin, old money and high society."

"Well, ain't we just going to fit right in?" Wilfred said.

Draven and Margaret both laughed.

Talen eyed them for a moment, unsure what they found funny. "We find the factory first," she said. "We cause enough of a ruckus, and it'll distract the whole city. Any Red Hands about should come running. That's when we'll pay a visit to Tuller."

"Assuming he's the one behind this," Margaret said. "I don't want to go after an innocent man, even if he is a robber baron."

Talen pointed to a spot south of the channel. "What's here?"

"Houses," Margaret said. "Immigrants mostly, Irish especially."

"Any chance you know of a 'less than legal' place to tie up?" Talen asked Draven.

She laughed. "In Boston, they're all less than legal. City has a long and proud history of smuggling. If you got gold, you can tie up right alongside the most reputable ships, no questions asked."

"Not greenbacks?" Talen asked. "Just gold?"

"They might take the paper, but they'd need more of it," Draven said. "What with the war over, paper is flowing heavy and not everyone likes it."

"You pick the spot then," Talen said.

"Aye. I'll see to it. And to be clear, I'm going with you this time."

"I'll take every gun we can get. Besides, if we come across any more inventions, having you along will be mighty handy."

"Is it safe to leave the ship with no one on board?" Margaret asked.

Draven smiled. "It isn't just debris my spindles keep the deck clear of. My ship will be just fine. I can't say the same about any damned fool tries to come on board though."

"How far out are we?" Talen asked.

"We had to shift routes a bit to avoid a summer storm to the south. Nothing to worry about, but it'll cost us a few hours. I figure we'll be there tomorrow by supper time."

With the planning done, the conversation settled into casual, easy talk. When they finished eating, Wilfred and Margaret went back up top for more target practice. Talen and Draven shared a few drinks in silence, each mourning for their own reasons, and in their own way.

Talen refilled their cups. "If it comes to it, I need you to see that Margaret and Wilfred get out safe. Will you do that for me?"

Draven nodded. "More than that, I'll see to it they get wherever they want, safe and sound. Swear it by my bare chin."

"Much obliged. I got some savings in my saddlebags. If you could—"

"She'll get every penny," Draven said and lifted her glass. "To friends, the old and the new, always faithful and true."

"May our enemies never know such friends." Talen tapped her cup to Draven's.

They both drank.

~

Hours later, Talen stood at the rail again, watching the storm in the distance. Wilfred and Margaret were sleeping. Draven, as ever, stood watch on the bridge. Another of the Great Lakes drifted below, the far shore just visible ahead. Talen thought back to the elemental, her hand touching the crystal in her side. She took the unused bounty crystals from her coat and eyed them. One by one, she let them fall into the lake.

Only seems right to give them back. I damned sure won't ever use one again.

A little after midnight, or so she guessed, Talen went below to spend some time with Gaoth. She fed him and the other horses some purloined apples from the galley.

"I know I said we'd be back on the road by now," she said, stroking the horse's neck. "But the job ain't quite done yet."

He nuzzled against her hand and looked at her with loving, ever-patient eyes.

"I ain't got no clue as to how this ends. But Margaret and Wilfred will take good care of you if anything happens to me."

He snorted and shook his head.

"I know you want to come. But you can't. I need you here. Who else will mind this ship and look after Joseph and Elise?"

He gave a low nicker.

She sighed. "I ain't looking to die. I just got a dark feeling. I know something new is out there. I go no notion what it is, but I know it's bad."

He just looked at her.

"We ain't never wasted time sweeting the truth so it went down easier. You've been a damn good friend, and without you, I wouldn't have made it this far."

Gaoth stepped close and pressed himself to her, his cheek to hers.

"I love you too, old friend." She kissed his cheek.

Rather than going to her room, she pulled herself onto his broad back. She turned herself around and stretched out, her legs hanging off his hindquarters.

She felt more than heard his strong heart thudding, slow and steady. Such a sense of peace and contentment settled over her that all she could do was sigh. It might not smell like roses, but Draven's spindles did a fine job turning and replacing the straw as needed. She didn't care though. Gaoth's strong back was a damn sight more comfortable than any bed.

She closed her eyes and slipped easily into sleep.

The next morning, she arose before dawn and went to watch the sunrise. To her surprise, she found Wilfred standing at the rail, puffing on his pipe.

"Morning," he said and motioned to a cup on the railing. "Coffee?"

She took it and drank, nodding her thanks. She didn't much care for coffee if given the choice, but the company and scenery made it a damned fine drink. She leaned against Wilfred and gazed at the sky.

Neither of them said anything. They didn't need to. They just stood there, savoring the quiet peace of predawn. Soon the fiery colors on the horizon spread, and the dark of night gave way to a spectacular dawn. Without a word, they went below and had breakfast ready when Margaret joined them.

The day passed with little said, each of them preparing in their own way. Farms and small towns passed below, so instead of target practice, they just watched an oblivious world go by.

No one had much of an appetite when lunchtime came.

When the sun began its slide down to the western horizon, they all went below. They went over Draven's map, and with Margaret's help, devised routes to take if things went bad. After that, they set to checking and double checking their gear. Margaret cleaned and oiled her rifle, Wilfred tended to his pistol, and Talen saw to her spell irons. She loaded a single basilisk charge into each, saving the other two. She did not skimp on fire charges this time, and slid extras into the slots on her gun belt. She'd see that factory burn, along with every dark creation in it. If the rest of the city went too, well then, so be it.

"Ain't you going to go above?" Talen asked Margaret. "I'd have figured you want to see your old home."

"I'm keeping myself distracted," Margaret said, reassembling her rifle. "I can't let myself start thinking about mama, or William and Charlotte. I need to keep focused."

"That working any better for you than me?" Wilfred asked.

"I doubt it," Margaret said.

"You know you don't have to go," Talen said to them. "With Draven along, I'll have another gun watching my back. Two, actually."

Wilfred gave her an easy smile. "Yeah, but you'll miss us something terrible. Besides, I got no place else to be."

"Can't let you get all melancholy," Margaret said, forcing a smile. It didn't last. "I need to see this through."

"We'll be setting down in fifteen minutes," Draven's voice said through the tube. "Since we're docking, we won't be using the boarding door. They'll lay out a gangplank at the top deck."

Talen looked from the speaking tube back to Wilfred and Margaret. "Take a deep breath. Just follow my lead. Stay close, and don't throw down unless, and until, I do."

They nodded.

"I need you both to do as I say, when I say," Talen said. "If I say duck, run, or jump on one foot, don't question. Just get to hopping."

"I might have trouble with that," Margaret said, smiling again, this time sincerely. "Depending on the foot anyway."

"Fair enough," Talen said, smiling back. "I'll be sure to specify."

She went to the cupboard, retrieved the near empty whiskey bottle, and three cups. She filled each, emptying the last of the bottle into her own cup.

"Mind if I did the honors?" Wilfred asked.

"Not at all."

Wilfred lifted his glass. "Health to the sick, honor to the brave, success to the lover, and freedom to the slave."

They clinked cups and drank.

Fifteen minutes later, the Cumulus touched down.

"Once more unto the breach, dear friends," Margaret said, and everyone stood.

Margaret pulled on Wilfred's coat and tucked her repeater into the makeshift holster she'd fashioned. Wilfred slipped the rucksack Talen had pilfered, now filled with his wares, over one shoulder. Talen pulled a glamour stone from the pouch and put it in her mouth. Once more, she shaped the magic as it settled over her. She considered a police uniform, but didn't know if they varied from city to city. Instead, she went with something she'd hoped would let her blend in more.

"That is some mighty red hair," Wilfred said.

"You're going fit right in," Margaret said.

Chapter Twenty-Six

As in Chicago, the stench nearly brought Talen to her knees. Ships of all sorts packed the harbor, which smelled even worse than the city. Dozens of airships came and went, most—like the steamers—spewed foul black smoke into the hazy sky.

"I'll still take the lead," Talen said and then turned to Margaret. "Your job is to make sure I'm headed the right way."

She nodded.

Together, the four of them descended the gangway and stepped onto the bustling dock. Through a tangled horde of workers and sailors, a grizzled but well-dressed man emerged and approached them.

"Evening," he said, giving them an officious smile. "I'm Harbormaster Coid. What's your business and how long will you need a berth?"

Talen reached into her coat, palming four hundred dollars in greenbacks, and offered her hand to the harbormaster.

"Call me Smith," she said, affecting a slight brogue. "And we're just stopping in for a bit of tourism. Won't be more than a day at most."

Coid shook her hand, glanced down at the money, and gave her a smile. "Welcome to Boston, Mr. Smith. Enjoy our fair city." He turned and walked away.

"Hope you didn't overpay," Wilfred said in a low tone.

"I'll call it cheap if it keeps the ship safe and ready to go." Talen pulled her coat closed to hide her irons and led the way, weaving through the mass of dockworkers.

Wilfred got more than a few insults and taunts. Lewd remarks and offers were sent Margaret's way. Talen gave hard looks to the worst and ignored the rest. Any other day, she would've fed each and every one their teeth, and happily so, but today, they couldn't. Besides, filthy as most of the men looked, she figured it best to avoid any physical contact.

The bustling madness didn't let up once they reached the narrow streets. Talen's heart beat faster as a cold stone settled in her stomach. With some effort, she fought back the panic, but it took all her resolve to breathe steady and keep focused.

Bad as Chicago had been, at least the streets had been wider. In these tight confines, the noise reverberated to near-deafening levels. A million sounds piled onto each other, an ear-splitting carol of utter insanity.

The four of them must've been an imposing sight, or queer at the least. The crowds parted as they went, giving Talen a respite from the claustrophobia.

"Watch the alleys," Margaret said. "Ruffians and muggers—"

Talen turned and looked at her. "Why didn't you say something on the ship?"

"It's not our safety I worry about," Margaret said. "I just imagine you'd rather not draw too much attention, or worse, have the police get involved."

"Sorry," Talen said. "You got the right of it."

Ringing bells cut through the clamor of the city.

"Six o'clock," Margaret said, when the cacophony faded.

"Is it always this loud?" Talen asked. "How did you ever manage living here?"

"Like anything else, you grow accustomed to it. When George and I first moved to Kansas, the quiet nearly drove us crazy."

Talen shook her head. "You are strange creatures."

"I am exceedingly average," Wilfred said.

"All evidence to the contrary," Draven said through a smirk.

Margaret directed them through the winding urban pathways. As it happened though, she didn't need to say much. The streets tended to be long, and while not straight as such, they didn't diverge.

Though not as large as Chicago—if Talen could be any judge of such things—it still threatened to overwhelm her. Thankfully, they reached Fort Point Channel before that happened.

Factories and mills lined the channel, all with massive brick stacks spewing black smoke. It reminded her of the river inlet in Chicago, with water just as foul. Her hand went to her side and touched the crystal beneath her coat and shirt.

What if this place had a resident elemental? Was all the filth slowly poisoning it? So much foulness. How could the residents not see they were destroying what kept them alive?

Talen came back to herself and realized she'd stopped, and everyone with her.

"Which way?" she asked, as cover. "It all looks the same."

All around them, people in grimy, tattered clothes poured from the massive buildings. Everyone looked utterly exhausted, as if they might collapse then and there. None met her gaze, but she could see their eyes held no light.

Inch by inch, these people were being worked to death. They were little more than living machines—nameless, faceless, and entirely disposable. She imagined they'd drag away any man who fell to fatigue or injury, quickly replaced by another.

Some humans were decent enough, Talen knew that. She walked with two now. Even so, she struggled to see humanity as anything but a vast machine, one that chewed up all life, including its own.

Margaret motioned to the left, away from the harbor. "That way. It's not far now."

Talen continued on, conscious to keep an easy pace for Margaret.

She scanned up and down the street as they went, looking for anything out of place. She spotted a trio of men standing just outside the front doors of a factory. Unlike those flowing past them, these men wore very fine, and very clean, suits.

Margaret lifted her hand to point. "I think that's—"

Talen took her arm and gently pushed it down. She pulled Margaret around a corner and down a side street. Wilfred and Draven following close.

"What are you doing?" Margaret asked. "That was the factory."

"I know." Talen checked all around them, several times. "Those three standing outside are guards. I got no notion if they heard about Pratt, but if they did, might be they're expecting trouble here. Either way, I just as soon not draw attention from them."

"They Red Right Hand?" Wilfred asked.

Talen shook her head. "No gloves, and I ain't never seen a Red Hand duded up like that."

"Pinkertons," Draven said and spat.

"Reckon so," Talen said. "Ain't no surprise really. Red Hands are stalkers and dedicated to their cause. They don't take to guard duty, no matter the pay."

"Is that better or worse than Red Hands?" Margaret asked.

Talen ducked her head out and looked the men over. They all had iron on their hips, at least two were spell irons. One, the leader she figured, kept eyeing some rough sorts loitering across the street. Thankfully, she didn't see no eyepieces.

Another suited man came out and said something about the inside being all clear. It was impossible to hear the words, but Talen read his lips. The leader nodded and said something in reply she couldn't make out. His bushy mustache hid his lip movements. The new arrival went to the doors and locked them.

Talen turned back to Margaret. "Not better, that's for sure. Aside from them three, there's hired thugs across the street, and they just locked the doors. Didn't set no wards though."

"I don't expect wards would react well if they got stained magic inside," Wilfred said.

"Lots of folks wandering about," Draven said. "Draw plenty of attention if we took them thugs down, even if we were quick about it."

Talen nodded. "I ain't risking no fight in the street." She turned to Margaret. "And I ain't going to risk them recognizing you. They ain't stalkers, but it might not matter."

"Would there be a back door to a place like that?" Wilfred asked.

"Might be," Margaret said. "Some places do, but they're usually kept locked or barred, or both, all the time. Bosses don't like their workers being able to leave before their shift is over."

"Locks and bars ain't a problem," Talen said. "We'll head around back and see if there's another way in. There's like to be guards there as well, but hopefully less of them. Even if there aren't, at least we won't be in the middle of a busy street. Keep your head down and don't look at them. Wilfred and I will keep ourselves between you and them. I don't know as they'll be looking for you, but you're the only one here anyone would recognize. No reason to take chances."

Margaret nodded.

"If something starts," Talen said, "let me and Draven handle it, you two get to cover."

Margaret and Wilfred shared a look, then nodded, if reluctantly.

Talen led them back to the street and toward the factory, Wilfred at her shoulder, and Margaret tucked behind them. The entrance to the alley sat less than a dozen paces from the main entrance, and closer still to the nearest guard. They kept their pace leisurely. Talen watched the Pinkertons, never looking right at them. Two of the men chatted, less focused on their task. The third, a hulking brute, cast his beady eyes over everyone that passed by. His meaty paw rested on the spell iron at his hip, index finger tapping it.

Talen slowed her pace, and when the Pinkertons turned away, she turned down the side street, the others right behind her. Little illumination from the streetlights, and even less noise, made it into the narrow, empty alley. The giant buildings towered on either side, the only windows too high to provide any escape. Talen hurried them along, checking ahead and behind the whole way. If they got caught here, this alley would become a kill box.

When they reached the far end, Talen motioned for them to wait. She poked her head around the corner, surveyed the street then ducked back in.

"More guards?" Margaret asked.

Talen nodded. "Four of them."

"At least now we know there is another door," Wilfred said.

"Ain't no getting around them," Talen said. "I'll bet they got sentries anywhere someone can get inside." Talen studied the windows again. "Maybe."

"Reckon you might be able to climb up there," Wilfred said, "but I damn sure can't."

Draven and Margaret nodded their agreement.

"You might be able to let us in from the inside," Draven said.

"I got no notion what's on the other side," Talen said. "Might well be empty air all the way down to ground level." She shook her head. "It's a door or nothing."

"It's your call," Draven said. "How do you want to play it?"

Talen checked the alley and then the walls for surveillance wards. She hadn't seen many, but knew they existed. Wards like that weren't cheap, but if someone shelled out for Pinkertons, they wouldn't blink at the cost of wards.

That meant they were alone, for now, but someone could come along any time. They needed to do something, and right now. She checked the back street again, just long enough to get a read on things.

Aside from the guards and some rubbish piles, the street was clear. Two Pinkertons leaned against the factory wall, smoking and chatting away. The other two had keener eyes and watched in either direction. She ducked back behind the corner as one turned to look her way.

"Only way in is through those guards." She didn't give a damn about killing them, but she didn't want to risk them calling for help.

"So, what's the plan?" Draven opened her coat and tucked it behind her pistols.

"When I tell you, make your way up to them and wait for my move." Talen turned to Margaret and Wilfred. "You two stay here till I tell you to come out."

Everyone nodded.

Talen spit the glamour stone onto the ground and crushed it. As soon as the magic slipped away, she wrapped herself in shadow and drew the knives from her back.

"Go," she said to Draven.

The dwarf strode around the corner, and headed straight for the Pinkertons, as if she didn't have a care in the world.

Talen sprinted past her, careful to avoid puddles or any debris that might give her away. When she reached the men, she slowed and gave them a wide berth so they wouldn't feel her pass.

"You lost, stump?" one of the men asked Draven.

He and his companions reached for their irons but didn't draw.

Draven smiled cheerily. "Fine evening, isn't it, boys? Charlie Pratt sends his regards."

The men exchanged a look.

"Who the hell is—"

Talen kicked the back of the Pinkerton's knee. As he collapsed, she wrapped an arm around his neck, catching him and covering his mouth. Before he could make a sound, she rotated her hips, tilting his head to one side. She drove a knife into the base of his skull and into his brains.

She let go and the man fell to the ground in a limp, dead heap.

"Holy shit!" another called out, drawing and igniting his iron.

Draven drew her pistols faster than Talen would've expected and fired at the man in front of her. No flash, no smoke, and aside from a low whump, no noise. The Pinkerton jerked twice and fell back.

The remaining two drew down, pulling their irons and lighting them up. Talen slashed along the wrist of the first one, cutting deep and driving the second knife into his chest.

The second fired at Draven, sending an invisible blast of kinetic force at her.

She'd already moved, and the shot only tore up the street where she'd been standing.

He rolled the cylinder and made to fire again. Talen spun and heaved his dead compatriot, still impaled on her knife, at him. The corpse drove the man into a wall. His shot went wild, and a second force blast hit the far wall, knocking several bricks out.

Draven gave him both barrels. His head snapped back, and he jerked to one side, spinning as he fell.

Talen checked the street. Still empty. She dropped her veil and grabbed one of the men by his jacket collar, hauling him from the ground.

"We got to get them out of sight," she said. "Empty streets draw less attention than them littered with corpses."

"There," Draven said, nodding at a garbage pile.

Talen smiled. *Seems about right.*

They piled the bodies and covered them with refuse. They'd be visible to anyone that happened by, but they'd be hard to spot at a distance.

Talen whistled and motioned for Wilfred and Margaret. They hurried over, both with their guns out and ready.

"We best be quick," Talen said. "No telling when or if anyone else will be along."

"We were damn quiet," Draven said.

"We were, but they might need to check in, or could be a roving sentry along any minute. Point is, we need to not be here." She looked at Wilfred and Margaret. "Don't shoot unless you got no option. Ain't nothing like gunfire to bring all manner of attention."

They both nodded.

"Any idea what's on the other side of that door?" Draven asked.

"None," Talen said. "Could be nothing, could be a dozen more of them on break."

"No wards on it," Wilfred said.

"Be ready." Talen wrapped herself in shadow once more, drew back, and kicked at the door. It buckled but held. She kicked again, and on the third kick, it came away, sailing into the building.

Someone cried out in surprise but went quiet when the door crashed into him.

Talen leapt, catching the man as he bounced off a wall. She drove him to the ground with both knives in his chest.

"Down!" Draven shouted.

Talen threw herself onto the body.

Another whump, and someone grunted and then fell to the floor.

Talen looked up.

A second man lay sprawled on the ground not ten feet away. He bore a quarter-size hole in his chest and stared with dead eyes.

Draven stepped inside the building, followed close by Wilfred and Margret.

Talen released the shadows and stood. "Much obliged."

"Glad you move as quick as you do," Draven said.

"Me too."

Talen's heart beat slow and steady

She drew both spell irons and took in the room. It was small, maybe twenty by twenty, had two doors and no windows. The remaining door, still closed, sat opposite the one she'd kicked in. Half a dozen chairs were around a table near one wall. It bore all the signs of an interrupted poker game: cards, coins, and a half-empty bottle of bourbon. She couldn't be sure, but it looked like just the two had been playing.

She closed her eyes and listened. The only breathing came from her friends, so she focused on what lay outside the room. Four men. Walking fast. She held up four fingers, pointed to the door, and motioned for Wilfred and Margaret to move to a far corner. They did so, their shooters aimed at the floor.

Draven took up position a few feet to the right of the door. Talen matched her on the left. Both raised their weapons. Talen rolled her cylinders to force loads, lit her spell irons, and they waited.

Despite the anticipation, her heart beat slow and steady, and one side of her mouth pulled up.

The footsteps came to a stop just beyond the door.

Pinkertons weren't stupid. She'd bet they were listening at the door. But unless they had a charm—or an elf—they wouldn't hear anything.

Seconds passed, slow as sap in winter, but neither Talen nor Draven so much as twitched.

"Jeb, Charlie, everything all right?"

No one answered.

"They might be outside taking a piss," whispered someone to the left of the door.

Talen took aim.

"Both of them?" whispered someone else from the right side of the door. "At the same time?"

Draven took aim.

Talen looked at her and gave a silent three count.

On one, both fired. Twin blasts of kinetic force hit within in an inch of each other, punching a hole in the brick two feet across.

Draven fired four shots, two high, two low, a foot between them.

"Shit!" someone shouted from the right side.

Talen rolled her cylinders to fresh charges without changing aim.

A head poked around the edge of the hole she'd made, but before she could fire, Draven put a bullet between his eyes.

The head snapped back, and his body fell to the ground.

The door kicked open.

Another Pinkerton stepped into view, a spell iron in his right hand, a mundane Colt in his left. "Die, you sons of—"

Talen fired her right-hand iron as she turned, narrowing herself as a target.

A pulsing green ball of light shot from the barrel and hit the Pinkerton right over his heart. In less time than it took to blink, he turned to a statue of red brick stone.

Left-hand iron ready, Talen rolled the right to a fresh chamber and waited. She hoped the sudden petrification would serve to terrify any Pinkertons on the other side of the door that were still breathing. At the very least, the statue almost entirely blocked the doorway.

No one else moved or made a sound.

Talen gestured for Draven to wait.

She nodded.

Talen doused her irons but kept them out and wrapped herself in shadow. She rushed toward the hole in the wall, leapt through, and tumbled to her feet on the other side, irons up and ready. Nothing but three corpses.

She looked over the factory.

Only the ten-foot walls—far from ceiling height—broke up the open space. A catwalk wrapped around the entire interior, just below the windows. Some kind of room sat high on the far wall, its windows dark.

Talen turned backed to the bodies. Two were sprawled, dark blood oozing from Draven's bullet holes. A third lay crumpled beneath a pile of bricks and dust, his head bent at an unnatural angle. A glance at the statue sent a shiver down her spine.

Man still knows his craft.

"All clear," she said in a harsh whisper, releasing the shadows.

"Mother of God," Margaret whispered, squeezing past the statue.

"You going to be okay?" Talen asked. "It ain't gonna get any prettier."

Margaret didn't look at the bodies. "I'm fine."

Draven carefully pushed the petrified Pinkerton to one side, clearing the doorway and allowing easier passage for her and Wilfred. Thankfully, it didn't make much noise.

Talen scanned the catwalk.

"See anything?" Wilfred asked.

"It looks clear. Best keep your eyes and ears open all the same though."

"This is a big place," Draven said. "We splitting up?"

"Hell no," Talen said. "Better to spend a little longer looking than risk them catching us separated. We'll gather up anything we find, make one big pile, and burn it to ash." She looked at Draven and Wilfred. "If either of you see something of interest, speak up."

They both nodded, and then everyone fanned out and walked onto the shop floor.

They rounded the first partition wall and froze.

"I reckon that qualifies as something of interest," Wilfred said.

"What are those?" Margaret asked.

"Those thieving sons of bitches," Draven muttered.

Talen couldn't think, much less form words. Wave after wave of pure, icy terror washed over her. Her chest tightened, her heart pounded, and her whole body began to shake. She could only stare at the iron behemoths, four of them in a line. And then she was back at Whitestone Hill. All around her, sisters and Lakota died screaming as spells and bullets bounced off the impenetrable hide of the Dwarven Leviathans.

Chapter Twenty-Seven

Talen?" Margaret asked. "Can you hear me?"

Talen blinked away the memories and came back to the here and now. Her hands ached and when she looked down, she saw why. She tried and failed to ease her grip on her irons. They burned with so much spell fire they lit the darkening factory floor.

Margaret stepped close. "It's okay," she said softly, putting her hands over Talen's. "This isn't the war. It's over, and you're safe."

It took nearly all she had, but Talen drew in one slow breath after another. Eventually, she got control of the terror eating her insides and drove it into submission. When her heartbeat slowed, she doused her irons and managed to ease her hold on them. Try as she might though, she couldn't keep from staring at the machines of death.

"No, you're wrong," Talen shook her head. "I ain't safe. Not sure anyone is."

Margaret put a hand on her arm. "Well, you're not alone."

Those simple words echoed off Talen's heart and filled her with more comfort and peace than she expected. She looked at Wilfred and Margaret in turn, and each nodded. Neither of them were fighters, but they'd come along all the same, insisted actually. Wilfred might've seen horrors and hell but not war. Not like Whitestone Hill.

Had anyone?

Yet, here they were, shoulder to shoulder with her. Even knowing they might not survive, they took up arms to fight against darkness. And they trusted in her to do the same and to keep them safe.

The anxiety melted away under the warmth of their love and their faith in her. She wouldn't—couldn't—let fear stop her from giving as much as them. Even Draven, her newest and most unexpected friend—

Talen looked around. "Where's Draven?"

Wilfred nodded at the nearest leviathan. "In that thing."

"What? How long was I gone?"

"A few minutes is all," Wilfred said.

"I had to say your name a dozen times before you snapped out of it," Margaret said.

"I'm sorry," Talen said. "It won't happen again."

"I know you've got some terrible scars," Margaret said. "I can't imagine what you've seen. You don't need to apologize. Not to me."

"Or me," Wilfred said.

Draven stuck her head out of a hatch on top of the metal beast. "I think I got some answers." She climbed up and out, as if she'd done it a hundred times before, and leapt to the ground from the large metal wheels.

"They ain't dwarf make, are they?" Talen asked.

Draven shook her head. "They got some features of our work in them, but these are human designed and built."

"Find anything?" Talen asked.

"Good news or bad?" she asked.

"I could do with some good news," Wilfred said.

"No dwarven iron in it. Not even an ounce." She looked at Talen. "It'd take some work, but your spell iron could turn this bucket to slag given enough time. They've got a lightning rod system mounted to the bottom, but it'd melt quick enough. Without it, a single bolt could make a very bad day for the crew."

"What's the bad news?" Talen asked.

"I found out what they're using those new crystals for."

Talen's stomach dropped to the floor. She looked again at the machine. A renewed dread rose up but drowned under a tide of unbridled fury. They were killing innocent people, stealing their souls, to power war machines? These bastards made stained seem decent in comparison.

"Why would they use the crystals to power it?" Margaret asked, her face pale.

"I told you, earth fire is deadly to humans," Draven said. "It takes a lot of power to move something heavy as a leviathan. Since they're made of regular iron, these monstrosities are three times the weight if they're an ounce. Only way to generate that much power is with an earth fire reactor. Since they don't have one and couldn't use it if they did, they found a way to use the crystals as a power source."

"But railroads use regular steam engines and they're a lot bigger than this thing," Margaret said.

"Bigger, not heavier," Draven said. "A railroad engine is mostly boiler, and it'd take one big as the thing itself to move this. Even then, you'd need to haul coal or wood to keep the fire going." She scowled. "I don't know how they figured out how to do it, but I found a panel inside that'll hold six of those new crystals."

"What about the guns?" Talen asked, looking at the half dozen barrels sticking out in all directions.

"Nah, they're all mockups."

"What's that?" Margaret asked.

"Placeholder," Draven said. "These are nothing but carved and painted wood."

Talen looked at Wilfred and knew he figured it out too.

"The rifle you got from Pratt," he said.

Talen nodded. "They'll mount them, or something like them."

"Merciful Jesus," Margaret said. "With four of these things armed with those rifles, they could roll over whole armies."

"Damn near any army," Draven said.

"How do we destroy them?" Talen asked. "Not just kill the crew, but make the machine itself useless?"

"You'll need fire," she said. "Lots of it and burning hotter than the fires of hell."

"What about ice?" Talen asked. "That's how I destroyed the rifles in Chicago."

Draven shook her head. "These are too big. I doubt you could make them cold enough to even break, much less shatter." She shrugged. "Won't help now, but ice might stop them if you froze over the wheels."

"I got an idea," Wilfred said and looked at Talen. "How many loads you got?"

"Three basilisk," she said. "Two dozen fire and force charges, and a dozen arctic."

"Too bad you used one of the basilisk loads," Margaret said. "I doubt these would be any good turned to stone."

"They only work on living things," he said. "But, if you'd part with two of them, along with a dozen fire, and half a dozen force loads…"

"What're you thinking?" Talen asked.

"Recall that time we got pinned down on the Kentucky/Tennessee border?" he asked. "We had them five kids with us."

Talen smiled. "You called it a spell bomb."

"Bomb?" Margaret asked.

"Of a sort," Wilfred said. "You set it off with magic, which normally ain't a good idea. Except I work a kind of fuse into it that slows the magical ignition. It'll be big and mighty hot."

"How long do you need?" Talen asked, pulling the charges from her pockets and gun belt.

"Reckon thirty minutes should do." He looked out the windows. "Ain't got much more than that before it's too dark to see."

Draven produced a metal rod with a glass ball on one end. She flicked a switch and it cast bright white light in all directions. "Electric torch." She handed it to Wilfred, produced another, and handed it to Margaret.

"You stay with him," Talen said to Draven, replacing her spent force charges. "Margaret and I will see if we can find the rifles, stones, and the designs to add to the kindling pile."

"I'll watch him," Draven said, replacing her spent rounds too. "Don't you worry none."

"You good with coming along?" Talen asked Margaret.

Margaret looked a little ashen. But she swallowed, clenched her jaw, and nodded.

Talen took the lead, careful to use the partition walls as cover. She didn't hear anything but wouldn't be careless, not with the end in sight.

They came upon two dozen crafter stations, just wooden worktables with collections of tools hanging on sideboards. Half the tables had only the barest hint of use, the rest looking entirely untouched.

"These look new to you?" Talen asked, looking the unmarred tables over.

"They do. And no tools."

"Might be they're having trouble finding crafters."

"I don't see any supplies," Margaret said. "Not at any of the stations."

Talen crouched but didn't see any drawers. "Ain't none."

"They might lock them up at the end of shift. Keep the workers from making off with the valuable stuff."

Talen looked around. "Wilfred said a stained crafter made the stones. I don't imagine no stained works at stations like these, much less goes home at the end of the day."

"No." Margaret sniffed the air. "And I don't smell any corruption. Do you?"

"Nah. But keep your eyes open."

They continued their search, both quiet as they could manage. Talen heard Wilfred working, Draven pacing, and Margaret breathing, but nothing else. Rather than being comforted, she found it unsettling.

They came upon a line of machines.

"These must be for making the rifle parts," Margaret said.

They were all connected with belts to massive flywheels, now still, that powered them. Like the crafting stations, the machines looked new, their enamel still gleaming.

"Looks like they're gearing up for a major increase in their output," Margaret said.

"You seem to know more about all this than I do," Talen said. "Any notion how long it'd take a build a rifle?"

She shrugged. "George worked in a factory before we moved to Kansas, but I've no idea how long the crafting would take. How long to craft a spell iron?"

"Near on a month."

"These things have to be quicker, right?" Margaret asked. "But even if they aren't, two dozen a month is an awful lot."

"Yes, it is." Talen looked over the machines, all cast iron and steel. Wilfred's bomb might not destroy them outright, but the fire would melt them nicely, even this far away. Of course, they didn't need to melt, just soften enough to put them beyond repair. "Let's keep looking." The next section seemed to be the assembly area. A dozen wooden crates sat to one side. Three were full. Talen did some quick math: a dozen rifles with Pratt, eighteen here. Figuring it took a month to make one, and half a dozen workers, that meant they'd been making them for five months.

"We need to get these crates to Wilfred," Talen said.

"There's a cart over there."

Talen retrieved the thing, a table-like top over four wheels; two larger at each side, and two smaller at either end that could rotate. "Keep an eye out," she said and then made quick work of loading the crates. The boxes were lighter than she would've thought. To be sure, she pulled open each one after setting it down to make sure the contents were as expected. They were.

"Do we wheel it back now?" Margaret asked.

They were nearing the front of the building. Talen looked up at the office. As she did, she heard something new and froze.

Margaret lifted her rifle, not making a sound, and scanned for a target.

Talen closed her eyes and focused.

There! A soft scraping. She turned her head trying to place the source, but it seemed to be coming from everywhere. After a long minute, she opened her eyes.

"Look for a trap door," Talen said in a whisper. "There's something beneath us."

After near on ten minutes, Margaret spotted seams in the floor around a heavy-looking cabinet. Talen examined it and spotted hinges on one side.

"Get back," she whispered.

Margaret did so and took aim with her repeater.

Talen gingerly tilted the cabinet until it lay on its side, revealing a roughhewn staircase that descended into darkness.

The scraping got louder.

Talen peered down, but her vision couldn't penetrate the gloom while she stood in even the dwindling light.

Margaret produced Draven's electric torch, clicked it on, and held it over the opening. The stairs went down ten or twelve feet to a tunnel.

"Stay behind me," Talen said, drawing both irons. "Keep the light high and if I tell you, douse it quick and get low. You'll be blind, but so will whatever we come across. I'll only need a second or two before I can see enough to shoot."

Margaret nodded, taking the torch up in her left hand, the repeater in her right.

Talen went down the stairs, slow and silent. She had to duck at one point to get below a low beam. She reached the bottom, Margaret on her heels. The brick-lined tunnel went twenty yards and stopped at a door.

Talen lit up her irons and crept forward, scanning the floor and walls. They reached the door without finding any traps or wards. The door was old oak, reinforced with iron around the edges. Through it, she heard the scraping and faint, almost wheezing, breaths. She moved closer and made to put her ear to the door, but drew up short. The reek of corruption seeped through the edges.

She drew back, almost bumping into Margaret.

"What?" Margaret asked in a barely audible whisper.

"Stained," Talen mouthed and pointed to the door.

The color drained from Margaret's face, but she hefted the rifle and nodded.

Talen slipped back into her role as a Shadow Warden, a destroyer of stained, and then leaned back and put a boot to the door.

It was solid, but the frame wasn't. The door tore from the old wood frame and fell in. Talen stepped into the room, irons leveled and ready to fire.

Her fingers twitched, but she didn't shoot.

Eight emaciated things, in the ragged remains of clothing, sat chained to tables, working away on stones. The stench of corruption mixed with the feces collecting at their feet. Above them, a single crystal hung, casting pale white moonlight on the room.

"Oh," Margaret said, covering her mouth and gagging as she stepped up behind Talen.

The stained crafters turned away from the brighter light of the torch. Even so, Talen could see their eyes were pools of swirling black.

"Monsters enslaving monsters," Talen said.

"Food," one rasped. "Water. We work. You bring food and water." It shook a tray to its left, rattling the stones inside.

"They're starving," Margaret said.

"No," Talen whispered. "They're starved. The only thing keeping them alive is the corruption. They ain't much more than animals now."

She stared unblinking at the pathetic creatures, more than a little taken aback with what she was feeling. Stained were abominations that had to be destroyed, and she'd killed more than her share. But this… She couldn't even find words for it. Abhorrence? Cruelty? Nothing could encompass the sheer wrongness of what she saw.

"Food," they all began to chant. "Water!"

Talen took aim with her irons and fired, hitting two with force spells. Their heads vanished, replaced by a red/black spray that coated the walls and the stained behind them.

None of the others so much as flinched, just kept chanting.

Only indignation kept her from vomiting.

One by one, Talen put each of them down. She'd never killed a stained so easy or felt so hollow after. She damned sure wouldn't feel hollow when she killed the man behind this horror though.

When all the stained were dead, Talen collected the stones from the tables, pouring them into a single tray. When she and Margaret got back to the main floor, even the city air tasted fresh and clean.

"Was that crystal producing the moonlight?" Margaret asked.

Talen nodded. "I'd wager. I once saw something similar but for sunlight. You charge it up during the day and it shines through the night."

"Someone put a lot of planning into this."

"They surely did." Talen nodded back the way they'd come. "Let's get these stones and the rifles back to Wilfred. He ought to be about done now."

Talen set the tray on the stack of crates and started pushing. Margaret kept her torch high and her repeater ready as they walked. Before coming around the last partition wall, Talen paused and gave a whistle.

"Come on," Draven said. "I won't shoot."

Talen pushed the cart up next to one of the leviathans.

"Sacred stone," Draven said. "You two look like you saw a ghost."

"Damn near," Talen said and then turned to Wilfred. "How much longer?"

"Just about done."

"What the hell happened?" Draven asked.

Talen filled her in.

"Whoever's behind this is in desperate need of killing," Draven said.

"No mistake," Talen said.

"All done." Wilfred got to his feet.

Talen eyed the bomb. "Work like the other?" It looked like an enlarged spell charge with etched symbols along the outside. Though not much bigger than one of Wilfred's hands, she knew from experience what it could do.

He nodded. "Put a magic heavy fire load into it and then run like hell. You got two minutes to get gone before it goes up. It ain't gonna explode exactly, but it will make a big, hot fire ball. You'd best be someplace else when that happens."

"When it's time, you all go first," Talen said. "When you're clear, I'll set it off. Two minutes is more than enough time for me to get clear."

"We ain't leaving?" Wilfred asked.

"Not yet," Talen said. "We didn't find no designs, but there's an office. I want a look-see before we go."

"Lead the way," Draven said.

Talen reloaded her irons as they walked, replacing the force charges in kind.

"How long you reckon it'd take to craft the magic parts of them rifles?" Talen asked Wilfred as they passed the stations.

"They're unique. But don't look overly complicated. I reckon I could do one in a week, two at most."

"So, two for an average crafter?"

Wilfred smiled. "Maybe three."

"Call it four months then."

"Pardon?" Wilfred asked.

"That they've been at this." Talen explained her math.

"Yep, these are for the mechanisms," Draven said, examining the machinery. "This setup looks to make the barrels." She gestured at some other machines. "Those likely do the connections and the rest."

Talen nodded at Wilfred. "Think his big ball of fire will see to them?"

"Might," Draven said and looked at Wilfred. "How hot you suspect it'll get?"

Wilfred shrugged. "Don't know as the number, but plenty hot. Reckon this whole building will be a furnace."

Draven nodded. "Assuming they don't get the fire out too quick, it should do fine."

"Good." Talen led on.

"I'm guessing that's where you found the stained crafters?" Wilfred asked, covering his mouth as they came to the cabinet, still on its side.

Talen nodded. "I'll put a fire charge down there before I set off the bomb. Between the bodies and the shit, a single shot ought to do it."

"I confess," Wilfred said. "There're times I'm mighty glad I can't use a spell iron."

"Douse your torches," Talen said to Wilfred and Margaret. "I don't want the boys out front seeing any light if they happen to look up at the windows."

They did so and proceeded up the stairs single file, Wilfred bringing up the rear. When she reached the door, Talen motioned for them to be silent.

She listened but didn't hear anything. She tried the knob. No surprise, it was locked.

"Allow me," Draven whispered.

Talen and Draven squeezed past each other, the dwarf's broad frame took up almost the entire stairway.

Draven produced some tools and set to work on the lock. In a matter of seconds, she nodded and then examined the door edge and the knob itself.

"No traps," she said in a whisper.

Talen drew her irons and nodded for Draven to open the door.

She did, and nothing happened.

Inside they found a large, well-decorated office. A massive wooden desk occupied most of the room. A line of cabinets sat along the wall opposite the windows overlooking the factory floor.

"Let's get to work," Talen said.

"Y'all might see just fine," Wilfred said. "But we humans are damn near blind in here."

"No torches," Talen said. "They're too bright."

"Pass it here," Draven said and held out her hand.

Wilfred handed it over, and Draven turned a dial near the top. When she switched it on, it gave only a faint glow, little more than a candle. Draven passed it back to Wilfred and then did the same to Margaret's.

"The windows face the factory," Draven said. "We should be okay."

"Unless someone comes inside," Talen said. "Let's be quick about it."

The four of them set to work, starting at the desk, but the drawers were locked. Draven found, and then quickly disarmed, the traps on each. Talen busted them open—no point in being gentle when the whole place would burn.

Wilfred and Draven searched through the cabinets.

"Well, hello there," Wilfred said.

"What'd you find?" Talen asked.

"A whole mess of crafting wares." He began filling his bag. "I'll just be helping myself, if you don't mind."

"Careful they ain't stained," Talen said, flipped through papers. She couldn't make sense of any of them.

"Accounting records," Margaret said, after a glance.

Talen tossed them aside and kept searching. She came across a letter. "Listen to this. *Mr. Tuller, we are very interested in your proposed solution to our reliance on dwarven armaments. I have secured, in your name, a grant from Congress. It should provide for your initial experiments. We look forward to hearing of your results as soon as possible. Sincerely yours, William W. Belknap, Secretary of War.*"

"The government knows about this?" Margaret asked. "Supports it even?"

"I ain't surprised," Talen said. "It's a new and terrible weapon. One they can use and ain't got to pay the dwarves for."

"I imagine the Dolomite would be interested in that," Draven said.

"I don't know," Margaret said. "I don't trust most politicians, but I can't imagine they really understand the whole truth. How do you defend using innocent people as…well, fuel?"

"Reckon it depends on who the innocent are," Wilfred said. "Some folk count for less than others."

Talen passed the letter to Draven. "It'll do more good with the dwarves. At least now we know Tuller is the one behind it all."

Draven took the letter and stuck it in her jacket. "Aye, I'll see to it."

"I'm not finding any designs," Margaret said. "Anyone else?"

Everyone answered no.

"Might be he keeps them at home," Wilfred said.

"Not likely," Draven said. "He'd have to haul them in any time the engineers needed them. They're here. We just haven't found them yet."

"Reckon he'd keep them in a safe?" Wilfred asked a moment later.

"I would," Draven said.

"Good, 'cause I just found one."

Everyone stood and turned. Wilfred had pulled a false front away from the bottom two shelves of a cabinet to reveal a steel safe.

"Allow me," Draven said.

Wilfred stepped aside. "You ever considered bank robbery as a profession?"

"As I understand it," Draven said, placing another tool over the dial, "Human law says I don't have to answer a question that might incriminate me."

Wilfred chuckled.

Draven turned some dials and then hit a button on the device. It whirred softly, like a hummingbird's wings. Five seconds later, the locked clicked and Draven pulled the door open.

"I do believe we found what we're looking for." She pulled a stack of papers from the safe and set them on the desk.

They were drawings, but Talen couldn't make head or tails of them.

Draven flipped through the pages, scanning each for a second before going to the next.

"Is that what we're looking for?" Talen asked.

"It is. And they're brilliant, for a human. Working within their limited technology, it's mighty impressive."

"Admire later. Put them in Wilfred's bag and let's get gone. I still plan on paying Mr. Tuller a visit."

They packed up and made their way to the back door. They found it, and the bodies, just as they'd left them.

"We'll meet you across the river," Margaret said. She gave Talen directions, repeating them until she had them memorized.

"I'll give you ten minutes before I set it off," Talen said. "Best get a move on."

The three left, Draven leading the way.

Talen watched them go. They went to the far end of the next building over before turning down a side street. When they were gone, she made her way back to the underground crafting chamber.

The smell had gotten even worse. The bodies, kept alive only by the corruption, had already begun to putrefy. She stood in the shadows, watching for unexpected arrivals as she counted the time. When she reached 600, she went down the stairs, sent a fire charge into the room, and turned her face away.

Air sucked past as the charge exploded and set the room to burning. She bolted up the stairs, taking them two at a time and sprinted for the waiting bomb.

"Son of a bitch!" someone shouted from the back of the building as Talen neared her destination.

"Look at Joseph!" another said. "He's a Goddamned statue!"

"Get around front," the first voice said. "Tell Jessie and the others to get their asses back here, right now! Come around, not through."

Talen chanced a glance around the wall, spotted three Pinkertons, and cursed silently. At least the others were well away by now. She looked at the spell bomb. Could someone cut the fuse—as it were—before it blew? She couldn't take the chance.

She holstered her irons, drew her knives, and wrapped herself in shadow. Then she sprinted around the partition wall toward the Pinkertons. The one at the lead turned at the sound of her footsteps.

He wore a brass eyepiece and stared right at Talen.

"Elf!" he shouted, raising his spell iron.

The other two turned.

Talen went to her knees and slid the last few feet. He fired, sending a blast of force over her head, and demolishing the wall behind her. She drove one knife into his groin and cut across the inside of his thigh as she pulled it out.

He stumbled past Talen as she got to her feet.

She kicked at his back, and he fell hard, his face smacking the floor.

The other two—neither had an eyepiece—looked around, pointing their lit spell irons in desperation. Talen danced between them, cutting the throat of one as she spun past, and shoving her blades into the other's chest, piercing his heart.

They both fell.

On instinct, she spun to her right, sheathing her knives and drawing both irons.

Another force blast tore away a section of wall behind where she'd been standing.

She stepped from the shadows, lit her irons, and gave the Pinkerton on the floor both barrels. The arctic spell hit him full on, turning him into an iceberg. The force blast hit half a second later, shattering the ice and the man inside.

She doused her irons, stepped back into the shadows, and waited.

Silence.

She didn't wait to see how long it would last. She bolted for the bomb, rotating the cylinders as she did. Fifteen feet away, she took aim with her right-hand iron. In a single stride, she dropped her veil, poured as much magic into the iron as she could, and fired into the bomb. Then she doused the iron and stepped back into shadows.

Three small comets streaked forward, trailing crackling sparks. They exploded on impact, engulfing the spell bomb in blue-tinted flame. When the fire dissipated, the bomb smoldered, casting blue sparks in every direction.

Talen waited a thirty count and then turned and ran as fast as she could, continuing the count in her head.

Forty-five.

She leapt out the back door and planted her feet on the far wall. She pushed off at an angle and hit the ground running.

Sixty.

Pounding footsteps came up the side street.

Seventy.

She reached the alley and turned. The four Pinkertons from the front, and three of the hired thugs, were running right at her.

None had eyepieces.

Seventy-five.

She drove an elbow into the lead man, shoving him hard into the wall, and slamming his forehead against the brick. She pushed away and into the next, hammering her knee into his crotch.

He doubled over.

She grabbed his coat, spun, and hurled him into the wall. He hit hard and crumpled.

Eighty.

The others came to a stop and spread out, weapons up, searching for a target.

Talen drew her knives and began the dance again. She spun, slicing and cutting.

The men started firing their mundane shooters. Shots bounced off the walls and her coat.

Ninety.

She kicked out low, knocking the last man's legs out and sending him crashing to the ground.

He fired wild. The bullet passed so close to her cheek, she felt it.

She drove her blades home, as he struggled to kick or pistol whip her. It took her several tries to finally get his heart, and he went still.

She rolled to her feet and ran for the street. She kept herself wrapped in shadows but didn't bother to keep silent or avoid puddles.

One hundred-ten.

She reached the street and turned, following what she prayed were Margaret's directions. A few people meandered about but only a few. Hopefully they wouldn't get hurt or killed, but she didn't have time to worry much.

One hundred nineteen.

She ducked down an alley and put her back to the wall.

One hundred—

A literal earthshaking boom sounded briefly, before being replaced by a ringing in Talen's ears. Broken glass and brick dust rained down on her. She stood and looked back, brushing the debris from her coat with one hand, bracing herself against the brick wall with the other.

A pillar of flame had punched through the roof of the factory and reached high into the night sky like the hand of some colossal, fiery god. She could only stare for a handful of heartbeats, exalting in the terrible magnificence. The ringing in her ears was slowly replaced by the sounds of horses neighing their dismay and people shouting for the fire brigade.

She stepped from the shadows before remembering the glamour was gone. In a panic, she looked around but didn't see anyone else in the alley. The fire had everyone's attention. She put the second to last glamour stone into her mouth and did her best to shape a matching image to the last one. Once it settled over her, she got her bearings and hurried off to meet the others.

Chapter Twenty-Eight

The city grew more frenetic as Talen wove through the mass of people in the streets. The flames from the factory were still visible, more so as night settled in. It seemed the whole city had left their homes to see the spectacle.

After fifteen minutes, she found Margaret, Wilfred, and Draven.

"You had us a might worried," Wilfred said.

"Had some late arrivals to the party."

The three shared a look.

"I'm fine, though I can't say the same for them," Talen said. "Time is wasting though. We need to move." She looked at Margaret. "Lead the way."

Soon they'd moved far enough away from the fire that the gawking crowds thinned out. The quality and size of houses changed. Tenement buildings in various states of disrepair gave way to large manor homes. Talen ignored the almost obscene displays of wealth amid so much suffering. She saved her anger—currently smoldering beneath a controlled calm—for Tuller.

"Do we have a plan?" Draven asked, as they rounded another corner.

"Find the rabid dog and put him down," Talen said.

"Just kick in the door, shoot the man, and move along?" Wilfred asked.

"You disagree with that?" Talen asked.

"Just wondering if we oughtn't to have a plan," he said. "I mean to say, if it gets loud, we set for a quick escape?"

"If that's an attempt to get me back to the ship," Margaret said. "I politely decline your invitation."

"I wasn't suggesting no such thing," Wilfred said. "Rather, I didn't mean it as such. Just saying we're a goodly distance from the Cumulus."

"That's a reasonable concern," Draven said.

"You're right." Talen stopped.

The others did as well.

"Don't you dare send me back," Margaret said, meeting Talen's gaze.

The shining streetlamps and faint sheen of moisture made Margaret's eyes look like glass. Talen marveled for half a moment. They were lovely.

Talen placed a hand on Margaret's shoulder. "I won't. You deserve to see this through. You ain't a child, and you understand what's ahead. Isn't my place to stop you." She looked at Wilfred. "But you're right. We're bringing down a rich and powerful man. We'll like as not need to get gone, and right quick."

Everyone looked to Draven.

"Ah, hell," she said. "This has been the most fun I've had in months. Shame to quit just before the last dance."

Wilfred shrugged. "Suppose I could take a hand at—"

"Last man that tried to pilot my Cumulus lost more than his hands," Draven said. She sighed, pulled one of her dwarven pistols, and passed it to Wilfred. "Take this. At least it'll be like something of me is there."

"Work like a regular shooter?" Wilfred asked, looking it over.

"Safety catch is part of the trigger mechanism. You got seven shots, and it does have a kick."

"I'll take proper care of it." Wilfred tucked it into one of his pockets and pulled his shirt down to cover the exposed handle.

"See that you do, and that it gets some use." Draven turned to Margaret. "Where do you want me waiting when it's done?"

Margaret considered. "South of the West Boston Bridge, at the bend in the Charles. You know where that is?"

"I'll find it easy enough."

"It's all mudflats," Margaret said. "You'll need to put down close to the roads for us to get on board."

"Won't be a problem. I'll need about twenty minutes to get back to the ship and ten more to get the meeting location."

"We'll give you the time," Talen said. "Be careful."

Draven chuckled. "Aye, 'cause I've surely got the worst of this. Don't have too much fun without me."

"Ain't gonna be no fun without you," Wilfred said.

Draven winked and then left.

"Let's get to the house and make sure there ain't no surprises waiting," Talen said. "I've had about enough of them tonight."

"I suppose a girl can hope," Margaret said.

Ten minutes later, they came to another corner. Just as she rounded it, Margaret stopped and stepped back out of sight.

"A surprise?" Talen asked.

Margaret nodded.

Talen moved past her and looked. Five men in rough, road-dirty clothes stood outside a very large house. They were smoking and talking, not focused on watching the street, and all wore red gloves on their right hands.

"Five Red Hands," Talen said. "Don't reckon they're guards."

"Why else would they be here?" Margaret asked. "Just having them outside his house will cause a scandal, and I can't imagine Tuller will be happy about it."

"Pratt met with a group of them," Talen said. "Might be someone wants a word with the boss."

"Maybe they came for the same reason as us," Wilfred said. "If the

Hand learned all Tuller had his fingers into, I don't expect they'd be too supportive. Ain't they fanatics?"

Talen shook her head. "They didn't want nothing to do with them rifles, but they didn't get indignant neither. Once a stained is in a crystal, they like as not see anything that happens as part of divine judgment."

"Even if they ain't really stained?" he asked.

Talen shrugged.

"I, for one, am not fond of the idea of having common cause with them," Margaret said. "So, what are we going to do? Your 'kick in the door and shoot him' plan seems to have hit a complication."

"We got time before Draven can meet us," she said. "And that fire will burn for a long while yet. We'll sit and see if they clear out. Waiting don't cost us nothing but time."

"I just want all this done with," Margaret said. "Though I'm not sure what I'll do when it is. The bounty will still be on me, even if the Red Hand won't be able to cash it in."

"You're welcome to join me in Lawrence," Wilfred said. "I could use some help running my shop. Pay ain't great, but it's something."

Margaret smiled. "Thank you for the offer. It's kind of you."

"That's an awful polite 'no,'" he said.

She shrugged. "I don't know if I want to go back to how things were before all this. So much has changed, myself included."

Talen wouldn't let her mind wander to the after. Plenty of work left to do before she could indulge in that. "You'll find your place," she said, still watching the Red Hands. "It might take some time, but you will. Just do what makes you happy."

"I'm not sure I know anymore," Margaret said. "I like it on the Cumulus. Think Draven would let me stay?"

"She seemed happy enough alone," Wilfred said. "But I confess, she do seem happier now."

"Maybe 'cause she can finally be herself," Talen said. "None of us care she ain't a man. There's something to be said for the simple joy of not having to hide who you are."

Margaret nodded. "There certainly is."

The conversation dwindled and they waited in silence.

"Still there?" Wilfred asked sometime later.

Talen nodded.

"How long we been waiting?" he asked.

"Long enough, I reckon. Time to make our move."

"You figure we can take on five?" Wilfred asked.

"Wait," Talen said, as a young boy came running up to the house.

Wilfred and Margaret stepped over to peer around the corner.

The Red Hands went to draw their irons, but seeing a child, held back. They just crossed their arms and took up an imposing posture.

Brave man that intimidates a child.

"Looks like a messenger," Margaret said. "He could be sending word of the factory fire."

"We got to move now then," Talen said. "If he decides to see for himself, we ain't going to be able to finish this. Get your guns out but keep them low and stay behind me. Wait for me to move."

"You plan to just walk up and say good evening?" Wilfred asked, drawing Draven's pistol.

Margaret pulled her repeater from her coat.

"Ain't that the polite thing to do?" Talen stepped around the corner and walked with purpose toward Tuller's house and the waiting Red Hands.

Margaret and Wilfred took up behind her, their hearts pounding.

Talen kept a close eye on the Red Hands, but also noted any movement in her peripheral vision. With luck, the street would remain empty.

"But I got a message for Mr. Tuller," the boy said. "Please, sirs, you must let me by."

"And we done told you," one of the Red Hands said. "Ain't no one getting inside till our boss finishes with him."

"Sir, this is urgent."

"I don't care, boy," the man said. "You get now, 'fore I find a switch and tan—"

"Don't touch him," Talen said, pitching her voice low.

The Red Hands looked to her, hands going to their irons.

"Mind your own, Paddy," the Red Hand said. "This ain't none of your concern."

From his swagger, Talen guessed he'd been left in charge while his boss was inside. "Head on home, child," she said to the messenger. "I'm here about the same business as you."

"I don't get paid if I don't deliver," the boy said.

Talen held out a five-dollar coin. "Here's your pay. Now get on home."

"Thank you, sir." The boy took the coin and hurried off.

"Now you need to do the same, Irish," the Red Hand said. "Get, before you and your—"

Talen drove her fist into his throat.

His hands went to his neck as he gasped and took a step back. His companions stared in stunned confusion for a full second. More than enough time.

Talen spit the glamour stone at one of the Red Hands as she drew both her irons, lighting them up as she did. Her glamour collapsed just as her irons leveled.

She put a force blast into the two nearest their choking leader, knocking them back and into a low iron fence. One slammed his head against a protruding spike and went still. The other flopped on the ground, trying to draw air into his ruined lungs and chest.

Wilfred fired, eliciting the now familiar *whump*. His shot went a little wide, catching the Red Hand at his left shoulder. It pulverized the joint and collar bone and sent the man spinning to the ground.

A lightning charge erupted from the barrel of his iron, as he tumbled, and shot into the open sky. The resulting thunderclap shook the windows in the nearby houses.

Margaret stepped from behind Talen and fired her repeater. Her shots went low and caught a Red Hand in the guts. He doubled forward, gripping his bleeding belly and took aim.

Talen fired, sending a torrent of arctic winds at him.

His iron spat fire.

Their magic collided in midair. A cloud of steam exploded out, knocking Talen back a few steps and hiding everything in a thick mist.

The moment she found her balance, Talen fired her right-hand iron. A trio of flaming comets streaked from the barrel. They exploded, burning away the mist and enveloping the Red Hand.

His charred and still-burning body fell to the ground.

Talen turned to check on her friends to find Wilfred aiming right at her. She spun away and saw the Red Hand with the mangled shoulder take another hit. This shot hit just below the neck. Blood painted the outside of the house, and he fell back, unmoving.

She turned back to Wilfred and nodded her thanks.

He returned the gesture.

"Made one hell of a ruckus," Talen said, replacing her spent charges. "Reckon the law will be here damn quick."

Wilfred and Margaret took up step behind her, and they walked to the front door. It opened an instant before they reached it.

A slender, grayed haired man in a butler's uniform gave them a once over. "Who are you ruffians? Are you responsible for that noise? The police—"

Talen punched him in the face, pulling it a little.

He fell back onto an exquisite marble floor and didn't move.

She stepped over him and into the house, irons held high and searching for a target.

Margaret and Wilfred followed, weapons ready.

The large entryway had a room on either side, both empty. A wide staircase sat opposite the door. Halfway up, the stairs split and connected to a landing on the second floor that overlooked the entryway.

Talen took aim there and took a step forward.

"Eugene, what was that noise?" a woman called out.

A moment later, a well-dressed human woman stepped onto the landing. When she saw Talen, Wilfred, and Margaret, she put a hand to her chest.

"Oh, my goodness!" she said. "Who are you? What do you want?"

"Mrs. Tuller, I presume?" Talen asked.

"Elizabeth Marie Hunter Tuller," she said proudly. "Yes, and who are you?"

"We're here for your husband, not you," Talen said.

"Elizabeth?" A man called out from the opposite side of the landing. An instant later, a balding man in a smoking jacket stepped into view.

"That's him," Margaret said.

Tuller gaped at Talen and company. "What's the meaning of this?" He turned to his wife. "Elizabeth, are you all right?"

"Your factory is burning," Talen said. "Your machines, rifles, designs, even that collection of monsters in your basement. It's all going up in smoke."

He stared at her. "What—"

Talen fired her left-hand iron. A green ball of pulsing light streaked toward Tuller.

An inch from his chest, his wife caught the spell.

Talen's blood went cold as the woman's arm slowly turned to marble. When it reached her elbow, she made a face, and it began to recede until her arm was flesh once again.

Elizabeth looked from her hand, still grasping the green orb, to Talen. Her blue eyes filled with swirling black, and the stench of corruption erupted from her, filling the house.

Talen blinked, hoping something was in her eye and she hadn't just seen that. Unfortunately, she knew that even if her eyes lied to her, her nose didn't. She struggled to come up with some explanation, any explanation, as to how any of this was possible.

Tuller stood unmoved by his wife's remarkable effort.

"You?" Talen whispered.

Elizabeth just smiled.

"Damn it, Tuller," another man called from down the hall. "What in tarnation is the hold up? I ain't got all night!" A broad, rough-looking man emerged. He glanced down at Talen, did a double take, and then made to draw his iron.

Elizabeth tossed the green ball of light at the Red Hand leader. In the blink of eye, he turned to white marble.

"Oh, dear me," Elizabeth said, looking from the statue to Talen. "Looks as if you killed the local leader of the Red Right Hand. I think they will be quite displeased with that, elf."

"You're a stained?" Margaret asked.

Elizabeth rolled her black eyes. "Please. Stained are animals, driven by instinct and their baser desires. I'm more, shall we say, evolved."

Despite the impossibility of it all, Talen finally understood.

"You were behind everything," she said.

"My dear puppet husband did the dancing," Elizabeth said, nodding at Tuller. "But yes, I pulled the strings."

Her husband just stood there, impassively staring off into space.

"Why?" Margaret asked, taking a step forward. "You're a woman. You know what it's like. Why would you do this?"

Talen put an arm out, stopping Margaret and putting herself between her sister and the stained.

"Of course, I understand," Elizabeth said. "Why do you think I needed a puppet? As to you, like all the others, you're nothing. A worthless piece of rabble I can make use of." She straightened, standing proud. "And I do it because I'm a patriot."

Despite the tightening in her chest, Talen couldn't hold back a laugh.

Elizabeth scowled. "And that is the problem. You elves and the red savages fill this land that's rightfully ours. It is God's will that we seize the whole of this continent. Of course, we must first remove any and all"—her lips curled into a sneer—"infestations."

Talen swallowed. "Afraid your toys are all broken," she said, still holding the woman in her sights.

Elizabeth shrugged. "Easy enough to collect new ones. Any designs you think you destroyed can be remade. It'll take time, yes, but my plan will succeed. It's ordained by our Heavenly Father." She smiled, eyeing Wilfred and Margaret. "I will, of course, need new crafters and fresh crystals to work with."

Talen fired, right-hand iron first, the left a second later. A ball of force leapt at Elizabeth, a single fireball on its heels.

Elizabeth batted away the force blast, which pulverized the petrified Red Hand leader. The fire didn't go so easy. It exploded, setting the walls, stairs, and Elizabeth herself ablaze.

"Run!" Talen said to Wilfred and Margaret as she rolled her cylinders to fresh charges.

Elizabeth, wrapped in flame, crouched to leap.

Wilfred emptied Draven's pistol at her.

Quarter-size holes tore through the walls and floor of the landing, but none hit home.

Elizabeth dove at Talen.

Talen fired, sending twin blasts of force at the burning woman.

She batted one away, sending it into a wall. The second shot slipped by and connected with her shoulder, sending her off at an angle. She crashed to the ground floor, smashing a table and the finery upon it.

She stood and stared at Talen with hatred and corruption-filled eyes.

Margaret fired off her repeater, sending a hail of bullets at Elizabeth.

Several rounds ripped through burning cloth and charred flesh. The stained women jerked but didn't seem otherwise bothered.

Talen fired again and again. This time a flurry of arctic spells struck Elizabeth, extinguishing the flames and shrouding her in ice.

"Get the hell out, now!" Talen said to her companions. "That ain't going to hold her long."

"I'm not leaving you." Margaret began frantically reloading her repeater.

Wilfred drew his revolver. "Got no place else to be."

Talen opened her mouth to protest, but an explosion of icy chunks brought her up short.

Wilfred emptied his revolver into Elizabeth, but he might as well have been tickling her. He hit all six times, but Elizabeth only jerked with each shot. Already the woman's burned flesh was healing.

Cold tendrils of fear tried to claw up from Talen's guts, but she fought them back.

The house around them wasn't as lucky as its owner. The fire spread to most of the upstairs, including Franklin Tuller. Even burning, he just stood there, impassive. A faint twinge of pity for the man rose inside Talen but died quick enough.

She pivoted back and fired the last of her charges. The movement made her aim awkward and hard to track. A force blast hit Elizabeth's right leg, snapping the thigh in half. The second shot struck her shoulder, tearing the joint free and sending her tumbling backward.

There's no winning this fight. But maybe I can make sure we both lose.

With that realization, the persistent fear and doubt that had besieged Talen melted away.

"You ain't doing nothing to her," she said to her friends. "Get out! I got no idea how long I can hold her back."

"Not long," Elizabeth said, through the sound of her bones snapping back into place.

Talen holstered her spent irons, drew the knives, and wrapped herself in shadow.

"I might not be able to see you, little elf," Elizabeth said, getting to her feet, "but I can sense you clear enough—"

Talen leapt and spun, cutting down the woman's chest and neck. Far too dark red blood oozed, rather than sprayed, from the wounds.

Elizabeth swiped at her.

Talen ducked back, just avoiding the strike. Elizabeth's fist hit the wall, knocking a hole in the plaster and wood frame behind it.

The stained woman was fast, faster even than Talen. But it was obvious she didn't know how to fight.

Talen stabbed, slashed, punched, and kicked, turning and twisting between blows to keep out of reach. A distant corner of her mind noticed no more gunshots. She hoped that meant Wilfred and Margaret finally did what she'd asked.

A lucky blow caught Talen's jaw. Her vision went white as her head snapped to one side, and next thing she knew, she was tumbling through the air like a tossed rag doll. The shadows slipped away from her, and she crashed into a wall, almost going through it.

A thousand flashes of intense pain shot through her whole body, and she fell to the ground, gasping for breath.

On instinct, she rolled away, just as Elizabeth stomped down, smashing a marble tile to powder. Talen kept rolling and then twisted her hips, kicking her legs out and regaining her feet.

"It's been a very long time since we killed a Shadow Warden," Elizabeth said, in a voice not entirely her own.

"I ain't dead yet, stained." Talen lunged forward.

As Elizabeth swung.

Talen dropped to her knees, and slid past her, avoiding the fist by inches.

As she went by, Talen turned and slashed out with her blades. Deep cuts appeared at the backs of Elizabeth's knees, severing the tendons. More almost-black blood leaked out like molasses, and she fell to the ground.

Elizabeth cried out, more in anger and frustration than pain.

Talen made to drive both knives into the prone woman's skull.

Elizabeth swung out her legs like a flail and caught Talen's side. The blow sent her into a table, knocking the wind from her lungs and the knives from her hands.

Talen worked to get her breath and looked down. Her shirt had torn open, exposing the crystal set in her stomach.

Elizabeth looked from the crystal to Talen with a mix of fear, hatred, and confusion.

Yeah, you ain't the only oddity here.

Talen straightened, pulled off her coat, and let it fall to the floor.

Elizabeth leapt at Talen on her already-healed legs.

Talen stepped to one side and grabbed a marble bust from a table to her left. She brought it down as hard as she could onto the back of Elizabeth's head. Talen missed, striking Elizabeth's neck instead, but still sending the woman to the floor.

"Talen, move!" Margaret shouted.

Margaret stood in the doorway, a burning spell iron in her right hand.

Talen tumbled back into one of the side rooms next to the entryway and covered her ears.

Margaret emptied her spell iron. Fire, lightning, and force magic rained down on Elizabeth, setting her aflame and hammering her against the floor. The windows blew out from the thunderclap, raining glass onto the street.

Elizabeth lay, smoldering and twitching, on the floor.

Talen got to her feet and went to Margaret's side.

Margaret kept turning the cylinder and pulling the trigger.

Talen recognized the iron as belonging to a Red Right Hand.

"It's empty," she said, taking the iron from her friend and dropping it to the floor.

"I did it," Margaret said, smiling wide. "I can't believe I did it."

"No, you didn't," Elizabeth said, her voice rough and dry.

Talen sighed and turned. "Damn it, lady, die already."

The stained pushed herself up from the floor, joints popping into place and skin healing.

Before Elizabeth could stand, Talen threw herself atop the woman.

Elizabeth hammered her with fists as Talen squirmed and twisted, trying to press the crystal against Elizabeth's exposed flesh.

Her ribs cracked, but Talen gritted her teeth against the searing pain, and pushed on.

At last, the crystal touched Elizabeth's skin.

She screamed and bucked like a wild mustang.

Talen's vision darkened, and she gasped for air, but every attempt was answered with a sharp, stabbing pain, and she came up short.

Elizabeth kept bellowing and struggling.

Talen locked her arms and legs around the stained woman and pressed the crystal harder into her skin. A new pain, this one on the inside, tore through Talen like a stampeding herd of buffalo covered in flaming spikes.

Her guts twisted, and she had to fight not to vomit. She felt the crystal grew hot as—she hoped—it drew the corruption from Elizabeth and into itself. It burned Talen's insides, and her mouth filled with a rancid taste.

Time lost meaning, and she almost slipped away but held tight, keeping the crystal pressed again Elizabeth's skin. It felt like trying to swim and breathe amid an ocean of foulness.

I may not survive this, she thought and smiled. *But I damned sure ain't going alone.*

Elizabeth gave a final scream and then Talen found herself atop a thick pile of ash.

She rolled to her back, coughing painfully, and struggling to breathe. All she could manage were small gasps of air as her insides seemed determined to see how tight a knot they could make. She vomited, twice, but managed to turn her head before she did. Above her, the flames were swimming over the ceiling of the house beneath a sea of smoke. She could hardly breathe and couldn't move at all.

Everything hurt and she had neither the strength, nor the will, to even try to move. She was so tired. Weary to the very soul, and she wanted nothing more in that moment than to sleep.

The light from the flames dimmed.

Talen smiled, content, and tears slipped from her eyes.

Mother, I'm coming home.

Chapter Twenty-Nine

Talen opened her eyes, surprised, and more than a little disappointed, to find she wasn't dead. Slowly, the sensation of her body came to her, and she blinked her vision clear. She lay in a bed, in a windowless, stone-walled room.

Margaret sat at her bedside, holding her hand.

"Where am I?" Talen asked.

Margaret gasped. "Oh my God. You're awake. Thank God." She turned away. "Wilfred, Draven, come quick."

Talen tried to sit up, but a sudden stab of intense pain stole her breath and brought her up short. She fell back and, thankfully, the pain faded.

"Don't move. You're still healing." Margaret gently pushed her back down onto the soft bed.

Now you tell me.

"Water?" Talen asked, glad to see it only hurt a little to speak.

Margaret held a large stone cup to her lips. Remembering last time, she sipped instead of guzzled. The cold, clean water slid down her throat and sent waves of euphoria coursing through her.

Wilfred and Draven came into the room, both smiling like fools.

Talen's heart swelled at seeing her friends, but the joy was tainted by more than a little regret that she hadn't died. She tried not to think about her sisters and mother, at having to wait to see them again.

"I knew you wouldn't go down so easy," Wilfred said. "Though you gave us one hell of a scare, again."

"Easy? I ain't sure we're talking about the same thing." She looked at Margaret. "Well done with that spell iron. You didn't just save my hide, you saved us all."

"No, you did all the work."

"If you hadn't softened her up, I never would've gotten hold of her. Thank you, sister."

Margaret smiled and squeezed her hand.

Talen pushed away the thought that it was the same hand Margaret had used to hold the blood-marked iron.

"Now, could someone please tell me where the hell we are? And why I ain't dead?"

"You're an honored guest in the home of the Granite Lord himself," Draven said. "And, in point of fact, you almost were dead."

"After you saw to Mrs. Tuller," Wilfred said. "Margaret and I got you out and back to the ship."

"He did," Margaret said. "I carried your coat and knives."

"We had no idea what you'd done or how," Wilfred said. "Imagine our surprise when we learned you had a damned bounty crystal in you."

Talen explained to them about Pratt's bullets, her failed attempts to heal, and the elemental's help.

"I told them as much," Draven said.

"You have rather impressive friends," Margaret said.

Talen nodded and smiled. "I do, at that."

"You were fading fast," Draven said. "So, I brought you here. I couldn't think of anything else to do."

"I'm surprised they even let me inside the door," Talen said.

"Oh, they weren't too keen on letting you in," Draven said. "They were actually dead set against it. It took nearly a day to get here. By then, you were stinking of corruption."

Talen's blood ran cold. Her hand moved, without her telling it to, to the crystal in her side.

"The crystal, not you," Draven said. "When I showed the guards, and told them how you got it, they changed their minds quick."

"Simple as that?"

"Well, I might've had to swear on my mother's bare chin a couple times," Draven said and then nodded at Wilfred. "And he might've threatened to blow up the whole damn mountain."

"Blow up the mountain?" Talen asked. "How the hell did you plan to pull that off?"

"Didn't," Wilfred said, grinning a little. "Course, they didn't know that. I'm a crafter and they ain't got no magic. I reckoned they didn't rightly know what I could and couldn't do."

"They were still more than a bit nervous," Draven said. "But they set to fixing you up. Before they finished asking if any elemental would help, two made an appearance."

"Two?" Talen wasn't sure if that had been a sign of respect, or how bad the corruption was. She decided it best not to dwell on it.

Draven nodded. "Not old ones, mind. Younger earth elementals—a granite and a sandstone. But understand young is a relative term. They might be only ten or twenty thousand years old."

"They couldn't remove the crystal," Margaret said.

Talen pulled the blankets away and lifted her shirt. The crystal looked different somehow. As clear as a still lake. Cleaner was the only way she could think to describe it.

"They did manage to transfer the corruption to a new crystal," Draven said. "Wove one together right then and there. Hell of a thing to see."

"Transferred?" Talen asked. "How?"

"No idea. They just formed it between them, touched it to yours, and the black just flowed from one to the other."

"What did you do with the new one?"

"We cast it into the kingdom's reactor," a low but powerful voice said from behind her friends.

They turned, and Draven bowed at the waist.

A dwarf, bare-chinned as Draven, stepped into the room. He only had an inch or so on her in terms of height but several inches at the shoulders.

"My Lord," Draven said and then looked at Talen. "May I present the Granite Lord, Torren of the Beardless."

Talen glanced at Wilfred and Margaret. Both smiled and gave her a reassuring nod.

"A new title, but one I'm rather fond of," he said, smiling. "Shadow Warden Talen, I'm delighted to see you recovering so well."

"Thank you for your hospitality and assistance," Talen said. Even knowing the circumstances, it felt damn strange to be thanking a dwarf for saving her life.

"I imagine it must be more than a little awkward for an elf to thank a dwarf for anything, much less saving her life," he said, his smile fading.

Talen made a noncommittal shrug.

"Allow me to offer our sincerest apologies for the actions of our brothers and sisters," he said. "Words fail, but I hope we can do more."

"More?"

"Draven shared that letter and the corrupted stones with me," Torren said. "Told us about the human leviathans and the rifles, as well. We've dispatched an emissary to our bearded kin, asking to meet over a matter of urgency. If anything could reunite the dwarven people, this could be it."

Talen bit back an angry reply.

"If it does," Torren said. "A requirement would be an unbreakable alliance with the remaining elves. Never again will we sell our honor for gold or treasures."

Talen wanted to believe that, or that the bearded would agree to such a thing, but she didn't have the optimism. "What if they say no?"

Torren looked at Draven and then back to Talen. "War, almost certainly."

She shook her head, suddenly very tired.

"We'll talk another time," Torren said. "I just wanted to thank you in person and tell you that you are welcome among the beardless and will forever be a friend."

Talen nodded. "Thank you."

Torren turned and left, Draven once more bowing deep.

"You need to rest and heal," she said. "When you're mended, I'll take you wherever you want to go. But know you're welcome on my ship anytime, for as long as you like."

"Much obliged."

"I'll be checking on you often enough to annoy you, of course," Wilfred said. He bent low and kissed her forehead.

"Get the hell out," Talen said through a smile.

"Draven's letting me stay on the Cumulus," Margaret said. "We, um, make a good team. All of us, I mean."

"I reckon we do," Talen said. "But I got things to tend to, and I can't be in that ship all the time." Her heart tore a little, so she decided to change the subject. "Speaking of which, how is Gaoth?"

"He's fine. Grazing outside with Joseph and Elise," Margaret said. "I'll be going to see him right now and let him know you pulled through."

"Tell him I'll be along as soon as I'm able. And maybe bring him an apple if you can find one."

"I will." Margaret stood, bent over, and, very carefully, hugged Talen. "Thank you, for everything. I'll never be able to repay you. You didn't just save my life. You gave me a new one."

"Make it a happy one and we'll call it even," Talen said, hugging back. Until that moment, she'd forgotten how much she'd missed hugs from a sister. Or rather, she hadn't let herself remember.

Margaret straightened, wiped at her eyes, and laughed. "I think I'm going to take a break from bawling for a while."

"Don't," Talen said. "Ain't no shame in tears. You earned every one."

Margaret took her hands away from her eyes. "I'll be back to check on you later."

Talen nodded.

Margaret left, leaving Talen alone.

"Thank you, for everything," she said to the empty room. "You saved my life, too."

Epilogue

Talen lay back against the pillow. Her whole body ached, and the crystal felt strange, as if her body hadn't healed to it like before. She hoped the dwarven reactor destroyed the other, and the corruption in it.

She closed her eyes, wanting to sleep for a week. Or forever, if she were honest about it. She felt unmoored again, drifting on the tides and waiting for a wind to blow her one way or another. The last time she'd felt like this had been when she'd lost her family and everyone she loved. Well, not everyone, she conceded, thinking of Wilfred. How odd to feel the same when the opposite happened.

Everything had changed and it disquieted her. She'd never flinched away from change before, but maybe she just wasn't used to so much of it so fast.

"We make a good team. All of us, I mean," Margaret had said.

And she'd been right. Part of Talen wanted to stay on the ship, stay with her new friends. Maybe even convince Wilfred to join them. But more of her wanted to go. Maybe "wanted" wasn't quite the right word. It just felt like the right thing to do.

It certainly wouldn't be fair to keep Gaoth in those stables. He needed to run, be free, and feel the wind in his mane. Part of her needed that too.

She didn't know what to do. There was work to be done and promises to keep though. She needed to learn where the bounty crystals came from, and there'd always be stained.

Her thoughts turned to Elizabeth and the temperature in the room seemed to drop several degrees. Tuller hadn't been an ordinary stained. But had she just been a singular monster? Or the first of a new breed?

Talen hoped for the former, but deep down, she knew the truth.

She stood at a crossroad, several paths before her. Each pulled at her heart, her mind, her soul or all three. But sleep called to her and pushed the making of long-term decisions aside. She closed her eyes and sank into a peaceful sleep, filled with happy dreams.

After two more days, Talen felt well enough to get outside and use a healing prayer to finish what her body had started on its own. It took almost two weeks to fully recover. During that time, she came to a decision.

True to her word, Draven didn't flinch when Talen asked to go home. Margaret, now part of the crew, and even Wilfred, went along to see her off. Talen couldn't find words to express her gratitude. The trip took longer than needed. Several times she asked to stop so she could ride Gaoth for a few hours. It got tense crossing the Rockies. If the Bearded knew the Cumulus passed overhead, they did nothing to stop it. Draven played it off, but Talen saw the worry in her face.

When, at long last, the redwoods and sequoias rose in the distance, Talen's heart stirred with both joy and sadness. The once massive forest, though still expansive, had acres of ancient trees missing; casualties of the human lust for lumber.

"Take care of yourself," Draven said, offering her hand.

"And you, my friend." Talen took the hand and pulled the dwarf into a hug.

"My offer doesn't expire. If you ever change your mind, I'd be glad to have you aboard again."

"I'll remember that." Talen turned to Wilfred.

He wrapped her in his arms and held her close. The smell of tobacco, leather, clean wool, and his own unique scent surrounded her in the light and joy of memories past. She kissed his lips softly.

"Keep a light in the window for me," she said. "Might be, I'll stop by Lawrence and see you again."

He shrugged. "Not sure I'll be there."

Talen smiled. "Margaret convinced you to join the crew?"

"For a spell, I reckon. Feels a bit like I found a home here, and I suspect I can do a lot of good."

"Of course you can, my *sans shulla*. You're a good man." She kissed him again.

"A better one for knowing you."

A few tears slipped down Talen's cheeks.

"It's not too late to change your mind," Margaret said, hugging her tight. "I don't want to lose my sister."

"You never lose a sister," Talen said, pressing her cheek to the top of Margaret's head. "But like I said, I got things to see to."

Margaret stepped back and nodded. "I understand. I'll miss you."

"I'll miss you, too," Talen said and kissed her cheek.

With nothing more to say, she turned, climbed onto Gaoth, and rode off. She only looked back once to see her friends waving goodbye.

She arrived at her home just as the sun started to sink into the vast Pacific. Only it wasn't home, anymore. In the years since the slaughter, nature had reclaimed the land. There were no structures left and no bodies. No sign at all her people had ever been there.

She drew in a slow breath. That was as it should be. How the elves had always intended. All that remained of her home, of her family, were the memories: centuries of laughter, tears, joys, and sorrows.

She sat at what had always been her favorite spot—the top of a high ridge overlooking the endless blue Pacific—Gaoth at her side, and watched the sun sink below the horizon. She wept, sobbed even, for all she'd lost and for what she'd found. She chewed ferns, having almost forgotten how sweet they were, and looked back on her long life. She saw a long winding path behind, but shadows and darkness clouded the way forward.

Even so, she smiled. On that shadowed trail were lights of bright hope, holding back the darkness. She let out a breath and stood.

She knew what to do now, but more than that, she was ready to do it.

"Mother," she said, her voice filling the forest. "I miss you and while I long to join you and my sisters, I know that isn't for me. Not yet at least." She drew in a long breath, savoring the scent of the trees, the earth, and ocean. "I'm not alone anymore. I found a new family, a strange and wonderful family. There's a storm coming, a rising darkness I can feel in my soul. You said I had a fight ahead of me. I think I'm ready to face it now."

She looked around, seeing her home again. She smiled and wept at the sight of it, but after a few minutes, let the memory fade. The good settled into her heart where she'd keep it close, right alongside a new collection of memories made just recently. The bad, she'd leave behind, never letting it weigh her down again.

Well, she'd sure try.

One last time, she drew in a slow breath, savoring the familiar smells.

"Give my love to my sisters. Tell them I'll be along when it's time. But now, there are things that need doing."

Gaoth snorted happily and nudged her with his cheek.

"I'm coming," she said and then climbed onto his back and stroked his neck. "I said we'd go home. Best we get moving. They got one hell of a head start."

Glossary

Juarchian *Elven* – "English Ivy." An unwanted invader that chokes out surrounding life

Shanzi fetsuian *Elven* – Someone or something that wallows in shit or other filth

Terisan ut marrin *Elven* – Bugger me blind

Dani orin *Elven* – Weevils take you

Sans shulla *Elven* – Cherished heart, most beloved, my love

Acknowledgments

My deepest gratitude goes to all those who helped this book come to realization. Thanks to the Knights of Powhatan: Kenda and Mike; the Knights of Olney: Dustin, Stephanie, and new arrival Parker; the Loughrey clan: Casey, Geoff, Geofferson, Delaney, Callahan, and Maguire; and the newly formed Mattis coterie: Kristin and Rodney Mattis. Thanks to my stalwart sidekick, Ed Blaylock (my book, which means you're the sidekick) and his podcast compatriot and pun master-supreme, Damian Harmony. Thanks to Margaret Bail for your hard work and support in helping this book find a home. Much thanks to Wilfred Berkhof for his generous donation to Worldbuilders. And last but not least, thanks to the Falstaff team of misfits for your faith and hard work: Venessa and John.

About the Author

Bishop O'Connell is the author of the American Faerie Tale series, a consultant, writer, blogger, and lover of kilts and beer, as well as a member of the Science Fiction & Fantasy Writers of America. Born in Naples Italy while his father was stationed in Sardinia, Bishop grew up in San Diego, CA where he fell in love with the ocean and fish tacos. After wandering the country for work and school (absolutely not because he was in hiding from mind controlling bunnies), he settled in Richmond VA, where he writes, collects swords, revels in his immortality as a critically acclaimed "visionary" of the urban fantasy genre, and is regularly chastised for making up things for his bio. He can also be found online at A Quiet Pint (aquietpint.com), where he muses philosophical on life, the universe, and everything, as well as various aspects of writing and the road to getting published.

Blog – https://aquietpint.com/
Facebook - https://www.facebook.com/AuthorBishopOConnell
Twitter - https://twitter.com/BishopMOConnell
Instagram - https://www.instagram.com/bishopmoconnell/
Amazon Author Page - http://www.amazon.com/-/e/B00L74LE4Y

Friends of Falstaff

Thank You to All our Falstaff Books Patrons, who get extra digital content each month! To be featured here and see what other great rewards we offer, go to www.patreon.com/falstaffbooks.

PATRONS

Dino Hicks
John Hooks
John Kilgallon
Larissa Lichty
Travis & Casey Schilling
Staci-Leigh Santore
Sheryl R. Hayes
Scott Norris
Samuel Montgomery-Blinn
Junkle